Finding Meaning in the Age of Immortality

T.N. Eyer

STILL
HOUSE
PRESS

Stillhouse Press
4400 University Drive, 3E4
Fairfax, VA 22030
www.stillhousepress.org

Stillhouse Press is an independent, student- and alumni-run nonprofit press based out of Northern Virginia and operated in collaboration with Watershed Lit: Center for Literary Engagement and Publishing Practice at George Mason University.

Library of Congress Control Number: 2023935443

ISBN-13:   978-1-945233-22-7 Paperback
                 978-1-945233-23-4 eBook

Cover Design: Megan Lynn Brooks
Cover Art: tk
Clock Face: ONYXprj/Adobe Stock
Interior Layout: Scott W. Berg

To my husband, Danny.

Life's highs are even higher and its lows are never as low with you by my side. You're my everything. I love you.

PROLOGUE

It begins with a dead body.

Zeke finds it slumped against a dumpster in an alley and starts screaming, a high-pitched, nasal whine his siblings would recognize anywhere. They come running, his howl serving as their beacon, wondering, as they approach, what they are in for, how bad it will be.

The Hudsons have lived on the streets for six years. They have grown accustomed to rats nibbling at their toes while they sleep and cockroaches treating their arms as interstates. They've stepped in vomit and slipped on blood; they can smell urine-stained cement a block away. They've even seen bodies before, clammy and unrousable, sprawling at inconvenient angles behind businesses and in parking lots. None of it fazes them anymore.

When they find Zeke staring, dumbstruck, at the body, they can't figure out why he screamed. A mental breakdown, they think. Zeke has always been more sensitive than the rest of them. But when they get closer, they understand.

"Oh, my god. Is it—?" Remy begins.

"No," Henry says. "Weaker chin, no scar on the neck. See? Close, but it's not him."

Zeke has stopped screaming and is gaping, slack-jawed, at his discovery.

Henry shakes him. "Zeke," he says. "It isn't him."

But Zeke doesn't seem to hear.

"Damn. It sure does look like him, though, doesn't it?" Ben mutters.

The dead man, whoever he is, bears a striking resemblance to their dad.

And then Remy realizes he could be. She turns to her brothers. "Guys, do you see what this means? This could be our chance." She licks her lips, eager, anticipatory. This could work; she knows it could.

Her brothers are staring at her blankly.

"You guys," Remy says, willing them to understand. "This man could be our ticket to getting off the streets."

Gradually, they comprehend what she is suggesting—first Henry, then Ben, then Zeke. They smile at her and then at each other. "It could work," Henry says.

They search the body for identification and find an expired California driver's license. The dead man is Robert Ritter, born May 2, 1991, a year and a half before their dad. Henry tucks the ID in his back pocket.

"Anything else on him?" he asks. But there is nothing—no cash or credit cards, no wedding ring or cell phone, only a corpse in tattered jeans, a stained T-shirt, and grime-crusted sneakers that reeks of mildew and sweat.

Remy stops a woman on the nearest street and asks her to call 911. "Please," she begs, forcing high-pitched urgency into her voice. "My dad is in the alley, and he's not breathing."

Two cop cars, an ambulance, and a firetruck show up ten minutes later. Henry and Ben kneel beside Robert Ritter, shaking him gently as though they are trying to revive him. Zeke looks on behind them, shifting nervously from foot to foot.

"Step aside, please," barks one of the paramedics.

They expect chest compressions, defibrillators, mouth-to-mouth, but the paramedic only reaches for the dead man's wrist and checks for a pulse. "I'm sorry," he says less than half a minute later. "He's gone."

"Great," says a cop, well over six feet tall, with gangly limbs and thinning hair. "Just great. He got any ID on him?"

The paramedic searches the body. "Nothing."

The cop turns to the Hudsons, who are gazing at the ground, attempting to look traumatized. "You know this man?"

"Yes, sir," Henry says, answering for all of them. "He's our dad."

"Perfect," the cop says, relieved. Then he remembers he's with the dead man's family. "Shit. I'm sorry."

None of them say anything. He softens his voice and continues. "Hey, if you can give me his legal name and birthdate, I can get you his death certificate today. Otherwise, I'll have to run his prints, and with the backlog, it could take months."

"Sure," Henry says, stepping forward. "He was Vance Hudson, no middle name, and he was born in El Desierto, California, on October 27, 1992."

When the cop has all the information he needs, he looks at the children Vance Hudson has left behind. They are short and thin with large, chestnut-colored eyes. The youngest, the girl, keeps squinting, a sure sign that she could use some glasses. The poor things. They are good kids. The cop can tell. Polite and helpful. "Do you have a mom?" he asks.

Henry shakes his head. "She left us a few years ago when times got tough."

The cop doesn't bother to hide his disgust. "Any other relatives?"

"No."

"What will you do now?"

"I don't know," Henry says. "Take things a day at a time, I guess."

The cop can see the girl's bones protruding through her chest, and the youngest boy has a stunted, malnourished look about him. Their hair is matted, and they reek, a stale, putrid stench that reminds him of a locker room seldom cleaned. It isn't any way for children to live. "Have you thought about going to a Compound? You're of age, aren't you?" he says to Henry.

"I am, and Ben is, but Zeke and Remy are minors, and we can't leave them behind."

"I don't see why you'd have to," the cop says. "It seems to me that you're their legal guardian now. The Compounds should admit them as long as they're with you."

Henry looks at his siblings, then back at the cop. "We don't have any of the paperwork."

For the first time since he arrived, the cop smiles. "You leave that to me."

PART I

CHAPTER 1

Then

Remy only understands bits and pieces of the news.

"Hemodyne—Compounds—free housing—blood—Immortality—"

Normally, Remy watches the faces of her parents and brothers to see whether the news is good or bad (usually bad), but tonight, their expressions conflict. Her brothers have dewy eyes and soft, hopeful smiles, but her parents are all frowns and glares and snarls.

"What's it mean?" she asks, tugging at Henry's shirt. "What's happened?"

"It means we're saved, Remy," Ben says, scooping her up in his arms. "We're saved." He swings her around, more playful than he's been in weeks, months. She clings to him, giggling, even though she still doesn't understand what's going on or what exactly it means to be saved.

When her mom uses that term, it means 'to love Jesus,' but she has gathered that her brother has a different definition in mind. Saved. She pictures Superman arriving with bags of food and toys, like Santa but less seasonal. The thought thrills her, and she lets out an enthusiastic squeal.

Her jubilation is short-lived. Her dad knocks Ben upside the head with the back of his hand. "We ain't going to them Compounds, ya idiot," he says.

Ben stumbles from the unexpected blow and drops Remy. She lands hard, her bum crashing into the threadbare carpet, her elbow colliding with Zeke, who is sprawled on his belly atop the floor, ignoring the commotion and staring at the television. Both of them start crying.

"Now look what you've done," her parents say simultaneously. It is unclear whether her mom is talking to her dad or her brother.

Henry rushes over to comfort Remy, but Ben stays where he is, clutching his head and staring at their dad as if he can't believe what he's hearing. "What do you mean we're not going?" he asks. "Why not?"

"Why not? Why not?" Their mom is pacing back and forth across the living room, agitated. "Because it's the devil's work. That's why not." She begins rubbing the cross around her neck as though it's a magic lamp, but neither genie nor Jesus emerges.

"And besides," their dad says. "We're no dupes. Free housing and food for a pint of blood a week? I don't think so. They'll lock us up and drain us dry." His hands have curled into fists, and his eyes are darting around the room as if he expects Compound employees to emerge from the shadows with handcuffs and chains.

"I don't think we have a choice," Henry says. "We don't have any food. We don't have any money. And come next month, we won't even have a home."

The eviction notice appeared on their door last week, and Henry, taut with stress, had explained to Remy that it meant they would have to move out of their house.

"How come?" Remy had asked.

"Because we don't have any money to pay the rent."

This Remy knew. Her dad had lost his job as the high school janitor the year before, replaced by a team of mop-wielding robots. Her mom, a housekeeper, had mostly been replaced by robots, too. They weren't the only ones. Most of Remy's friends' parents didn't have jobs. The factory where Mark's dad worked had moved to China. The gas station that had employed Jenny's mom was all machines now. Fast food restaurants all had ordering kiosks; grocery stores were self-check-out. Everyone Remy knew was poor and hungry and scared.

"I want to go to a Compound," Remy volunteers now. She rubs her growling tummy, imagining a place where her mom is not angry and her dad is not ashamed, where they can be a normal family like the ones on television.

Vance shoots her a look of pure fury, and Remy buries her head in Henry's stomach.

"There will be no Compound, and that's final," Vance growls.

"Then what will we do?" Henry asks. "Where will we live?"

"We'll manage," Vance says. "Move to LA, maybe. Ain't no jobs in El Desierto no more."

"What makes you think there are jobs in LA?" Ben asks.

"It's a city. There are always jobs in the city."

But this time, there aren't. This time there aren't jobs anywhere.

Now

The Hudsons stand apart from the other passengers as they wait for the shuttle. Remy is struck by how clean the Compound residents, or Cruors, look. How well-fed, how happy. How tattered and pungent she is by comparison. She tells herself that they were like her once, that they understand and sympathize, but from the way they are glancing at her and her brothers, she isn't sure that's true.

The shuttle approaches, and the small crowd shifts, standing, collecting their belongings, jostling for a place in line. Although the bus stop is the Los Angeles Public Library—a beautiful Art Deco building dwarfed by skyscrapers—Remy notices that none of the passengers are carrying books.

"This is an unusual bus stop," Henry remarks to another passenger as they move to the end of the line.

"It's one of Nathan Odili's quirks," the passenger replies. "Every Compound shuttle around the country deposits its passengers at a public library.

Every Compound has a library, too. Odili seems to think that mere exposure will persuade his poor, undereducated Cruors to pick up a book every once in a while. He's sorely mistaken, of course. Who needs books when there are so many less effortful diversions?"

"You don't sound undereducated," Henry remarks.

"Me? No, I'm not. I was salutatorian of my high school and then dropped out of Princeton."

Henry has never heard of Princeton, but Remy has.

"If you got into an Ivy League school, what are you doing here?" she asks, squinting at him skeptically.

He turns to her. He is about Henry's age and good-looking, with broad shoulders and expensive clothes. "It all became too much for me," he confesses. "The pressure, the expectations. I would have had a heart attack by thirty if I'd stayed."

Henry gawks at their new acquaintance. "You chose to live on a Compound even though you had an alternative?"

The passenger shrugs. "It's a good life."

Ben nudges Henry in the ribs. "Told you so."

"You going for the first time?" the passenger asks.

They nod.

"You'll love it there. You'll see."

"Are there many Cruors like you?" Remy asks hopefully.

"No," he says, looking right at her. "Most people like me wouldn't be caught dead on a Compound."

The bus door closes at 4 p.m. on the dot. At 4:01, as the bus idles by the curb, waiting for an opportunity to merge into traffic, a young woman with short spiky hair comes running up and pounds on the door. It doesn't budge. She will have to wait for 5 p.m.

"I guess that's the downside to self-driving vehicles," Henry remarks as they watch the woman throw her hands up in frustration. Ben waves goodbye to her as the bus pulls away. She gives him the finger.

The bus crawls through downtown Los Angeles until it reaches Interstate 10, where traffic isn't moving much faster than it had been on the city streets below. None of the other passengers seem bothered by the pace of progress—they are probably used to it—but Remy is eager to leave the city behind. It hasn't been kind to her family. They were homeless the entire time they lived there, and they rarely had enough to eat. They never had a steady income, and they never managed to attend the same school for an entire academic year. Good riddance, Los Angeles, Remy thinks. She subtly raises her finger to the window and flips the city off, imitating the woman who'd missed the bus half an hour before. She smiles at the gesture, her own minor act of rebellion.

The skyscrapers give way to strip malls and suburbs, brightly painted cellblocks with colorful signs out front advertising restaurants Remy will never eat at, and department stores that sell clothes that cost more than her family spends on food in a month. Some of them Remy recognizes. In Santa Monica, the beachside suburb where they most recently resided, there'd been a Dim Sum Palace and a Gap. But most are unfamiliar. She wonders if Red Lobster is a pet store or a restaurant. She's always wanted a pet, but she's partial to jellyfish.

At first, Remy is disappointed by how little of the city she's explored, but after a few miles, she notices that, for the most part, she is seeing the same stores over and over again. She hopes the whole world is not a series of Starbucks, KFCs, HomeRobots, and Wal-Marts duplicated a million times over.

Beside her, Zeke has fallen asleep and is snoring, his head tipping onto Remy's shoulder, his mouth wide open like the street performers downtown who are so hungry they offer to catch the leftovers of passersby with their lips as long as they get to eat whatever they catch. Human seals, they call themselves.

Zeke had tried to imitate them once, but he was too clumsy to catch anything. His face had come to resemble a Pollock painting, streaked and splattered with an array of brightly-colored food. After a while, passersby had stopped aiming for his mouth at all and had instead thrown their food at his clothes, the back of his head, his face, laughing viciously as he stumbled about, his head tossed back, his mouth open, as though he were trying to drink rainwater falling from the sky. Remy cringes at the memory.

At five-foot-five, Zeke looks younger than Remy, even though he is seventeen, three years her senior. He is awkward and unaware but sweet, a pint-sized version of Lennie Small from *Of Mice and Men*.

Across the aisle, Ben and Henry are having trouble sitting still. Ben stares out the window, his asymmetric chin jutting forward, his wiry limbs tense with anticipation. Beside him, Henry is ponderous, uncertain. With his dark, unkempt hair and the worry lines around his eyes, he resembles an absent-minded professor twice his age. The brothers are both anxious, but for different reasons. Although they are headed toward the same fate, Ben feels like he's won the lottery, while Henry worries that he's making the biggest mistake of his life. Ben's cocksure grin gives Remy confidence; Henry's reluctant eyes make her afraid.

Ben is retelling the story of his sole visit to the Compounds, the time he'd run away at fifteen. He had been there less than half a day, but that had been long enough for him to fall head over heels for Compound life. He mentions the warm welcome, the new buildings, the lemonade, but mostly he dwells on the cafeteria, describing the food he'd eaten in painstaking detail.

Remy ignores her brother and focuses instead on the landscape, which is transforming before her eyes. Both traffic and the cluster of buildings have thinned, and Remy feels as though she has been transported to the set of a John Wayne movie, surrounded by a puce desert, barren and dry.

The bus exits the freeway, exchanging six lanes for two. They go twenty minutes without passing a single building. The air shifts from the grey-yellow, pollutant-laden smog of Los Angeles to the unquenchable thirst of the desert, and even the odors change. The city smelled like people—sweaty, greedy, tempestuous—while the desert smells like a mixture of gasoline and gunpowder. No wonder they vote so differently, Remy thinks, when they breathe such different air.

Ben spots the Compound first, even though Remy has been looking for it.

"That's it, right?" he says to no one in particular, pointing out the window and bouncing up and down in his seat like a child.

That's it? Remy thinks, staring at a uniform cluster of buildings in the distance. Her heart sinks. For a decade, the country has been praising the Compounds—their livability, their convenience, how much nicer they are than they need to be—and in her mind, that translated into the sort of quaint, planned community portrayed in classic television shows set in tidy suburbs or charming towns. She had expected tree-lined streets and single-family homes, each with a patch of grass out front. Instead, she is getting concrete, fifteen or twenty stories high, not a tree or plant or flower in sight. It is a prison or a Soviet exurb, a community planned by frugal engineers, not artists or architects. She wants to tell her brothers that they've made a terrible mistake; they can't live here.

The Princeton dropout notices her disappointment. "Don't worry," he says, leaning forward and resting a fraternal hand on her shoulder. "It's not as bad as it looks."

Remy turns to him. "Promise?"

"Promise," he says. "You know, I think you may be the first newbie who's cared about aesthetics. Most are just grateful for a good meal and a warm bed."

Remy blushes. "I am grateful for a good meal and a warm bed," she assures him. "But I guess I'd imagined something different, something a bit more *Anne of Green Gables* and a bit less Chateau d'If."

"What's your name?" he asks, looking at her with furrowed brows as though he can't quite figure her out.

"Remy," she tells him. "Remy Hudson."

"Well, Remy, I'm Caleb," he says. "When you realize that you don't fit in here, come find me, okay?"

Remy frowns. "What makes you think I won't fit in here?"

"I've lived on the Compound for three years, and I've never heard anyone else mention Chateau d'If."

The bus comes to a halt outside the cold steel wall that surrounds the Compound. It is ten feet tall, unmanned, and unadorned. The wall makes Remy nervous. This is neither a prison nor a military base, just fifty- or sixty thousand people swapping blood for a bed. She wonders why this level of security is necessary, what Hemodyne is trying to hide.

"Home sweet home," Caleb says.

The other passengers begin to disembark.

"Zeke," Remy says, elbowing her brother in the stomach. "Wake up. We're here."

Zeke opens his eyes and looks around, disoriented.

"We're here," Remy repeats.

Zeke stands to get off the bus but trips on someone's shoe and stumbles into Henry. Everyone turns to stare at Zeke, and he offers a dopey, apologetic grin. Nobody smiles back, but they don't taunt him either. Remy is relieved; Zeke has been mocked all his life.

They wonder what happens next. It is not obvious. There is nothing outside except the steel wall and beyond it, the tops of dozens of concrete apartment buildings.

"They used to send someone to greet each bus and welcome the newbies, but these days, there aren't many of you," Caleb explains. "Everyone who wants to be here is here already."

Remy sinks her teeth into her lower lip, worried that they are too late, that Compound 78 is already full.

But Caleb doesn't look concerned. "Come on," he says. "I'll get you sorted."

They follow him off the bus and into the evening air. Remy had forgotten how hot summer in the desert can be. It feels like someone has deposited them in a massive oven and closed the door, leaving the sun to slowly bake them to death. Sweat seeps from Remy's pores, and her knotty hair feels heavy against the nape of her neck. When she reaches back to pull it up into a messy bun, she catches a whiff of her underarms and nearly gags. She can't remember the last time she had access to a bath or deodorant.

The other passengers from the bus, about nine in total, have queued along the steel wall. The first in line, an oversized man with a bushy beard, places his left index finger against a small metal pad.

"Welcome home, Spencer," a shrill, maternal voice says. The metal door slides open, and Spencer disappears inside.

Home, Remy thinks. She hasn't had a home since she was eight years old. Sometimes she dreamed about what a home might look like if she ever got one again, but it never looked anything like this.

Caleb approaches an entry phone that's attached to the wall. He presses a button and then speaks into the receiver. "Hi, there. This is Caleb Wentworth. I've got four newbies here who could use some sort of orientation."

The person on the other end must be apologetic because Caleb says, "That's okay. Just get here now," and then, "Thank you," before hanging up. Remy is surprised by how authoritative he sounds, like he is the boss, and the person on the other end is his underling, even though Caleb is a Cruor and, in the modern-day caste system, Cruors are at the bottom, America's very own *Dalits*.

Caleb turns to the Hudsons, who huddle together, uncertain and pathetic. They have nothing but the clothes on their backs. They have not bathed for days. Their stomachs form a choir singing in growls instead of notes. Ben and Remy's are basses, while Henry's is a tenor, and Zeke's is a shockingly high soprano; he's so hungry his stomach is whining.

Caleb's expression softens when he sees them. He's looking at them with more tenderness than anyone has for a long time; he pities them. How strange, Remy thinks. No one has pitied the poor in years.

"They're sending someone now," Caleb tells them. "Don't worry. They'll take good care of you. You'll like it here. Everyone does. I've got to get going, but if you need anything, I'm in Building 17. Caleb Wentworth."

Remy doesn't want him to leave. In her mind, Compound 78 is like

Los Angeles, large and crowded and mobile, and unless she stalks Building 17, she'll never see him again.

Her brothers must look as reluctant as she does to see Caleb go because he smiles at them and says, "Jesus. You guys are looking at me like I'm abandoning you outside an orphanage. You'll be fine. Trust me. And I'll see you inside once you get settled."

Henry nods. "Thanks for your help."

Caleb shrugs, presses his index finger against the metal pad and vanishes inside the impenetrable steel wall. And then it's just them, standing outside a fortress in the middle of a barren desert.

Ben does his best to reassure the others. "Wait 'til you see the cafeteria," he says. "I've never seen so much food in my life. And we'll actually get to choose what we eat, like in a restaurant."

Remy and Henry look at each other and roll their eyes, sick of hearing about the Compound cafeteria.

The metal door that Caleb and the other passengers had used to enter the Compound slides open again, making the Hudsons jump. This time, a man walks out. He is dressed in a red linen shirt tucked into creased khakis that are half an inch too long. His white face is bright red in the desert heat, and his blonde hair is plastered to his damp forehead. He's short, even shorter than Zeke, but as he walks, he tilts his head back so far that the only way he can see the Hudsons is to shift his gaze downward. Despite being shorter than them, he has found a way to look down on them.

"Hello," he says. "I'm Dallas. Welcome to Compound 78."

Henry extends his hand, determined, as always, to show that poverty and good manners aren't mutually exclusive. "I'm Henry, and these are Ben, Zeke, and Remy."

Dallas ignores Henry's hand and openly assesses the others. Remy can only imagine what he sees—street urchins, filthy and malodorous, a modern-day equivalent of Fagin's gang in *Oliver Twist*. But surely, he must be accustomed to that by now; it's hard to believe that many people who volunteer for the Compounds look much better.

"You're all related?" he asks, wrinkling his nose.

Remy glares at him. Back before the Compounds opened there had been a lot of negative press about the poor having children they couldn't afford, as if people without money didn't have the right to have a family, to have love.

"Yes, we're siblings," Henry says without a trace of shame in his voice.

"And your parents?"

"Our father is dead. Our mother left us years ago. We have the paperwork."

Dallas nods. "Great. Fine. First time at a Compound?"

Ben speaks up. "I've been here before. Ran away from home six and a half years ago." He says this with pride, as though running away to a Compound is a sign of remarkably good judgment.

But Dallas doesn't look impressed. "We give you a good meal and drive you home?"

Ben grins. "Best meal of my life."

Dallas winces the way adults do when kids say that McDonald's is their favorite restaurant. "I hope the food is as good as you remember.

"So, let me tell you what's going to happen," he continues, turning away from Ben and toward the others. "Tonight, we'll show you to a guest room where we'll have clean clothes and a hot meal waiting. In the morning, we'll do your Intake and then get you settled in. Does that sound okay?"

They nod at the rhetorical question and follow Dallas through the gate with their breaths held and their fingers crossed, hoping they aren't making the biggest mistake of their lives.

That night, showered and dressed in brand new salmon pink pajamas, tucked in between the clean sheets of a twin bed in a room that is refreshingly odorless, noiseless, and equipped with blackout curtains, Remy is unable to sleep.

It's the silence. She is so unaccustomed to it she finds it smothering. It is as though someone has pressed a pillow over her mouth, nose, and ears, dulling her senses until there is nothing. She takes several deep breaths to reassure herself that she is alive, but for a long time she can't seem to relax.

When she finally does drift off, there is the nightmare. In it, she is strapped to a concrete altar, a sacrifice to anonymous vampires who swarm overhead in anticipation of their feast. She attempts to free herself, but her bindings won't give. The more she struggles, the tighter they become.

Remy sits up, panting. Vampires. That's what her mom had called Immortals. "They feed off other people's blood, don't they?" Stupid, really, comparing one of the greatest scientific advances of all time to the fantastical creatures of horror movies.

Henry rolls over in his twin bed across the room from hers. "Remy? Are you okay?"

"Nightmare," she explains.

She gets out of bed and moves toward him, missing the warmth of his body against her back, but he puts his hand out to stop her.

"No," he says. "Not here. They'll think it's—"

"Perverted," she finishes, realizing he's right.

On the streets, it had made sense for Henry and Remy to sleep cuddled up together. Henry had protected her and kept her warm. But here, she doesn't need his protection, and there are blankets on the beds. Here, a fourteen-year-old girl sleeping in the same bed as her twenty-three-year-old brother will only raise questions. Remy returns to her own bed, embarrassed.

"Why are you awake?" she asks.

"I don't know. Worried, I guess. I know we need this. We need to be here. I mean, what's the alternative, starving on the streets? But at the same time, I'm afraid to believe that things will be better now."

Remy has had the same thought. They've been fooled before. When they moved to Los Angeles, their dad said things would be better. When they relocated to Santa Monica, he practically guaranteed streets paved with gold. There had been promising job advertisements and well-intentioned charities, all offering a salvation that never came and enough false starts to dash the hopes of even the most persistent optimist. Those mirages in the desert of their devastation make it hard for them to believe they have actually found water this time. But what choice do they have but to try to drink?

Despite her own misgivings, Remy tries to comfort her brother. "Henry, where do you want to be five years from now? What do you want to be doing?"

Henry doesn't hesitate. "I want a job. Not Cruor. A real job. One where I make or do something. And I want you to be in college. At Harvard, maybe." Harvard is the only school he can name.

"That sounds like a good future," Remy says. She means it; it's the future she wants, too. "You know none of that's ever going to happen if we go back to the streets," she whispers. "But here. I don't know. Maybe it could. I can go to school, the same school, every day, and you can focus on something other than scrounging up food and keeping Ben out of trouble. This could be good, Henry."

When Henry responds, he sounds more resigned than enthusiastic. "You're right," he says. "This could be good."

The next morning, they are awakened by an alarm none of them set. "Rise and shine. You have a meeting in one hour," a woman announces. She seems to be the voice of the Compound, and when Remy pictures her, she imagines someone loving and competent, like the 1950s stay-at-home mom who cooked, cleaned, and raised perfect children all while wearing pearls and high heels.

"Isn't that cool?" Ben says, appearing in the doorway of Henry and Remy's room in nothing but a new pair of Compound-issued boxers. "We'll never have to worry about being late again."

"It is useful, I guess," says Remy, though she thinks there is something Orwellian about an uninvited woman commanding you to get up, no matter how melodic her voice.

19

Henry stumbles out of bed and over to the next room to check on Zeke. Remy closes the door and removes her Compound-issued pajamas, dropping them carelessly atop her unmade bed. She wraps a towel around her body and grabs a vial of soap from the welcome kit. She is beginning to think the hot showers alone might be reason enough to stay. She has spent most of her youth dirty—oily skin, crud under her nails, debris in her hair, and, for the last year or two, a stench from her armpits that led her to keep her arms pressed firmly against her sides, which localized the odor but also made it worse.

When she was able to clean herself, it was most often at a public bathroom sink, splashing cold water across her body, scrubbing her skin with her hand or a paper towel. Hot water and soap and shampoo are luxuries. She would stay in the shower all day if the water didn't automatically shut off after ten minutes.

She plods out into the common room and toward the apartment door. The women's communal bathroom is down the hall.

"Remy," Henry calls, stopping her.

"I know," she says. "I just showered last night, but I have to take another one. I think I'm addicted."

Henry looks amused. "It's not that," he says. "It's," he pauses and comes closer. "I thought you should know that, well, most women, they, you know, shave their legs."

"Oh," Remy says, blushing. She looks down at her own legs. They are skinny and bronze and coated with soft dark hairs. She goes to the welcome kit and retrieves a razor.

Henry is not finished. "Yeah. And, um, also under the arms. Like here." He points to his own armpits to show what he means.

Remy is mortified. She doesn't have to look at her own underarms to know that they resemble a gorilla's. "Uh, okay. Thanks. I'll take care of it. Anywhere else?"

Henry hesitates, reddens, and then shakes his head. "No," he says. "That's all."

She thanks him again and hurries to the shower. She doesn't miss her mother often, but now, she thinks, while they're adjusting to this new, civilized world, it would be nice to have her around.

Dallas comes for them at nine o'clock sharp.

"I hope you slept well," he says.

Henry shrugs. "What's with the alarm?"

"I know it's a little strange, but we found that a number of Cruors had trouble getting to where they needed to be on time. So now, we take care of that for you. Isn't that great? One less thing to worry about."

"Infantilizing," Remy mutters under her breath.

"What?" Dallas asks.

"Tantalizing. This technology is tantalizing," Remy says.

"Well, wowie. Will you look at that vocabulary?" Dallas remarks, flashing Remy a smile that is surprisingly genuine.

Remy forces herself to smile back.

At 9 a.m. on a Friday, the Compound is a ghost town. The businesses are shuttered. The streets are deserted. It is so silent that Remy can hear the wind whistling gently between the buildings. She moves closer to Henry, discomfited by the emptiness.

When they arrived last night, it had not been like this. Then, the streets had been crowded, humming with music, the clack of high heels, the holler of drunken voices. They had gone to sleep in a thriving metropolis and awakened in an abandoned settlement.

"Where is everybody?" Ben asks.

"Well, students are already in school, and everyone else is still asleep. Donation doesn't start until ten," Dallas explains.

The Hudsons look at each other. They cannot imagine sleeping this late. Shelters would have kicked them out by now; realtors might have brought prospective buyers through the foreclosed homes they'd squatted in; garbage trucks would be growling through alleyways, emptying the dumpsters that blocked them from public view. Outside, staying put so long was dangerous.

21

Dallas mistakes their perplexity for disdain. "Yeah. Not the most ambitious people on the planet, but then again, what is there to wake up for? You'll see how it is soon enough."

"Do you live on the Compound?" Remy asks Dallas, stepping up to walk beside him.

Dallas snorts. "Of course not," he says. "There's a town about ten miles east of here, Crystal City? It's where a lot of the schoolteachers, doctors, and administrators who work here on Compound 78 live."

Remy senses that it's important to him that she knows this. He may work here, but he's not one of them.

The Intake room is on the third floor of a large administrative building. It is designed to resemble a cozy middle-class living room, with a tasteful plaid sofa, two overstuffed armchairs, a wooden coffee table, and a fireplace. The scent of coffee brewing wafts in.

Being in this room, clean and wearing new clothes, feels like coming home after fighting in a war, and Remy finds herself flooded with emotion. Relief dominates, but disbelief, exhaustion, and wariness linger in the background. She knows she once fit in in a place like this, but she wonders if she can now, after all she has been through. She wonders if her brothers share these sensations or if they have already adjusted to this more comfortable replica of their old lives. They seem tense but not as tightly wound as she is. Or maybe they are just better at hiding it.

A robot brings breakfast in, and Remy watches as her brothers visibly relax. She stares at them in disbelief, wishing food was all it took to calm her nerves. Even Henry looks more at ease than she has ever seen him, as if, after months on patrol, he can, at last, let his guard down. She attempts to emulate them, both in sentiment and in appearance, but everything about her performance feels wrong. She is an actor in a stage play with all the right props and dedicated co-stars, but she can't seem to get into character.

As they are eating, Dallas begins their Intake. "Can you all read and write?" he asks as he passes out several forms.

They are insulted. "Of course," Remy says.

Dallas shrugs. "About forty percent of the people who come here can't."

"Adults?" Remy asks.

"That's right."

"Well, can they learn to read here?"

"Hey, trust me, Dr. Odili is a huge proponent of education. Every Compound in the country used to offer classes in basic literacy and numeracy. But attendance was dismal. And by dismal, I mean non-existent, so we couldn't justify the cost. Shut the program down. Really, it's a miracle we still have libraries."

Remy is troubled by this, though she can't say why. If there's one thing she's learned in her fourteen years, it's that adults can't be forced to do anything they don't want to do.

They complete the forms, which ask for detailed histories of their lives, including a year-by-year account of their whereabouts and any previous job experience. There is a space for medical history, too, but they are informed that this will be supplemented by a physical exam performed by Compound doctors. For the most part, it is standard stuff, and they breeze through it.

"Great. This all looks great," Dallas says, glancing at their forms. "Now, let's see your documents."

Remy digs her fingernails into her thighs as Henry reaches into the back pocket of his jeans and produces a folded stack of paperwork. "It's all here," he says.

Dallas takes everything—the form assigning legal guardianship to Henry, the official declaration that their mother is a missing person, their father's death certificate listing the cause of death as alcohol poisoning—and promises to return in a few minutes.

There shouldn't be any problems. Their paperwork is all legitimate and police-issued. But there is always a chance that the police officer ran the dead man's fingerprints after all or that their real father, awaking from a drunken stupor in a parking garage a few blocks away from where they found Robert Ritter, wondered what had become of his children and reported their disappearance to the authorities. They look at each other nervously but don't say anything. They know the room could be bugged.

When Dallas returns, he is all smiles. "Your paperwork checks out," he says. "Let's get you settled."

First, their fingerprints are taken.

"You're not in the system," Dallas remarks. "How unusual." Fifteen years ago, Congress passed a controversial anti-crime measure requiring anyone who received government aid to get fingerprinted. Most Cruors would have fallen into this category; the Hudsons did not. Vance Hudson believed in both privacy and self-sufficiency. Welfare was not an option.

Next, their photographs are taken and printed onto plastic identification cards. In hers, Remy's lips creep up in a closed-mouth grin, a skeptical girl told to smile by a bored photographer.

They are each given a cheap cellphone and a bank account, then they are led through the Compound to a warehouse filled with clothes, inexpensive but new and surprisingly varied, and told that they may each select five tops, three bottoms, two pairs of shoes, and a jacket, along with ten pairs of socks, ten pairs of underwear, and, for Remy, two bras. She has no idea what her chest size is, and there is no one to measure her. She eyeballs the inventory, discreetly holds the cups against her breasts and picks two nude bras that she thinks, hopes, will fit.

"You get new clothes once a year," Dallas tells them. "And, of course, you can buy additional items. You'll find our prices are very competitive."

Later, they are separated. Henry and Ben are taken to the Donation Center where they will be Donating a pint of blood every week for as long as they reside in the Compound. Their first Donation is next week. Today is an information session of sorts, where they'll learn what they should and should not eat, drink, and do within forty-eight hours of giving.

Zeke, who is a senior in high school, and Remy, who should be in the ninth grade, are kept together at first. They are given aptitude tests and personality assessments. After this, they, too, are separated. Remy is given an eye exam—which results in a new pair of wire-rimmed glasses with thick, round lenses—and then a physical, where she is asked if she would like either the IUD or the Implant.

"We're big believers in long-term birth control here," an overweight blonde nurse explains.

"I'm not sexually active," Remy tells her.

"Yeah, but you're what?" She checks her records. "Fourteen? Oh, honey, you and I both know if you're not now, you will be soon. Anyway, it's free. Why take the risk?"

Remy hesitates.

"It's long-acting, but it's nothing permanent. If you decide you want to have a baby, we're happy to remove it for you, no questions asked."

At last, Remy agrees. Between her brothers, who scared away any guy who got near her, and her mother, who would have put a real, chainmail chastity belt on her daughter if she could have, Remy has never considered having sex, but she is a sensible girl, and she remembers well the sorry sight of girls her age tottering down the street with bulging stomachs and drooping eyes and no prospects for the future.

"You're going to love it," the nurse says, inserting the implant into her upper arm. "It's one less thing to worry about, you know?"

Lunch is in the cafeteria, a sprawling, windowless structure that resembles an aircraft hangar. As Remy approaches, her anticipation builds. Ben has been so effusive about the Compound cafeteria she wonders how it could possibly live up to expectations.

And yet, somehow, it does. As Remy steps inside, she gasps. She has never seen so much food in her life. It lines three walls of this massive structure, piled high in large metal trays: pastas and soups and salads and deli meats. She begins to tremble at the sight; it's almost too much food, too much choice, and she wishes she could have eased into this experience somehow instead of being tossed into it unprepared.

The cafeteria is noisy, even though it's half empty. The hum of the frozen yogurt machine, the conversations of other people, the whirring of robots as they replace and remove food are not only audible but amplified so that Remy has to fight the urge to cover her ears.

She follows an oblivious Zeke over to the food and watches as he helps himself to a heaping spoonful of each item, then becomes dismayed when his plate fills when he is not even an eighth of the way through the buffet.

"Here," Remy says, passing him her empty plate. She is no longer hungry.

Zeke squeezes her plate onto the tray beside his and resumes scooping food. Remy wonders how much he'll end up wasting, how much the Compound throws away each day.

Something about this scene makes her childhood feel impossible like she must have imagined the persistent hunger pangs, the gnawing obsession with finding her next meal because she cannot imagine how starvation could exist there when there is such abundance here.

Tray empty, Remy follows Zeke to a tangerine orange table, where their brothers are already stuffing their faces. Remy, who has been worn down by examinations, both academic and medical, is surprised by how much energy Henry and Ben have. Their eyes are shining with anticipation. Of what? Surely not of having blood siphoned from their bodies like gasoline from an abandoned vehicle. She doesn't have to wait long to find out.

"They pay us," Ben blurts as soon as Remy and Zeke are seated.

"What?" Remy asks.

"They pay us," Ben repeats. "Seventy dollars every time we Donate."

"Seriously?" Zeke says. His eyes have brightened, too, and Remy can see that he can't wait until he can put his education behind him and become a Donor, too.

"Seriously," Ben says. "Seventy dollars! To spend on whatever we want!"

Remy understands why this means so much to Ben. On the Outside, they'd always pooled any money they earned, and every cent had gone toward their survival. Ben, who was cunning and quick, consistently brought in the most, but he'd never gotten to enjoy his money or even determine how it was spent. To have his own discretionary funds, to be able to select what he eats, to decide how he uses his time, all of these new choices are giving him a sense of control over his life for the first time. Poverty had been a brutal slave master; now, at last, he's free.

Henry is excited, too. He has never been as vocal as Ben, but he is smiling, and his eyes have become distant and dreamy.

"You're happy, Henry?" Remy asks.

"They pay us," he says, echoing his brother. "Do you know what that means? It means we can save and eventually have enough money to get out of here. Maybe buy a house somewhere, start again."

Remy doesn't say anything, but she does the math in her head. Seventy dollars a week is about $3,500 a year. Even if Henry saves every cent, it will be a very long time before he can afford to leave, especially if he doesn't have a job waiting on the outside. But she knows better than to rain on her brother's parade. "That's wonderful," she says at last, forcing a smile.

"Yeah," he agrees, still beaming. "It is. I feel a lot better about being here now."

Remy continues to grin at him, wishing she felt the same way.

CHAPTER 2

Then

It is Connor Davenport's sixtieth birthday. To celebrate, he is throwing a party befitting a sixty-year-old: at 5 p.m., in the dining room of his country club, with a smattering of stodgy hors d'oeuvres followed by a fixed three-course dinner.

His youngest daughter, nineteen-year-old Sabrina, had urged him to do something more fun. Tech mogul Roger Greenberg's sixtieth, for example, had been on his private island, catered by a celebrity chef, with live music by Roger's favorite classic rock band, Imagine Dragons. Why couldn't her father do something like that?

Instead, Sabrina is stuck at a table with sixty-five-year-old Brian Mc-Gill, ignoring his leg, which keeps brushing up against hers and trying to suppress a yawn as he rambles on about his Swiss watch collection. Her dad doesn't even like Brian, but he's the only billionaire in a club full of millionaires, so excluding him was not an option.

Sabrina notices Brian's wife, seated on his other side, rolling her eyes and stroking her diamond necklace as if to remind herself that beautiful, expensive things are her consolation prize for being married to the big oaf with the wandering eye. Sabrina pities her and wonders what kind of terms the prenup must contain to induce her to stay with a creep like Brian McGill.

She glances around the room in search of her siblings, the only other people under fifty in attendance. Her brother Prince, over-dressed in a three-piece suit, is standing behind her, talking to a cluster of old women who all want him to psychoanalyze them.

"But why am I so attracted to younger men? They're less mature and more likely to cheat on me. Yet every man I've been with is at least a decade my junior. My current husband was born the year I graduated high school."

Sabrina suppresses the urge to gag, but Prince has never seemed to mind banal chatter. He listens attentively, never interrupts, and always says the right thing at the right time. Sabrina supposes that's what a master's degree in clinical psychology trains you to do.

Sabrina's sister Darcy is harder to locate, somehow. She is fully twice Sabrina's size, and yet she has mastered the art of making herself invisible. It's her dull wardrobe, her wash-and-go hairstyle, the way she hunches her shoulders and keeps her eyes on the ground. If she were to murder somebody in front of a dozen witnesses, not one of them would be able to describe her to the police.

Sabrina eventually spies Darcy squeezed into a corner by herself, holding a plate loaded with carbs. Sabrina watches as she flags down a server and helps herself to several crab cakes slathered in some mayonnaise-based sauce. She consumes each one in a single bite, barely bothering to chew. Disgusted, Sabrina turns away.

When it is time for dinner, Connor claims the seat on the other side of Sabrina. Prince jockeys to sit beside his dad as well, but Connor makes no effort to save a seat for his son, so Prince ends up a table away. Sabrina glances around for Darcy but doesn't see her. She is probably at the back with the other misfits, wolfing down rolls from the breadbasket.

Next to Sabrina, Brian is yammering on about some rare Rolex when he falls silent mid-sentence. He pulls his phone out of his pocket, reads a message, and then calls out, "Turn the television on, Francisco."

The room falls silent. The other guests are appalled. They know Brian is accustomed to getting his way but ordering the television on during someone else's birthday dinner is crossing the line even for him.

"Brian," his wife says in the same voice she probably uses to chastise her shih tzu.

"What?" Brian says. "It's important."

As if to confirm this, phones begin buzzing throughout the room, like a plague of locusts descending on the country club. Sabrina frowns at the cryptic message she's received from her agent. *History is about to be made*, it says. *Turn on the TV.*

Sabrina assumes the worst. Another terrorist attack or nuclear war. Maybe even a zombie apocalypse, she thinks, remembering a movie she'd seen a few nights before.

The other attendees confirm Brian's instruction. "Go ahead. Turn on the television, Francisco."

"What channel?" Francisco asks.

"Any of 'em," says Brian McGill.

On the screen is an empty podium. Behind it, the words HEMODYNE ENTERPRISES, in gold against a black background.

Connor leans across Sabrina to Brian. "You ever heard of these guys?"

Brian nods. "Pharma start-up. They do vaccines through blood transfusions or some crap like that. Approached me for an investment, but they were too new at the time."

A minute later, a man walks across the stage toward the podium. He is in his early forties, with dark curly hair and tortoise shell glasses. He's grinning like he's won the lottery, strutting like he's been elected president. He's good-looking, Sabrina thinks, like the classic film star Denzel Washington.

Two seats away, Brian McGill mutters, "African. He's too dark to be African American." Beside him, his wife buries her head in her hands.

"Good evening, ladies and gentlemen," the man begins. Brian McGill's assertion is confirmed by his slight accent. His voice is rich and melodious. He might be a father singing a lullaby to his child, and Sabrina finds herself thinking that if something terrible has happened, this is exactly the man she wants in charge.

"I am Nathan Odili, the founder and CEO of Hemodyne Enterprises. Tonight, I am pleased to announce that thanks to the efforts of our exceptional scientists and researchers, Immortality has become a reality."

"Oh my god," Sabrina says, covering her mouth with her hand. She turns to her father, certain she has misheard, but he looks flabbergasted, too.

"Immortality?" she says to no one in particular. "Like eternal life?"

Around her, the members of the West Side Country Club murmur amongst themselves. They are giddy and anxious, wondering aloud if this is real. They'd better hope it is, thinks Sabrina. Almost everyone in the room is over sixty. They're on the last leg of life, winding down, increasingly irrelevant in their companies, treated like children by their kids, and subjected to a million little humiliations—senior discounts, extra-large print, child-proof pill bottles they have to ask their grandchildren to open—every single day. If this is true, it will have a far greater impact on them than it does on the population at large.

Sabrina's dad reaches for her hand. "Can you believe this?" he asks her with wide eyes and a tooth-bearing grin. She hasn't seen him this happy since before her mother died.

On television, Nathan Odili has been taking questions from an incredulous press pool. He is thoughtful and thorough, and with each answer he delivers, Sabrina squeezes her dad's hand a little tighter, believes in Immortality a little more.

"How much will it cost?" one reporter asks.

For the first time, Nathan Odili hesitates. "Although we hope to make it more affordable in time, for now, the cost of producing the Infinity Serum is extremely high. Consequently, the price of Immortality is high, far higher than we would like it to be."

"How much?" the reporter presses.

"It will be $6,300 per week or approximately $327,000 per year."

The press room descends into chaos. The journalists are grumbling to each other, complaining to Odili. To them, Immortality is no longer salvation; it is a cruel tease, a winning lottery ticket dangled in front of them and then shredded. They will never have that much money; most people won't.

The voice of a female reporter rises above the crowd. "In the U.S., the unemployment rate is at forty-three percent. Families are struggling to make ends meet. How can you justify this?"

Nathan Odili adopts a somber expression. "All I can say is that I hope Immortality will become more affordable in the future," he repeats.

"It's good to be rich, ain't it, boys?" Brian McGill booms.

A number of people at the country club chuckle at their good fortune, but others are ominously silent. One man seizes the arm of the woman to his left and moans, "I gave my entire fortune to Stanford in an annuity. My wife and I get $300,000 a year. I never thought we'd need more than that. But now—I've killed us." Panicked, he shakes the woman's arm. "Oh, God, I've killed us."

Around the room, others are voicing similar concerns. They had retired too early; they hadn't saved enough; they'd given in to midlife crises, buying expensive cars or losing half their wealth in expensive divorce settlements. They'd donated too much to charity, made too many bad investments, tried too hard to keep up with the Joneses. Had they known, they would have made other choices, but how could they have known? Immortality isn't the product of incremental advances accumulating over decades; it is a giant leap forward.

Sabrina watches the scene, amused and unconcerned. She assumes her father will pay for her Immortality, just as he has always paid for everything. Immortality, Sabrina thinks, trying to come to terms with this new and improved reality. It's almost as impossible to believe as a zombie apocalypse.

Now

Prince Davenport's car pulls into the driveway of his father's Bel-Air mansion. He pops a couple of Altoids into his mouth and double-checks his appearance in the rearview mirror before stepping onto the pavement. He has been looking forward to this family dinner since the last one, two months prior. He hopes it will go better this time. He knows it won't.

His dad opens the door, and Prince reaches for him, pulling him into an all-encompassing embrace. If Prince's enthusiasm alone could forge a family, they'd be the Brady Bunch.

"Dad," he says. "It's good to see you."

Connor pulls away, coughing. "Have you been drinking?"

"I met a couple of friends for happy hour," Prince lies.

Connor nods. "Can I get you something else?"

His father's bar is stocked with top-shelf liquor. "I'll have a vodka martini. Grey Goose, please."

"Sure." Connor moves into the kitchen to make the drink while Prince wanders around the living room, looking at the art he's seen a million times. His mom had selected the bright, avant-garde pieces herself. When she was alive, she would put up new works every spring, an expensive habit that Connor would occasionally grumble about but never attempted to curtail. In the decades since her death, the art has remained unchanged. Prince is glad. He wasn't close to his mom, but he still feels a pang of nostalgia when he sees traces of her in these works.

"How's retirement, Dad?" he asks when his father returns, martini in hand.

Connor had retired the month before after working as a corporate lawyer for forty years. He had stayed at his firm just long enough to establish a fortune of ten million dollars, roughly the cost of Perpetual Immortality for one person.

Connor forces a smile. "Fine. Good. Great. I'm doing all the things I never had time for before."

It's a lie, Prince knows. Connor hates retirement. Sitting home bores him. Travel is too much of a hassle. He can only golf for so many hours a day. But as much as Connor hates retirement, he'd hated his job more.

The doorbell rings again, and Connor springs to his feet to answer it. It must be Darcy, Prince thinks. Sabrina is never on time.

Darcy is dressed in a black suit so boxy she might have gotten it in the men's department. She wears no make-up, does not tweeze her unibrow, cuts her own hair whenever it starts getting too long. It is her own little rebellion—against the beauty industry and against her sister; she rejects them, so they can't reject her.

Connor puts his arms around his daughter in a perfunctory hug, but Darcy doesn't return it. Her arms remain at her side, and she stiffens as though Connor is not her father but an over-familiar boss.

"What can I get you to drink?" Connor asks, ignoring the slight.

"Red wine, please. Whatever you have."

While he gets her a glass, she eyes Prince warily. "How's Dom?" she asks, sidestepping his outstretched arms and settling on the couch before he can insist on a hug.

"The same," he says. "Thanks for asking."

Their dad returns, hands Darcy a glass, and takes a seat himself. He looks uncomfortable, impatient. Probably anxious for Sabrina to arrive, Prince thinks. Their father has always been closest to her.

In between sips of their drinks, they offer each other close-lipped smiles, but nobody says anything. Prince's heart slides into his stomach. They haven't seen each other in months. How can they have so little to talk about?

"Hey, how was Brian McGill's funeral, Dad?" Prince asks, pleased with himself for remembering the death of his father's friend.

"Haunting," Connor replies. "The single most terrifying funeral I've ever attended."

"Because he was Immortal?" Prince asks.

Connor nods. "I think so. He's the first Immortal I've known to kick the bucket. I'd understood that it was possible, of course, that Immortals can die from accidents or injuries, but I don't know. I guess I've chosen not to think about that, to pretend Immortality really is immortality."

"It is, Dad," Prince assures him. "Brian shouldn't have flown that day. Conditions were bad. Visibility was low. But he didn't listen."

Connor mulls this over, then shakes his head. "In Brian's specific case, maybe, but plane crashes happen. Car crashes happen. Murders and mass shootings and fluke accidents happen. I looked up the statistics. On average, sixteen hundred Immortals die every year. Sixteen hundred. Our rate of death from accidents, suicides, and murders is slightly higher than it is for the population at large."

Prince shrugs, much less perturbed by this statistic than his father. "Over-confidence probably."

Connor shudders. "Maybe."

"It's hard to feel sorry for an ass like Brian McGill," Darcy says. She swallows the rest of her wine in one giant gulp and stands to get more.

Prince glares at her, but Connor chuckles. "More than a few people were whispering that at his funeral, especially the Mortals. It reminded me of the old times, before Immortality, when all of us put up with Brian but talked shit about him behind his back. I even thought his death might unify us all again, erase the division between Mortals and Immortals."

"And?" Prince probes. "Did it?"

Connor shakes his head. "No, it appears it was a temporary ceasefire. The next day, everything was as segregated as before."

Connor has been complaining about the country club's division for years. "It's not that I blame the Mortals," he continues. "They aren't doing well."

"Well, of course, they're not," Darcy says. "A bunch of them have died, and the rest are ten years older now."

"Yeah, but it was bad right from the beginning, from the moment the Infinity Serum was announced. Their pace slowed; their appetites diminished. Their golf games got worse overnight. At the same time, we Immortals, I swear, something happens to us when we receive that first injection. We stop aging and ailing, obviously, but it's more than that. I feel younger and stronger. I have the energy of a forty-year-old." Connor flexes a flabby arm as if this is somehow proof of his vitality.

Prince nods. "You've been given eternal life while they were instantly diagnosed with a terminal disease."

"Yes," Connor agrees, pleased with this analogy. "I think that must be what death feels like to them now, not an inevitability but a condition."

Connor ponders this a moment, then continues. "They've taken it so badly. They glare at us when they think we're not looking, as though we're the ones who have done this to them. They're so bitter, but they claim we're the ones who have changed."

"To them, it probably seems like you have," Prince explains. "Comments that you make without thinking – about future plans or your health or your great-grandchildren could feel like a slap in the face to them."

Connor looks at his son thoughtfully, then shakes his head. "Whatever," he grumbles. "I'm not going to walk on eggshells around them."

Prince sighs. No, of course not. His father has never been sensitive.

Connor changes the subject. "You know Brian didn't even have a will?"

"You're kidding," says Darcy. "How could anyone with as much money as Brian McGill die intestate?"

"It's true," Connor insists. "Apparently, when he became Immortal, he invited a couple of the guys over, lit the fire pit in his backyard, and watched his will go up in flames. Afterward, he broke out a bottle of Glenfiddich and proposed a toast to eternal life."

"Ugh," Darcy says. "Could he be any more intolerable?"

Sabrina arrives then, ten minutes late, which is about twenty minutes early for her. From the living room, Prince and Darcy watch the expression on their father's face change. Before, he'd been tense and uncomfortable, like a man enduring a colonoscopy. When Sabrina arrives, he beams with joy and relief as if she is a doctor who has pronounced him in perfect health.

Sabrina, dressed in a form-fitting teal dress, black stockings and knee-high boots, is as radiant as ever, permanently frozen at nineteen, a top model just a step below the household names like Annika Swan and Carlotta Dominguez but still profitable enough for the Xiomara Khan Agency to sponsor her Immortality.

Prince sometimes wonders about the details of her arrangement with the Agency. What will happen when, despite her eternal youth, designers grow tired of her? Will Xiomara Khan cut her loose, subject her to the horrors of Mortality? Or do they have some sort of pension plan that will give her Perpetual Immortality in exchange for, say thirty or forty years of service? If not, he hopes she's saving. He knows she's not.

Connor turns to his other children, his arm still wrapped around Sabrina. "Well, now that you're all here, let's eat."

He leads them to the formal dining room, where a marble table that can seat sixteen rests regally beneath a crystal renaissance chandelier.

"What's the occasion?" Prince asks. Family dinners usually take place on the patio beside the pool, at a table that seats six.

"No occasion," Connor says, sitting at the head of the table. "Just wanted to have a nice dinner with my children. Is that a crime?"

"No," Prince says, taking the seat to his father's left. Darcy sits beside Prince, using him as a buffer, while Sabrina sits to her father's right.

"Well, now, tell me what you've been up to," Connor says once they've made themselves comfortable. "Sabrina?"

"Everything's good, Daddy," she says, nibbling at her kale salad. "I'm moving in with Hayes."

"Who?" Connor asks.

"Hayes Harris. My boyfriend?"

"You're dating a guy named Haze? God, that is too perfect," says Darcy, helping herself to a roll. "Is he a drug dealer, or does he just smoke a lot of pot?"

Prince winces. "I think his name is probably spelled H-A-Y-E-S, right, Sabrina?"

"Of course," says Sabrina, who has missed the joke.

"I thought you were dating some other guy," Connor remarks. "Todd something or other."

"Tad. And no, we broke up three weeks ago."

"Three weeks ago? And you're already moving in with some other guy?" Darcy says, scrunching her nose as though she smells something rotten. "Do you even have your own place, or do you just go from boyfriend to boyfriend?"

"This coming from someone who's never had a date in her life?" Sabrina replies. She is pointing her fork at Darcy accusatorily. Her sister's acerbic tongue has never intimidated Sabrina. She may not be as smart as Darcy, but she has always known how to get under her skin.

"What does Hayes do?" Prince asks, cutting off his sisters' exchange, attempting, as always, to preserve the peace.

"He's British."

Everyone stares at her, but she doesn't notice. She is looking down at her fingernails, examining the polish for chips.

"Last time I checked, that isn't a profession, honey," Connor says patiently.

"I know that, Daddy," Sabrina replies. They wait for more, but nothing is forthcoming.

"So, what does this Tad fellow do, Sabrina?" Connor asks again.

"Hayes, Daddy. Tad was the last one." She gives him an exasperated look as though he is the one who requires an unbearable amount of patience.

Connor corrects himself. "Sorry. Hayes. What does Hayes do?"

Sabrina shrugs. "I don't know. I think he probably has a trust fund or something. He's never mentioned a job."

Connor frowns. "Darcy? Are you dating anyone?"

He knows she is not, and she knows he knows she is not. She shoots him a nasty look. "No, I'm not. But I am working on a particularly important case."

Prince offers an encouraging grin. Darcy is a lawyer for a human rights firm where her specialty is Immortality. As far as Prince can tell, her job entails two tasks: writing reports on the evils of Immortality and helping 'victims of Immortality' obtain legal status. When pressed, she'll say she doesn't hate Immortality itself, only the wrongs that are perpetrated for its sake, but Prince wonders how anyone could write up incident after incident of abuse—the blood of poor Eastern Europeans being forcibly extracted and trafficked to wealthier Western Europe, hungry Bangladeshis turning their children into blood banks, armies in Nigeria killing entire villages by draining the people of their blood the way you might drain a swimming pool for the winter—without developing some kind of antipathy toward the underlying cause.

"Tell us about it, Darcy," Prince says. He sets his glass down and leans forward as though whatever she is about to say is the most important thing in the world.

Darcy, who spends her life as an overlooked blade of grass, stepped on, shit on, and ignored, is clearly grateful for Prince's interest.

"I'm representing a group of Mexican immigrants who were recruited to come to the U.S., where, they were told, there's a shortage of blood. They expected to be housed on Compounds, but the Americans who approached them weren't with Hemodyne, and they didn't take them to Compounds," Darcy explains. "Instead, they were locked in an abandoned warehouse outside San Diego where they were held as, well, slaves, essentially. Blood slaves. They were kept in terrible conditions—no indoor plumbing, no beds, very little food—for six years before investigators found them."

"So, what's your role in this saga?" Connor asks. "It sounds like the work has already been done, the people saved."

"I'm fighting for their right to remain in the U.S.," Darcy explains.

"Why should they be allowed to stay here?" Connor asks. "I mean, what happened to them was terrible, and they should certainly receive some kind of compensation, but why should we let them stay?"

Darcy shifts in her seat, and Prince can see she is struggling to control her temper. "Well, Dad," she begins. "The U.S. has an interest in successfully prosecuting criminals, but it can be difficult to get undocumented immigrants to report criminal behavior or to testify in court because they're afraid of being deported. To combat this, the U.S. offers a visa for those who are willing to come forward. I'm working to ensure everyone in that warehouse gets one of those visas."

Sabrina, who usually ignores any conversation that is not about fashion, pop culture, or her, sits up in her chair. "Hey, you know, something like this happened to my friend Katja. She came over from Russia as, like, a mail-order bride for this multi-millionaire who was a total dog. He'd, like, slap her around and stuff. Anyway, same thing. She thought the only way to remain in the country was to stay married to this guy, but one of our friends put her in touch with, like, a really good lawyer who was able to get her another kind of visa, so she could stay in America and divorce the jackass."

Darcy raises her eyebrows at Sabrina, clearly surprised that she has managed to make a substantive contribution to the conversation. "Right," she says. "Slightly different scenario, but similar concept."

"That's wonderful, Darcy," Prince says. He is beaming at her, aware that his sister derives self-worth exclusively from her work.

He turns to his father, hoping Connor will say something complimentary, too, but instead, Connor steers the conversation to his son. "Prince, what are you working on these days?"

"Oh, nothing as interesting as Darcy," he says. "But work is fine. The usual."

He is an Immortality Therapist, which is more a marketing ploy than an official specialization, but it works, attracting wealthy clients and enabling him to charge double the going rates.

"Any interesting clients?" Connor asks.

"Hardly," Prince says. "Today was my third session with a woman who can't decide whether to get Immortality for her dog."

"Does the Infinity Serum even work on animals?" Connor asks.

"It hasn't been extensively tested," Prince replies. "They know it won't harm dogs, but it's not clear whether it will extend their lives indefinitely. They tell pet lovers they can try it at their own risk."

"But really, isn't that the same as Immortality for humans?" Darcy points out. "I mean, when it was approved by the FDA, Hemodyne only had five years of clinical trials. They couldn't know with any certainty whether it would keep humans alive forever. They still can't."

"With each passing year, it looks more and more like Immortality is the real deal, Darcy," Connor says. "I mean, hell, I haven't aged in a decade. My buddy Larry, his wife had cancer. Six months to live when Immortality was announced. She's still alive today, and her health hasn't gotten any worse."

"I guess what bothers me," Prince says loudly, attempting to redirect the conversation, "isn't that the Infinity Serum may not work on her dog, but that she's willing to spend over $300,000 a year to get Immortality for a pet."

"Well, that's not fair," Sabrina remarks. "Some people are very attached to their animals."

Prince and Darcy both stop eating and glare at their sister. Even Connor looks embarrassed by her remark.

"What?" Sabrina says. "It's true."

Prince bites his lip in consternation. Has Sabrina forgotten about Dom? Prince pictures his son, diagnosed the year before, deteriorating every day, destined to die before he can graduate from high school. His only hope is Immortality, and Prince can't afford it.

Prince opens his mouth to explain this to his sister, but the words don't come. In the end, it falls to Connor to enlighten Sabrina.

"Sabrina," he says. "Prince's son has a terminal disease. The money his client is using to save her dog's life could be used to save Dominick's life instead."

"But she doesn't know about Dom," Sabrina says.

Prince grips the underside of the table and squeezes with all his strength. His sister is oblivious, not cruel, he reminds himself. He can't get angry. He can't let another family dinner spiral out of control.

"She may not know about Dom specifically, but surely she knows that children are diagnosed with terminal illnesses every day," Connor explains. He is so patient with her, far more patient than he is with Darcy and Prince.

Sabrina starts to say something else, but Connor cuts her off. "And on that note," he says. "I have an announcement to make."

Prince raises his eyebrows. Connor is not the sort of father who makes announcements. Typically, he tells Sabrina any news and then it gradually trickles down, first to Prince and then to Darcy. But Connor is standing now, and his expression is unusually grave.

"Brian's untimely demise has made me think," Connor says. "Since his funeral, death has felt like a rapidly encroaching force, a wave biding its time until I go out to sea, where it will swallow me whole."

"Daddy, you're being ridiculous," Sabrina interrupts, waving her hand dismissively.

He ignores her. "When I think about what will happen to our family if, or when, the time comes, I feel unsettled. As you know, right now my estate is divided into even thirds, one share for each of you. That's always seemed like the fairest way. The trouble is, I'm worth about $10 million dollars, which means that if I die, you'll all be wealthy, but none of you will be able to afford eternal life."

Prince's breath catches in his throat. If this is headed where he thinks it is, it could save his son. He leans forward, pressing his palms against the tabletop.

"Brian's funeral made me realize that Immortality is not only the greatest medical advance in the history of the world, it has also separated the winners from the losers starkly, permanently, some would even say cruelly. I'm a winner, and I want my family to be winners, too. If you're on a sinking ship, and you have one life vest, you don't cut it up and give a third to each of your kids. You save one. Otherwise, they all die. What I'm trying to say is," he pauses, looking at each of his children in turn, "I've decided to change my will."

CHAPTER 3

Then

Oz, Ben thinks, the first time he sees a Compound. Vast in scope, otherworldly in nature. His little sister, Remy, would be proud of the reference. Those are her favorite books, her latest literary obsession, and Ben makes a mental note that if he ever goes back for his family, he can probably lure her to the Compound by comparing it to this beloved fantasy land. But then it's not Remy he'd have to convince.

The Compound's buildings—identical in size and height, too numerous to count—are shiny and bright. They glisten in the sun, the way only new things can, before they dull, lose their luster, become the second-hand toys of Ben's childhood.

Ben is so excited a small squeal emanates from within him. He glances around the crowded bus, embarrassed, but no one has noticed. They are as exuberant as he is, these economic refugees who have struggled for years, decades. Seeing their new home has reduced them all to children, gasping and clapping, abandoning reticence for unrestrained delight.

Ben smiles, swept up in a feeling of oneness with these strangers, and when a small cluster near the front begins to sing a hymn of salvation, Ben, pleased he knows the lyrics, sings along, even though his relationship with Jesus is tenuous at best.

"Why didn't we come sooner?" the skeletal woman behind Ben asks her husband, a hint of accusation in her voice.

"We had to be sure," her husband replies, and though the comment isn't directed at Ben, he nods. He can hear his father in this man – the caution and skepticism, the unwillingness to be made a fool of again.

This is the second wave of mass relocation, the people who had let their family or friends lead, then waited for their reports. They had expected horror stories, midnight escapes, cautionary tales. Instead, the joke is on them. They have spent years barely scraping by while the others settled into the Compounds and established lives—real lives.

The bus stops in front of the Compound wall, steel and intimidating and ten feet tall. Ben is impressed. To him, the wall is a symbol of security, a sign that there is something worth protecting inside.

A quartet of Compound employees, dressed in matching emerald polos and khaki shorts, welcomes them and hands them Dixie Cups of ice-cold lemonade as they disembark.

Ben accepts a cup from a ponytailed woman in her forties and chugs it, certain, as soon as it hits his tongue, that he has never tasted anything so good. His mother makes lemonade sometimes, squeezing drops of juice from shriveled lemons into a pitcher of tap water, stirring in some sugar if they have any. But her drink bears little resemblance to this one, doesn't even deserve the label 'lemonade.'

While the new arrivals finish their refreshment, a Compound worker presses his index finger against a digital screen attached to the wall. A metal door Ben had not noticed slides open, and the ponytailed woman beckons, "Come see your new home."

Inside, two rings of skyscrapers surround an attractive town center. Ben is in awe of the uniformity of the buildings, their factory-fresh look. They are all grey and clean, no graffiti, no signs of wear and tear. Ben smells food and his feet begin moving in that direction, propelled by the angry urges of his underfed stomach.

The ponytailed woman steps in front of him. "We'll just do your In-take first," she says. "Do you want to go wait with your parents?"

Although this is phrased as a question, it's a command, and Ben nods before moving away from her, amongst the four-dozen other new arriv-als, until he finds a family that could pass as his. The man is bearded; the woman is matronly. They have five children already, and Ben thinks that maybe he can slip through with them.

He listens as the man gives his name and as he introduces his wife and children. The Compound employee summons his family forward one by one, recording their fingerprints on a digital screen. Ben hopes she'll over-look him, but she doesn't. She glares at him now, recategorizes him. Be-fore, he had been an over-eager kid; now, he is a trespasser, a rule-breaker, a stowaway.

Ben looks around, feigning confusion, and starts to back away.

"Not so fast," she says as she lunges across the table and seizes his arm.

The security guard is middle-aged with thick, dark hair and a small paunch. He might be Ben's dad, except his eyes are kinder. Kinder, too, than any law enforcement professional Ben has ever seen.

"Come on, kid," he says to Ben, who is sitting on a metal folding chair in an administrative office, his head in his hands.

Ben stands and holds out his wrists, frustrated by his failure. Getting this close is so much worse than never trying at all.

Instead of cuffing him, the man rests a hand on his shoulder, firm, fa-therly. "Let's get you something to eat."

Ben nods, his eyes still on the floor. He had gotten himself arrested once, thinking juvie might be worth it for the regular meals. It had not been, and he'd been relieved when the judge gave him a suspended sentence and told him not to get in trouble again.

Ben expects a stale sandwich, a mealy apple. Instead, the security guard leads him to the Compound cafeteria. Ben has never seen any place like it. It is the size of four football fields, with food lining three of its walls. It smells of home, not Ben's home, which smells of cheap beer and bleach, but the middle-class home of Ben's dreams, with normal parents who barbecue and bake bread and make him eat his vegetables. He looks from the food to the guard and back again, trembling with hope and fear and disbelief.

"Get whatever you'd like," the guard says, gesturing at the splendid buffet.

Ben helps himself to lasagna and rotisserie chicken, fajitas and six different deli meats, a snow mound of mashed potatoes, and a pair of golden-brown dinner rolls that look like sunbaked breasts on his plate. When he sits down, he gropes each of them with one hand, smirks at his private joke, and begins devouring them, sinking his teeth into one and then the other.

He eats every bite of food on his plate and then returns for seconds, even though his stomach, unaccustomed to such bounty, is already cramping in protest. He stops only when his body physically rejects the food, his gag reflex sending the bite of peanut butter cookie he had swallowed back up into his mouth and out onto his plate. Ben scowls, not ashamed, only disappointed.

The security guard, who has been sitting beside him, watching him eat, pats his back. "We'll get you some food to take home."

Home is a two-bedroom hovel, with duct tape sealing a window Zeke had broken with a broomstick. The paint is peeling; the front step has fallen in. Black mold spatters the once-white front door like smudged mascara against an ashen face. It's a crap hole, Ben acknowledges to himself as they pull into the driveway, but it's a home, for now anyway. They have received six eviction notices over the years, but somehow, they have always managed to avoid getting kicked out. Ben is not naïve enough to think their luck will last forever, and he sometimes marvels at how seldom his parents seem to think about the future or prepare any kind of contingency plan.

Zeke answers the door when they knock. He looks from Ben to the Compound guard, then yells, "Mom! Dad! Ben's home."

They hadn't noticed he was gone. It has been less than twenty-four hours, and Ben has a history of disappearing for days at a time, only to reappear well-fed and happy, sometimes with food or money in tow.

For half a second, Ben thinks he might get away with this, that he might slip into the house unnoticed and stow the food he has brought home with him beneath his bed. But after acting like an ally all afternoon, now the security guard betrays him. "I'll need to speak with your parents," he says to Zeke.

Ben curses under his breath, wishing this man wouldn't interfere with what he doesn't understand.

"Mom! Dad!" Zeke yells again.

"What?" Vance Hudson yells back, wrapping his head around the kitchen wall to see what all the fuss is about.

"Oh, shit," he grumbles when he sees the uniformed man next to Ben.

He storms toward the door in paint-stained jeans and an undershirt, smelling of body odor and beer. The rest of the family follows—his mom Ilene, with her mouth pinched in disapproval. His older brother Henry, not surprised but disappointed, and his little sister Remy, clutching Henry's hand.

"What'd you do this time, boy?" Vance asks, coarse and weary.

The guard steps forward. "Mr. Hudson? I'm Paco Hernandez, a guard at Compound 264. Your son turned up at our gates tonight."

Ben stares past his family into the house beyond. He could be moving into a new apartment right now, eating a second meal at the cafeteria. Instead, he is back here with the parents he is growing to hate, the siblings he is coming to view as a burden.

"Thank you for bringing him home," Ilene says. Her voice is flat, and her eyes are hollow. She has deadened herself to him, to the world, the way she does when she is so enraged that screaming will not do. It is not that he ran away. It is not that he has gotten in trouble or that he has been escorted home by this intrusive security guard. It's where he ran that has infuriated her. He had delivered himself to the enemy, offered up his soul for an all-you-can-eat buffet.

"It's no problem, Ma'am," Paco is saying, with hat-tipping respect that only makes Ben's parents more suspicious. "We fed him a good dinner, and we've brought some food for the rest of your family, too."

He gestures at the paper bags he and Ben are carrying, each stuffed to the brim with cans of vegetables, bags of rice, loaves of bread. More food than they usually eat in a week. His siblings' eyes are glued to the bags, their yearning palpable.

"No, thank you," Ilene says, crossing her arms.

Ben's heartbeat becomes plodding and heavy. This is what he had been afraid of. But she's not serious. She can't be. They don't have the luxury of turning away free food.

The security guard, Paco, is visibly astonished. "Please, ma'am. It's free. No strings attached."

"She said we don't want it," Vance says. Although he is not a large man, there is something intimidating about him. It's his bearing, maybe, or his rage. Or possibly, Ben thinks, the fact that he has nothing to lose.

"But—" Paco begins.

"But nothing." Vance knocks the bag from Ben's hand then cuffs the back of his neck and pulls him into the house in one swift, angry motion. "Thanks for bringing my boy home. Now get the hell off our property."

Ben catches one last glimpse of Paco Hernandez before Vance slams the door. The guard's face is awash with self-incrimination. But Ben doesn't blame Paco. He blames himself. He should have been quicker and craftier. He'd had the food to feed his family literally in his hands, and he'd let it slip through his fingertips.

Now

Before they are shown to their new home, the Hudsons are given a tour of the Compound. Dallas leads them around at a leisurely pace. He seems to have acquired an iota of respect for them—perhaps because they're all literate and articulate and cooperative—but he still walks with his head tilted back abnormally far so that he can look down on them.

"At maximum capacity, each Compound holds between fifty- and sixty thousand people," he tells them. "We're currently at 48,000 or so. Every Compound comes with certain amenities: park, swimming pool, gym, library, schools, movie theatre." He points to each in turn.

Remy lights up when he mentions the library. Large, impersonal, inner-city libraries have always felt like home to her; she had spent a good portion of her youth nestled in a corner of the children's section, making her way through stacks of books.

"Can we check books out?" she asks. This was the one privilege that had always been denied her in Los Angeles. Checking books out required a membership, and a membership required proof of residency.

"Of course," Dallas says. "And if there's ever a book you want that we don't have, send in a request form. We'll get it for you. Dr. Odili is very generous when it comes to books."

For the first time, Remy feels the stir of excitement that has already overtaken her brothers. Life may not be perfect here, but it will be better.

Main Street runs through the center of the Compound. The buildings there are concrete, absent architectural detail, devoid of color. Functional but not picturesque. The result is that Main Street is overwhelmingly grey, as though it is permanently stuck in a cloudy day.

Remy can see through the glass windows of the Burger King, and she scans the menu to see how prices here compare to the Outside. The Value Menu at Burger King had been one of the best deals around back in LA For two dollars, she'd been able to get a Whopper Jr. But here, there is no Value Menu, and the Whopper, five dollars in Santa Monica, is ten dollars here.

"Why are prices so high?" she asks Dallas.

"To discourage over-consumption," he explains. "We want to encourage healthy behaviors without restricting choice, so we incentivize and disincentivize accordingly. The gym is free. Fast food is marked up. But remember, the cafeteria is always free, so it's not like anyone's going hungry."

The markup doesn't appear to be much of a disincentive. The Burger King is packed.

Dallas points to several bars on the street, and Remy wonders if alcohol is marked up, too. She pictures her dad getting them kicked out of a shelter for harassing the staff, pissing in alleyways that would otherwise have made reasonable places to sleep, slumping in a corner all day with a bottle of cheap vodka when he should have been working, and she hopes so.

"The legal drinking age on the Compounds, as in the rest of the country, is twenty-one, and we prohibit drinking the twenty-four hours before Donation," Dallas tells them.

"Is that much of a problem?" Henry asks.

"You know, early on, we were concerned about enforcement, but it turns out we didn't need to be. Cruors tend to use their weekly allowance within two days of Donation. There's no money left to buy booze by the time Donation rolls around again, and on the rare occasion that someone does manage to drink within twenty-four hours of giving, well, the hangover that results ensures that never happens again."

"You mean nobody saves anything?" Henry asks in disbelief.

Dallas thinks about it. "Sure. Sometimes a guy will save up to take his girlfriend out to a nice dinner, or a mom will put away a few dollars to get her kids something for Christmas," he concedes. "But they're not exactly establishing rainy-day funds. And really, why should they? Everything they need is taken care of here."

Henry frowns. He is naturally frugal, attempting to put away a few dollars even when his family was at their poorest because he subscribes to the view that tomorrow might be worse. It's a lesson he learned from his parents' mistakes.

Remy understands this and whispers, "Don't worry, Henry. Just because they're not saving doesn't mean you can't." But she is troubled, too. She doesn't understand the people here. They seem to have forgotten the way things were before the Compounds—the widespread poverty and unemployment, the mass evictions and unbearable hunger, charities' inability to provide sufficient help and the government's failure to do so. Henry is right; they should be saving. They should remember how insecure security can be.

Dallas continues their tour. "There are forty-two apartment buildings on Compound 78. Each is twenty stories high, and each story holds fifteen apartments and sixty people."

Twelve hundred people in a single building, Remy thinks. She can't even imagine.

There are two rings of apartment buildings. The inner ring, closest to the Donation Center, Main Street, and the cafeteria, is comprised of eighteen buildings. The outer ring, at the very edge of the Compound, along the steel wall, has twenty-four, six along each wall, even though the Compound is not a perfect square but a rectangle, longer on the north and south than it is on the east and west. The excess space along the north and south walls is occupied by one-story security buildings.

"Is safety much of a concern?" Remy asks, surprised that in addition to the steel wall, the Compound has two fully staffed security offices.

"Oh, not yours," Dallas says, chuckling. "You're perfectly safe here. But we have to protect our blood supply. Immortality is big business these days, and the hardest part is procuring enough blood to make it possible."

That is why they are here, of course. Remy had researched the Compounds once before delivering a makeshift presentation to her parents in a desperate attempt to convince them to move to one. She had started with information her parents already knew, that Hemodyne had invented Immortality, delivered via a horrifically expensive weekly injection of Infinity Serum. That Infinity Serum required mass quantities of human blood and that attempts to find an effective substitute – animal or synthetic –had failed. As a result, Hemodyne needed people, hordes of them.

At some point, Hemodyne's economists must have done some number crunching and come to the conclusion that the best way to secure a sufficient blood supply was to secure the poor, and the cheapest way to secure the poor was with free housing and food. They'd termed the Donor class 'Cruors,' an obsolete Latin term referring to coagulated blood. She had thought that once her parents understood Hemodyne's motivations they might relent, but she'd barely made it through a sentence of her presentation when they'd cut her off, hostile, disinterested, unswayable.

The apartments are assigned at random. The Hudsons have drawn one on the eleventh floor of Building 19, looking back into the Compound, not out to the desert beyond. Remy would have preferred a view of something other than another apartment building, but she is not going to complain. A bed is a bed, and she is grateful.

"Your fingerprints should work now. Why don't one of you try to open the door?" Dallas suggests.

Ben steps forward and places his left index finger on the pad outside the building door. The door slides open, and a woman's voice says, "Hello, Benjamin."

Ben turns to them, baring his teeth in an exaggerated grin as he takes an oversized, ceremonial step into his new apartment building.

The others follow him into the lobby, another colorless space that Remy guesses is supposed to look modern. Instead, it just looks cold. To the right is an electronic bulletin board announcing various events: Children's Movie Night, a grunge band playing at the dive bar, a sale on women's cosmetics. To the left are mailboxes for every apartment in the building, all three hundred of them. Straight back are two elevators, one in motion, the other holding at ground level in anticipation of the Hudsons.

"There's a basement, too," Dallas tells them as they walk toward the elevator. "That's where the laundry room is. It's free, of course, not coin-operated. There are very clear instructions posted down there, but if you need help, just hit the call button. Please. The number of times we've had people break our machines…"

Remy looks at Dallas curiously. Has he forgotten that two in five Cruors are illiterate? Of course, they can't understand the instructions.

They ride the elevators up to the eleventh floor, and Zeke, at Dallas's prompting, presses his left index finger against the pad next to their apartment. The door swings open. "Welcome home, Ezekiel," the automated voice says.

The apartment is dusty with disuse, and the air is thick and chalky.

It is cheaply furnished and has just three rooms: a living space and two bedrooms. The bathrooms are down the hall. Still, it has all the essentials—beds and bedding, a sofa, a television, a plastic table and chairs, a computer atop a desk. The floor is linoleum disguised as hardwood; the walls are white and unadorned.

"What do you think?" Dallas asks once they have had a chance to look around.

"There's no kitchen," Remy remarks.

"No," Dallas agrees. "Compound 1 had kitchens, but so few people used them that it didn't make sense to continue including them. Most people prefer to take their meals in the cafeteria."

"Does the computer move?" Zeke asks. Everyone turns to look at him, bewildered.

"Well, it's a desktop, so, not easily," Dallas says.

"Oh," Zeke replies. His eyes scan the apartment anxiously as though he is trying to locate something he has lost.

Ben bursts out laughing. "Oh, come on, man. You've charmed the snake in more public places than this."

Zeke turns bright red. Dallas looks uncomfortable, and Henry and Remy exchange looks. They had been doing so well until now, dispelling the notion that the poor were ill-bred and uncouth, and now Ben has managed to negate their efforts with a single comment.

"Well, if that's all, I'll be leaving you." Dallas looks like he can't get away fast enough. "My number is in your orientation packets. Call me if you need anything."

After he's gone ("That guy could use a little more snake charming if you ask me," Ben remarks as soon as the door is closed), they stand crowded in the doorway, gazing at their new apartment. After six years on the streets, they finally have a place to call home.

The minute her brothers' heads hit their pillows, they are out. Even Henry, who the night before had been so uncertain, seems to have come around to the idea of living here. But Remy finds herself unable to sleep for the second night in a row. Something unidentifiable is nagging at her, a siren she can't quite locate, and until she does, she can't know how to react.

Restless, she slips out of bed and into some jeans and a sweater. Dallas said the Compound is safe. She decides to see for herself.

Outside, the Compound is dark but for the streetlights shining down on the sidewalks. At three o'clock in the morning, everyone is asleep. It's not like Los Angeles. There are no restless vagabonds wandering aimlessly through the streets, no businessmen arriving home after a late flight into LAX, nobody so downtrodden or important that they remain awake while the rest of the city sleeps. Even the parties appear to have died down.

Remy stays in between the two rings of apartment buildings, following the path that winds its way around the entire Compound. The desert is pleasant at this hour. It is warm but not hot, and there is no wind, in contrast with Santa Monica, where the ocean breeze had been pervasive, chilling.

She can't get over how still it is here. Between the silence and the abundance of concrete, she feels as though she has been buried alive. The Compound isn't heaven; it's a necropolis, its inhabitants zombies. She turns this idea over in her mind, amused at first and then unnerved. She knows now what's been bothering her.

On the worst nights of Remy's childhood, when she was so hungry her stomach sounded like a fireworks display, one unexpected burst after another, when she was tired or dirty or sick, Henry would hold her close and whisper, "You don't like this? Then get out of here. Go to college, get a job, and never look back."

She had been willing to come to Compound 78 because she'd seen it as a trampoline, a springboard to the future. Here, she'd thought, was a place where she could focus on school so she could go to college, an opportunity to restart her life. But after only a day, the Compound seems more like a whirlpool than a trampoline. Everyone else has been sucked in, can't get out, and is forced to see the same thing day after day until they drown in their complacency.

She sees a wooden park bench and collapses onto it, panting, not because of her pace but because she is afraid of dying here. In the labyrinth that is her life, she has escaped one dead end only to find herself heading straight for another.

The high school counselor, Julia, is a Midwestern transplant in her mid-forties with big blue eyes, thick red hair, and flawless porcelain skin. Remy stares at her hair enviously. She had hoped conditioner would tame her own wild locks, but her dark curls remain as unmanageable as ever, as dry and frizzy as a worn-out toothbrush. Julia looks from Zeke and Remy to her computer screen and back again as though something is confusing her. Finally, she asks, "Zeke, are you planning to take the National Placement Exam at the end of the year?"

"No," Zeke says at once.

Julia has no intention of trying to persuade him otherwise, but Remy is disappointed. "Zeke," she says, punching him in the arm. "Why not?"

He shrugs. "I don't want to. I don't have to, do I?"

"No," the guidance counselor says. "No, of course you don't. Most Cruors don't. If you're happy here on the Compound, you can become a Donor the week after you graduate, no exam necessary." Her tone is encouraging. She reminds Remy of a used car salesman hawking her wares.

"Is there any way I can become a Donor sooner?" Zeke asks.

Julia smiles. "I'm afraid not, but you're not the first student to ask." She assigns Zeke to remedial classes across the board.

"You're behind in pretty much everything, but we'll get you caught up," she says. Remy doubts that. Zeke hasn't attended school in nearly a decade, and he's never been interested in learning. He will leave Compound 78 High as uneducated as when he entered.

Julia turns to Remy. "You, on the other hand," she begins, "read and write at a college level, and your analytical skills are excellent. You're behind in math, but otherwise, I think you should be fine in regular freshman-level courses."

Remy, who had been beaming with pride at her results, is crestfallen at her course assignments. "Regular?" she asks. "Not honors?" She has managed to test into honors classes her entire life despite illiterate parents and irregular school attendance. She doesn't understand how she is falling short here.

The question irritates Julia. "We don't offer honors classes here," she says drily. "There isn't enough demand."

Remy is dumbstruck. She knows what students in other places do in preparation for the National Placement Exam. They enroll in the most rigorous courses their schools offer. They sign up for extra test prep sessions beginning in the seventh grade. They take old exams and pay actual exam graders to give them feedback, and when they don't perform as well as expected, they hire private tutors. They get diagnosed with learning disabilities that entitle them to accommodations on the exam itself: extra time, longer and more frequent breaks, private rooms. They know what the stakes are, and they give themselves every advantage.

Remy doesn't need all of that. She just needs a curriculum that will prepare her for the exam. She glares at Julia. "Without honors classes, how are we supposed to be competitive on the NPE?"

"You study hard, that's how," Julia replies, meeting Remy's gaze. "There are plenty of test prep books in the library."

Remy senses the futility of this conversation and falls silent.

When Zeke and Remy's schedules are finalized, Julia gives them a tour of the school. It is modern with clean hallways and state-of-the-art science equipment. Even the lockers that line the hallway are opened with fingerprints. Remy knows she is supposed to be impressed, but she feels about the high school the way she does about everything else on the Compound; it's a façade without substance. She blinks back tears. She is quickly growing to hate it here.

By lunchtime, the other students have already pegged Remy as a nuisance. She asks and answers questions; she participates in demonstrations;

she elicits hopeful smiles from previously uninspired teachers.

"Why's she trying so hard?" Remy hears one girl whisper to another.

Remy doesn't expect them to understand. She is accustomed to not having friends. Her life has been too transient for sustained, meaningful relationships outside her family. At her past schools, she could never really be herself; she'd had too much to hide. She'd lied about where she lived and about her parents. She'd had to make excuses for things other students didn't even have to think about. "We can't work on the project at my house because…"; "I missed the last week of school because…"; "You haven't been able to reach my mom or dad because…"

Everyone had always believed her. It was the underperformers—behavioral or academic—that teachers and administrators questioned. They overlooked the fact that her armpits stank of sweat, that her clothes were threadbare and soiled, that she was the thinnest girl in a school full of anorexics.

Her classmates had noticed. They eyed her warily as she approached, fanned their hands in front of their noses if she got too close, kept their distance if they could manage it. But none of them thought of helping her. They didn't realize anything was wrong beyond her deplorable personal hygiene. As a result, she was ostracized; no one wanted to be friends with the smelly girl. Here, it is the same but different. Here, no one wants to be friends with the nerdy girl who tries too hard.

She makes her way to the Compound cafeteria, helps herself to a bowl of raisin bran and a carton of milk, and looks around for a place to sit. She sees Zeke at a fire engine red table with a cluster of guys who are all larger and more muscular than him. She knows if she goes over, he will make room for her, but she also knows how hard it is for her brother to make friends, and she is reluctant to taint him by association. Instead, she makes her way to an empty table and keeps her head down as she eats. Tomorrow she will bring a book.

She is almost finished when a voice above her says, "Is this seat taken?"

She looks up and sees Caleb standing before her, eyebrows raised, a bemused expression on his face. She hadn't noticed it on the bus, but he looks different from everyone else here. His hair is silkier; his skin is clearer. He is cleaner, somehow. If the rest of the Cruors are tarnished silverware, Caleb is the shiny, polished alternative.

"Caleb, hi," she says. "Yeah. Of course. Sit."

He takes the seat across from her.

"So," he says, taking a bite of his BLT. "Your first day of school and you've already set yourself apart."

Remy snorts. "Is that a nice way of saying I'm a pariah?"

Caleb shrugs. "Little bit."

"How did you know?"

"I hear things," he says cryptically. He reaches for his chocolate milk and studies her over the rim of his glass as he drinks.

"How do you stand it here?" she blurts. She has been wondering about this since the bus ride. How could he go from Princeton student to Cruor, from someone who could have done anything to a Donor whose greatest contribution will be his blood? How can he bear to live the same life as her classmates who scoff at learning or as her brother Ben, who aspires to nothing?

"There it is," he says. He leans back in his chair and grins.

"Well?" she demands.

"Remy, I'm not like you," he says. "Yeah, I'm smart, but I'm also lazy and scared. Before, my whole life was planned out. I was supposed to go to Princeton, major in econ, get my MBA, then take a job in my dad's private equity firm. And the pressure, the expectation, it all got to be too much. So, I rebelled. But not by doing something useful like writing a novel or starting a non-profit. No, instead, I came here, essentially choosing to do absolutely nothing. You think you and I are alike, but we're not. Not really. You're here because you have nothing; I'm here despite having everything. There probably aren't two people on this Compound who are more different than you and me." He is emphatic, but something in his tone suggests he wants her to challenge his assertion, to tell him he is not as pathetic as he thinks he is.

Remy doesn't speak at first. She looks at his clear skin and expensive clothes and thinks about his words. Eventually, she whispers, "Then why do I feel like you're the only one here who gets me?"

Caleb looks away.

"Help me, Caleb," Remy says. "I want what you had. I want to go to Princeton or Harvard or Yale. I want to get out of here and never come back. I want a shot, just a shot, at a future."

"So, what's stopping you?" he asks, but they both know the question is disingenuous.

"Do you know what NPE test prep is like here?"

"Abysmal," he replies. "Know why?"

"No. Why?"

"Because every year, a maximum of ten students on Compound 78 take the NPE. Ten. Maximum. For everyone else, school is just something to endure. This is the downside of being run by a corporation. Everything is about maximizing efficiency, and in Compound schools, that means helping the majority of students eke out a high school diploma, not ensuring the handful at the top are competitive on the NPE."

"What I'm hearing is that I don't stand a chance without your help."

He opens his mouth, closes it again. She doesn't take her eyes off him. "I'll think about it," he mumbles.

"Thank you, Caleb," Remy says. She leans across the table and throws her arms around him. "Thank you so much."

CHAPTER 4

Then

The halls smell of urine, and the carpet is splotched with flaxen stains.

"The previous owners had cats," their real estate agent, Opal, explains.

"No kidding," Prince remarks.

"It's a dump," Tina says.

"It could use some work," Opal agrees. "But for this neighborhood in your price range, it's really the best we can do."

She crinkles her nose as she says this as if it's their budget and not the cat piss that stinks.

Every house she's shown them has been a dud. They've been tiny or in disrepair, adjacent to a freeway or in the middle of a slum. Each time they reject a place, she reminds them of how little money they are bringing to one of the most competitive markets in the country. "If you try to race a Chevy Malibu against Porsches and Ferraris, you shouldn't expect to finish first. You should be glad you're in the race," she tells them.

Tina, three months pregnant and cranky, plans to fire her as soon as the day is over. "I won't have my real estate agent make me feel like she's doing me a favor," she tells Prince as they follow Opal to one last house.

Prince doesn't argue. One of the reasons he'd married Tina is that she has the courage to do things he wouldn't dare.

When they stop in front of a large Victorian in a good neighborhood, Tina thinks Opal is taunting them. "That bitch," she grumbles. "I swear to God if she says, 'This is what you could have if you paid a little more,' I might have to slap that condescending smirk off her face."

But the Victorian is not a tease. It's not within their budget, but it's close, and it's so beautiful it makes them giddy. They run through the house like school children, imagining a future in each room.

"We'll host dinner parties," Tina purrs in the dining room that can seat eight.

"And have movie nights," Prince says when they see the spacious den.

"I'll bake in here," she says in the kitchen with dual ovens, a six-burner stove, more counter space than she knows what to do with, even though she hates baking. Even though every cake and cookie she's ever attempted has been a gooey, runny mess.

Upstairs, she places her hand on her stomach and breaks into a grin. "This is where Dominick will put up pictures of half-naked girls and play music we hate."

In the next room: "We'll paint these walls pink for our daughter when she's small, and she'll paint them black when she's a teenager."

In the third room, Prince chimes in. "The twins will have to share this room. We'll put in bunk beds for them, and they'll fight over who gets the top."

Tina kisses him with tongue right in front of Opal, intoxicated by how quickly the future she dreams of has gone from out of reach to imminently possible. They duck into the next bedroom, the master, and Prince pulls Tina onto the bed, where they paw at each other playfully. Like teenagers, Prince thinks.

"And this," he whispers, tickling her ear with his tongue, "is where we'll make all those beautiful babies."

"I take it you like it?" Opal asks from the doorway, her arms crossed in disapproval.

"What's wrong with it?" Tina asks, sitting up, tidying her short, dark hair with her hands.

"Nothing," Opal assures her.

They wait. With Opal, there's always a catch.

"Really," she promises. "It's been on the market for two years, and the owner's desperate."

It's the kiss of death in Southern California, staying on the market too long. Everyone starts to wonder why it isn't moving, what other buyers are seeing that they're not.

"Nobody wants a Victorian in Southern California," Opal explains. She says it in such a way that they can tell she thinks they have terrible taste, but they don't care.

"We'll take it," Tina says with a brief, decisive nod.

"It's over your budget," Opal points out.

"We'll manage," Prince tells her.

"That's right," Tina adds. "I hate being a social worker anyway. Maybe I'll become a real estate agent like you. Good commission, right?"

Opal raises her left eyebrow and smirks.

"And Prince can stop counseling at-risk youth and open a practice targeting millionaires," Tina continues.

Prince laughs because he thinks she is joking. Later, he discovers she is not, that her solution for coming up with the unbearably steep mortgage payments is for them to become Immortality specialists in their respective fields, the first of their kind. But that day, in that moment, he thinks she is just talking, spewing a series of meaningless words at a woman who doesn't matter.

The next week, when their offer is accepted, they buy a bottle of Martinelli's and drink it in their small West Hollywood apartment, toasting their good fortune.

"God, Prince, can you believe it?" Tina says. She gets up from the couch and twirls around in circles, her white maternity dress floating up in waves around her. For a moment, it looks like she has wings.

Prince rises and takes her in his arms. "We're really doing it, aren't we? We have a beautiful house, a son on the way, each other. God, what if it's all a dream?"

Tina wraps her hands around his neck and smiles, her white teeth yellowing beneath the halogen bulbs of the ceiling fan. "It is a dream," she says. "We're making our dreams come true."

Now

Prince's new patient is Alan English. Prince expects an older man, uptight, academic, but the man relaxing in his waiting room, ankle over knee, couldn't have an Immortal Age of more than forty (Actual Age fifty, probably). He is dressed in designer jeans and a cashmere sweater. He is handsome, with a full head of hair, dark and wavy, and a face that's all lines and no curves, drawn with a ruler, not a protractor.

"Alan?" Prince says. "How can I help you?"

"I hate my life, and I don't know what to do about it," Alan spits out before Prince manages to close his office door.

Prince nods. This is how almost every conversation in his office begins. For people who have everything, his clients are surprisingly miserable. "Tell me about it," he says, leaning back in his chair.

Alan summarizes his early life in six sentences. He was born into money, attended private schools, got a high-paying job, married a daddy's girl with even more money than him, two kids, huge house, more private schools. He sounds so caustic it's as though he is mocking his own existence.

"That sounds nice enough," Prince remarks. He wonders if other therapists have to fight off a strong sense of loathing every time they meet with a client.

"Yeah, it was," Alan admits. "Until Immortality came along." He and his wife had begun getting the Infinity Serum almost immediately. Their kids' college funds became Immortality funds because eternal life is more important than education, but otherwise, life had gone on very much as before. He'd gone to work. His kids had gone to school. And even though ten years had passed, he hadn't aged.

"And then last month, we took a trip to Paris. Went to the Louvre to see the Mona Lisa. My wife's godmother is friends with the curator, so we got in early, before the crowds. We stood there with this masterpiece that we had all to ourselves, and I thought, Da Vinci created this, the Last Supper, the Vitruvian Man all in a single lifetime. Sixty or seventy years. I have infinitely longer. What am I going to do? Keep making money? Getting the occasional promotion? It all seemed so meaningless suddenly. I mean, if I'm going to keep taking up oxygen, shouldn't I be doing something more?"

He stands and begins pacing the room, restless, agitated. "I've tried to talk to my wife about this," he continues, "but she doesn't get it. She thinks this is a midlife crisis. Tells me to get it together. Buy a convertible if I have to. We fight all the time now."

Prince listens, asks questions. By the time Alan has finished describing his life, the hour is up.

The trouble with his clients, Prince thinks after Alan has gone, is that they all want to believe they're special. If these people read a little more, they'd know that scarcely a month passes without *The Atlantic* or *The New Yorker* printing an article penned by some well-intentioned Immortal lamenting the fact that nothing he accomplishes feels good enough anymore. It is the curse that accompanies the blessing of eternal life.

Prince understands the dilemma, but he doesn't pity it. Before becoming an Immortality specialist, he'd worked with at-risk teenagers, kids who'd grown up with alcoholic mothers and abusive fathers, a brother who'd killed or been killed or killed himself, absent parents, senile grandparents, too much on their plate, too little money. Health, love, food, shelter—those are necessities. Meaning? Even the search for meaning, that's a privilege.

It's only three o'clock, but Prince begins to pack his belongings. Alan was his last appointment. His wife, Tina, is concerned that he hasn't been bringing in quite as much money lately. He tells her it's the economy. "Everyone I talk to says their client list has shrunk."

Tina, a real estate agent specializing in 'forever homes' for the Immortal, has been doing well despite the downturn. "When the stock market takes a tumble, people turn to real estate," she explains. "It's a safer bet." He doesn't remind her of the housing crisis four years ago, when real estate values, too, had sunk to historic lows.

He walks out of his office and into reception, where his secretary Blair is on the phone. "I'm afraid Dr. Davenport is booked up for the next two months—Anything sooner? I'm afraid not—Oh, wait. Here. I have a cancellation next Thursday at one o'clock. Does that work for you? Great. Perfect. I'm so glad we were able to work something out. Can I get a few details from you?"

Prince shakes his head. Blair is an expense he wishes he could cut. Receptionists are extinct at all but the most upscale establishments. Appointments can be made online; kiosks take care of check-in; credit card machines handle any payment due. But Tina says Blair is essential to his image. "You want to attract a wealthy clientele? You have to look like you've already made it," she insists. A receptionist, along with the expensive leather chairs she made him buy for his office, the $3,000 watch she'd gotten him for his birthday, and the self-driving BMW that totes him around, are signs that he has.

The overbooked schedule is part of the ploy, too. He's never full more than a week in advance. His regulars take up seventy to eighty percent of his time, but that still leaves him with plenty of availability for new clients. "Doesn't matter," Tina argues. "Let them see how desirable you are. They should feel lucky to get an appointment with Prince Davenport."

Sometimes his entire career feels like a sham.

Blair hangs up and turns to Prince. "Heading home, Doc?"

He has told her dozens of times that he only has a master's, but she insists on calling him doctor anyway. ("Smart girl," Tina had said when Prince complained about this. "People want doctors; they trust doctors.")

"I think so," Prince says. "I know it's not great for business, but I want to spend as much time as I can with my son."

Blair places her hand over her heart. "Of course you do," she says. "How's he doing?"

"A little worse every day."

"We are now approaching Home."

Prince sits up, momentarily disoriented. It is 8:17 p.m. His head is pounding, and his mouth is dry, but he knows in a few minutes he will have to pretend he's had a drink or two, not seven or eight, that he stopped at the bar for one hour, not five. If Tina believes he had a quick drink after work, she is sympathetic. If she were to learn he has stopped scheduling clients after three so he can spend hours in a bourbon-colored haze, she would throw a fit.

He searches his bag for Advil, finds it, and swallows six pills without water. A couple of them lodge in his throat, but he ignores this. They'll make their way through his digestive system eventually.

The car rounds the corner and his house comes into view, the sole Victorian nestled amongst ranch homes and haciendas.

"We hate your house," one of the neighbors had said right after they'd moved in. Her tone had been jocular, but Prince suspected she was telling the truth. The Victorian ruins the cohesion of the neighborhood. In this suburban community, it feels garish and out of place.

Of course, that is why they love it. It's so different from all the other desert-friendly California architecture. They had fallen hard for its wrap-around porch, its turret, the two ornate fireplaces they'll never use. When they'd bought it, the house had been a symbol of their aspirations. Now, a dozen years later, it is a reminder of their failures.

Tina's Mercedes isn't in the garage. She's working late again. She has never been someone who shies away from long hours, but lately, they've been longer than usual, more often than not.

Inside, Dominick sits beside his nurse, Davida, watching TV. When he hears the door close, he turns, sees Prince, and springs to his feet. "Dad," he says, throwing his arms around his father.

Dom never used to be like this. He loved his parents, but he didn't embrace them every time he saw them. He's eleven, too old to be that attached to mom and dad. But since the diagnosis, he's become more affectionate. He reaches for their hands and rests his head against their shoulders. If they are home, he is glued to their side. Prince isn't sure whether his son is lonely or afraid to die.

Davida stands, too, slowly, with effort. She slides her feet into her clogs and slings her faux leather tote bag over her shoulder. "Mr. Prince, may I have a word?" she says.

Prince releases his son. "I'll be right back, buddy," he says. The boy turns his attention back to the television, where a spandex-clad teenager is beating up a thug twice her size.

Prince follows Davida into the kitchen. She has her hands on her hips, and she is not smiling. "Mr. Prince, you're late again," she tells him. "I was supposed to leave at six."

"I know you were, Davida," Prince mutters. "I'm sorry."

Davida recoils at the stench of his breath. "Mr. Prince," she says. "I know this is hard for you and Mrs. Tina, and I know you're doing the best you can. But it's not good enough. Dominick needs you. You need to be there for him, Mr. Prince."

It's a lecture Prince deserves. He sees the way Davida is looking at him, with a mixture of pity and disdain. He can see their family through her eyes: a sickly son who remains sweet and good-natured and only wants love. A mother with a short temper who struggles to show affection, who buries herself in work and avoids her home and her husband and her son. A father who reeks of booze, who claims to love his son but would rather spend his evenings in some seedy bar, drinking with strangers. A cold, empty house, haunted by dashed hopes and eviscerated dreams. They are coping. They are not coping well. A dying boy deserves more.

He promises Davida he will do better and shows her to the door.

"Dad!" Dom says again when Prince re-enters the room. He doesn't get up this time, but he's clearly happy his father has returned.

"How was your day?" Prince asks over the din of the television.

Dom shrugs. "Good. Well, mostly good. I fell again." He holds up his arm. His wrist has been splinted and wrapped.

"Oh my god, Dom," Prince says, inspecting the injury, for what, he isn't sure.

Dom pulls his arm away. "It's just a sprain, Dad," he insists.

It's happening more and more now, as the doctor had said it would.

Before they knew better, they had assumed Dom was a klutz. He would trip going up the stairs, drop the milk he was pouring, slip on the dry grass at the soccer field. Then he started slurring his words. They'd thought it was something minor, that he was developing some sort of speech impediment that could be easily corrected with therapy. They had been completely unprepared for the diagnosis.

It had been the worst day of Prince's life. Sitting beside Tina in the doctor's office after they'd sent Dom out of the room. Studying the diplomas behind the doctor's head—the bachelor's degree, in Latin, from Harvard, the medical degree from UCSF. A faint scent of cinnamon in the air from the doctor's breath. He'd been chewing Big Red.

The look on the doctor's face had sickened Prince. He'd felt like the father of a fallen soldier, opening his door to find a uniformed officer standing before him with his hat in his hand. Helpless. Hopeless. Aware of the news he was about to receive but desperate to forestall it.

Juvenile Tay Sachs.

Prince didn't know what that meant. He had clutched Tina's hand hard. Too hard. She had pulled away and wrapped her arms around her chest, and he hadn't been sure if it was a protective gesture or if she'd been trying to discourage his desperate attempts at affection.

Tina confessed to a great aunt with Tay Sachs who had died in the 1960s. "But I didn't know Dom was at risk," she insisted. "I thought both parents had to be Jewish." But it turned out French Canadians were susceptible, too, and Prince's mom was from Montreal.

They'd peppered the doctor with questions, implored him to offer them a smidgen of hope.

"Immortality," he'd said. "It's the only chance he has."

"He's not eighteen yet," Tina had pointed out. "He isn't eligible."

"He'd qualify for a compassionate exception," the doctor had assured her. "If you can afford it, let's start him on injections right away."

But they couldn't afford it. Prince's dad could, but he'd declined to help without apology or explanation, even after Prince had groveled before him, offering him anything, anything the old man wanted. He would have killed for his father if it would have saved Dom. Connor had looked embarrassed for him, and he had understood that his father didn't see him as a parent willing to give up everything for his child but as a beggar demeaning himself.

Aside from Immortality, there was no cure for Tay Sachs, just a gradual worsening of symptoms. First, the clumsiness and slurred speech. Eventually, an inability to walk, to eat, to communicate. Dom would slowly stumble toward his death.

How do you tell a ten-year-old he's going to die? You don't, Prince and Tina decided. They told Dom he'd been diagnosed with Tay Sachs and that, over time, he would become clumsier and clumsier.

He shrugged, "Well, that's not so bad," and ran outside to play.

But in time, he grew curious, and, in the age of the internet, it wasn't hard for him to learn more about the disease. One evening, when Tina was working late, Dom looked at Prince in between slices of pizza and asked, "Dad? Am I going to die?"

Prince hadn't had the wherewithal to lie.

Once Dom was aware of his impending death, he began to decline more rapidly. There were more breaks and sprains and more trips to the emergency room. His words slurred more often; his handwriting became indecipherable.

Prince and Tina changed, too. Before, they'd tried to stay upbeat for

Dom. They fought back tears with over-enthusiastic smiles, resisted the urge to hold their boy all the time by kicking a ball back and forth with him instead. They'd done their best to push Tay Sachs out of their minds. It wasn't hard. Because Dom still looked and acted healthy, it was easy for them to forget about his death sentence.

After he knew, their floodgates opened. Tina buried herself in work, claiming they could use the extra money to help cover Dom's medical expenses, even though their insurance took care of most of his costs. Prince turned to alcohol. He didn't want to feel anything. He wanted to be numb, blurry, hazy, sick. Anything but the parent of a child whose days were numbered.

Prince knows that he is drinking too much. When his clients—Immortal but sad, confused, lost—confess to an alcohol problem, he suggests AA or asks them how they think their behavior is affecting their family. He has never tried any of that himself. He isn't ready to talk himself out of drinking yet.

"But Dad. Guess what, Dad?" Dom is saying now.

Prince looks over at him. "What is it, Dom?"

"I heard from the Make-A-Wish people today."

Prince high-fives him. Dom has been hoping for this. He's known what he would wish for since the moment he learned he might be eligible. "That's great, Dom. So? Do you get to make a wish?"

"Not yet, but I will. Know what I'm going to wish for, Dad?"

"What?" Prince asks, even though Dom has repeated his wish so often, he's begun to sound like a broken record.

"I want to go to London to watch Arsenal play." He is so enthusiastic Prince half expects him to jump up and run into the backyard, where his soccer ball, untouched for months now, still lies in the hedges.

"I think that's a fantastic wish, Dom. Can I come, too?"

"Of course, Dad. They're not going to fly me out there alone."

Prince encourages his enthusiasm, asking him questions about London and Arsenal and soccer, thinking all the while that this is a good goal. This is attainable. This will keep Dom occupied while, behind the scenes, Prince battles to save his life.

The family dinner at his father's had been full of surprises, volatile and emotional, not a rollercoaster but an accelerated drop tower. His dad wanted a single heir to pass on not just wealth but everlasting life. Dom was the obvious choice.

Prince knew his sisters would back him. They loved their nephew. He was dying, and they had no children of their own. He had looked to them both expectantly, but their eyes were elsewhere, anywhere else. "Darcy?" he'd said. "Sabrina?"

They had been embarrassed at first, apologetic, but they had quickly turned argumentative. He recalls Sabrina's sense of entitlement, Darcy's smug superiority. Their unexpected betrayal knifed through his insides until he felt like a gutted fish, the life slowly seeping out of him, out of Dom.

"How can you not want to save my son?" he had asked his sisters, blinking back angry, incredulous tears.

It was his father who had answered him, his voice cold, his stare penetrating. "You do realize that for Dom to get Immortality, I would have to die?"

He did realize that. Of course, he did. And he doesn't want his dad to die. But he does want Dom to live. That's what he's rooting for, not Connor's death but Dom's life. That's the natural order of things, isn't it? You reluctantly accept that your parents will die, but you don't expect to outlive your kids.

He had fought for hours, but he hadn't made any headway. They were all so stubborn, so selfish. He has never hated anyone, but he hates them—his sisters, his father. He never wants to see any of them again. But he knows he has to. He has to change their minds, to convince them his boy is worth saving. Just thinking about it makes his palms sweat. He shouldn't have to fight to save his child's life.

CHAPTER 5

Then

Henry lies awake in bed listening to the thunderstorm in his stomach. When he is this hungry, sleep becomes impossible, and the night becomes endless and unbearable, an eight-hour stretch in which food is unattainable except in dreams or nightmares, which torment a starving child equally.

The front door opens and closes.

"There you are," Henry's mother, Ilene, says. Henry can hear the hope in her voice, and he shakes his head at her foolishness.

His father offers some reply that Henry can't hear, but he knows it's not Vance's words that matter; it's the stench of his breath.

"Have you been drinking?" Ilene asks, her voice high-pitched and incredulous.

"Just one," Vance says. "I swear."

Henry expects his mother to reprimand his father, but instead, they fall silent. The faucet in the kitchen is turned on, and the sound of running water, audible through the thin wall that separates the bedroom Henry shares with his siblings from the kitchen, makes Henry aware of his bloated bladder. He must have drunk three or four gallons of water tonight trying to make his empty stomach full. He has been to the bathroom twice in the past hour, and he needs to go again now, but if he can, he will hold it until his parents have finished their conversation. He doesn't want to get trapped in the middle of one of their fights.

As the faucet is turned off, Vance says, "I saw Jane Johnson today. Remember her?"

"Sure, I do," Ilene replies. "She used to babysit the kids. Sweet girl. God fearing. Where'd you see her?"

"Coming out of the alley behind Main Street."

"No. Her? Of all the women—her? I never thought she'd sink that low."

"She has two boys under five and a husband who put a bullet in his head last year. What choice does she have?"

"I don't know, but not that. Anything but that."

"She did seem embarrassed," Vance acknowledges. "She wouldn't even look at me."

"Well, of course she's embarrassed. What woman wouldn't be?"

"Some aren't. To some, it's a job, same as any other."

"That's not what the Good Book says."

"I think there's something to be said for a woman taking some initiative," Vance remarks.

Henry groans inwardly. Sober, his father would know better than to say something that can only lead to a fight. Drunk, he seems to relish the opportunity to verbally duke it out with his wife.

Ilene obliges. "What exactly are you trying to say, Vance? You think I don't work?"

"You try to get work. Sometimes. Sure. But you also spend a hell of a lot of time in that church house praying for a miracle that'll never come. At least when Jane Johnson gets on her knees, she gets paid for it."

An odd, offbeat sound emerges from the living room as if someone is erratically clapping their hands. His mother is slapping his father, Henry realizes, over and over again.

"Knock it off," Vance yells. The slapping ceases, and Henry imagines that his father has caught his mother's wrists and is holding them still in his big, bear-like hands, restraining her as he might an over-aggressive dog.

"How dare you?" his mother yells. "How dare you suggest those women are somehow better than me? Is that what you want? A whore for a wife? If so, you married the wrong woman."

"I don't want you to be a whore—"

"You spend what little we earn on beer while your children starve to death, and I'm the problem? Because I won't sell myself for ten dollars? Why don't you stop drinking and get a job? A man is supposed to take care of his family, and you fail. You fail. You fail."

"Oh, please. I work ten times as much as you."

"You fail," Ilene chants. "You fail. You fail. You fail."

Now

Forty-eight hours after his second Donation, Henry has a pretty good sense of how an old car feels. No matter how hard he tries to get his body to turn on, to move, to show even the slightest sign of get-up-and-go, the old clunker remains haplessly slumped over in a chair, looking much older than its twenty-three years.

The first Donation had gone well. He'd been back to normal within an hour, running on a treadmill within two. But this time has been different. He's felt lightheaded since the moment the extraction machine began drawing his blood.

Before Hemodyne and Compounds and Immortality, blood donation had only been permitted every fifty-six days. Now, Cruors are expected to give once a week. To enable this, Hemodyne has developed some mystery concoction, bright yellow and tangy, that Donors must consume every morning. Henry isn't sure what this drink is supposed to do exactly, but it doesn't appear to be working for him. He wonders how he can go through this every week. He feels depleted. It is an effort to walk down the hall to the bathroom.

Losing two pints of blood in two weeks doesn't seem to have taken much out of Ben, who is already at a Compound bar drinking away his meager earnings. But Henry has barely left the apartment. He looks for any sign he may be getting stronger, but so far, there is none. He is a couch potato who has attempted a marathon; he wonders if his body will ever forgive him.

He slumps in the living space watching an old episode of *Law & Order: SVU* with Zeke. Since arriving at the Compound, Zeke has developed a penchant for detective shows. He watches them for hours on end, voicing aloud his suspicions that the pretty girl is the killer or that the man in the train station isn't what he seems.

At first, Henry was amused by how absorbed Zeke became in these dramas, but now he has begun to worry. He has yet to see Zeke open a textbook, and when Henry casually asks whether he has any homework, Zeke shrugs without taking his eyes off the TV. Henry is in unfamiliar territory. Part of him thinks he should force an answer out of Zeke, and if his brother does have homework, order—or at least encourage—him to do it. That's what a real parent would do, isn't it? Say something like, 'No TV until you finish your homework'? But Henry isn't a real parent; he's a brother, and he's uncomfortable taking on too much of a parental role.

"No, Olivia, don't go in there alone," Zeke cautions *SVU*'s Detective Benson. Of all the detectives on all the shows he watches, he is most protective of her.

"Be careful, Olivia, please," Zeke urges.

Henry rolls his eyes. Sometimes he can't believe how quickly he's shifted from grateful—for the Compounds, a home, a rest—to bored. If you had told him even a month ago that his life would be reduced to this, he would not have believed it. He feels like he has been moved to a retirement home to while away the remainder of his days. He need not work or contribute. All anyone expects of him is good behavior and a healthy appetite. Eat three meals a day. Drink your energy drink. Do what the doctor says. It's depressing to be as useless as a geriatric at twenty-three. And then, as if to underscore the point, *Law & Order* ends, and *Matlock* takes its place.

"That's it," Henry says. "I'm out of here."

He forces his leaden body off the couch and makes his way back to the bedroom he shares with Remy. It's ten o'clock, a perfectly reasonable time to go to bed, he decides. He is relieved Remy isn't home, so he can change into his pajamas in the bedroom instead of having to trudge down the hall to the bathroom. He gradually lifts his shirt over his head, then freezes, topless, in the center of the room.

It's ten o'clock on a weekday, and Remy isn't home. That isn't like her. He pulls his phone from his pocket, but she hasn't messaged him. His heart starts racing. He knows the other kids don't like her. What if they've beaten her up or trapped her in the janitor's closet or—stop, he tells himself. She's probably at the library. She just lost track of time. He sends her a quick text and waits, breath held, for her reply, but minutes tick by and he doesn't hear from her. He pulls his shirt on again and lumbers back into the living space. "Zeke, do you know where Remy is?"

Zeke, caught up in his show, ignores Henry.

"Zeke!" Henry calls, as though his brother is across a crowded room. When still no response is forthcoming, he claps his hands together twice.

Zeke pauses his show and turns toward Henry, not bothering to hide his irritation.

"Remy?" Henry asks.

Zeke lets out an exaggerated sigh. "She got invited to Jody Ryland's party."

"Who's Jody Ryland?"

"A girl we go to school with. She throws the best parties. I had a threesome at the last one."

"You what?" Henry is so unprepared for his brother's pronouncement that he loses his balance and has to steady himself against the back of the couch.

"That's all anyone does at these parties," Zeke says. "We've been here three weeks, and I've already slept with four different girls." He holds up the four fingers on his left hand for emphasis.

Henry's head is swimming. "What are you talking about? You're in high school."

"I'm telling you," Zeke reiterates. "That's all these parties are." He recounts in graphic detail the rules of a popular party game, a bawdy version of seven minutes in heaven, with oral sex instead of tender kisses and an element of competition, too. Seven minutes to get a guy to orgasm. The girls who manage are the most desirable. A skilled tongue can compensate for an ugly face.

Henry starts coughing. The thought of his little sister on her knees in a closet before guy after guy makes him ill. For the first time, he understands the anxiety a father feels when his little girl goes out on her first date, when she stays out later and later with her steady boyfriend, maybe even on her wedding night. He understands the desire to threaten every guy who comes near her with a shotgun and to beat the living daylight out of any guy dumb enough to break her heart. And then Henry realizes that, like it or not, he is Remy's father now. Ben is grown, and Zeke, at seventeen, is close enough, but Remy still needs a parent, and there is no one but him.

He moves toward the door with surprisingly little effort, propelled by the need to save his sister. "Zeke," he says. "Show me where Jody lives."

Henry has to bribe Zeke to get him to agree—ten dollars from Henry's next paycheck. It could be worse, he tells himself. Ben would have charged twenty.

Henry moves as quickly as he can, aware that every minute he is delayed is a minute Remy could be fighting off some boy or taking off her clothes. He shudders.

By the time they get to Jody's apartment, Henry is sweat-drenched and shivering. He isn't well enough for this. He shouldn't have come. He had to come.

Zeke refuses to go in with him—"Even I know that would be social suicide"—so Henry barges in alone. The skunky smell of weed assaults him as soon as he opens the door. The room, lit only by small multi-colored Christmas lights stapled to the wall, is thronging with teenagers, smoking, grinding, kissing, petting. The raging hormones smell almost as strong as the pot.

Henry takes a deep breath and wades in, scanning the crowd for Remy. Within seconds, he is offered two beers and a joint and has his ass groped by an unseen hand. He shrugs it all away, worried about the consequences if he is caught here, at a party full of underaged kids. On top of a table, two girls in bras and miniskirts dance provocatively. In a nearby chair, a pigtailed girl is giving a chubby, grunting fellow a lap dance. He can't believe Remy is at a party like this.

The room is hot, and it is hard to breathe, and before he can locate his sister, Henry finds his energy faltering. He looks for a place to sit down, just for a minute, but every available surface has a body on it, sometimes two or three. He leans up against a wall instead, panting and dizzy, trying to summon more energy, but he is only getting weaker.

He remembers Remy telling him once that when mountain climbers get above a certain elevation, they have a limited amount of time to summit and begin their descent because the oxygen level is dangerously low. That is how Henry feels. He has only a few more minutes to find Remy and get out, or he will pass out right here on the sticky floor. He pushes off the wall and resumes his search. Remy has to be here.

And then he sees her, sitting in a circle with five or six other teenagers, a bottle in the center. At first, Henry is relieved. Spin the bottle is relatively innocuous; he has no objection to his sister sharing a few tentative kisses. Then he remembers what Zeke had told him about seven minutes in heaven, and his stomach turns.

He trudges over to his sister, shoving at anyone who gets in his way. She sees him coming and scrambles to her feet.

"Henry," she yells. "What are you doing here?"

"Let's go, Remy," he barks.

"What?"

"I said, 'We're going.' Come on."

"Henry, I can't just—"

"Now!"

The other kids are staring at him now, and Remy looks mortified. She gathers her backpack and starts toward the exit. As her friends watch her go, they mock her, yelling to make sure she can hear them over the music.

"Oh, did daddy come to get little Remy?"

"Poor little Remy has to go home now. It's a school night."

Their laughter rings in Henry's ears, taunting and cruel, and he begins to wonder if he's made a mistake. He doesn't want to embarrass his sister. He just wants to keep her safe.

She tugs at his arm, trying to get him to leave before he does any more damage. He goes willingly, hating this party, hating himself.

As soon as they are in the hall, Remy starts yelling at him, asking him what he was thinking, why he would do something like this, but Henry can barely hear her. The exhaustion and dizziness that he had been fighting overtake him, and he lurches to the wall as the world goes black.

He awakens to the smell of bacon, a rumbling stomach, a pounding headache. He feels groggy and disoriented, and when he tries to remember the night before, he discovers that he can't. He opens his eyes and squints, attempting to recall anything after watching *Law & Order* with Zeke, but there is only Detective Benson in pursuit of a suspect and then nothing.

"Oh, good. You're awake."

"Remy?" he says. His voice is faint and raspy.

Remy is sitting on her bed, watching him, her brows furrowed with concern. "You need protein, Henry," she says. "Have some breakfast."

She passes him a paper plate covered in foil. Beneath it, several strips of bacon lie atop a sea of scrambled eggs. He reaches for the bacon, which is all the things bacon should be—crispy and salty and greasy—and takes a generous bite. Remy nods with approval.

"What happened?" Henry asks.

"You humiliated me in front of my classmates at Jody Ryland's party, then passed out as soon as we left, probably so you wouldn't have to hear me yell at you."

His headache intensifies, drilling away at his temples like a jackhammer. He remembers everything now. "I was scared," he says, sinking his teeth into another strip of bacon. "Zeke told me what happens at those parties."

"They are pretty bacchanalian," Remy admits.

Henry has no idea what that means. "So why did you go?"

Remy shrugs. "I don't know. I guess I thought I should at least try to make friends here. It was a disaster, of course. I'm clearly not going to meet my Diana Barry at a party."

"So, I saved you?" Henry says hopefully.

"You humiliated me," Remy repeats. "I can take care of myself, Henry."

He knows that's true. His sister has always been resourceful, and she's never cared much about what others think of her. "I messed up," he admits.

"Obviously," she says.

Henry hangs his head. "I'm sorry, Remy." He hopes he can make this right. "How did I get home last night? Did you and Zeke carry me?"

"Zeke?" Remy says. "No. I called Ben, but he didn't answer. I didn't even bother with Zeke. You know he never picks up when he's watching his detective shows."

Henry had thought Zeke would wait for him in the hallway outside of Jody's apartment, but that had been a stupid assumption. As soon as Henry had gone inside, Zeke had probably hightailed it back to the apartment to see the rest of *Matlock*.

"I called Caleb," Remy is telling him. "He helped me get you back here."

"Oh," Henry says. He wonders if he has gotten it wrong. Maybe it isn't her classmates he has to worry about. "Is anything going on there?"

Remy rolls her eyes. "He's my tutor, Henry. That's all. And he's like your age. He's not going to hit on a fourteen-year-old."

"Twenty-something men hit on teenage girls all the time, and you know it," Henry says.

Another eye roll and a snort, loud and exasperated. "Caleb doesn't see me like that. I touched his arm by accident once, and he pulled it away like I'd burned him."

"Well, that's a relief."

"What's going on with you, Henry? Why are you so worried about me?"

Henry shakes his head, frustrated with himself. "I don't know," he says. "Nothing feels right here."

Remy gazes at him thoughtfully. "It has been an adjustment," she acknowledges. "But give it time, Henry. It'll be okay."

"Yeah," Henry says, though he isn't sure he believes her.

"I have to get to school, but here's something to help you pass the time." She extracts a thick paperback from her backpack and tosses it to him.

"*Less Miserable*?" He glances up at his sister. "A self-help book?"

"That's *Les Misérables*," she says. "It's French."

"You're giving me a book in French?"

"It's translated into English. I was going to return it to the library, but I think you'll like it."

"It's long," he says, fanning its six hundred pages with his thumb.

"That's the abridged version," Remy tells him. "Give it a try. You don't have anything better to do."

She's right, of course. He doesn't feel well enough to go out, but the thought of ensconcing himself in the living space, watching detective shows with Zeke for the third day in a row, sounds about as appealing as watching paint dry. "Thanks," he says at last.

After she leaves, he chokes down the rest of his breakfast. The food doesn't taste bad, but he hasn't had much of an appetite since their third or fourth day here. His body, used to existing on so little, seems to reject his attempts to gorge.

When he's finished, he tries to sleep, but sleep evades him. Reluctantly, he turns to the book Remy's brought. How had she pronounced the title? *Lay Miserable*? No, that isn't right. It's strange to be reading a book when he doesn't even know how to say its name, but he knows it will mean a lot to his sister if he can get through it, and he is bored. He sighs and turns to the first page, wondering how his life came to be reduced to sitting in his bed for days at a time, reading books with fancy French names.

CHAPTER 6

Then

"—such a relief. They don't sponsor just anyone, you know."

"Who's sponsoring you for what?" Darcy asks.

There had been a line in the ladies' room, but she hadn't minded. She had appreciated the break from her family, from the stuffy ambiance of the Dorothy Chandler Pavilion, from the man seated beside her who kept glaring at her polyester blouse as though he couldn't believe management had let her in. Why had she agreed to come to the opera tonight anyway? She doesn't even like *Madame Butterfly*.

Sabrina, who is sitting on the other side of their father, hesitates. "My agency," she admits. "They've agreed to sponsor my Immortality."

"Right," Darcy says, crumpling the program in her hands. "Of course. Nobody sponsors the Immortality of talented engineers or teachers or doctors, but God forbid we let our models die."

Predictably, Connor defends Sabrina. "The Xiomara Khan Agency is a business, Darcy, not a charity. They're choosing to make their top models Immortal because it makes financial sense to them. Engineering firms or hospitals could do the same."

"Doctors and engineers don't have fan clubs or followers, no matter how talented they are," Darcy retorts. "People want them to be good at what they do, but their patients or clients don't feel particularly attached to them, and their employers know that. Let them die or retire. Someone else is waiting to take their place."

"Someone else could take my place," Sabrina argues.

"That's not the point," Darcy says, exasperated. "We shouldn't be sponsoring the Immortality of doctors or engineers any more than we should be sponsoring the Immortality of models because when push comes to shove, they're all interchangeable. To the extent Immortality exists and costs as much as it does, it should be reserved for exceptional people: each generation's Einsteins and Ataturks. The people who will continue to drastically improve society as long as they live."

They've heard it all before. Darcy has been ranting against the implementation of Immortality since the night Nathan Odili announced it. She is not opposed to it the way some religious groups are, preaching fervently to anyone who will listen that only God should determine matters of life and death. Nor does she share the concerns of her only friend Warner, who worries obsessively about Immortality's implications for population growth. No, Darcy hates that Immortality is available to only a select few and that those lucky few are determined not by merit but by wealth.

She worries, too, about new human rights abuses resulting from Immortality. She has written reports on this topic, carefully documenting the black market for blood that has emerged in China, Venezuela linking rations to Donation without monitoring how often people give, household staff in Saudi Arabia being forced to Donate so much blood that they die. In its current form, Immortality rewards the wrong people, furthers the wrong goals, and seems to Darcy little more than another unfortunate extension of capitalism, where money determines worth, where the mistreatment of others is incentivized, where the poor get screwed again.

"You're so naïve it pains me," Connor is saying. "What world are you living in? If I can afford something, I should be able to buy it, and if the Immortality of certain key players will strengthen my business, I should be allowed to sponsor them, plain and simple." He is fed up with Darcy, as usual. They've never been able to have a reasonable discussion about anything. He hadn't even told her he is Immortal. She'd found out from Prince, who hadn't realized it was a secret.

"Why?" Darcy asks. "Why does our entire society have to be based on the principle that if I like something and I can afford it, I should have it? Why is everything centered around money and selfishness? Can't you ever think beyond yourself to what would be best for the world? You shouldn't have Immortality, Dad. What are you going to do with it? Work for a few more years, then retire? Spend eternity playing golf? What makes you any more worthy than a dedicated nurse who saves hundreds of lives every year? The whole system is fucked up and you can't even see that."

Now

Darcy hasn't slept well since the dinner at her dad's. She is haunted by Prince, his immense pain and sense of betrayal, the way his eyes had darted from Sabrina to their father to her, finally coming to rest on her because he had trusted her the most, believed she would be his ally. She always had been. But not this time. Not when it mattered most.

Et tu, Brute?

She has picked up the phone to call him a dozen times, but she can't bring herself to speak to him. What would she say? She hasn't changed her mind, and there's no point trying to explain her position to Prince. He wouldn't understand. What father would? I'm choosing my principles over your son's life. It's a privileged position, really. One that no parent could possibly take. She'd probably feel different if Dominick were hers.

Fighting with Prince has left Darcy untethered from her family. She has never talked to her father or sister regularly, only her brother and nephew. Now that they have stormed out of her life, she has a lot more free time. With no hobbies and few friends, Darcy redoubles her efforts at work. This is good, she decides. She's up for a big promotion; increasing her productivity can only make her a more desirable candidate.

Two weeks after her father's dinner, Darcy's boss, Elwood, steps into her office and closes the door. He is an aging hippie, overweight, with a blond ponytail and ill-fitting, thrift shop clothes. When he speaks to his employees, his voice is barely above a whisper. When he speaks in the courtroom, his voice booms.

"Darcy, I was going through the applications for the Assistant Director position and saw that you'd tossed your hat in the ring," Elwood says, squeezing into the folding chair that has been crammed into her office.

Darcy nods. She knows she's well-qualified. She's been a Program Officer for eight years and has always had top performance reviews. "Yes, sir," she says. She sits up straighter and tucks her hair behind her ear.

Elwood smiles, a withholding little grin that strikes her as pitying. It is the grin Prince offers whenever they are discussing her love life. "I'll cut right to the chase," Elwood says. "Darcy, you're a strong writer. You excel at analysis. You notice trends no one else does. You're hardworking and efficient. Between you and me, you're probably the best Program Officer we've ever had. But you'd make a terrible Assistant Director."

Darcy interlaces her fingers and squeezes her hands together to keep them from shaking. There's nothing quite like being told you'll never advance in the organization you've devoted your life to. Elwood, who was singing her praises only a moment ago, is now spelling out her shortcomings one by one, the same list of disappointing adjectives that peppered her report cards all through school: anti-social, defiant, stubborn, insular, negative, disagreeable, unpleasant, strange. It all amounts to the same thing: nobody likes you.

Darcy has a million arguments on the tip of her tongue—she has spent her life countering accusations like this—but she doesn't get the chance to utter a single one. Elwood holds his hands up to silence her and says, "Now, I came to say that although I won't be considering you for this promotion, I would like to offer you a raise. You've been with us for a number of years now. Your work is excellent. You deserve it." He looks so pleased with himself.

"I see," Darcy says.

Inside, she is fuming. She wants to tell Elwood to take his raise and shove it. She wants to quit and storm out of the room. But there is no point in anger or in arguing. In her eight years at the Human Rights Alliance, she has never seen Elwood change his mind.

Defeated, disappointed, she offers a meek smile. "Thank you, Elwood," she says. "I appreciate the raise."

After he leaves, Darcy buries her head in her hands. She'd thought investing in a job, in a cause, was safe. The more she put into it, the more she would get out. Devotion is rewarded with success. Competence produces positive results. Foolish, really. She's given everything she has, and after eight years, all she has to show for it is one lousy raise.

Darcy wants to spend the weekend at home with a bottle of expensive wine and a sizable wedge of triple-cream brie, but she has plans to meet her best friend Warner at an Immortality protest outside the Wilshire Federal Building. She reluctantly drags herself into a hoodie and a pair of well-worn jeans.

"Going with the tumbled-out-of-bed look again, are we?" Warner says when he sees her.

"Dressed to pick up men again, are we?" she retorts, eyeing him up and down. Warner laughs and gives her a hug. His cashmere sweater, designer jeans, and suede shoes are too fancy for a protest—possibly, Darcy thinks, too fancy for LA—but he is of the belief that you never know when you might meet the man you're going to marry, and when you do, you want to be dressed for it. Darcy thinks that if a man cares that much about what she's wearing, he probably isn't the man for her.

The turnout is small. There are a couple dozen protestors, and Darcy recognizes several of them as Serials, people who turn up at every march or rally, not because they are passionate about the cause, but because they enjoy the act of dissent or like to feel as if they're a part of something bigger than themselves.

The leader of this protest hands Darcy a digital petition. "Get as many people as you can to sign this," he instructs, as if she is stupid and doesn't know how a petition works.

She takes it and glances over the language. It is a standard petition, urging the California legislature to continue to ban the mentally ill from Compounds as they lack the capacity to consent to blood Donation.

She begins to approach people on the sidewalk, thrusting the document in their face. Most of them are so relieved she's not asking for money that they sign the petition without reading it. They are distracted, happy to feel like they're making a difference, eager to get on with their day.

"I'm not going to get any spam from this, am I?" asks a middle-aged woman in skinny jeans.

"No, ma'am," Darcy assures her. "We're not interested in harassing you. We just want to make sure the government doesn't harass the mentally ill." The woman nods, signs, and walks away. She's asked the only question Darcy has gotten all day.

Toward the end of the protest, a scruffy guy in his twenties walks by. Grad student, probably. They're near UCLA. She allows herself a little grin. Grad students are liberal, political, eager to protest the government.

"Sign our petition," she says, thrusting the clipboard toward him. It is a statement, not a question, and he looks taken aback by the directive.

"What's it for?" he asks, slowing slightly.

"The government wants to commit the low-risk mentally ill to Compounds without their consent. Nobody should be forced to give blood unless they agree to. We're out here fighting on behalf of people who can't fight for themselves."

The grad student looks at her with a mixture of amusement and disdain. "When you say the mentally ill, I'm guessing you don't mean the ones who have nice families to look after them?"

"No, they're not at risk. The law would be targeting vagrants, the most vulnerable among us."

"Let me get this straight. The government wants to take the mentally ill homeless and relocate them to Compounds, where they'd have a warm bed to sleep in, all the food they can eat, and regular access to mental health care instead of leaving them on the streets to fend for themselves, and you're opposed to this?"

Now it's Darcy's turn to be taken aback. She hadn't expected an argument. "I'm in favor of liberty, and this is taking theirs away," she counters.

"If the government was trying to do something that would harm them, I'd sign your petition in a heartbeat, but this would actually improve their situation."

"Theirs or Hemodyne's?"

"Both," he says with a shrug. "They're not mutually exclusive. Now if you'll excuse me, I've got to get going." He hands the petition back to her unsigned and continues down the street.

"You people are all so afraid," she yells after him. "You'll sacrifice liberty for security."

The grad student turns to her. She expects to see smugness, defiance, some intolerable expression of disagreement on his face, but instead, he looks pained. "Yes," he agrees. "That's exactly what I've done, but until you've lived on the streets, doing things you never thought you would just to survive, you really aren't in a position to judge."

She watches him walk away, unnerved. Had he just hinted at being a Cruor? If so, he's not at all what she imagined. No, she thinks. He couldn't be. He was so robust, and Cruors are weak and tired and timid. At least she thinks they are. She's never actually met one.

Warner comes up behind her. "What was that all about?"

Darcy shakes her head. "Nothing," she says. "Just some guy who doesn't get it."

After the protests, Darcy and Warner go to a wine bar, where a stainless-steel machine dispenses exactly 125 milliliters of Argentinian Malbec into a glass for Darcy and the same amount of Chablis for Warner. They take a table by the window, looking out at the parking lot of a strip mall.

"Unbelievable," Warner sneers as they watch a Ford Future pull into the lot. "We've invented Immortality, but we still can't manage to get rid of the architectural monstrosity that is the strip mall."

Darcy rolls her eyes. Warner has always been more of an aesthete than she is. To her, beauty is a non-issue, a triviality that's been made important by a handful of shallow people who don't have anything more import-ant to worry about. But she's willing to grant that she may not appreciate beauty because she doesn't possess even an ounce of it herself, and she's never been allowed to forget it.

"So, you and Prince still aren't talking?" Warner asks, pushing his chair back a few inches and crossing his ankle over his knee. She has told him about her father's will, his sudden desire to bestow Immortality on one of his offspring in the event of his untimely death.

"No," she says. "And I can't say that I blame him. His son's life is at stake."

"It's not too late," Warner says. "You can still change your mind."

"I've thought about it," Darcy admits. "But I can't."

Warner nods. "Darned principles."

"You know, when Dom was first diagnosed, Prince went to Dad and asked him to sponsor Dom's Immortality, but Dad refused."

"I remember," says Warner.

"Well, afterward, he came to me, and he was so angry. He called Dad so many names, said so many angry things about him, and the thing is, I didn't disagree. What kind of man saves himself over his dying grandson? And I said that to Prince, almost word for word. But he took it to mean—"

"That you thought your dad should save Dominick," Warner finish-es. "When what you really meant was that if your dad insisted on saving someone, it should be Dominick, not himself."

"I've been consistent in my position," Darcy says. "I disapprove of wealth-based Immortality, and I don't see why Dom, as much as I love him, should be saved when so many kids like him will die just because their families are poorer than we are.

"Is it awful that I put my principles above the life of my nephew?" Darcy asks. "God, of course, it is. Principles are one thing, but what's more important than the life of a child? I really am a heartless monster."

"Actually, you're what policymakers should be," Warner says. "Detached from personal pet issues and more in tune with what makes the most sense for the nation."

"Tell that to my brother," Darcy mutters. "You know what the worst part is?"

"What?" Warner asks. He leans in, expecting something juicy.

Darcy looks out the window, too ashamed to meet his gaze. "I couldn't even bring myself to tell Prince the truth. I told him that I was in favor of Immortality for Dom a year and a half ago when he was first diagnosed, but now his quality of life has diminished so much that I don't think it makes any sense."

"Oh, Darce. You didn't."

Darcy lowers her head.

"Jesus. Is Dom's health even that bad?"

Darcy shrugs. "He slurs his speech and falls a lot."

"Oh. So, you're basically saying that if someone is handicapped, their life isn't worth living?"

"I know. It sounds awful. I don't even believe that. But at the time, it seemed easier than telling Prince the truth."

"Darcy, Darcy, Darcy," Warner mutters.

She still can't bring herself to look at him. "I know."

"You want your dad to give his money to a Foundation, right? Sponsor the Immortality of someone who truly deserves it?"

"That's right," Darcy agrees. "They could name the sponsorship after him, which would preserve his legacy in another way."

Warner rests his elbows on the high-top table, his chin in his hand. "That's noble. It really is, but it's never going to fly."

"What do you mean?" Darcy asks.

"You're putting an idea up against people. When you do that, people win every time. Ideas are too abstract and too difficult to grasp. People are concrete, real, right in front of you. Principle seems a lot less compelling in the face of someone's suffering."

Darcy squirms in her seat, uncomfortable, unhappy. Even if no one else understands her, she needs Warner to. He is her only friend.

"I know it's easier to value the needs of people," she begins, "but—" She falls silent, grasping at words, trying to explain. "Have you ever seen *The Way We Were*?" She knows he has. Warner is madly in love with Robert Redford.

"Of course," he says in a tone that suggests the question is an insult.

"Of course," Darcy echoes. "There's a scene toward the end where Redford and Streisand are fighting for the zillionth time. Redford wants Streisand to prioritize their relationship, so he tells her that people are what matters. People, not principles or causes. And she replies that people are their principles. She's not willing to stop fighting for hers even if it costs her the man she loves."

"God, you're her," Warner says.

"I am," she confirms. "And I can't do it. I can't give up my principles, not even for my nephew, the person I love most in the world."

"Because without your principles, you're nothing," Warner says.

"Because without my principles, I'm nothing."

CHAPTER 7

Then

The cowbell itself is not especially loud, but rung less than an inch from Zeke's head, it is deafening. His palms move to his ears as his eyes open. His mother is leaning over his bed, her dark eyes boring into him, her tongue traversing her chapped lips.

"Rise and shine," she demands. "The Lord has blessed you with another day."

It is 5:45 in the morning, and school doesn't start until 7:30, but Ilene Hudson always makes time to pray. She rings the cowbell again, its rusted, tinny sound falling flat in the over-furnished room all four of her children share. Zeke's siblings are already out of bed, taking turns in the bathroom, pulling on the cleanest clothes they can find. But Zeke knows he is slow in the mornings, so he sleeps in the clothes he will wear the next day.

He watches, groggy but awake, as his mother retreats to the living room, where she will kneel on the worn carpet, reading her grandmother's leather-bound Bible and waiting for her children to join her. She expects them to be kneeling around her in a circle by 6:15. The punishment for arriving late is no breakfast, a cruel punishment considering there is often no dinner, leaving the tardy with only the school-provided lunch, which is hardly sufficient.

They all try to be on time, but delays happen. Today, Remy comes running in last and drops to her knees beside Henry, who puts his arm around her protectively.

"Six thirteen," Ilene announces, pleased. "Let's begin."

When Ilene prays, it is as though she is in a trance. Her body and tongue, typically rigid and constrained, become loose, and she sways back and forth and speaks without ceasing, as though she is possessed by some invisible body sent to oversee her worship. She prays for an entire hour, never once asking for any of the countless things they need, only singing God's praises in a reverential ode.

Zeke doesn't know how the others do it. To him, her words are rambling and meaningless, but their rhythmic cadence is comforting, and he cannot make it through prayers without drifting off.

His siblings are sympathetic. They seem to understand that he can't help falling asleep, that his body reacts to prayer as to a lullaby, and they do their best to nudge him awake before their mother notices. But today, his sleep is too deep, his dreams too enchanting. By the time Ben manages to rouse him, Ilene is already looking at him as though he'd nailed Jesus to the cross himself.

The penalty for sleeping during prayer is the same as the penalty for being late. Zeke will not receive breakfast. Instead, he is forced to watch as Ilene distributes a single slice of stale white bread to each of her other children. Ben's has a splotch of green mold on it. He nibbles around it. Zeke is so hungry he considers asking for the mold.

Ilene makes them eat in front of her so she can be sure that none of them share their meager breakfast with Zeke. His stomach roars, audible and angry, and they toss him apologetic, guilty glances, but he is not upset with them. He has done the same whenever any of them has upset their mother. But Zeke goes without breakfast about three times a week, as often as the rest of his siblings combined.

They leave the kitchen and trudge toward the schoolhouse, Zeke's stomach protesting with every step. He is weaker than usual today and struggling to keep up. He falls behind his siblings. They don't notice or care.

He is four or five blocks behind when his father appears from a side street, a half-rotted apple in his hand.

"Here you go, Zeke," he says, extending the pathetic piece of fruit towards his youngest son. "Something tells me you need this today."

Zeke seizes the apple and gnaws away at the good parts. It's not much, but it will sustain him until lunch.

"Your mom wasn't always like this, you know," his father is saying, ashamed and apologetic. "All the prayers and that, it's just her way of coping."

Zeke hears him, but he isn't really listening. He is devouring the apple as quickly as he can, half-afraid his mom will appear and take it away from him. He goes through the good parts first but then decides to eat the rotten bits, too. Within a minute, only the core remains.

Zeke looks up at his father, satiated, grateful, and is surprised to find his old man gazing up at the sky with tears in his eyes.

Now

Except for school, Zeke likes Compound life. He likes waking up in a warm bed and knowing he'll get a hot shower. He likes the automated voice, prodding him to rise with the patience and persistence of a sitcom mom. He prefers her to his own mom, who would ring that awful cowbell in his ear if he slept too late.

Zeke likes eating on the Compound, too, although he doesn't praise the food as much as Ben, or care about it as much for that matter. As it is, he eats only when he needs to, and then he gorges, stuffing his stomach until he feels like he is on the brink of explosion. He is like an automobile at a gas station, filled to the brim to avoid more frequent refueling. Food is necessary, but it's not something he savors.

He has friends on the Compound, too, for the first time in his life. He fits in here, behind these walls, where listlessness is normal and indifference is expected.

Between food, school, and socializing, Zeke finds he doesn't have nearly as much time as he would like to watch his detective shows. *Law & Order. The Immortal Murders. Another One Disappears. Criminal Minds. In Plain Sight.* These are what he loves more than anything in the world, even if he's honest, more than partying. There's something satisfying about watching the predictable formulas play out in show after show: the crime, the obvious suspect, the likable character who has really committed the crime, the ingenuity that enables the detectives to discover the truth. After six weeks of watching these shows every day, Zeke, who's no great thinker, can solve the mystery nine times out of ten.

"Zeke, don't you have to study?" Henry sometimes asks, in those not infrequent moments when guilt demands he attempt to be a better parent. Zeke shrugs.

"Hey, Zeke, want to come to a party?" Ben asks, trying to add a spark of excitement to the life of his dormant brother. Zeke shakes his head.

"Are you going to sit there all day, Zeke?" Remy asks about once a week, a trace of disgust in her voice. Zeke nods.

In time, his family comes to accept that if Zeke is awake and in the apartment, he will be on the sofa in front of the TV. "I dread the day he graduates and can do this all day long," he hears Remy say to Henry.

"I just hope he graduates," Henry replies.

One evening, Zeke is stretched across the sofa, half dozing and half watching a *Victims and Villains* marathon. He has not left the living space since breakfast. His siblings have wandered in and out, speaking to him occasionally, though he doesn't pay attention to what they say. It's never anything important—greetings and rhetorical questions mostly.

A new episode starts, one Zeke hasn't seen before. A man has been found dead in an alley with no identification on him. The detectives are trying both to identify him and to figure out what happened to him. The dead man reminds Zeke of his father—the same age, the same coloring, even the expression on his lifeless face mimics the contemptuous, confused look that so often overtook Vance Hudson, especially when he was drunk.

About an hour later, the detectives determine that the man was killed by an old homeless woman because he wouldn't share his bottle of whiskey. They track down the man's adult children, who hadn't seen their father in over a decade, and reluctantly break the news to them. But his children are indifferent to his death. "He was an alcoholic," his son says. "We didn't want anything to do with him." To them, he had been dead for years.

Watching the episode is like discovering a seashell from some long-ago beach vacation, where the lingering scent of the sea brings forgotten memories crashing back. Except the memories Zeke recalls aren't of sunshine and sandcastles, but of his father, slumped in an alleyway, stinking of day-old vomit, yelling out nonsensical demands as spit dribbled down his chin.

The last time they had seen Vance, a few hours before the discovery of his dead doppelganger, Robert Ritter, he had been passed out cold on the oil-stained ground of the abandoned parking garage where they'd been living since their mom left. They'd tried to wake him, first calling his name, then rocking him gently, then slapping his clammy skin, but nothing had roused him. At last, they had left him there, intending to return later that day, but of course, they never had.

Now they've been at the Compound for six weeks, and it hasn't occurred to any of them to take the shuttle back into Los Angeles to check on their dad. Vance hadn't been much of a parent their last year on the streets, had, in fact, been a hindrance with his persistent inebriation and unwillingness or inability to sober up, but before that, before their mom disappeared, he'd done all he could for them. He'd loved them. Now, he remains somewhere in that vast metropolis, drunk and hungry and all alone.

That evening the Hudsons eat dinner together, a new initiative of Remy's who is concerned that they're growing apart. "A meal together, once a week," she'd begged, and her brothers had complied with varying degrees of enthusiasm.

Tonight, they have a table to themselves, Zeke and Remy on one side, Henry and Ben on the other. Remy has brought a study guide in case the others were late and, Zeke notices, Henry has a book, too, a paperback. He glances at the title. *The Count of Monte Cristo*. Zeke has never heard of it.

Ben arrives last, carrying a tray piled high with food. He still treats every meal at the Compound like it might be his last.

"Do you think we should check on Dad?" Zeke asks once Ben is seated, with no preface or introduction. Too oblivious to wade into the shallow end, he has dived right in.

His siblings play with their food, refusing to meet Zeke's gaze, and wait for each other to speak.

"He is our dad," Zeke says when the silence has stretched from seconds to minutes.

"Some dad," Ben remarks, stabbing his lasagna with a fork. "He let us starve on the streets for six years. I don't feel any obligation to him. Not after what he put us through."

Zeke is caught off guard by his brother's hostility. Their dad hadn't been perfect, but he'd tried.

Henry speaks up. "You're right, Zeke. We should check on Dad, but we can't."

"Why not?"

"You're not of age yet, and neither is Remy. We came here with documents claiming that our dad is dead and that I'm your legal guardian. If Dad sees us, who knows how he'll react? He could try to force you and Remy to stay with him. He could go to the police. He could notify the Compounds that we're here against his will. We could be tossed back onto the street with nothing but the clothes on our backs and a sandwich for the road."

"Dad wouldn't do that," Zeke protests.

Henry shrugs. "Maybe. Maybe not. But it's too much of a risk. I'm sorry."

"But—" Zeke begins.

"Why?" Ben asks, interrupting him. "Why do you want to go out of your way for a man who never bothered to do the same for you?"

"He's our dad," Zeke says.

"A dad is just the man who knocked up your mom," Ben retorts. "Stay away from him, Zeke. Dad is nothing but trouble."

Zeke wakes early the following Sunday, in time to catch the first shuttle into Los Angeles. As he is leaving the apartment, Ben comes home, reeking of sex and alcohol. "Where're you going?" he slurs as he stumbles to his bed. He falls asleep before Zeke can make up a response.

Zeke walks across the deserted Compound to the bus stop where the bus is already idling. There is no one else on board at this hour.

When the bus arrives in Los Angeles, Zeke heads toward the metro. He uses the ten dollars he had procured from Henry to buy a metro ticket, then rides the Expo Line to Santa Monica. He walks south to Pico Boulevard and the abandoned parking garage where, six weeks ago, he and his siblings had deserted their father.

Zeke remembers arriving in Santa Monica for the first time, how different it was from Downtown Los Angeles, or El Desierto before that. Santa Monica had continued to thrive even when it seemed the entire country had been swept up in an unstoppable hurricane of poverty. It was geography that saved the city; everyone was clamoring to be near the beach.

Vance had moved his family here because he had heard Santa Monica was 'homeless friendly.' But Vance had misunderstood. He'd expected soup kitchens and homeless shelters, after-school programs for kids and job training centers for adults. Instead, he'd gotten a city that was mostly indifferent to its poor, that was reputed to be friendly only by contrast to its neighbors, many of which would discreetly arrest and expel the homeless or harass them until they left on their own.

Nonetheless, they'd stayed. The schools were good, and the district didn't do residency checks. The weather was pleasant, and Santa Monica continued to attract tourists, which meant people with disposable income who would occasionally toss a dollar or a doggie bag their way. It wasn't bad, Zeke thought, recalling his time there. But it wasn't the paradise they'd expected.

It has occurred to Zeke that the parking garage where they left their father might be a pile of rubble by now, their father displaced and lost forever, but he tells himself it's unlikely. The owners of the garage had been threatening demolition for at least a year by the time the Hudsons left for the Compound; it seems unlikely that they'd finally gotten around to it in the past month and a half.

Sure enough, when he arrives, it is still there, a layered concrete cake crammed between a defunct department store and an ill-advised roller rink that had failed half a year after it opened. The demolition notice is still attached to the parking garage entrance, three feet tall with bright red lettering, warning away would-be trespassers.

The front is boarded up, but the sides are not. Zeke walks around to the right of the structure, in between the garage and the roller rink, through the weeds that have cropped up in the cracks of the sidewalk and climbs over the concrete barrier that once walled in cars.

The garage is as they left it, dark and heavy, stained with car oil and tread marks. Although it has not welcomed a vehicle in years, it still smells like a gas station, of fuel and exhaust and cigarettes. Zeke climbs the stairs apprehensively, wondering what he'll find when he reaches level four, not sure what he's hoping for. He tries to proceed in silence, in case someone else has moved in, but the garage is an echo chamber, alerting anyone or anything that may be lurking here of his presence. This simple trip to check on his father has become an act of bravery.

The stench hits him as he reaches the fourth floor. Rotting meat, sticky and pungent. Zeke tries to breathe through his mouth, but he can still smell the putrid aroma.

He rounds the corner and sees a stack of blankets piled haphazardly atop each other, but there is no sign of his father. He's too late. His old man has left, probably driven away by the revolting smell.

And then Zeke realizes his father is the smell. The body of Vance Hudson is slumped against the garage's concrete barrier, black and bloated and almost unrecognizable.

Zeke creeps closer, his hand over his nose, his eyes flickering shut against his will. Up close, his father is grotesque. His eyes bulge out of their sockets; parts of his skin have peeled away from his face. His tongue, more than double the size it was in life, flops out of his mouth and down against his chin, resembling a child's imitation of death, but infinitely more repulsive. The scar on Vance's neck is still visible, and there are shards of broken glass scattered to the right of him. A vodka bottle, probably, though the smell of alcohol has been subsumed by the odor of decay.

Trembling, Zeke retreats. In his rush, he stumbles into a concrete pillar, thick and unyielding, and he crumples to the ground. He tries to get up, but instead, he falls apart, vomiting on the ground, the column, his jeans. He has seen dead bodies before, but never anything like this.

He loses track of time and his sense of place. The world spins and turns black, and Zeke feels as though he's been cast out into space, dizzying and endless, oxygen-free.

Later (minutes? hours?), he stumbles out of the garage, makes his way back to the metro and then to the Los Angeles Public Library to await the shuttle back to the Compound. He can't stop shaking. When he closes his eyes, he can still see his dad's bloated corpse. And the stench. He is convinced the stench has clung to him, for even here, miles away, it smells as if he never left.

He keeps thinking that will be him someday, a putrid mass of rot. He has never feared death before—has never thought about it much one way or another—but now it stalks him, teases him. Terrifies him. He doesn't want that end. He doesn't want any end. Ever.

CHAPTER 8

Then

Ben wakes with a start, but he doesn't open his eyes. He has learned to feign sleep until he has assessed his situation as fully as he can. Twice he has awakened when someone was in the process of robbing him and gotten the shit beaten out of him for his trouble. The third time, he kept his eyes closed until his assailants were gone. He'd lost money and some over-the-counter pain pills, but his body was otherwise unmolested, his limbs left intact. Now, he never opens his eyes until he remembers where he is and listens to what's going on around him.

He determines he has slept inside, for there is no breeze, and in a cot or bed because his back isn't aching the way it does when he sleeps on the ground. He is either squatting or in a shelter. Squatting, he decides, because shelters come with odors, and this place smells of nothing at all.

He eases his eyes open, prepared to shut them again if the situation warrants it. He sees his dad slumped over in a chair, his eyes open but sagging. Henry is beside him in another chair, snoring softly.

He's in a hospital, he realizes, even though he's never seen one before in real life, lying in a bed with clean sheets, with tubes and wires adorning him like tribal body art. Funny. He doesn't feel sick.

"Ben," his dad exclaims, so boisterous he wakes Henry.

"Hi, Dad," Ben croaks. "What happened?"

He'd contracted a flu that had turned into pneumonia, Vance explains. They had left it too long, not realizing it was severe, and by the time they had taken him to a hospital—via an ambulance they could not afford, to an emergency room that had already presented them with a bill they could never pay—he had been so near death that his doctor could not guarantee he would survive the night.

"They kept asking why we didn't get you help sooner," Vance says. "Even threatened to call CPS." He cannot meet Ben's eyes.

It is nearly two weeks later now, and Ben is expected to make a full recovery. His doctor, in a fit of humanity, gave his family the entire hospital room. His dad pushes back a curtain to reveal Remy and Zeke asleep in a bed identical to his, his mom dozing fitfully in the chair beside them.

Ben's father has more news. "The doctor's been talking to me about going to a Compound," Vance whispers. "He says it isn't safe raising you kids the way we do, or fair to you neither. And I've been thinking, and Henry agrees, he's probably right. It's been a real wake-up call nearly losing you, Ben. I don't want something like this to happen again."

Ben wonders if, now that he's awake, he's become delirious. His parents have said in the past that they'd rather see their kids die than watch corporate America enslave them.

"How'd you get Mom to agree?" Ben asks.

His dad and Henry exchange looks. "She doesn't exactly know yet," Vance admits.

"So, we're not going," Ben says, annoyed that his father had gotten his hopes up. His father doesn't believe in a whole lot anymore, which has left him untethered and unpredictable, but it has also left a void, which Ben's near death and the doctor's timely intervention had managed to fill with the notion that the Compounds are a necessary evil. But Ben's mom is different. She has closely held, unwavering beliefs, among them that only God should control when man lives or dies. To her, Immortality and everything connected to it exists in contradiction to God. She will never agree to go to a Compound. Never.

"We're going," Vance assures him. "Your mom will come around. She has to. She brought four children into this world. It's time for her to do right by them."

But Ilene does not come around. She listens as Vance attempts to justify the move, his voice supplemented by the pleas of his children, and her face transforms from surprised to angry to hurt.

When Vance falls silent, having made the best argument he could, Ilene glares at him. She is an angry minister silently condemning a reproachable congregant. Vance cowers, gives in.

"Ilene," he whispers. He is prepared to repent and apologize, but she shakes her head. It's too late for him, for all of them.

"He that believeth on the Son hath everlasting life: and he that believeth not the Son shall not see Life; but the wrath of God abideth on him." She looks at each of them as she quotes the New Testament, her cold, unforgiving eyes boring into them, damning them.

"You will not drag me down with you," she says with finality, and then she turns and walks from the room.

When she has not returned two hours later, they search for her, checking the overcrowded cafeteria, the gift shop, the waiting rooms filled with loved ones anxiously awaiting news. They interrogate nurses and receptionists, doctors scurrying from patient to patient, security guards pacing up and down the halls, but no one has seen a petite brunette with frizzy hair and a look of chronic constipation on her face.

They wait for Ilene in Ben's hospital room until Ben is discharged and then loiter in the lobby until security asks them to leave.

"What now?" Henry asks as they step outside into the stifling after noon heat.

"Maybe we go back to the garage," Vance says. "Give her a week or two to come to her senses."

They return to the condemned parking garage they'd been living in before Ben got sick. They are relieved to see it's still standing after their two-and-a-half-week absence and pleased that their makeshift home—the boxes, clothes and blankets they'd left behind in their haste to get Ben to the hospital—remains untouched.

"We won't stay long," Vance promises. "Only until she comes back."

Two weeks pass and she doesn't return, and Vance turns to vodka to dull the pain.

Every now and then, after a month, then two, then six have passed, one of his children approaches him and asks about moving to a Compound, but Vance always refuses. "Just another week or two," he says. "She'll be back by then. She can't stay mad at us forever."

Ben turns eighteen and considers leaving for a Compound by himself, but by then, his family is worse off than ever, and it seems heartless to leave his siblings behind. Vance has become a burden. He still needs to be fed, but he no longer attempts to contribute. He drinks vodka like it's water, begging cheap bottles off liquor store patrons or manipulating Zeke into handing over whatever he has earned panhandling. Jobs remain impossible to come by; charities are over-subscribed; ordinary people and the police are hostile, assuming everyone who qualifies for a Compound has relocated to one, and that the people who remain are the felons, the druggies, and the nut jobs. The children tell Vance it's time to go; they beg him to take them to a Compound, but without Ilene, he won't budge.

Now

Ben used to sit with his back against the wall of the local drugstore and watch people walk by. He watched the men in their shirts and ties—jackets flung over their shoulders, armpits damp with stress-induced sweat—rushing from meeting to meeting. He watched the women trying to silence their crying babies while participating in conference calls and juggling groceries. He heard barked commands and sycophantic responses, saw bags under eyes and creases in foreheads. Tense fists and pounding feet and furrowed brows. Phones flung to the ground in frustration, tires kicked and curse words uttered, adults throwing temper tantrums and having meltdowns, taking their rough day out on whoever happened to get in their way.

Since coming to the Compound, Ben has thought about those people often, and he can't figure out what induces them to remain on the Outside. He compares their lives to his: he has a comfortable bed and all the food he can eat, a hot shower and clean clothes, access to bars and movie theaters. But he also has something they don't: time. He has time for his family and friends, time to work out, time for his hobbies and interests, time to improve his basketball game. He always gets at least eight hours of sleep, and he hasn't once felt stressed since coming here. To him, Compound life is a dominant option.

Sometimes when he comes home, he sees Remy hunched over her books, studying. She is inexplicably determined to return to the Outside, to become one of those stressed-out women in a business suit and high heels. Ben tries to deter her without much success. She's approaching the entrance to the labyrinth, and once she steps inside, she may never find her way out again. Instead, there will be wrong turns and dead ends, a life full of frustration.

"Why is this so important to you?" he asks.

"I want choices," she says. "I don't want my life to be determined by default."

"Living on the Compound is a choice," he says.

She thinks about this for a moment. "Yes," she agrees. "I suppose it is."

She returns to her books, and Ben leaves her in search of someone or something more interesting. Remy has always been odd. On the streets, she'd preferred hidden alleys with working streetlights to homeless shelters. Better for doing homework, she'd explained. Quieter. Fewer distractions.

That she could focus on fractions when their family was perpetually on the verge of extinction had always perplexed Ben. But then, at least, there hadn't been anything better to do. They had no money for movies or

TV, no friends or neighbors. But here, she could be relaxing by the pool or going to a party. How can she focus on schoolwork here?

Most of Ben's time is spent working out, watching sports, drinking, having sex. In the past, he was a thwarted hedonist. Now, he's living the dream. The day of and the day after Donation are Ben's recovery days. He uses them to get over not just his loss of blood but also the excitement of the previous week. He doesn't mind taking a break. There is something pleasant about stretching out on the sofa and watching detective shows with Zeke. Henry used to join them, too, but these days he stays locked away in his room.

"Hibernating for the winter?" Ben asks. Henry just shakes his head.

Then one day, Ben comes back from Donation and finds the television off, the room silent but for the scratching of a pencil against paper. Zeke and Remy are sitting side by side at the table. Zeke writes something while Remy looks on, biting her lip and shaking her head.

"Not quite," she says. "You forgot to carry the one."

Zeke frowns, tries again.

"Better!" Remy exclaims.

"What are you doing?" Ben asks.

"Studying," Remy replies in a voice that suggests it should be obvious. Zeke avoids Ben's eyes.

"Try this one, Zeke," Remy urges, oblivious to her brother's discomfort.

"Maybe we should take a break," Zeke mutters. He twirls his pencil between his fingers and stares down at the table.

Remy is incredulous. "Zeke, you've got to take this seriously if you want to pass the NPE. You don't have much time."

Zeke lowers his head, and, for a second, Ben thinks he's going to crawl beneath the table. Ben is amused until Remy's words sink in.

"Wait, you're taking the NPE?" For as long as he can remember, his younger brother has hated school. Zeke has treated his education as a prison sentence and acted accordingly, keeping quiet and trying not to cause trouble, counting down the days until he's released into the real world.

Zeke manages a brief nod but can't bring himself to say anything. To him, ambition is as shameful as bedwetting or nose-picking. Ben understands this in a way that Remy does not. He's an active member of the world they inhabit, while Remy watches it disdainfully from the sidelines.

"Why?" he asks Zeke.

Zeke shrugs.

Ben scoffs. "This is so stupid, Zeke. I mean, you hate school. You're bad at it. You're going to make yourself miserable for the next six months, take this exam, and then you know what's going to happen? You're going to fail."

"Don't listen to him, Zeke. If you work hard enough, you can pass," Remy tells him, glaring at Ben.

"Okay," Ben says. "Let's say you do pass. Then what? You go to college? Four more years of school? And then some office job where you spend hours behind a desk doing work you hate? For what? You like hanging out with your friends and watching TV, both things you can do here, on the Compound, without wasting time on this bullshit."

Something flickers in Zeke's eyes. Sadness. Regret. But still, he doesn't say anything. He has become a cornered animal, uncertain how to proceed. His eyes dart back and forth between Ben and Remy. He doesn't want to upset either one of them.

"Did she put you up to this?" Ben asks. A tinge of resentment stirs within him, a desire to swat at his sister, to shoo her away from hapless, impressionable Zeke.

But then Zeke mumbles, "It was my idea. I asked her to help me study."

Ben shakes his head in disbelief. Zeke is hopeless. "Of course you did. Well, can you go study somewhere else? I want to watch TV."

"Sure," Remy says, but Zeke looks mortified by the thought of leaving the apartment with his books in tow. Remy rolls her eyes. "Don't worry," she says. "We won't run into any of your friends in the library."

Zeke begins filling his backpack, keeping one apologetic eye on Ben as he does.

When they have left, Ben shakes his head and turns on the television. He can't imagine what has motivated his listless brother to voluntarily take an exam.

Henry stumbles in an hour later, gaunt and sickly, unsteady on his feet. Donation always seems to take more of a toll on him than on anyone else. Ben helps him to the couch.

"How you feeling?" he asks.

Henry grimaces. "I've been better. I keep waiting for this to get easier." He surrenders his body to gravity, letting it pull him down to the couch with a thud.

"You're not eating enough," Ben tells him. "I've seen your dinners. You pick at some fruit, nibble on a roll. If you eat more, your recovery time will be shorter." Ben hears himself and winces. He sounds like a nagging mom.

But Henry only nods. "I know. I'll try to do better." He glances around the room and seems to realize something is amiss. "Where's Zeke?"

Ben snorts. "You're not going to believe this. He's studying for the NPE with Remy. As if he has a snowball's chance in hell."

Henry looks up, surprised. "He's really doing it, huh? I didn't think he would."

"You know about this?" Ben asks. Henry keeps tabs on Remy. He knows her comings and goings, her feelings and friends (or lack thereof), but with Zeke, Henry is usually oblivious.

"He started talking about it after he found Dad," Henry explains.

Zeke had come back from Los Angeles delirious and incoherent, mumbling streams of words that didn't form sentences. Eventually, they'd managed to piece together that he'd ignored their objections and gone into the city, where he'd found their dad dead and decomposing. The discovery has destroyed Zeke. He showers as often as he can now. He complains about an odor the others cannot smell. His eyes have changed, too, their boyish simplicity replaced by some lingering horror. Fear. Disgust. Inevitability.

He is recovering gradually, but he has yet to return to the happy-go-lucky kid he'd been before his ill-fated adventure.

"What does Dad have to do with the NPE?" Ben asks. It must be a distraction, something to take Zeke's mind off their father's bloated body.

"Oh, he concocted this crazy plan. Pass the NPE, go to college, study business, and make enough money to afford Immortality."

"Zeke wants Immortality?" Ben says. He starts to laugh. "He'd be better off robbing a bank."

Ben expects Henry to reprimand him, to insist Zeke's problem is serious, but Henry laughs, too. "God, please don't suggest that to him. You know how impressionable he is."

Ben pictures Zeke attempting to rob a bank. He imagines a toy gun, a cheap mask that falls off halfway through, a paper bag with a green dollar sign drawn on the side that can't handle the weight of the bills Zeke has stolen and splits down the middle as he's trying to escape. Zeke has always been willing to try everything, but he's never been much good at anything.

"Hey," Ben says. "Remember the time Zeke decided to run a lemonade stand?"

Henry smiles. "How could I forget? He dropped a lemon rind into a jug of water and mixed it with a spoon." He sticks his tongue out, and Ben laughs.

"What about the time he heard Dad say we needed to start bringing home some dough, so he snuck into the school cafeteria and filled his backpack with bread dough?" Henry says.

Ben doubles over with laughter, clutching his stomach as it starts to cramp.

"The dough got all over everything, his books, his clothes, his hands. We called him the Pillsbury Doughboy for weeks," Ben remembers.

His eyes meet Henry's and they smile at each other. It's a moment of rare camaraderie at their brother's expense, but Ben appreciates it. He wishes they had more times like this.

As their laughter fades, Henry becomes serious again, and Ben half expects an admonishment for making fun of Zeke. Instead, Henry says, "That's why I worry about him, you know. He's so impressionable. What if he does something stupid to get Immortality?"

Ben feels a strange sense of pride. Henry doesn't usually share his concerns with anyone. As the second oldest, Ben might have helped out more with Zeke and Remy, especially after their parents ceased to parent, but Henry had so dominated that role that Ben had never felt there was room for him. "Yeah, I get it," he says. "But if there's one thing I remember from being his age, it's that no one can tell you what to do."

"I know. But I guess I feel responsible for him now."

Ben gazes at his brother. Henry has aged since coming to the Compound. He has bags under his eyes and worry lines on his forehead. He hasn't gained any weight either, in stark contrast to Ben, who has put on nearly twenty pounds. Henry probably looks worse than usual now, less than an hour after Donation, but even accounting for that, his brother clearly isn't doing well.

"You shouldn't feel responsible for him," Ben says. "He's grown. We have to let him be."

"You're right," Henry agrees. "I know. But keep an eye on him for me, will you?"

Ben is surprised by the request. Nobody has ever asked much of him. "Sure," he says, sitting up a little straighter. "Of course."

They watch a few minutes of the Lakers game in companionable silence, and then Ben, hungry for more of his brother's confidences, asks, "What have you been up to this week?"

"Reading," Henry says. He holds up his book so that Ben can see the title.

"*The Stranger*," Ben reads. "Any good?"

"Yeah, not bad."

Ben feels something stir in his stomach. "Why do you read so much these days? You never used to."

Henry extends his arms toward the ceiling in a long, drawn-out stretch. When he lowers them again, his demeanor has changed. He's quieter, more pensive. "You know, I never got much of an education, Ben, so I guess I'm trying to educate myself now. Read some of the books I should have read in high school."

"What for?" Ben asks. He isn't sure why, but this bothers him. What's wrong with Henry as he is? What's wrong with any of them?

"I don't know," Henry says. "Why do you spend all your free time at the bar?"

"Because drinking is fun. Sex is fun. TV is fun. There's nothing fun about reading."

"Why do you care what I do?" Henry asks.

Ben falters. Why does he care? He never has before.

"Because you're changing," he sputters. "Everyone is changing. You and Zeke and Remy. It's like you're all trying to be something you're not."

"Let me ask you something, Ben," Henry says, eyeing his younger brother. "Are you bothered because we're changing, or are you bothered because you're not?"

Three nights later, Ben makes his way to the Compound pub. This is his watering hole of choice. He appreciates the dark interior, the mossy greens and woodsy browns, the smell of cheap beer seldom mopped from the sticky floor. Even the remote-control-operated fireplace—which others mock as old-fashioned and unnecessary in the desert heat—makes him feel at home.

He arrives at 3:30 p.m. because he knows this is when Caleb Wentworth drinks. Caleb avoids bars at night when they are crowded with drunks and people who aspire to be drunk. When starry-eyed girls encircle him and try to command his attention. When everyone seems to remember that he's not really one of them, that he comes from money, that he might, no, should, buy them a drink. When he is labeled a jerk or a jackass if he declines as if he owes them somehow. So, Caleb drinks early when his only companions are a random assortment of misfits—middle-aged, socially awkward, in search of a drink, not a night out.

Caleb prefers this scene; Ben does not. He likes to drink later, when the Compound bars are packed to capacity with scantily clad women and cocky guys, flirting and petting and whispering and kissing. Shots circulated. Another round. Everyone drinking to get drunk, to have fun, to have sex. It's all impulse and indulgence, life at its best.

Ben can't understand why Caleb avoids it even if it does cost him a little more. But then, Caleb is an enigma. He's friendly. He plays and watches sports. He works out. But he has also been known to disappear for days at a time. He doesn't attend parties, and he doesn't have casual sex. He seems to enjoy Compound life, but he remains separate somehow.

Today, Caleb is tucked away in a corner booth perusing an old-fashioned print magazine with lots of words and very few pictures. He looks unnatural, by himself, in a bar, reading instead of staring at a screen. Ben is pleased with his timing, glad he can rescue his friend from his solitude.

"Hey man," he says.

Caleb looks surprised to find someone sitting across from him. "Oh, Ben. Hi." His voice is strained.

"Whatcha up to?" Ben asks.

"Nothing much."

Ben waits for Caleb to say more, but he doesn't, and now they are staring at each other in a silence that is fast becoming uncomfortable, like teenagers on a blind date.

"Can I buy you a round?" Caleb asks at last.

Ben agrees, requests a Corona and waits in the booth while Caleb goes to the bar to order two cold ones from the vending machine.

"Thanks, man," Ben says when he returns.

"Anytime," Caleb replies. "How's Remy?"

"You probably see her more than I do." Caleb has, somewhat reluctantly, agreed to prep his sister for the NPE.

"Yeah," Caleb mutters. "First, it was her. Now it's four others, too."

"Really?" Ben says, surprised. "Who?"

"Malachi Williams, Miguel Bernardo, Becky Chin, and your brother, Zeke," Caleb lists.

"Zeke the worst of them?"

"Between you and me, he doesn't stand a chance," Caleb admits.

"No surprise there. I can't believe he's even taking the damn thing."

"Yeah, it's weird. Like, it's clear he cares about passing, but he doesn't know how to study or focus or remember much of anything. Even when he knows an answer, he has trouble putting it in writing, and he doesn't seem to have any ideas or opinions of his own. He's an unusual guy."

Ben feels uncomfortable discussing his brother with Caleb. He's spent his life defending Zeke against people who thought he was deficient, retarded, dumb. "How are the others?" he asks.

"Mixed," Caleb replies. "Becky Chin is taking the exam for her parents. They want her to become a doctor, but I've never seen anyone with less aptitude for science. Miguel would probably test into college with good schooling. As it is, I'm not sure I can get him there. Remy is fantastic. She's both smart and determined. She's a shoo-in for college, but I'd really like to get her into an Ivy. And Malachi Williams, well, he's another level entirely. He's wasted here. Honest to God, if I didn't know any better, I'd say he's Nathan Odili's illegitimate son. He should be able to write his ticket to any university in the country. Another round?" Caleb asks.

Ben has downed his beer in several long gulps. "Yeah, thanks," he says.

Caleb returns half a minute later with another Corona.

Ben takes a swig without tasting it. "I don't get it," he says to Caleb. "Why are they all so determined to leave? It's awful out there. You hated it, too, right? I mean, you chose to come here, and you weren't even on the streets."

Caleb raises his eyebrows, surprised by the turn the conversation has taken. "Yeah," he says thoughtfully. "I remember the exact moment I made the decision. Spring semester, I was up at three in the morning, writing a paper on George Eliot, and I realized I was miserable. I didn't care about anything I was learning or doing. I was sick of being stressed all the time.

And I decided I didn't want to do it anymore, so I stopped. I closed my computer and went to bed. I never turned in the paper or took any of my finals. I went home, and when I got Incompletes in all my classes, I explained to my parents that I wasn't going back."

"I'm sure they took that well."

"Oh, they told the school I'd had a panic attack and got a therapist friend of theirs to certify as much. Then they took me from psychiatrist to psychiatrist, trying to get someone to 'cure' me. You know what the psychiatrists did? They prescribed pills. Lots and lots of pills." Caleb laughs, a cold, bitter laugh that sends chills down Ben's spine. "Can you imagine? Like trying to heal a stab wound with a Band-Aid."

"But life on the Compound is better, right?" Ben prods. "It sounds a lot better than what you were going through in college."

Caleb shrugs. "I guess so, although I'd be lying if I said that the burden that's been weighing on me my entire life has finally been lifted."

"What do you mean?" Ben asks.

"My friends mock me. My parents are ashamed of me. No one in my extended family knows I'm here. My mom tells them that I've joined the Peace Corps, that I'm in Malawi building schools and feeding starving orphans."

"What's wrong with the Compounds?"

"Nothing," Caleb says. "And don't let anyone tell you otherwise."

Ben nods. He is happy here, and so is almost everyone he knows. Unfortunately, the exceptions are his siblings. "Then how come Henry's miserable here, and both Zeke and Remy are trying to leave?"

Caleb tears a napkin into shreds with his fingers, leaving a pile of small white paper atop the table. Ben imagines him repeating this a thousand times, then throwing the shreds into the air, making it snow in the desert. Ben's never seen snow. He probably never will.

"You know what I think, Ben?" Caleb says, looking past Ben and through the pub door to the Compound streets outside. "I think we're all just trying to find meaning in life. If you find it here, great, stay here. If

Remy can't, well then, she should go. Everyone should have the freedom to determine their own course."

Ben nods. He likes that. His choices aren't better or worse than his siblings'. They're different. They're what's right for him.

Meaning, Ben decides, is overrated. People spend too much time inside their heads asking difficult questions, pondering issues that are so much larger than themselves, when really they should take a deep breath, look around at what they have, and be grateful. The Cruors have stumbled upon a kind of paradise that their wealthy counterparts will never enjoy. For once, the poor have it better than the rich. It must be divine justice, the meek inheriting the earth, enjoying lives of leisure while the wealthy slave away.

After Caleb leaves, Ben remains in the bar, mooching beers and groping girls, taking shots when they're offered and having nonsensical conversations he'll have no recollection of come morning. By eight o'clock, he's drunk, and he stumbles out of the pub, his arm draped around Angela or Andrea. Whoever she is, she seems delighted to be with him.

The next morning, he wakes up hungover but happy in her bed. Across the aisle, another couple is spooning. Were they here last night? If so, he hadn't noticed.

The room is messy. Clothes are piled on the floor. Every inch of the wall is covered with posters of male celebrities. On top of the dresser, dozens of bottles in all shapes and sizes—hair sprays and perfumes and face creams and lipsticks—are crammed together, a colorful bouquet of items into which a woman can dive and emerge, if not beautiful, then certainly improved.

He wonders if the two women who live here knew each other before coming to the Compound, if they are sisters or best friends, or had worked together at some seedy Hollywood brothel. If not, then Hemodyne had paired them up. His friend Jamie says that roommates are assigned without regard to compatibility. When she'd first arrived, she'd had to share a room with a compulsively tidy girl who'd gotten angry over unmade beds and refused to allow food in the apartment, who'd once interrupted Jamie during sex to have her pick up a condom wrapper, casually tossed on the floor in the heat of the moment.

"I switched roommates as soon as I could," Jamie had told him, which apparently was allowed. Find someone you'd rather live with and you can move in with them on the first day of the next month.

The girls who share this room seem similar enough, or, at any rate, they both have men in their beds. Angela or Andrea is still asleep beside him. He can feel her breath, warm and steady, on his back. He slips out of bed and into his clothes without looking at her face. Better not to know, he's found. Better to assume the best.

In the living space, a wiry redhead is watching a talk show. She turns when he opens and closes the bedroom door, rotating her head at a glacial pace. When she is facing him at last, he sees that her eyes are vacant. A drug addict, he realizes. He'd seen plenty of people like her on the Outside, slumped against walls on nearly every block, more ubiquitous than Starbucks and Dime-a-Dozen combined. The eyes. It's always in the eyes.

If she's caught, she'll be given one shot at rehab, but if she relapses, she'll be banned from the Compounds forever. Like being cast out of Eden, Ben thinks, but at least Hemodyne gives you a second chance.

He waves at the redhead, but if she notices, she doesn't respond. He stays where he is for a few more seconds until she turns back around and resumes watching television, and then he makes his way to the apartment door and leaves.

It's 11:52 a.m., and the sun is blazing. Ben ambles toward the cafeteria, craving something greasy. He hasn't made it far when he hears a woman say, "Excuse me?"

He turns around and finds himself face-to-face with a slender, pretty woman in her late twenties. Her hair is bobbed, her smile disarming. She wears some makeup, but not much, and her dress is form-fitting but professional, the only splash of green in the arid desert. Dallas is beside her, his nose twitching slightly like a cat assessing something he isn't sure he can trust. This is the first time Ben has seen him since Intake. He looks different when his head isn't tilted back.

"Hi," the woman says. "I'm Wei Wei Sung with *The Atlantic*. The magazine? I'm writing a piece about life on the Compounds. Would you mind if I ask you a few questions?"

In the background, Dallas's mouth has stretched into a taut, close-lipped grin, and his nose is twitching more vigorously.

Ben ignores him. "Sure," he says. "Happy to help."

"Great," Wei Wei replies. "How much time do you have? Could you show me around, maybe introduce me to some people?"

"Yeah. Absolutely," Ben says. He wonders what his odds of getting her into bed are.

She turns to Dallas. "Thanks for your help, Dennis, but I'm fine from here," she purrs.

"Ms. Sung, I'm your escort. I'm supposed to stay with you at all times," Dallas protests. His voice is a full octave higher than usual.

Ben, who has never cared for Dallas, grins. "Don't worry, Dennis. I'll take good care of her."

Dallas's eyes turn murderous, but his smile remains. Wei Wei is watching. He opens his mouth to protest again, but Wei Wei cuts him off. "Honestly, Dennis, if this place is as safe as you say it is, I'll be fine."

It's a trump card. Dallas has two choices: relinquish her to Ben or admit that the Compounds aren't as safe as Hemodyne claims. Neither will please his higher-ups.

"Okay, fine," Dallas relents. "But please be back to the administrative building by a quarter to five."

"We promise," Wei Wei says, making the sign of an X across her heart.

"Thanks for helping me shake that guy," she says after Dallas has gone. She smiles at Ben, a big, beautiful smile, and he feels his heart start to pound. It's not that Wei Wei is so much more attractive than the best-looking Cruor girls, but there's something about the fact that she's an Outsider.

"No problem," he says, smiling back at her. "You want to get something to eat?"

They walk to the cafeteria. He helps himself to a burrito but directs her toward the dishes he thinks she'll like—the salad bar, the fruit, the stir fry. "It's better than I expected," she admits.

"I've put on twenty pounds in two months."

"My god, how skinny were you before?"

"Skinny," he says. "Scrawny."

She asks him about life on the Compound, and he answers truthfully. It's safe. The people are friendly. The amenities are impressive. He couldn't be happier. "Honestly," he gushes, "I can't imagine a better life."

When she seems suspicious, he shows her around. The swimming pool, the schools, the movie theatre. At the pub, Ben introduces Wei Wei to a quartet of permanently laid-off ex-professionals who talk about their experiences on the Outside: the education they'd gone to the trouble to attain, the unexpected lay-offs, the crippling debt.

"Everyone thinks Cruors are fuck-ups," says Paul, a burly fellow who used to be a pharmacist. "But we did everything right. Went to college. Majored in something practical. Got good jobs. Then those jobs disappeared, and nothing replaced them."

"It's not like we didn't try," his friend Leo chimes in. "I worked in advertising first, then digital marketing. When I was laid off, I found something in PR that lasted about two minutes. Finally, I got a job delivering mail for the post office. It didn't require a degree and it only paid a third of what I'd earned at my peak, but it was something. Six months later, they replaced me with a drone."

Wei Wei records their words on a small digital device. She asks follow-up questions and listens with interest and empathy. When she is done, she buys them a round of drinks to thank them for speaking with her.

"No need to thank us," says Paul. "It's nice to have someone listen for a change."

As it approaches five o'clock, Ben tells Wei Wei it's time to go. They say goodbye to the group at the bar and wander out into the afternoon sun. Wei Wei babbles as they walk, and Ben, who is accustomed to chatty girls, is happy to let her.

"You've shown me a different side of the Compounds. It's so wonderful," she rambles. "It's true what that Paul said. I did think you were all miscreants. Or losers. Or druggies. That's what we're told, you know. A shocking lack of empathy, really. I think my parents did it to assuage their guilt. Like, they wouldn't feel so bad walking by all the starving children if they could tell themselves that their parents were slackers who deserved this. Personal responsibility and all that, you know? But obviously, it wasn't like that. People wanted to work. There just weren't enough jobs."

Ben looks at her, amused. "None of it matters now," he assures her. "We're okay."

"I know you are. I can see that. But what would have happened if Hemodyne hadn't come along?" She'd come to the Compound skeptical of Hemodyne, determined to uncover the seedy underbelly of the corporation, to write an exposé detailing its countless shortcomings. Instead, she's been converted.

The next month a glowing article about Compound 78 appears in *The Atlantic*. Two days later, Dallas calls.

CHAPTER 9

Then

Nine-year-old Sabrina is in her room, nestled atop a pink tufted chair that resembles a throne, reviewing her spelling list again. The school-wide bee is tomorrow.

Sabrina is a good speller. She always gets one hundred percent on weekly spelling tests. Every report card she's had since kindergarten has praised her accuracy. She isn't sure why she's so good at knowing the order letters should go in to form a word. It isn't that she reads a lot (she doesn't) or that she's good at memorization (she isn't). But there is something about words that sticks with her. She can sense whether they are spelled correctly the way a good chef knows which ingredients to combine to elevate a recipe.

The school-wide bee is held on stage in the auditorium as though it is a play or a talent show. Students, teachers, and sometimes parents sit in the audience, cheering the competitors on. This makes some students nervous, but not Sabrina. She has always loved being the center of attention.

Her mother raps on the bedroom door as she is opening it, her knock not a request but an announcement. Christie Davenport is expertly made up, draped in loungewear that costs more than most wedding dresses.

Sabrina has never seen her mother look less than perfect, and her mother makes sure Sabrina always looks perfect, too.

"Hi, darling," Christie says, beaming at her favorite child. "Want to watch a movie?"

"I can't," Sabrina replies. "Spelling bee's tomorrow." She looks up at her mother hopefully. "Will you help?"

"Love to," Christie says, winking.

Sabrina brightens; her mom isn't usually interested in her schoolwork. She extends the spelling list toward Christie, anxious to show how much she knows, ready to spell 'abundance' and 'arduous' and 'edifice.' But Christie walks right past Sabrina, straight to her daughter's walk-in closet.

"Now, this is gorgeous," Christie says, selecting a black velvet dress with a white lace collar. "But it may be a bit much. You don't want to be overdressed."

She puts the dress back and continues rifling through Sabrina's closet, extracting then rejecting outfits, searching for the perfect look. Sabrina watches her, awestruck. This, she realizes, is what makes her mother so exquisite. She never thinks the event for which she is dressing is more important than what she wears.

Sabrina glances down at her spelling list, the columns of black words printed on dull yellow paper. Then she looks back to her closet. It is crammed full, a rainbow of beautifully made clothes, none of them dull yellow. In her rush to join her mother, she lets the spelling list fall to the floor.

"What about this?" she asks, pulling out a red knit sweater. "With a black skirt, maybe."

Her mother strokes the sweater as though it's a pet. "That could work, Sabrina. Try it on. I'll come up with a few more options."

Sabrina pulls on a black A-line skirt to pair with the sweater. She lays them both out on her king-sized bed and begins to change, eager for her mother's approval, determined to hear the parents in the audience tomorrow whisper, "Would you look at Sabrina Davenport? She could have stepped right out of *Vogue*."

"What do you think, Mom?" she asks once she's changed clothes. She spins in a slow circle, so her mother can assess her from every angle.

"Wait. Stop right there," Christie orders. She is holding four or five additional outfits by the hanger. "Here, take these," she says, passing the clothes to Sabrina. "An event this significant calls for a fashion show."

Sabrina claps. She loves it when her mother sits on the sofa in the living room and watches as Sabrina sashays and poses, imagining that she is a model strutting down a Parisian runway.

"Add shoes to that outfit," Sabrina's mom orders as she leaves the room. "I want every look to be complete. Sell me on it. Let me see how gorgeous it will make you look tomorrow."

Sabrina giggles. "Okay," she promises, rushing back to her closet in search of her patent leather Mary Janes.

In her hurry, she tramples over the spelling list, which lies forgotten on the floor.

Now

Sabrina used to sit in the window of her mother's boutique on Melrose and watch the shoppers walk by. They were mostly wealthy. Trendy. Thin. The men wore leather shoes, and the women had extensions in their hair. Some were famous and afraid to be alone. They would come into the boutique with entourages and escorts, a burly bodyguard with an earpiece, an assistant talking into a phone. Others craved privacy. They would slip into the shop discreetly, ask for the store to be locked until they were finished, and make so many purchases they paid the boutique's monthly rent.

When business was slow, Christie would join Sabrina at the window, and they would rate the attractiveness of passersby on a one-to-ten scale. When someone fell below a six, Christie would wrinkle her nose until she could no longer see them. Ugliness disgusted her. She found it as offensive as a racial slur.

When she stood to go back to work, she would run her fingers through

Sabrina's hair and whisper, "You're more beautiful than any of them, sweetheart. You're the most beautiful girl in the world."

A decade and a half later, as Sabrina is packing up after a photo shoot that has run late, the photographer, a wiry chain smoker named Gil, whispers that to her, word for word. "You're more beautiful than any of them, sweetheart. You're the most beautiful girl in the world."

Sabrina freezes, her eyes locked on her own face in the floor-to-ceiling mirror in front of her, Gil behind her at her ear. She dabbles in the supernatural—séances, psychics, religion—and she wonders for a moment if her mother could be channeling her through this unexpected medium. "What did you say?" she asks, turning to face Gil.

"You're beautiful. Gorgeous. Sexy. What do you say we go back to mine?"

Sabrina's heart sinks. "Sorry, Gil. My boyfriend's waiting for me, but you're a real doll." She kisses him on the cheek and leaves, hoping he isn't the vindictive sort who'll refuse to work with her if she doesn't sleep with him. It's happened before.

Her car, a leased Tesla that she can't afford, is waiting out front. "Home," she says as she reclines her chair and closes her eyes.

The longer she is in this industry, the more she hates it. It has consumed her life from the moment she signed with Xiomara Khan at twelve years old. It has given her the validation she craves—*Yes, Sabrina, you are beautiful*—but, in exchange, it has claimed her youth, her dignity, her future. She never went to college. She can't do anything else, and she can't age, or she won't be able to do this anymore.

She wonders sometimes about other paths she could have followed, but she's not sure she'd be much good at anything else. Almost every compliment she's ever received has been about her looks. But then, she supposes, better that than to go through life like her sister Darcy, never receiving a compliment at all.

She thinks she might have liked to be a writer, and sometimes, on those rare nights when she doesn't have an event to attend and Hayes is not around, she'll pull out a notebook and write short stories, mostly about the modeling industry, because that's all she knows. She finds writing therapeutic, so much so that she stops seeing her over-priced therapist. She types up a couple of her stories and submits them to competitions, but she never hears anything. That's okay, she tells herself. You didn't really think you were going to win, did you?

Sometimes she reminds herself that she's Immortal, that she has all the time in the world, but then she remembers she doesn't control her Immortality; it's owned by someone else. Increasingly, it has come to feel like a form of slavery, yet she is afraid to let it go because she doesn't know if she can survive without being young and beautiful. She is fairly certain aging is what killed her mother, and they are cut from the same cloth.

As her car maneuvers itself through traffic, she phones her father to pass the time.

"Sabrina. How are you?" Connor Davenport asks. He is always pleased when she calls, she knows. It's confirmation that she cares.

"Photoshoot ran long. I've been looking alluring and exotic for the last twelve hours."

"A photoshoot, huh? For whom?"

"Xanadu XY. You've never heard of her, but they're calling her the second coming of Alexander McQueen."

"Who's Alexander McQueen?"

"Never mind, Daddy," she says, smiling. She likes that he's not a part of this world, that she can have a conversation with someone that doesn't center around fashion.

"But she's a big deal, huh? I'm having dinner with the Levins tonight. I'll have to tell them about this."

She takes a deep breath and reminds herself that he's bragging because he's proud. She tells herself that all parents are like that, that at some point, they start to care more about what you do than who you are. "You do that, Daddy," she murmurs.

"I wish your mother could see you now," Connor adds. "She always knew you were special."

Sabrina's heart pounds. Her mother keeps coming up today. Sign or coincidence?

She tries to forget about her mom most of the time. For her, thinking about Christie is like scratching a mosquito bite: it only makes things worse, but once she starts, she can't seem to stop. She still misses her mom so much.

For a long time, she'd blamed herself for Christie's death. If she had only been more beautiful, she could have saved her mother; her mother could have lived vicariously through her.

In the months that followed the funeral, she had spent thousands on daily blow-outs, purchased top-of-the-line beauty products, watched hours of make-up tutorials online. Her schoolwork was neglected, then forgotten. When she signed with Xiomara Khan the following year, it had felt like atonement.

Afterward, she had handwritten a letter to her mother. *Guess what, Mom? I'm a model.* The next time she had visited Dior, she had slipped the letter into one of the handbags, which had seemed more appropriate than leaving it at her mother's grave.

"I wish Mom had been born later," Sabrina says now. "If she could have become Immortal at twenty-five or thirty—"

Connor doesn't say anything. They both know how much preserving her youth would have meant to Christie, how much aging cost her.

"Have you given any more thought to your will?" Sabrina asks.

"I think about it constantly," Connor says. She can hear him hesitating. He needs to say something but isn't sure he should. She waits.

"Sabrina, honey," he begins. "I hope you know how much I love you. I'm sure you must be wondering why I don't just give Immortality to you. Hell, you've always been my favorite. But the truth is, I'm having trouble leaving Immortality to you when you already have Immortality."

Sabrina nods, even though he can't see her. At dinner that night, she had behaved badly. She often does when she doesn't get her way. Tantrums, insults, threats. Darcy used to call her Veruca Salt.

That night she had felt like a knife-wielding madman, stabbing her siblings and her father with cruel, hurtful words. *It's too late for Dom, Prince. Of course, you don't want Immortality, Darcy. Your life is worthless. Why are you doing this, Daddy? You don't even like them.*

Prince had started crying at the table. Connor had yelled at him. *What's wrong with you? That's not helping anything.*

His son's dying, Daddy. That's what she should have said but hadn't. She hadn't said anything at all. Instead, she'd sat there smirking, delighting in her rival's failure, as if this were a sporting event or a casting call.

Darcy had begun lecturing them on the evils of doling out Immortality as if it were any other good or service—if you can afford it, you can have it.

If you don't want Immortality, you don't have to take it, Darcy, Connor had hissed.

Oh, I want it, Darcy had snapped. *But I want to give it to the next Alexander Fleming or Jonas Salk, not some ditzy model who whores herself to wealthy men.*

Ugh, stop, Sabrina had said. *You're the Miss America contestant who wishes for world peace. Nobody likes you, you self-righteous little snot.*

It had disintegrated from there. *Slut. Pig. Bitch. Shut up, Prince. No one wants to save Dom.* Was it Sabrina's fault? Maybe. But Darcy's insult, *some ditzy model who whores herself to wealthy men,* had hit a little bit too close to home.

Her dad is still waiting for a reply. Her instinct is to whine, a strategy she's found to be inexplicably successful with men of all ages, although she suspects it continues to work only because she still looks 19. But she remembers something else about that dinner. *Grow up, Sabrina. You're not a little girl anymore.* No, she's not. Even if they keep treating her like one. She takes a deep breath and says, "I might have Immortality, but I had to sacrifice my independence to get it."

Connor chuckles. "If you get Immortality from me, I'll have sacrificed my life."

"You'll have died, Daddy, but I'm not asking you to sacrifice your life, and you're not offering."

Again, there is silence, and then Connor says, "You know, Sabrina, sometimes I think I underestimate you."

Sabrina doesn't miss a beat. "I'm sure you do, Daddy. Everyone does."

Sabrina is half asleep when her car pulls into the driveway of Hayes Harris's ultra-modern glass and concrete house. He is home, unfortunately, his flashy red Maserati parked carelessly in the driveway. He doesn't value the car or anything else for that matter. He had told her once during a fight that nothing was irreplaceable, not even her. He has too much money, too little heart.

She is craving a hot bath and a cup of chamomile, but Hayes isn't the sort of man who ever likes a quiet night in. She takes a deep breath before opening the front door.

"There she is!" he calls out when he sees her. He is sitting on the sofa with three men she doesn't recognize, who leer at her openly as they drink imported beer from amber-tinted bottles.

"This line has your name on it, Sabs," Hayes says, pointing at a rail of white powder arranged with impressive precision atop the coffee table.

"Thanks, hon, but I'm not in the mood tonight," she says, giving him a peck on the cheek that she hopes will soften the petulance he often displays when she doesn't go along with what he wants.

"What?" he asks. He doesn't seem upset yet, just inquisitive.

"Long day. Shoot ran twelve hours, and all I want is a bubble bath. Hi, guys," she says, waving to Hayes's friends, who have been ogling her for so long they have crossed the line from admiring to inappropriate.

She heads to the master bedroom, closes the door, and sinks onto the bed. She has just begun to remove her six-inch heels when the door opens again, and Hayes bursts in. His face is determined, predatory, and at first, Sabrina thinks he's going to initiate sex. She will lay back, as compliant as an inflatable doll, and hope it does not last long. She has learned not to resist; he can be aggressive, especially when he's been drinking.

But instead of climbing on top of her, he sits beside her and rests his hand against her inner thigh. "Sabrina," he says. "My cousin Ollie and his friends are here from London. I've been bragging about LA for months now. This is my chance to show it off, but to do that properly, I need my gorgeous supermodel girlfriend by my side." He's being charming now, all grins and winks and subtle touches. He'll try honey first, but he's not averse to vinegar. She wants to make him happy, but she needs sleep.

"Of course," she says, placing her hand atop his and giving it a little squeeze. "I'll have a round or two with your friends, and then you guys can go out, and I can go to bed." It pains her to make this offer. The last thing she wants is to make awkward conversation with a trio of strangers who are probably already drunk, who will almost certainly try to grope her the moment Hayes's head is turned, but relationships are compromise. She is trying.

"Won't do," Hayes says. His tone is still flirtatious; his grip on her wrist is not. "You're going out. Now get dressed."

He lets go of her and leaves the room, slamming the door behind him. Sabrina remains where he left her, trembling. Her relationships all end up like this. Men who think they own her because they sponsor her Immortality. And, in a way, they do. She needs them far more than they need her.

It had all been going so well before Immortality. Her career trajectory was promising, and when she dated, she'd been the one with the power, able to make men do anything she wanted with a single look.

But Immortality had changed the game. The top models could remain eighteen, nineteen, twenty forever. They would never age out of the industry. They would never be replaced by younger, prettier versions of themselves. The path to success had always been narrow; with Immortality, it had become razor thin.

Recognizing this, Xiomara Khan had gathered her models and announced she was letting ninety percent of them go. She'd said it without introduction or conclusion, without anything to soften the blow. They had been stunned.

Xiomara had never run her company like the others, who kept every model they could on the books because doing so cost them nothing. Instead, she cut underperformers loose, encouraging them to go to college, get a job, marry a millionaire. "You're certainly pretty enough for that," she'd tell them.

After Immortality, the top models were kept, the bottom were cut, and those, like Sabrina, who were on the cusp, were called in for a discussion. It had been brutal.

"Sabrina," Xiomara had said, drumming her silver-tipped nails against her oversized desk. "You're so close. Had Immortality not come along, you would be replacing Azra Nassar or Carlotta Dominguez in two or three years. But now it's going to be so much harder."

Sabrina gulped.

"Honestly, in your case, I think there's only one possible solution. Get Immortality. Buy yourself more time. Eventually, the world will tire of Azra and Carlotta. They'll long for new faces, and if you're still young, you could be one of them. Can you afford Immortality, Sabrina?"

Sabrina had known her father wouldn't help her, but she'd asked him anyway, calling him right there in Xiomara's office while Xiomara waited.

"He won't do it," Sabrina had reported, hanging up. She'd had to blink repeatedly to stop tears from falling. Xiomara hated criers.

Xiomara had walked over to Sabrina and placed her hands—as soft as satin, as cold as ice—against Sabrina's cheeks.

"You want this, don't you?" she had asked.

"More than anything," Sabrina confirmed. She felt like she was on a reality show, trying to convince the at-home audience not to vote her off.

Xiomara had nodded at her, convinced, a benevolent judge granting a reprieve. "Then there might be another way."

The other way had been Brad, a millionaire who wanted a hot girlfriend and was willing to pay for her Immortality. Xiomara had shown her a picture. He was old—in his sixties at least—with liver spots on his face and three or four chins bunched up against his neck. Sabrina was repulsed.

"I can't," she'd said. "I'd feel like a prostitute."

"Don't think of yourself like that. At $327,000 per year, you'd most definitely be a high-priced call girl," Xiomara assured her.

Sabrina felt sick. "What would I tell my family?"

"Tell them the Agency is sponsoring your Immortality," Xiomara had suggested. "It's more or less the truth."

"The Agency is sponsoring my Immortality," Sabrina had echoed. It sounded believable enough.

"The Agency is sponsoring my Immortality," she repeated. She has been repeating it for the past decade.

Brad had lasted two miserable years. He was the only one who'd been physically abusive, slapping her across the face when she said something that displeased him, whipping her behind with a belt because it turned him on. She'd put up with him until she met Rick at a party.

From then on, she'd swapped one generous multi-millionaire for another, as easy as switching shoes. After Rick, there had been Dmitri, Parker, Li Wei, Tad, and now Hayes. Things always start the same—a rich man sees her, becomes obsessed with her, will do anything to have her. Things always end the same, too, with the men coming to believe they own her.

She'd love to pull out a couple of big suitcases, pack up and leave now. She can imagine the look on Hayes's face. Disbelief. Incredulity. Humiliation. If she were lucky, his friends would laugh at him. So much for the hot girlfriend.

But she won't do it. She never does. She'll stay with Hayes until she finds the next rich guy, and as soon as he offers her Immortality, she'll leave Hayes behind.

The next day Prince texts, asking if they can meet. Sabrina has no other plans, and she is grateful for an excuse to get out of the house. Hayes likes to day drink on Saturdays, and Sabrina, whose head is still throbbing from last night's misadventures, simply doesn't have it in her.

Hayes doesn't know about her father's will or even that her father is Immortal, but he does know about her dying nephew, and he's sympathetic.

"My sister died when I was young," he told her back when they were first dating. "I don't think I've ever recovered."

Today when she tells him she's going to see her brother, he assumes she will see Dominick, too. "Let me know how the little guy's doing, okay?"

Five years ago, a few kind words would have made her think that the relationship was salvageable, that last night was the aberration and a good man lurked beneath a harsh and entitled exterior. Now, she knows better. She's learned that a kind side doesn't compensate for a mean streak.

As she travels up to the Valley, Sabrina mentally prepares for the conversation with her brother. He hadn't specified the purpose of this impromptu get together, but she's sure it's Dom, their dad's fortune, Immortality. She wishes for a moment she hadn't told her family that Xiomara Khan was sponsoring her Immortality. They might be more sympathetic if they knew the truth, but how could she have told them that? Now, when Prince pleads—will he plead or yell? Be angry or desperate?—she will have to stick to the argument that she feels like the agency owns her, even though it sounds selfish and silly, even to her.

She checks the time as her Tesla pulls up to the coffee shop Prince has selected. She was so eager to get out of the house she has arrived early, for once.

The coffee shop is cozy and old-fashioned. Comfortable armchairs and sofas mingle with tables and chairs. Everything is leather or wood. It reminds Sabrina of the coffee shops of her youth. The ones she frequents these days are more modern, with a lot of stainless steel and an abundance of windows, for seeing and being seen. In this one, the sole touch of modernity is the absence of baristas, the hum of their mechanical replacements.

She orders an iced skinny latte at one of four large machines, each the size of an ATM but made of durable glass so that she can watch her drink's construction. Espresso, skim milk, and ice all go into one tall, cylindrical glass, where they are optimally blended before the drink slides out of the machine and into her eager hands. Sabrina takes a sip and smiles. The drink is perfect, and her headache is starting to abate already.

She doesn't miss baristas. For years, she had gone to the same coffee shop every day, and she'd never known how her drink was going to turn out. There might be too much milk or not enough. Sometimes, they'd forget to use skim. She appreciates the precision and consistency of a machine.

She sits down at a corner table with her back to the wall, giving her a view of the shop's other patrons. Watching people who don't know they're being watched feels almost embarrassingly authentic to her; it's compelling in a way performances for the benefit of a camera are not.

On her table is an abandoned print copy of the *Los Angeles Times*. She picks it up daintily, as though it is an ancient artifact, and turns it over in her hands. Print newspapers are rare these days. World affairs don't interest her, but the entertainment section does. She begins to flip to the back, but then something catches her eye. In the lower left-hand corner is an advertisement for a gossip columnist. She scans it. Social. Well-connected. Will blend in at parties with millionaires and celebrities. Strong writing skills. No experience necessary.

"Are you reading the paper?" It's Prince, curious, surprised.

Sabrina shakes her head. "I was about to throw it out."

"Don't," Prince says. "I may read it later. Kind of a treat to get to read the news the old-fashioned way."

"Will you have something?" Sabrina asks. She wants to distract him, just for a moment.

"I will," he replies. "Be right back."

While his back is turned, Sabrina rips the advertisement out and sets the paper down again. She tucks the ad into her handbag to revisit later.

Prince returns, carrying a muddy beverage in a mug. His hands are small and thick, and Sabrina finds herself staring at them sympathetically. She has always felt sorry for Prince. She inherited the height intended for him, standing 5'11 to his 5'8, and he has gotten the delicate features

Darcy would have benefited from, the long eyelashes, dainty mouth, and pointy chin. He's always looked to Sabrina like one of Santa's elves, and he behaves like one, too, industrious and over-eager, perhaps a tad pathetic.

"How are you?" he asks as he settles in.

"I'm okay," she replies. "What are you doing?"

He has reached into this black leather satchel and retrieved a miniature bottle of Woodford Reserve. He opens the bottle and dumps the contents into his coffee.

"It's one o'clock," he shrugs. "I thought drinking at lunch was in again."

"No, drinking at brunch is in. Drinking mimosas and daffodilites at a restaurant is in. Discreetly pouring bourbon into your coffee is vaguely alcoholic."

He downplays her accusations. "I like a stiff drink, but I'm careful. I don't imbibe at work or get drunk around Dom. I try not to get drunk at all. I just need a little something to take the edge off."

Dom's decline is costing him. Family, she knows, is Prince's world. She's often thought he'd make a good golden retriever. He's so loving and loyal; he needs so much affection. When Prince first introduced Tina to the family, Connor hadn't liked her. "Look at that. Did you see how she winced when he took her hand?" he'd whispered to Sabrina. "She's a gold digger. I'm telling you."

But Sabrina knew how emotionally demanding Prince could be. It would be a full-time job loving him.

"Do you ever think about Mom?" Sabrina asks now, out of the blue.

"Oh, no. No, no, no, Sabrina. Don't you dare." He raises his hands toward her, palms up, as if to stop this line of questioning in its tracks.

"What?" she asks, perplexed. Her mom has been on her mind since yesterday, when that creepy photographer had, for one golden moment, appeared to be channeling her.

"Don't you do that. Don't you compare me to her. I'm not Mom. Mom did drugs. Dangerous, illegal drugs. I have the occasional drink. I'm not going to end up like her. I'm nothing like her." Her brother looks spooked by the thought as if there is no worse fate than ending up like their dead mother.

"What do you have against her?" Sabrina asks.

Prince widens his eyes and raises his eyebrows as if the answer to her question is obvious. "Mom was silly and vapid. In all the years I've been a therapist, I've never met anyone with less depth than her. As far as I could tell, she only valued one thing: beauty. And when hers started to fade, she turned to drugs to dull the pain until she overdosed. It doesn't get more simplistic or shallow than that."

She is shocked to hear him speak this way, amazed at how different his recollections are from hers. "What do you know?" she asks. "Mom wasn't shallow. Loving beauty isn't shallow. Nobody says that appreciating a Monet or being in awe of Niagara Falls is shallow. What's wrong with valuing the beauty in everyday life, in the people all around you, in clothing or jewelry?"

Prince sighs. "The problem with Mom wasn't that she appreciated beauty, it was that she was enamored of it to the exclusion of everything else. I once heard her refer to me as an eyesore. She called Darcy 'spud' for crying out loud."

Sabrina giggles. *Why do you call Darcy 'spud,' Mommy? Because she's lumpy and dull, like a potato.*

"You think that's funny?" Prince asks. "Why do you think Darcy is so emotionally detached?"

Sabrina is taken aback by the harshness in his voice. Prince is almost never harsh. "I'm sorry," she whispers.

But he doesn't hear her. "You really are a spoiled brat, aren't you? Don't you know how charmed your life is, compared to Darcy's or mine? Darcy grew up believing she was the most hideous, unlovable person in the world, and now she can't sustain a relationship to save her life. All I've ever wanted is a loving family, and what did I get? Parents who so clearly preferred you, a wife who could only have one child before her hysterectomy and hasn't been the same since, and a son with a terminal disease. You had love and affection growing up. You have a successful career and men falling at your feet now. You've managed to get Immortality, locking you permanently at nineteen. And then Dad comes along, suddenly saying he wants to leave Immortality to one of us if, and only if, he dies and you want that, too. Even though you already have Immortality. Even though you already have everything. How selfish can you be?"

Tears are rolling down Sabrina's cheeks. She hadn't expected this. Questions, yes. Attempts at persuasion, absolutely. Maybe even a few angry words. But nothing like this. "Is this why you asked me here? To berate me?"

Prince looks away. "No," he says. "I came to beg you to reconsider your position. Ask Dad to leave his fortune to Dom."

"Why would I do that if I'm so spoiled and selfish?" Sabrina says. She expects him to apologize, to say he hadn't meant it, that he'd been angry.

Instead, he grabs her hands and looks at her with large, desperate eyes. "It's not too late to change. Please. Dom is getting worse."

"Dom is always getting worse." She winces as she hears herself say it. Cruel, even if it is true.

But Prince presses on. "No. No, this time it's a lot worse. They're fitting him for a wheelchair. He'll never walk again."

PART II

3.5 YEARS LATER

CHAPTER 1

Then

When Darcy arrives at the golf course, schlepping a borrowed set of clubs, her father is already waiting with his friend, Aidan Levin. Both men force smiles, but she can tell neither of them wants her there. Fair enough, she thinks. I don't want to be here.

She has come at her boss's behest. Golf is a great way to schmooze with rich people, and the fledgling Human Rights Alliance needs all the donors it can get. Darcy hates sports almost as much as she hates Immortality, but she'd do anything for the Human Rights Alliance.

"Thanks for letting me tag along," she says to her dad and his friend, trying to be pleasant.

"No problem," her dad replies. "Aidan's relieved to have you here. For once, he won't be the worst golfer on the green."

"Ha ha," Aidan says, but he is smiling, and for a moment, she thinks this might not be so bad.

Aidan is a talker. As they golf, he rambles on about sports, his car, his wife, his upcoming trip to Europe. Around the seventh hole, he brings up his daughter, who is waiting to hear where she's been accepted to college.

"She has her heart set on Stanford, but her NPE score is off by about two hundred points," Aidan says. He takes a swing at the ball and misses it entirely. "Jesus," he mutters and tries again. This time he connects, but the ball lands one hundred yards shy of the hole.

He turns to Connor. "Think it's futile?"

"Your golf game or your daughter's admission to Stanford?" Connor asks. He places his own ball on a tee.

"Funny," Aidan says, frowning. "But seriously, what if she doesn't get in?"

Connor seems unconcerned. "She'll have the Immortality edge, won't she?"

Darcy winces. It has been added to the list of "plusses" considered by university admissions committees: athletes, legacies, minorities, and now Immortals may enjoy a slightly lowered bar as a result of their status. This incenses Darcy. "Giving Immortals an admissions bonus is like giving tax cuts to the rich," she'd complained when the policy was implemented. But universities justify it by pointing out that Immortals can take advantage of the education they receive forever, while Mortals will benefit for seventy or eighty years at most.

"It's not enough," Aidan says, shaking his head. "Immortality can make up for a fifty- or one-hundred-point shortfall, but two hundred? My last name would have to be Bezos or Odili."

Darcy fights the urge to roll her eyes. If the little Levin girl can't manage a decent score with all the private schools and Ivy League-educated tutors she's had, she probably doesn't deserve a spot at Stanford.

"Well, she'll get in somewhere, right?" Connor says, indifferent.

"Yeah," Aidan replies. "Southern California State."

"Hey, nothing wrong with that," Connor says.

"Oh, please," Aidan mutters. "Between me and you, I feel like I let her down. She begged me to pay someone to take the exam for her. In retrospect, maybe I should have."

Darcy groans. Is that where we are now? she wonders, gazing at Aidan in disbelief. Has it come to that? Or maybe it had always been like that, and she hadn't realized it.

"What?" Aidan says, turning to Darcy with his hands on his hips. "You have something to say to me?"

She is surprised by his hostility. For her father's sake, she bites her tongue and turns away, but he persists.

"No, seriously. What is it?"

And then a lecture bursts from her like a bullet from a gun, carefully aimed and potent. "Your daughter shouldn't get into Stanford. Her score isn't good enough. But you're operating under the misguided notion that what she deserves is far less important than what she wants." Darcy shakes her head in disgust. "The world may not be fair, but we should at least pretend like it is."

Aidan is staring at her as if she's insane. She should apologize, but before she can, Aidan begins to laugh. "Don't be naïve, sweetheart," he says. "If I don't fight for my daughter, some other father will fight for his. We want our kids to have it all, and we'll do what we can to make sure they get it. The alternative isn't that they work hard and accomplish their goals. It's that they lose."

Aidan is too close to Darcy for comfort. She can smell the tuna fish he'd had for lunch on his breath, his expensive aftershave. She takes a step back, trying to decide how to respond. She knows things can only get worse from here. Her best option, she decides, is to go, but she can't resist a parting blow. "Your daughter may live forever, but regardless of where she goes to college, it's going to be an empty, meaningless life because you haven't taught her any other way."

She picks up her clubs and marches off, glancing back only once when she is almost out of sight. She isn't sure what she's hoping to see—maybe some sign that her words have had an impact. But no. The men aren't even looking in her direction. They have resumed their golf game. Aiden has probably already forgotten what she said, and soon, he'll forget her. Darcy sighs. No matter how hard she fights, nothing changes.

Now

Connor Davenport dies just before midnight on Independence Day. When Darcy receives the phone call at two o'clock in the morning, she doesn't believe it.

"You must have the wrong man," she says to the beleaguered nurse on the other end of the line. "My dad can't die. He's Immortal."

"I'm sorry, Ms. Davenport," the nurse replies impatiently. "But as I'm sure you know, Immortals can still die from accidents and injuries, and your father has been in a very bad car accident."

"Oh, God." Goosebumps begin to pimple Darcy's skin. She had never been close to her dad, but she hadn't wanted him to die.

"I really am sorry." The nurse sounds more sympathetic now. "You'll need to notify your siblings of your father's death and then send someone to the hospital to identify his body."

Her siblings? She doesn't want to break the news to them. "I'm not sure I'm the right person—" she begins.

But the nurse has already hung up.

Darcy isn't sure why she is her father's emergency contact. Prince is the oldest; Sabrina is his favorite. She can only guess it is because she is best in a crisis, the most competent generally. But it is a role she neither feels qualified for nor wants.

She arrives at her father's hospital room with a rip-roaring tension headache. She hates all of this. Prince would have been a much better choice. She takes a deep breath, pushes the door open, and charges inside. She is prepared to encounter her father's lifeless body, but the hospital bed is vacant. To Darcy, this feels symbolic. Connor is out of the room and out of her life.

She wishes she felt something—grief or loss or dread—but although she is shocked by her father's death, she is not saddened by it.

"Darcy Davenport?" a nurse asks, poking his head into the room. "I'm sorry about your father. He was hit by a drunk driver who'd deactivated his car's self-drive feature and was going ninety on Mulholland. He never stood a chance."

She nods, as indifferent to how her father died as she is to his death itself.

"We just moved his body. Will you identify it?"

"Later," she tells him. "My siblings are coming. I need to be here for them."

He nods. "No hurry."

She had invited her siblings here to the last room their father had ever occupied because she hadn't wanted them in her apartment. Here, she can walk away when they become exasperating, go home, shut the door, shut them out. If they'd met at her place, she'd never have been able to get rid of them.

Prince rushes into the room then, face wan, eyes wide with disbelief. "No," he whispers, staring, as she had, at the empty bed. He shakes his head vigorously, refuting the news.

"I'm sorry," Darcy mutters.

He puts his arms around her, reeking of booze and grief. She flinches. He clings.

She remembers Prince telling her once that he'd learned to cry silently so he would not disturb his wife. "Tina doesn't like tears," he'd explained. Now, he doesn't make a sound. She can tell he's crying only because her shirt is becoming damper and colder. She doesn't doubt his grief is sincere. He'd always loved their father far more than their father had loved him.

When Prince pulls away, Darcy hands him some tissues from a box beside the now vacant hospital bed. The sheets still have imprints from Connor's body. A small splotch of blood stains the pillowcase.

Prince takes the tissues with a grateful half smile and blows his nose. Next to him, Darcy feels hardened, cold. She can't even feign regret at her father's passing.

Prince stumbles into a chair and buries his head in his hands. Darcy sits beside him, wishing she could leave.

Ten excruciating minutes later, Sabrina arrives, her hair in disarray, a gold bandage dress plastered to her skin. Her eye makeup is smudged, and she is barefoot. Shiny metallic stilettos dangle from her hand.

"Daddy?" she says, as though she expects her father to be there, waiting for her with a mischievous grin on his face, telling her this has all been a joke or, knowing Connor, a test to see how much she loves him.

"Sabrina," Darcy says, standing. "He's gone."

Sabrina's knees go out from under her, and Darcy does her best to keep her sister from collapsing to the floor. She is not heavy, but she is tall, and Darcy, at five-foot-three, is struggling. Prince rushes to help, and together, they settle Sabrina on the bed. She's hysterical, crying the way Prince had wanted to, in jerks and spasms, alternating between low-pitched moans and high-pitched howls. It's so over the top that it feels like a performance, like a bad actor auditioning for a play. She is behaving how she thinks she should, Darcy realizes, and she chuckles.

Prince glares at her, but Sabrina doesn't notice. She is too wrapped up in her performance to gauge the reaction of the audience. Beside her, Prince pats her daintily on the shoulder and whispers, "There, there," as if she is a toddler throwing a tantrum.

Darcy takes a step back and rests her head against the wall. It isn't fair to judge her siblings or herself now, in the middle of the night, minutes after learning of their father's untimely demise, but as she observes the scene—Sabrina, over-dramatic and emotional, Prince desperate and ineffectual, herself detached and cold—Darcy finds herself thinking that none of them have grown into particularly well-adjusted adults.

In the days that follow, Darcy becomes the command center—the person to whom questions are directed, the person by whom decisions are made.

She identifies her father's body. She signs the requisite paperwork. She is tempted to donate his body to science, but she knows Connor wouldn't have wanted that. That is what happens to Cruor corpses, and even in death, he wouldn't want to be mistaken for one of them.

There is neither funeral nor memorial service. Connor hadn't wanted either, hadn't wanted anyone to know he'd died. He viewed it as a personal failure somehow, dying despite Immortality. Darcy doesn't particularly care—if anything, this makes her job easier—but Prince is distraught.

"I want to grieve with other people who loved him," he complains over the phone.

A few nights later, Prince stops by Darcy's apartment.

"I'm not sure why I'm here," he confesses. His eyes are bloodshot, his hair unkempt. Darcy lets him in and fixes him a drink.

"I'm starting to think I need a therapist," he says, sinking onto her couch. "I mean, besides myself. My feelings for him are like a three-way tug-o-war between grief, rage, and hope. It can't be healthy."

"Isn't anger one of the five stages of grief?" Darcy asks.

"Yes," Prince acknowledges. "But I'm not angry at Dad for dying. I'm angry at him for what a bastard he was when he was alive. And then I feel guilty for feeling that way. I mean, he did the best he could, right?"

Did he? Darcy wonders. It seems to her that with Connor, the path to decency was always one step forward, two steps back, the devil on his left shoulder too often overpowering the angel on his right.

"And the hope is for Dom?" Darcy asks.

Prince looks at her. "If this saves his life—I would still be heartbroken that Dad is dead, but God, if this saves Dom's life—"

Darcy doesn't know what to say. She doesn't want her father's fortune to go to Dom, but she wouldn't begrudge Prince if it did. She doesn't think it will. If she had to put money on it, she would bet it will go to Sabrina.

A car deposits Darcy in front of Kimball, Truly, and Watts. She makes her way to the top floor, where the conference rooms are. An automated voice welcomes her.

She is the first one there. She helps herself to a cup of coffee and a handful of cookies.

Prince arrives next in a dark suit a size or two too large for him. He is gaunt, with bags under his eyes and a stubbled chin. He is a convicted man, here for sentencing. Except it is not his fate that will be determined today but his son's.

Sabrina shows up fifteen minutes late, oblivious and unapologetic. She greets them with an upbeat hello and helps herself to a cup of coffee. Darcy pops another cookie in her mouth. Prince fidgets with his phone. We've recovered from our father's death so quickly, Darcy thinks.

The door opens again, and an older man walks in. He resembles a skinny Santa Claus with a thick white beard and wire-rimmed glasses. He introduces himself, but Darcy doesn't catch his name.

"I'm so sorry for your loss," he begins. "Connor was a good man, well-liked by colleagues and clients alike, and a hell of a golfer. He put me to shame on the course every time."

He glances around at them, expecting a chuckle or a grin, but nobody obliges. None of them are interested in this forced eulogy.

The attorney senses this and cuts his speech short. "Connor's will contains a single bequest. It's a little unusual. He's left a note here in an attempt to explain. It reads: 'In the end, I couldn't decide, so I leave the decision to you.'"

He looks around the room to evaluate the effect Connor's note is having. Bewilderment mostly. Prince and Sabrina are frowning. Darcy's stomach churns.

The attorney clears his throat. "The entirety of my estate will go to whoever is decided upon by my three children, Prince Michael Davenport, Darcy Rochester Davenport, and Sabrina Ann Davenport; provided, however, that (i) the fortune may not be divided but must go in its entirety to a single entity, and (ii) all three of my children agree on the bequest."

He peers at the Davenport siblings over his spectacles. "Got that?" he asks. "You can't divide the fortune, and you must all agree on who gets it."

Prince cries out, a singular, piercing yelp. "Dom." He turns wild-eyed, from one sister to the other. "Please."

Neither responds.

Prince sags, his hope shattered, his rage visibly mounting. "You can't do this," he cries, seizing Darcy by the shoulders. "I just lost my father; you can't kill my son. Please. Please."

Darcy pulls away, looks away.

"You monsters," Prince yells, sinking from his chair to the floor, reduced to a puddle of broken sobs.

CHAPTER 2

Then

"Dad, what are you doing?"

Remy looks up at the sound of her brother's voice. "Henry," she yells as she flings herself into his arms.

Henry absent-mindedly puts his hand on her head, but his eyes are locked on their father. "What are you doing?" he asks again. "Why isn't she in school?"

They are on the Third Street Promenade, a popular destination for tourists and beggars alike, a full two miles from Remy's elementary school.

Vance Hudson throws his hands in the air. He is fond of dramatic gestures. The more nervous he becomes, the grander his movements until, when he is backed into a corner, he resembles an orchestra conductor mid-concert. "It's third grade. What does she need third grade for? To learn cursive? Nobody uses cursive anymore. Third grade is a waste of time."

Henry's eyes narrow. "That's not the point. We talked about this. Remy gets an education."

"She's gotta eat. We all do. What good's an education if she's dead?"

But Henry isn't swayed. "We had a deal."

"That was before I knew," Vance protests. "I thought LA would be different. I thought we would find work here. But that hasn't happened, Henry."

Henry had been an 'A' student back in El Desierto. His teachers had spoken of college and scholarships and potential. But it wasn't to be. Henry's school attendance had been spotty since he was a boy, but when they'd moved to Los Angeles, just before his senior year, Vance had told him in no uncertain terms that his school days were finished; he needed to work.

Henry hadn't put up much of a fuss. He'd sacrifice his education for the sake of the family, with one condition: that Remy got to finish school. "Kindergarten through twelfth grade," he'd said. "And college if she can get in."

She had been so little then, so useless, that Vance had agreed. But the economy is different in the city. They are less able to hire themselves out as cheap labor and more likely to get food or money by begging, and when it comes to begging, who better to elicit pity than a malnourished little girl in pigtails, clutching a filthy, one-eyed doll?

"Our deal didn't hinge on you finding work," Henry says. "She's going to school, Dad, and don't you ever keep her out again."

"Or what?" Vance asks. He rolls his shoulders back and adopts a fighter's stance. He is feisty and unafraid, and he has a mean left hook.

But Henry has no desire to fight his father. Instead, he steps in front of Remy, locks eyes with Vance, and whispers, "Or I take Remy away from here, and we never come back."

Henry takes his sister's hand and leads her away, leaving their father behind, confused and defeated.

Now

Henry is home alone, reading, when someone knocks on the door. He sighs. The only visitors the Hudsons ever get are the young, starry-eyed girls that Ben has slept with. Ben treats these girls like condoms, using them for sex and then discarding them, and when they realize what has happened, they show up at the Hudsons' apartment, lovestruck and desperate, or sometimes angry and determined to give Ben a piece of their mind. But Ben is never home, and it is Henry and Zeke who bear the brunt of their emotions, often spending hours trying to convince these girls that they are better off without Ben. They should stop answering the door, Henry thinks, but they never do.

Henry reluctantly rouses himself from his latest book, agitated, like a bear prodded awake from hibernation. He opens the door, prepared to make excuses for his brother, but for once, it's not some sad, heavily made-up girl on the hunt for Ben. It's Caleb, his eyes red and weary.

"Hey, Henry," he mutters. "My roommates are having a video game tournament. There are twenty grown men in my apartment hooting at the television screen like overgrown monkeys. Do you mind if I stay here for a while? I just want to read."

Henry hesitates. He is reluctant to let anyone invade his space. But Caleb has been so good to Remy that Henry can't turn him away.

"Come in," he says. He turns and retreats into the living space, leaving Caleb to follow.

"Sparse," Caleb remarks, stepping into the room.

There is no décor, no personal touch. Others Cruors add rugs or art or indoor plants. They leave shoes and sweaters lying around, empty bags of potato chips on the sofa, soda cans on the floor. Here, there is nothing but a couple of textbooks on the desk and a plate of pretzels within Henry's reach. It's as if the Hudsons never moved in, or perhaps like they have one foot out the door.

Henry stretches out on the couch. Caleb settles into a chair. He sits still for a minute, taking in the scene, then says, "Thanks for this. Normally, I'd go to the library, but Remy and Miguel are studying there, and I don't want to interrupt."

"No problem," Henry says, and then, in an effort to be collegial, "What are you reading?"

"*Beloved* by Toni Morrison."

A smile emerges beneath Henry's beard, and he raises his book so that Caleb can see the cover. "Me, too."

"Coincidence?" Caleb asks.

"Remy," Henry replies. She had recommended it to them both.

They sit together in contented silence, each reading their copy of *Beloved*. It is the best night Henry has had in a long time.

The next time Caleb sees Henry, he asks him what he thought of *Beloved*. Henry discovers he has a lot to say. He is starved for conversation.

"Every time I try to talk to the rest of them"—the other Cruors, he means—"I'm reminded that I don't fit in here." Henry is full of thoughts and ideas and questions, and his only outlet has been his sister.

Caleb, who is also something of a loner, invites Henry to the pub. They talk until closing, then meet again the next day. Within a month, they have become inseparable.

"So, you and Caleb are friends now?" Remy asks Henry one evening when she comes in from a test prep session. The NPE is less than a week away. Caleb has extended his classes from two hours to four and has personalized assignments for Remy and Miguel, the two seniors who are taking the exam this year. He has had three pupils take the NPE so far, and every one of them has failed. He has confided in Henry that he is desperate to break his losing streak.

"Does that bother you?" Henry asks Remy. He doesn't want anything to distract her from the NPE. If he needs to put his friendship with Caleb on hold, he will.

Remy looks amused. "No," she assures him. "It's fine. I think it's good for you."

It's good for Caleb, too. When Remy goes off to college—as they are certain she will—Caleb will become Henry's new roommate. Henry doesn't know as much as Caleb, but he is smart and thoughtful. They discuss literature, religion, politics.

"How do you do it?" Henry asks Caleb one night.

They are hiding in the cocktail bar, hoping to avoid Ben, who has discovered that they drink together and started joining them. He is enthusiastic but disruptive; they can only tolerate his company so many nights a week.

"Live here, you mean?" Caleb smiles. "Remy asked me that once."

"And?" Henry prods.

"You know those competitions kids have to see who can hold their breath underwater the longest?" Caleb asks, gazing into his sunshine yellow cocktail. "Princeton was like that. Stay underwater. Hold your breath even if it hurts. Don't think about whether you're enjoying what you're doing or if you'd rather be doing something else. Just stay under that water. For me, coming to the Compound was like resurfacing and taking a big gulp of fresh air. And even though I'd lost, I felt like I'd won because I could just enjoy the pool again."

Henry removes the orange slice garnishing his cocktail, bites into it, and places the rind on a napkin. "Are you still enjoying the pool?" he asks.

Caleb hesitates. "Officially, yes," he says. "When I go to visit my parents or see my friends, I always praise Compound life as a kind of permanent vacation. But between you and me, something started to change in my fourth or fifth year here." He removes the napkin from beneath his cocktail and begins shredding it into uneven strips. "Lately, this has started to feel like a vacation that's gone on too long."

The day of the National Placement Exam, Henry and Caleb are both as nervous as Remy. Henry can't seem to stop his leg from trembling while Caleb keeps standing, pacing, and sitting down again.

"Will you guys relax?" Remy says to them over breakfast. Her plate contains a banana, a cup of yogurt, and a slice of wheat bread, toasted and buttered. It's the same breakfast she eats every day. Her notes and textbooks are at home; she is carrying only her ID.

"I wish I'd been as calm as you the day I took the NPE," Caleb says.

"Instead, I threw up. Twice."

Henry and Remy exchange a look and burst out laughing. They like Caleb, but they can't believe how little grit he has.

Remy finishes her breakfast, but neither Caleb nor Henry takes a single bite of theirs. "You two not eating doesn't help me pass the exam," Remy points out.

Henry understands this, of course, but he has no appetite. Even the smell of the bacon on his plate is starting to turn his stomach. He pushes the plate away. Across from him, Caleb has turned an unbecoming shade of red.

Remy shrugs and stands and hugs them both goodbye. "Wish me luck," she says.

"You don't need it," Caleb assures her. "You've got this."

When she is gone, he turns to Henry. "How are you going to get through today?"

"Take a sleeping pill and hope it lasts until the exam is over," Henry says. "You?"

"*Twilight Zone* marathon." Caleb is unsteady on his feet, and he looks like he might hurl.

"She really will be okay, you know," Henry says, gripping his friend's shoulder.

"I know," Caleb agrees, but Henry understands that Caleb feels as if it's his future on the line as well as Remy's. What kind of an NPE tutor is he if none of his students can pass the exam?

Afterward, she returns to the apartment, confident, elated. Nailed it, she says, and she throws herself into Henry's arms.

He is drowsy—his sleeping pill hasn't fully worn off—but she drags him out for a walk. "I've been sitting inside all day," she says. "I need the fresh air."

She hasn't stopped moving since she got back. She bounces, shimmies, squeezes and releases his arm. He has never seen her like this before.

"So? Tell me about it," he says once they're outside, weaving their way around the Compound grounds. It is chilly, and neither of them is dressed for it. Henry wraps his arms around his torso to keep warm, but Remy doesn't seem to notice the weather.

"It went well. Really well. I knew how to do everything it asked: analyze essays, design experiments, draft communications depending on the audience. But the best part was, remember that practice essay I wrote analyzing the factors that have destabilized the Middle East in the twenty-first century? One of the questions on the exam involved discussing how a major region has changed geopolitically over the past fifty years. I pretty much rewrote my practice essay. Caleb prepared me so well. Miguel said the same thing. We both walked out of the exam feeling like we'd aced it."

She is rambling, and she hasn't stopped grinning. Now Henry grins, too, hoping she can't detect that it's forced. He's proud of her; he really is. She's the seedling he has been nurturing for eighteen years now, so close to blooming he can see the petals. But she hasn't bloomed yet, and he finds any hint of celebration premature.

"I'm glad you feel confident about the exam." He keeps his eyes on the path, avoiding her gaze.

"You're nervous, aren't you?" she says. "Because of Malachi."

"Yeah, I guess I am."

"Me, too," she confesses. "But at the same time, I felt good during the exam."

"So did he," Henry reminds her.

It had been shocking, unfathomable. Malachi was the Compound's prize student, better than Remy, better, Caleb says, than he was at that age. He was a genius, plain and simple, with a mind so quick and complex it was like a sophisticated computer programmed by brilliant engineers. He should have aced the NPE even without Caleb's tutelage. He was the second coming of Einstein, Curie, Odili. He hadn't even made it past triage. He was among the one-third of NPE takers who'd been cut in the first round by a grader who'd viewed his performance as so poor it didn't warrant further consideration.

Malachi had been stunned. "I don't know how this happened," he'd repeated to anyone who would listen.

"Maybe something went wrong during the exam," Caleb had suggested. It happened sometimes. Bubbling in the wrong row on the multiple-choice portion. Repeating the error in every row thereafter. Part of an essay getting lost somehow. Misreading a prompt. Everyone had urged Malachi to start saving money to take the exam again the next year.

But Malachi had refused. "If I'm not good enough, I'm not good enough," he'd said. He graduated from Compound 78 High and began Donating his blood, no different now from Zeke or Ben or any of the other Cruors, everything that made him exceptional stamped out by one grader's indifferent boot. It has been nine years since someone from Compound 78 passed the NPE.

"I have to believe Malachi's failure was a fluke," Remy says now. "I have to."

They walk on in silence, Remy's jubilation strangled by Henry's caution. Both haunted by the memory of Malachi. Remy shivers, then quickens her pace whether to keep warm or to escape the discussion, Henry isn't sure.

"Hey, tell me something, Rem," Henry says, scrambling to keep up with her. "After you pass the NPE and graduate from college, what then?"

It's uncharted territory, talking about the future beyond college. It's always felt too presumptuous, too risky, as if daring to dream of life on the other side of the river could flood the bridge. "Do you ever think about it?"

Remy stops walking entirely. "Yes," she ventures. "All the time. I worry that the Outside won't live up to my expectations, that instead of varied and full of opportunity, I'll find it repetitive and oppressive. That Ben will be right, and I'll be miserable. Or that everything will be exactly as I hoped, but I won't fit in." She looks up at Henry with a tense, close-lipped grin. "I'm excited about the future, but I'm scared, too."

Henry isn't sure whether to be impressed or heartbroken by his sister. She's so mature for her age, so different from Caleb, who seemed to think that once he got into Princeton, the hard part was over. Remy will never believe that the hard part is over. To her, hope will always be tempered by reality.

"Okay," Henry says, fingering his beard. "Let's talk best-case scenario. How do you want your future to look?"

"I have this fantasy," she begins, but then she falters. "It's silly."

"Go on," Henry prods.

"Okay, well, I guess I go to college and get my degree, and then I start teaching."

"Teaching?" he says. He's not sure why, but this surprises him.

"Wait. There's more. After I've taught for a few years, I want to open a boarding school somewhere beautiful, surrounded by mountains and trees, like the boarding schools in the movies. Except this isn't a normal school."

"Wait. Let me guess. It's a school for wizards!"

She punches him on the shoulder. "This isn't *Harry Potter*." She grows serious. "It's a school for Cruors."

"What?" He turns to her, certain he's misheard.

"It's a boarding school for the top Cruor students from around the country, tuition free, paid for by people who believe in social mobility and giving the poor a fighting chance. Maybe Hemodyne would even fund it. And we'd recruit the best teachers and have amazing students, and we'd be, you know, doing a lot of good." She gazes up at him with large, timid eyes. "Is that stupid?"

"No," he says, wrapping an arm around her shoulders. "It's beautiful."

On a whim, Caleb invites Henry to Los Angeles to meet his mom. Henry agrees, but the night before, he is so nervous he can't sleep. His interaction with Outsiders is limited. He doesn't know how to dress or what to say or do. He visits the barber to have his hair cut and his beard trimmed and skims the internet for a crash course on etiquette, but he still feels unprepared.

He dresses up for the occasion in jeans and a collared shirt. He gets to the bus stop forty minutes early, then paces back and forth in front of the steel wall, trying to pass the time and calm his nerves. There are no benches, and he doesn't want to sit on the ground for fear of dirtying his clothes.

Gradually, others join him outside the wall. They sit directly on the road, unconcerned about ruining their pants, shading their eyes from the scalding sun with their hands, gazing out at the vast desert in the direction from which the bus will come.

Ten minutes before departure, there is still no sign of Caleb. Henry begins to panic, to worry that he has gotten the wrong date or time, to wonder if Caleb has changed his mind about this endeavor. Beads of perspiration dampen his dress shirt, and he fans himself with his hand.

Caleb appears just as the bus rumbles into view. Relieved, Henry hurries up to him. "Perfect timing," he says.

Caleb nods. "It takes seven minutes to walk from my apartment to the bus stop, and the bus reliably arrives five minutes before it's scheduled to depart. I don't like wasting time."

This strikes Henry as funny, but he doesn't say so. If there's one thing the Cruors have in abundance, it's time.

"I hate riding the damn bus," grumbles a woman with bloodshot eyes whose skin is blistered and peeling like paint on a neglected fencepost. "Reminds me of the dark days. Travelin' all over the city. Tryin' to find a damn job."

"I like it," says an old man, leaning on a cane. "Used to ride it all night long. It was nice and warm and them seats was cushioned. The motion lulled me to sleep, just like a baby."

Caleb had told Henry once that he'd never ridden a bus before moving to the Compound. In Los Angeles, buses were for poor people.

Now, Caleb prefers to sit in the front. In the back, the ride is noisier and bumpier, making it harder to read or think. He slides into the first row and pulls out a book. Beside him, Henry does the same.

Less than a minute before the bus door closes, Zeke scurries up the steps, sweaty and out of breath. He's wearing khakis and a collared shirt, and he's carrying an apple, a couple of muffins, and the Recovery Formula half wrapped in a paper towel.

Caleb and Henry exchange looks. When Zeke sees them, he looks dismayed, and when he realizes the only seat available on this unusually crowded bus is directly across from them, he becomes visibly distressed, his eyes darting anxiously around.

"Sit down, please," a voice orders. Zeke blushes and obeys, perching on the edge of his seat, legs in the aisle.

"Hey, Zeke," Henry says. Caleb, who has the window seat, leans around Henry and waves.

"Hi, guys," Zeke replies, offering a half-hearted wave of his own.

"What takes you into the city today?" Caleb asks.

Zeke lowers his head. "Trying to find a job," he mumbles.

Caleb and Henry exchange looks again.

Zeke's obsession with Immortality has swollen, festering like an infected bug bite and consuming him, one inch at a time. He has developed and hatched several plans designed to enable him to live forever, but each has failed more spectacularly than the last. He doesn't know it, but he's become something of a laughingstock on the Compound. He could have his own reality show: What will Zeke do next? Train monkeys to pick pockets? Dig holes in the desert in search of buried treasure? Trade everything he owns for a handful of magic beans?

Not all his plans have been so fanciful. Originally, he'd attempted the NPE, envisioned college, a high-paying job. When he'd failed the exam, to no one's surprise but his own, he'd decided to marry rich instead. He had, for months after graduation, taken the shuttle into Los Angeles and spent his pitiful weekly allowance in high-end bars, buying drinks for entitled princesses, hoping one of them would fall for and marry him.

It was the sort of idea that only worked in romance novels. Most women drank the cocktails Zeke bought, flirted with him, maybe even slept with him for the sheer novelty of having sex with a Cruor, but none of them had been interested in marrying him or even in seeing him again.

In the past few weeks, Zeke has resorted to a new plan: spending his weekly allowance on the Immortality Lottery. It's a long shot, but so is trying to find a job as an unskilled, undereducated Cruor.

"What kind of job?" Caleb asks.

Zeke shrugs, embarrassed. "I don't know," he says. "I thought I'd walk around, see who's hiring."

Henry shakes his head. It's as though Zeke is living one hundred years ago when a diner might advertise for a dishwasher by putting a sign in its front window. "You know, most businesses post their jobs online these days," he says, trying to be helpful.

Zeke shrugs again. "I figure it will be harder to turn me away in person."

Where does Zeke get these ideas? Henry wonders. Television probably. He sees something on one of his detective shows and assumes if it worked for the fictional character in the program, it will work for him, too. Even if Zeke could find a job, how much does he think it will pay? How long does he think it will take before he's saved enough for Immortality? Henry thinks about asking, then thinks better of it. Better for Zeke to waste time on innocuous, if foolhardy, schemes than to try something dangerous or demented. Not a year ago, a man desperate for Immortality had barged into an Eternity Clinic and taken everyone there—fourteen people in total—hostage for six days before police had stormed the building, leaving the man and two Immortals dead. Now, the price of Immortality has crept up as Eternity Clinics beef up their security. Zeke isn't violent—he's passive to the point of being pathetic—but desperation can play out in unpredictable ways.

When the bus arrives in Los Angeles, Caleb's mother is waiting, her black Lexus idling by the curb. Henry and Caleb say goodbye to Zeke, who

161

wanders off toward the high rises of downtown and step into the waiting car.

"Caleb," Jennifer Wentworth says, pulling her son to her in a warm embrace.

She is a thin woman with black bobbed hair dressed casually in leggings, a long t-shirt, and tennis shoes. She wears minimal makeup and no jewelry. She is not what Henry expected.

"Mom, this is my friend Henry," Caleb says.

"Hello, Mrs. Wentworth. It's a pleasure to meet you," Henry says, extending his hand.

"The pleasure is mine, Henry," Jennifer Wentworth replies smiling at him. "I've been begging Caleb to introduce me to his Cruor friends for years."

Caleb blushes. Cruor isn't quite a derogatory term, but it is synonymous with poor.

Henry isn't bothered. "Well, I'm flattered to be the first."

Jennifer Wentworth takes them to lunch at a French bistro near Pershing Square. Caleb has warned Henry that everything his mother does is a test. She owns a preeminent testing company and designs examinations for a living, thoughtfully crafted, laboratory tested, proven to predict future performance on the job, whatever the job may be. Growing up with her had involved a never-ending series of quizzes, measuring Caleb's intelligence, his progress, his adaptability. She'd tested his friends, too, sometimes because she was curious but often to see how they compared to him. Henry is her newest lab rat. She doesn't appear to expect much. She seems delighted when he's able to read the menu.

"So, tell me, Henry," she says, pushing the breadbasket away. "What do you do on the Compound when you're not Donating blood?"

"Well, ma'am, I read a lot," Henry says, helping himself to a slice of the baguette.

"Do you?" she asks, trying to contain her surprise. "What do you read?"

"The classics, mostly. First French, then British. Now American."

She doesn't believe him. Henry can tell by the way she purses her lips. "Oh? What's your favorite?"

"*Les Misérables*," Henry answers without hesitation. "But I may be partial to it because it was the first novel I read as an adult."

"I always adored *Madame Bovary* myself. Do you know it?" She remains visibly skeptical, and Henry gets the impression she is trying to trap him in a lie.

"I do," he tells her.

"And what did you think?"

Henry glances down at the table. "To be honest, I found Emma Bovary intolerable. Poor little rich girl, bored with her privileged life, whines about nothing for three hundred pages. But you have to understand. At the time, I'd been on the Compound for less than six months after six years on the streets. It was difficult for me to sympathize with someone who had everything but was still unhappy, when not long before, I'd never known where my next meal was coming from."

Jennifer starts to say something, but he goes on before she has a chance.

"More recently, I read Kate Chopin's *The Awakening*." He pronounces it 'Chop-in.' Out of the corner of his eye, he sees Caleb wince.

"Did I say it wrong?"

"It's 'Show-pan,'" Jennifer explains.

"Oh," Henry blushes.

"Don't worry about it," Jennifer says, patting his arm. "I thought lapel was pronounced 'lay pull' well into my twenties."

Henry nods, grateful for her magnanimity. "It's similar to *Madame Bovary*, as I'm sure you know. Another bored, wealthy woman lamenting the state of her life. But by the time I read it, I'd been on the Compound for three years, and instead of being repulsed by Edna, I found myself sympathizing with her."

"Tell me more," Jennifer says, no longer skeptical but curious.

"I feel frustrated with my life the way Emma and Edna did, even though all my needs are met. I'm not happy conforming to what the world expects of me as a Cruor. I understand now, in a way I didn't when I read *Madame Bovary*, that once you no longer need to worry about food and shelter, you begin wanting more out of life."

Caleb is impressed. His mother is awe-struck. "My god," she whispers. "You're not what I expected of a Cruor at all. Tell me," she leans forward, placing her hand on Henry's. "Why didn't you go to college? Or did you?"

Henry smiles. "A lot of Cruors did go to college, but I'm not one of them," he says. "I didn't even make it through high school."

"So you're self-taught?"

"Yes, ma'am. For the most part."

"My god."

"If you think Henry's impressive, you should meet his sister," Caleb says. "She just took the NPE."

"And thanks to Caleb, she could go to college," Henry adds.

Jennifer looks confused. "What does Caleb have to do with anything?"

"Didn't he tell you?" Henry asks. "The schools on the Compounds are terrible. There are no honors classes and no real way to prepare for the NPE besides a handful of test prep books. So, Caleb tutors the students who want to go to college. He started with my sister, but he's up to eleven students now."

Jennifer looks at her son. "Caleb, why didn't you tell me?"

Caleb looks like he's going to be ill. He shoves a hunk of bread in his mouth and chews with unusual zeal.

"Wait until I share this with the family," Jennifer continues. "They'll be so impressed."

"That's why I didn't tell you," Caleb sneers.

"Excuse me?"

"The Peace Corps was getting less believable every year. Now you have something new to feed your friends. 'Oh, Caleb works at the Compound tutoring Cruor children.' Better yet, 'Caleb has started a non-profit preparing under-privileged Cruors for the NPE.'"

His impression of his mother is uncharitable—the high-pitched, nasal voice, the way he crosses his eyes as he speaks.

"Well, why not?" Jennifer says. "It makes you sound accomplished, philanthropic even. Nobody can criticize you for that."

"You mean nobody can criticize you," Caleb spits.

Henry is desperate to disrupt this embarrassing exchange. "What do you do, Mrs. Wentworth?" he asks, even though he already knows.

She looks over at Henry as though she had forgotten he was there. "Call me Jennifer, please," she insists, tucking her hair behind her ear. "I run a testing company. We design examinations and assessments."

"Like the NPE?" Henry asks.

"Like the NPE," Jennifer confirms. "Although I primarily work for private organizations, helping them design exams for current or potential future employees."

Henry's face falls. "So, not the NPE?"

"No, not usually, though they do occasionally ask me to consult for them when some sort of problem arises. Four years ago, for example, they had an unusual number of regrade requests, and they asked me to see if I could find a glitch in the exam. Turns out the wording of one of the essay questions was ambiguous, which led to all sorts of problems." She smiles at Henry. "Have you taken the NPE yet?"

Henry shakes his head. "What chance do I have?"

"A very good one," Jennifer insists. "Especially with Caleb tutoring you. You have all the time in the world. You don't have to sit the exam this year or next. You could take it six years from now if you wanted."

"I don't know why we hadn't thought of it before," Caleb says. "She's right. Every American is entitled to take the NPE once free of charge." A retake costs $5,000, a second retake $10,000. Technically, a struggling student can retake the exam as many times as he or she wants, but the price rises each time. Eventually, the cost becomes prohibitive for most people; a single retake is a hardship for the Cruors.

"I don't know," Henry says. He struggles to articulate his concerns, his fear of failure, how intimidating he finds exams, essays, classrooms.

How much easier it is to accept that he's trapped through no fault of his own than to risk escape. Henry, who has always lived vicariously through others' dreams, finds he is afraid to dream himself.

CHAPTER 3

Then

The House of Unrealized Dreams, as Prince has taken to calling their once-beloved Victorian, is unprepared for a boy in a wheelchair. It's Prince and Tina's fault, really. They had known this day was coming for years but had done nothing to prepare for it. They had assumed it would arrive gradually, a friendly orthopedist warning them when Dom had only a year, a month, a week left to walk. Instead, Dom had become wheelchair-bound overnight after yet another fall had resulted in yet another broken leg.

They bring him home, wheel him over to the stairs. His bedroom—all the bedrooms—are on the second floor, as is every bathroom save a powder room.

"We'll have a chair lift installed," Prince says. But when Tina phones the company, the representative informs her that they cannot do the job because the Victorian is listed as a historic building to which this kind of modification cannot be made. They can't install an elevator either.

"We'll just have to carry you up," Prince says to his son. "A piggyback ride."

"I'm not a little kid," snaps Dom. "I'll move downstairs."

They move his bed to the living room and cram it in next to the sofa.

They rearrange the furniture downstairs to accommodate his wheelchair. Like a game of Tetris. Find a way to manage the latest complication falling from the top of the screen. Falling into their lives. They're becoming experts at Tetris.

The first time Dom needs to go to the bathroom, he navigates his wheelchair through the dining room and kitchen toward the powder room tucked at the back of the house. But the hallway that leads to the powder room is too narrow for the wheelchair. The closest Dom can get is the edge of the kitchen, a full six steps away. He reluctantly turns to his father, who helps him to the bathroom.

"Can you get your pants down?" Prince asks.

Dom looks like he wants to die. "Yeah, I'll be fine."

"Okay. I'll wait outside."

"No!" Dom snaps. His skin is growing warm beneath Prince's grip.

"Well, then, how will you—?"

"I'll text you when I'm done." He will not look at his father.

Prince leaves the bathroom, closing the door behind him. He waits in the kitchen and passes the time by unloading the dishwasher, sorting the mail, playing with his phone. He snacks on trail mix and pats himself on the back when he drinks a glass of water instead of bourbon.

Ten minutes pass and he hasn't heard from Dom. He doesn't want to embarrass the boy, but he's starting to worry. What if Dom has fallen? What if he's in a heap on the floor?

Prince raps on the bathroom door. "You okay in there, kiddo?"

"Fine!" comes the reply, humiliated, angry.

Prince retreats, belatedly realizing he should have texted instead.

When, three or four minutes later, Dom texts him, Prince opens the bathroom door to a revolting stench. Dom is scowling on the toilet seat, his pants bunched around his knees. Prince suppresses the urge to gag and helps his mortified son back to his wheelchair. Dom's illness isn't just taking his health; it's claiming his dignity, too.

Dom only lasts two nights in the living room. He has too little privacy there and no access to a shower. Reluctantly, he agrees to let his father carry him up the stairs, looping his legs around Prince's back, his arms around his neck.

They try to minimize Dom's trips up and down the stairs. They fit his shower with a small, plastic, removable bench, so he can bathe himself without help. They lower the rod in his closet so he can reach his clothes from his chair. They spare him as many little humiliations as they can.

Still, Prince can't help thinking that this process should be reversed. Dom should be getting stronger and becoming more independent. In three or four decades, he should be easing his aging parents into an uncomfortable second childhood. Instead, he peaked at ten and has been diminishing ever since. He will diminish until he dies.

Now

Darcy is waiting in front of the trendy popsicle shop in Beverly Hills, arms crossed in front of her chest, chin jutting out in distaste. She looks formidable, Prince thinks, and he tightens his grip on the handles of Dom's wheelchair. She hasn't noticed them yet.

"Darcy," he calls when he's half a storefront away.

Darcy turns. "Oh, look. You brought Dom," she says, forcing a smile. Prince's heart breaks a little. She used to be happy to see Dom, but Prince's relentless battle for his dad's inheritance has cost them that relationship.

Dom waves at Darcy from his wheelchair, oblivious.

"It's so good to see you, Dom," she says. She is trying to sound upbeat for his sake, and Prince is grateful.

"You don't come around anymore, Aunt Darcy," Dom says. His speech, which has been slurred for years, is almost incomprehensible now.

"I know, Dom. I'm sorry. Work," she explains. But Prince can see he doesn't believe her. Dom thinks she's avoiding him because of his disease. That's what's keeping everyone else away. His friends have stopped coming to visit. He is no longer invited to birthday parties. Spending time with him is too logistically complicated, too hard. He can't do much anymore—sports are out of the question; video games are a struggle. Easier to exclude him altogether than to relegate him to a corner to watch the other boys play.

Darcy visited long after the others had stopped. She is close to her nephew and isn't bothered by his increasing handicap. But since Connor's death, since she's found herself at odds with her brother, she has stopped coming, too.

Darcy must suspect her absence is hurting her nephew because she says, "I'll make more time for you, Dom. I promise."

He feigns indifference. "Don't worry about it. I'm not much fun these days anyway."

Darcy looks away, muttering something incomprehensible. Prince saves her. "Why don't we get some popsicles?"

They order, collect their frozen treats, and sit outside at a table in the sun.

"How's your popsicle, Dom?" Darcy asks. She bites instead of licking. Watching her eat makes Prince's teeth cold.

"Really good," he says. He has gotten dragon fruit because, at fifteen, he is obsessed with dragons. "You want to try?" He extends his arm toward Darcy, offering her the popsicle.

She smiles and reaches for it, but before she can take it, Dom loses his grip and it falls, shattering on the sidewalk, dyeing the ground bright fuchsia.

"Shit," Dom cries out. "I can't even eat a fucking popsicle."

"Dom," Prince says. "Language."

"Don't language me," Dom says, his lip curling in an angry sneer. "This is my fucking life. I can't eat. I can't talk. I can't walk. It sucks. It fucking sucks." He reaches for the only thing on the table, a stack of brown paper napkins, and throws them at his father. They separate and drift to the ground unhurried, a series of badly folded paper airplanes coming in for a landing.

Prince bends over and picks the napkins up. He's grown accustomed to these tantrums, but he still doesn't know how to handle them. Toddlers, yes. Dying teenagers, no.

Darcy remains in her chair, concentrating on her popsicle. She seems paralyzed by this scene, uncertain how to proceed. Eventually, she says, "I'll get you another popsicle, Dom."

"Don't bother," he replies.

When she gets up anyway, he yells it. "I said, don't bother."

She ignores him and returns a few minutes later with another dragon fruit popsicle. "They didn't even charge me." If she is trying to reassure him, it backfires.

"Of course they didn't. Nobody wants to double-charge the poor crippled kid." He reaches into his pocket and pulls out a crumpled ten-dollar bill. "Here," he says. "Take this and give it to them. Tell them I don't want their charity."

"Dom, they were trying to be—" Darcy begins.

"Take it," he screams.

Darcy's eyes grow wide. She looks to her brother for help.

"Dom," Prince says. "It's good customer service. If I dropped my popsicle, they'd probably give me a free one, too."

"Oh yeah?" Dom says. He reaches over and knocks the popsicle from his father's hand in one swift, angry motion. Prince doesn't react quickly enough. He can do nothing but watch it fall, the bright green of his basil popsicle intermingling with the magenta of Dom's, a sticky, distorted swirl that vaguely resembles Barney, the dinosaur Prince had adored as a boy.

"Why don't you get another popsicle, Dad?" Dom challenges.

Prince hesitates, afraid to be proven wrong.

"Well?" Dom chides. "Go on."

Prince stands slowly and pushes back his chair. If they won't replace his popsicle for free, can he slip them some money without Dom noticing? If so, would it be wrong to lie to Dom?

A car horn honks, and Tina's Mercedes pulls up. She's twenty minutes early, but they're all relieved to see her.

"Hi, there," she says. "Enjoy your popsicles?"

Nobody says anything. Tina senses something has gone wrong, assumes it's Prince's fault, and glares at him.

Dom rolls over to his mother's car without a word. Prince and Darcy help him in, fold his wheelchair, put it in the trunk.

"Is he always like that?" Darcy asks Prince after they have gotten Dom settled and closed the car door.

"He's been moodier lately," Prince admits. "His mom thinks I should discipline him, but I can't do it. Not to him."

"It isn't fair, is it?" Darcy says. "Not only does he have to die young, he doesn't even get to enjoy what little time he has left."

He offers her a conflicted smile. He's grateful she has excused Dom's bad behavior, but he's also annoyed by the presumption that she can even begin to understand what his son is going through.

As he gets into the car, she waves goodbye from the curb. "It was great to see you, Dom," she offers.

"Bye," he says, not bothering to make eye contact or even glance in her direction.

Tina and Prince smile apologetically as the car pulls away from the curb, leaving Darcy standing by herself, two half-melted popsicles in her hand.

On the ride home, they are silent, frustrated. Dom gazes moodily out the window. Prince fingers the airplane-sized bottle of Maker's Mark in his pocket and tries to ignore his wife's accusatory glances.

What could I have done? he wonders. I can't control Dom when he's like that. Tina wasn't even there. She doesn't know what happened. She doesn't understand.

But after a while, her disapproval gets to him, and he finds himself wondering if he could have done more. Stopped Darcy from replacing Dom's popsicle, maybe. Or not suggested the popsicle place at all. A movie would have been safer, with little time for conversation and a bucket of popcorn nestled snugly in Dom's lap. What was he thinking, suggesting popsicles? Of course, this is his fault.

When they get home, they fight, Tina in booming shouts that echo throughout the house, Prince in angry whispers, admonishing her to keep her voice down. In the next room, Dom urges the volume up on the television to drown out their voices.

Dom doesn't know about Connor's will. Prince and Tina can see no point in telling him. It would only get his hopes up, destroy his relationship with his aunts, and tarnish his memories of his grandfather.

"It's been three months," Tina reminds Prince for the umpteenth time. Three months since his father died. Three months of stalemate. The battle over Connor Davenport's will is beginning to resemble trench warfare. Prince skirmishes with his sisters once a week, and then they all retreat to the holes they've dug, damaged but not defeated, neither gaining nor losing ground. Like any war, theirs is taking its toll.

The worst part is Prince suspects it is all for naught. All his planning and strategizing, his fights and his fears and his rage. Deep down, he knows he is losing, but he can't bear to surrender.

The next weekend, Dom has friends over for the first time in months. Prince has bought him the latest video game, hoping it will encourage him to be social and encourage the other kids to socialize with him.

Prince is so excited he tiptoes into the dining room to eavesdrop, eager to hear his son happy for once, but the voices of his friends come through first, not enthusiastic but annoyed. Strained. Conflicted.

"No, Dom!"

"What are you doing?"

"You're going to get us killed!"

Prince cringes. Poor Dom. He used to be the best at video games, his thumbs gliding swiftly over the controls, his timing impeccable. Kids he didn't know used to ask him to beat levels they couldn't get through. His friends encouraged him to forget about soccer, become a video game star instead. After four years with Tay Sachs, it appears he can no longer do either.

"Damn, Dom. We're dead."

"Sorry, guys," Dom mumbles.

Prince, hidden in the dining room, can't see Dom, but he can picture him: head lowered, eyes focused on his hands. To his friends, he may sound contrite, but inside, he's fuming. Why can't he control his body anymore? Prince wants to bang his head against the wall. This was a terrible idea.

Mercifully, Dom's friends are supportive.

"Hey, that's okay, Dom."

"Don't worry about it. We can try again."

"I'm going to go to the bathroom first," Dom says. He navigates his wheelchair toward the bathroom. He can't get there without help, but Prince suspects he doesn't actually need to go; he just needs some space. The last thing he wants is to cry in front of his friends. He stops in the dining room, just shy of the kitchen and buries his head in his hands. He hasn't noticed his father sitting at the table, watching him with a look of immense sympathy. It's for the best. Dom hates it when people feel sorry for him.

In the living room, his friends begin speaking in urgent, hushed voices.

"Jesus Christ, he sucks."

"There's no way we get past Tarzamur with him playing."

"Maybe we can convince him to sit this level out?"

"And the next level? And the level after that?"

"It's his ViZion. He gets to play."

"But he sucks. He's even worse than Dylan."

"Shut up, Ike."

"Guys, I don't know if I can handle this anymore. Let's just go."

"What? Like, sneak out while he's in the bathroom?"

"Yeah. Why not?"

"Because he's like, dying, man."

"So?"

"Seriously? How big of an asshole are you?"

Prince hears a floorboard creek and looks over toward Dom, who is blinking back tears.

"Yeah, that's what I thought," he whispers as he turns his wheelchair around.

He takes a minute to pull himself together, and then he makes his way back into the living room, smiling as if nothing is wrong.

Prince arrives at the office the next morning dressed in his only remaining bespoke suit, hoping his attire will compensate for his otherwise disheveled appearance. His secretary, Blair, isn't impressed.

"No time to shave?" she asks, eyeing him critically.

"In the hospital with Dom all weekend," he explains. It's a lie that no one will think to question.

"No excuse for not looking professional," Blair says.

"Unavoidable, I'm afraid." He hurries to his office and closes the door.

Once upon a time, Blair would place her hand over her heart every time he mentioned Dom. She'd make excuses for him to clients, explaining in confidential whispers that he had a dying son. She'd throw her arms around him in long sympathetic hugs. Once or twice she'd even slipped him a bottle of bourbon. But lately, she's become critical and unforgiving. His practice is faltering; her job is on the line.

He sets his bag on the floor, his thermos of coffee on his desk. He turns his computer on, eager to check his email before his first meeting. While he waits, his eyes wander to his bottom desk drawer. No, he tells himself. It's too early. It's a line he's never crossed before, a line he doesn't want to cross now. He takes a tentative sip of coffee instead. When he looks down, he sees that his hands are shaking a little. Like an addict. He sits on them to keep them still.

His phone rings. Blair. "Mr. Davenport, Laine Hardaway is here."

God, is she his first client? What a way to start the day.

"Please tell her I'll be right with her, Blair."

Another sip of coffee, slower, longer. A few words of encouragement. You can do this. It's only three hours. You can do this.

He only sees three patients a day now, in the mornings, between nine and noon. "I want more time with Dom," he'd explained to Tina.

"Dom is in school until three," she'd snapped. "You want more time with the bottle."

He hadn't bothered to deny it. Their marriage won't survive Dom's death. He's certain of it now. He's not sure he will either.

Keeping an emergency bottle in his desk drawer had seemed like a good idea when he'd put it there. Just in case. To help him function. Now he wishes he hadn't.

He only has another minute or two to himself. He can't keep Laine waiting. He could use a drink to deal with her, but he doesn't want her to smell alcohol on his breath. If she did, she'd be about as forgiving as Blair. *That's no excuse for not being professional.*

He can see Laine's pinched little mouth and wrinkled nose now. The way she runs her tongue across her teeth whenever she finds something distasteful. God, he can just see her. He contemplates sticking his finger down his throat, making himself sick so he can go home, but he's afraid his vomit would smell of last night's bourbon. There's no getting out of this. He has to see her. If he starts hiding from his clients now, he may never stop.

Quick bit of liquid courage then, before he does. Rough night last night. Rough morning now. Just this once. He pours it into his coffee to disguise the smell. Swigs. Feels calmer already. He can do this. He can.

"I have some exciting news for you, Doc," Laine Hardaway says as she strolls into his office, tugging her indifferent Afghan hound, Kabul, along behind her.

"Oh?" Prince takes another sip of coffee. Brilliant move, spiking it. It will make this session much more tolerable.

"Frank proposed," she says, sitting delicately on Prince's settee. Beside her, Kabul collapses to the floor with a frustrated sigh.

Laine beams at him. "Yes, that's exactly how we feel, Kabul." She musses the hair atop the dog's head. "I've never seen such an intuitive animal."

"So, I shouldn't congratulate you?" Prince asks, looking from Laine to Kabul as if either one of them might provide the answer.

"No, I suppose you should. I did say yes after all. The trouble isn't that I don't love him or that I don't want to marry him. He's a good man. We have fun together. The trouble is Immortality."

"That you have it, and he doesn't?" Prince ventures.

"Well, yes, but it's more than that. He hasn't brought it up yet, but I keep wondering, what if he expects it now? I mean, I'm marrying him, and I have plenty of money. He probably expects Immortality."

"But you don't want to give it to him?"

"It's not that. Not exactly. It's—you know what it is? I've worked hard for this money. I've earned my Immortality, and it bothers me that he hasn't, that he would be benefiting from my success."

Amazing, Prince thinks. She actually believes her own drivel. He wishes Darcy were here. She'd destroy Laine's arguments in a minute. Frank is a hardworking, underpaid elementary school teacher. Laine hosts a talk show entitled *Dysfunction*. From society's standpoint, if only one of them can live forever, it should undoubtedly be him.

"I see," Prince says. "Why don't you think he deserves Immortality? Because he doesn't make enough money?"

"No. Sort of. Maybe. I mean, if he wanted Immortality, he should have picked a higher-paying profession."

Prince takes another sip of coffee. His stomach churns. He thinks of Frank, straining his back as he bends over child-sized desks, teaching schoolchildren to read. He pictures Laine in bright pink lipstick egging people on until they're screaming at their loved ones on national television. He imagines Dom, sitting at home in his wheelchair, diagnosed with a terminal disease through no fault of his own, destined to die before eighteen. Who deserves Immortality? In a just world, not Laine, that's for sure.

Prince is sitting on the bed, drinking a glass of wine and strategizing with Tina. They're having Sabrina over for drinks tonight in yet another bid to convince her to give their father's inheritance to Dom. Prince has bought top-shelf liquor for the occasion. Tina has been researching trendy cocktails all week. They've purchased a dark green sweater for Dom that brings out the color of his eyes and dragged him to the barber for the first time in months.

"Do I look okay?" Tina asks, staring at herself in the full-length mirror. She is fit but not thin and has always been self-conscious about her figure.

Prince doesn't have time for her insecurities. "You should be coming up with a strategy, not worrying about your mascara," he snaps.

"Looks matter to Sabrina," Tina insists. She smiles into the mirror, rubs some lipstick off her teeth, and smiles again.

"Not your looks," Prince says, carelessly swirling his wine. "Why would Sabrina care about your looks?"

"Why are you drinking?" Tina retorts, glaring at him in the mirror. "We're having cocktails in half an hour."

Prince turns his glass up and drains the contents before Tina can take it away from him.

"Oh, real mature, Prince," she scoffs.

"Dom. We're supposed to be talking about Dom," Prince reminds her, staring at his empty wine glass, wishing he'd brought the bottle upstairs.

Tina shakes her head. "That boy," she says warily. "We've got to make sure he's on his best behavior tonight."

"How do we do that?" Prince asks. "He's not a puppy."

Tina scowls. "Try to be helpful, Prince. Just once."

Downstairs, the doorbell rings. Tina glances at her four-thousand-dollar Cartier watch. "Is she early?" she asks, reaching for her perfume. "We don't even have a coherent plan."

"I'll get it," Dom yells below.

Prince leaves his wine glass on the bedstand and makes his way downstairs.

"You look good, Dom," he hears his sister say as he nears the foyer.

Dom will like that. When he was young, Darcy had been his favorite aunt, but as he's gotten older, Sabrina has supplanted her. "She's the only hot girl I'll ever be seen with," Dom had explained a year or two ago.

"Thank you, Sabrina," Dom says now. "You look gorgeous."

"Thank you, Dom."

"Will you pick me up at school sometime? I want the guys to see me with you."

When he speaks, his words behave like ingredients in cake batter, oozing and comingling until they're no longer distinct but part of one giant jumble.

"What?" Sabrina asks.

Dom repeats himself. He tries to take his time, enunciate each word. He's clear enough that Prince, accustomed to his speech, can understand him, but Sabrina is struggling.

"I'm sorry, Dom," Sabrina says. "I don't understand."

"He'd like you to pick him up from school," Prince explains, entering the room. "He wants all the other guys to see his hot aunt."

It's the perfect compliment, and Sabrina lights up. "I'd be happy to. But maybe we won't tell them I'm your aunt." She winks. Dom smiles.

"Sabrina!" Tina exclaims. She rushes into the room, arms extended as if she has unexpectedly encountered a beloved old friend.

"Hi, Tina," Sabrina says. Usually, she matches Tina's enthusiasm, but today she is withholding. Polite but not effusive. "Where are those martinis you promised?" She raises an eyebrow as if she knows the drinks are a ruse.

"Coming right up," Tina says as she heads into the kitchen. "You're not in a hurry, are you?"

"I'm meeting Leroy for dinner after this, and I can't be late," Sabrina explains. "Leroy hates it when I'm late."

"Leroy?"

"The latest boyfriend." She rolls her eyes as if her dating patterns have become absurd even to her.

"Come into the kitchen and tell me all about him," Tina calls. Like they are teenagers gossiping about high school crushes.

Sabrina turns to Prince and cocks her head to the side. Asking, is this the best you can do? Prince shrugs. No, he wants to say. It's just Tina. Tina is thoughtful and strategic, but she's better behind the scenes. She can't act to save her life.

They sit around the dining room table, sipping some gin-and-lavender concoction Tina had discovered on the internet. Beside them, Dom slurps Dr. Pepper through a straw. He is pleasant to be around for once, even charming; he smiles often and listens to Sabrina with obvious attentiveness. A teenaged boy in the presence of a beautiful woman, Prince realizes, and he feels strangely heartened by the normalcy of his son's behavior.

When there is a lull in the conversation, Prince attempts his newest tactic to persuade Sabrina to give his son Immortality, inspired by his session with Laine Hardaway. "Do you know, I have clients who can afford to give their partners Immortality but decline to," he begins, even though it is only Laine, no one else. He explains Laine's twisted logic, her belief that she is somehow more deserving than her dedicated fiancé.

"That's awful," Sabrina says, scrunching her nose in disgust. "I'd never be with a man who wouldn't give me Immortality."

Prince and Tina look at her curiously.

"Why would you need a man to give you Immortality?" Tina asks. "You already have it."

Prince and Tina gaze at her expectantly, willing her to understand that she's no different from Prince's clients, denying someone Immortality when she's in a position to grant it.

Sabrina turns beet red. "I mean, if I didn't already have Immortality," she stammers, reaching for her cocktail.

Under the table, Prince clenches his fists. He opens his mouth to berate Sabrina for her hypocrisy, but before he can, Dom speaks up, and for once, he is perfectly clear.

"If you learn one thing from spending a lot of time in the hospital, it's that nobody's entitled to Immortality," he says. "Nobody's entitled to life."

Prince downs the rest of his cocktail in a single gulp while Tina buries her head in her hands. Dom has undermined the case for his Immortality again.

CHAPTER 4

Then

The ruse is simple. Different name, different angle each time.

"'Compounds Save College Graduates, Too' was brilliant. *The Atlantic* ate it up. Next time maybe it can be something about fresh starts or families reuniting. Ooh, or support for single mothers. People love that stuff." Dallas licks his lips like a hungry wolf.

"So, I invent stories?" Ben asks, trying to make sure he understands.

"Invent? No. Absolutely not. There can't be any lies. Ever. You find a narrative about Compound life that's been overlooked. You guide the journalist to the people and places that display that narrative. The journalist has an interesting angle from which to approach an over-addressed topic; Compound 78 shines."

Ben pretends to think it over. "What's in it for me?"

Dallas rolls his eyes as if it's typical of a Cruor to want something for everything. "What do you want? Twenty per journalist?"

"A hundred," Ben counters.

"Done," Dallas says, so quickly Ben knows he should have asked for more. "But nobody can know. I'd be in all kinds of shit if anyone found out."

"Don't worry," Ben assures him. "Nobody will know."

He longs to tell his siblings. They've never thought much of him, he knows. On the Outside, Henry was responsible, Zeke was nice, and Remy was smart, while to them, he was nothing but a troublemaker. He wasn't a bad kid, just more willing to do whatever was necessary to survive. But they never noticed his resourcefulness, only his shortcomings, the handful of times they had to pick him up from the principal's office or convince the police that nothing like this would ever happen again.

But now, Ben has been singled out. He has been handpicked to be the voice of the Compound, to influence how they are perceived by the Outside. It's the single biggest honor he's ever received, and he can't tell a soul. He feels like a spy or a criminal mastermind, his name destined to go unuttered, his work forever concealed from the world.

Now

Ben rests his Compound-issued blue and white sneaker on the metallic park bench and pretends to tie his shoe. This corner adjacent to Main Street smells of barbecue, and his stomach purrs in response.

"Excuse me." A woman's voice directly behind him. Wealthy. Entitled. That's her.

"Yeah?" Ben says, turning to face her.

When he sees her, he struggles to keep his mouth from dropping. He wonders if he's misunderstood. Maybe they're filming a movie here, and she's an actress hoping to bum a cigarette. But no, she introduces herself as a journalist. Sabrina Davenport. *Los Angeles Times.*

"Do you have a few minutes? I'd like to ask you a couple of questions." She is more confident in her beauty than her reporting. She leads with her body, fingers her hair.

"Um, okay," Ben says. "Sure." He subtly shifts his gaze from her to Dallas, looming in the background. She takes the hint.

"David, can you give us a few minutes, please?" Her voice is sugary and hard to refuse.

Dallas puts up a half-hearted fight. Protocol. Supervision. Formal tour. Like any determined reporter, Sabrina is having none of it. She leans in, sexy and suggestive, promising something without promising anything. "Surely you can make an exception this once."

Dallas blushes and gives in. "Well, if it's our little secret."

Sabrina turns to Ben. "What's your name?" she asks as her fingertips graze his arm.

Ben is so smitten that he forgets to use an alias. "Ben Hudson," he says, lowering his voice an octave. When he realizes his mistake, he has to stop himself from slapping his forehead with his palm. In the background, Dallas is shaking an angry fist at him. How stupid could he be?

Sabrina is oblivious. "Ben will take good care of me, won't you, Ben?"

He swallows and nods. While she sends Dallas away, Ben tries to pull himself together. He's been with women as hot as her before. Almost as hot anyway. Well, hot, at any rate. He's seen women, and even a few men, flaunt their sexuality before, too, but never like her. If sex is power, she's a superhero.

She's speaking to him. He hasn't heard a word she's said.

"I'm sorry, what?" he asks.

She smiles. Used to this. "I said, 'Will you tell me about your life as a Cruor?'"

He takes it slow, shows her around. Lets her ask questions, makes her feel like she's in control. What he does is art. A play in two acts. First, cater to the oversized ego of the actor, then subtly take control as the director. Works every time.

Sabrina wants to sit on a bench in the shade and observe the Cruors before interrogating them. "I'm a people watcher," she confesses.

"So am I," Ben says. "When I was homeless, I used to sit with my back against the wall of a drugstore and watch people far more important than me rushing by. I'd wonder who they were and where they were going, and, more than anything, why they were in such a hurry."

He is trying to be funny. She doesn't laugh. "You were homeless?"

He studies the pavement, pretending his past is difficult to discuss. Reporters eat this up, the story of his six years on the street, his impoverished childhood in El Desierto before that. He never shares the same anecdote twice. He has a knack for picking the story best suited to each reporter, the one that will tug at their heartstrings the most. He looks up and gives Sabrina a pitiful grin.

"Yeah, for six years," he says. "It wasn't so bad for me, but I worried about my little sister. I saw the way guys looked at her. And the pimps. The pimps were so aggressive. For a virgin like my sister, they were offering top dollar."

Ben expects Sabrina to be horrified, but all she says is, "You know, sometimes I'm not sure the modeling industry is so different."

"Wait, you're a model and a journalist?" he says, surprised but not surprised.

She scrunches up her nose. "For now."

"You don't like it?"

"No, I do. Sometimes. But I've spent the last two decades working my ass off to become a supermodel, and it never quite seems to take. Close, but no cigar." She holds her thumb and index finger a quarter of an inch apart to show just how close she has gotten. She seems annoyed by her failure but, interestingly, not ashamed.

"That's hard to believe," Ben tells her. She is the most beautiful woman he has ever seen.

Sabrina shrugs. "Oh, I have a successful career, I suppose, compared to most. But I've never quite gotten to where I want to be."

"So now you're quitting?" He's not judgmental. He finds striving overrated, ambition exhausting. If life is short and we've only got one go at it, why not enjoy it, he thinks. Of course, her life is not short. If she's been an aspiring model for twenty years, she must be Immortal. She looks about eighteen.

"I don't know if I'll ever be able to bring myself to do that," she admits.

"So then, why are you here?" he asks.

"I stumbled into journalism by accident. Saw an ad in a paper for a gossip columnist and applied on a whim."

"You're a gossip columnist?" he asks, confused. What is there to gossip about here?

She shakes her head. "I was. Attended the same parties I was going to anyway, but I'd write them up afterward—who's fucking whom, who threw a tantrum, who got smashed and vomited all over the carpet—that kind of thing. Between you and me, it was kind of gross. One night I needed a break, so I went out and sat in the lobby. Started chatting up the doorman, a fellow named Tiberius. At first, we were just making small talk, but before long, we were exchanging shattered dreams."

She looks pensive, distant, like she is back in that lobby with Tiberius, reliving their conversation. "Tiberius wanted to play professional baseball. He should have been able to, too. He was that good. Star in high school, star in college. Made it up to AAA but could never quite reach the pros. Know why?" She doesn't wait for an answer. "Immortality, that's why. Poor Tiberius couldn't get a job because none of those fuckers in the majors ever retire. Don't have to. They make enough for Immortality and can keep playing baseball forever. In football, players still get injured. They retire and lose their contracts, not at the same rate as before, but it still happens. But in baseball, almost never. They just play and play and play. So poor Tiberius never got his shot."

He's surprised by her hostility, that someone so beautiful could be so bitter. "But aren't you Immortal?" he asks.

She assesses Ben warily as if trying to decide whether she can trust him. "I am," she admits. "But you don't know what I have to go through to get that Infinity Scrum."

What he imagines is probably worse than the truth. Still, he shudders. "Is it worth it?"

She looks off into the distance. "I'm starting to wonder."

She pulls herself back into the present and flicks her dark, silky locks behind her shoulder. "Anyway, I wrote Tiberius's story up and submitted it to my editor. I thought he'd toss it out, tell me to stick to gossip, but he loved it. Not only were they going to run it, he was reassigning me. I was no longer the gossip girl. I became the Eternity Columnist. It's my job to find unexpected ways that the advent of Immortality affects ordinary people."

"What's the best story you've heard?" Ben asks.

Sabrina doesn't hesitate. Her eyes light up as she says, "Keisha, a thirty-one-year-old mother of three, was diagnosed with leukemia the month after Immortality was announced. She was normal, middle class. No way she could afford Infinity Serum. But her husband shared her story on the internet and crowd-funded enough for her Perpetual Immortality. People still try that today, but it doesn't work anymore. Too many terminally ill people to choose from. But it worked for Keisha. She got to see her kids grow up. She watched them all graduate from high school and go onto college. And then once they had, she found another young, middle-class mother recently diagnosed with breast cancer and passed Immortality onto her."

Ben frowns. "So, she died?"

Sabrina nods. "She succumbed to cancer eight months ago."

To Ben, the story seems fictitious, the sort of tale that would appear in a children's book or a church periodical in a transparent attempt to convince people to be better than they are. "Did that really happen?" he asks.

"Of course," Sabrina says, offended. "Look." She pulls out her phone, fiddles with it, and passes it to Ben.

It's her article, complete with pictures of Keisha and the woman she'd passed Immortality on to, each with their families. "I don't believe it," Ben mutters. "Incredible."

Across from him, Sabrina is beaming. It's the first genuine smile he's seen from her since she arrived.

"So, you're here looking for another one of these stories, these Immortality tales of yours?" he asks.

"Exactly. Cruors have been almost as affected by Immortality as Immortals. A lot of people have covered the Compounds generally, but I want to zero in on a person or two specifically and share their story."

Ben smiles. It's too easy. He knows the perfect person.

It is only Ben's second time inside the library. In the past, he has avoided it as a scientist avoids a psychic—because he finds it inane and unnecessary, because it contradicts the very nature of who he is.

He has forgotten how still it is in here, how crude and inhospitable. It makes him off-balance and uncomfortable. He feels like he's having an allergic reaction. He doesn't like the smell of old books or the dust circulating through the air. The sight of so much tiny print makes his eyes water. He wonders why books haven't been phased out of existence, like puppetry and pantomime before them. There are easier, more pleasurable forms of entertainment now.

As usual, the library is empty but for eleven high school students and Henry, divided into teams of two, their heads bent over a series of rectangular wooden tables. They whisper amongst themselves, jot thoughts and ideas down on paper. They are preparing for the NPE. Caleb wanders among them, leaning over their shoulders, asking questions and nodding encouragement.

Remy is there, too, even though she has already taken the NPE and can no longer benefit from these sessions. She has become Caleb's assistant.

"What is this?" Sabrina asks. Like him, she appears out of her element in the library. She hovers close to Ben as if she may need his protection.

"This is the Compound Library," Ben explains. "Come on, we don't want to interrupt."

He leads her over to his sister, who has been watching them from across the room.

"Remy," Ben whispers. "This is Sabrina. She's a reporter with the *LA Times*. She's looking for an interesting story about Cruor life, and I thought yours and theirs," he indicates the other students, "might be just the thing."

Remy looks at Ben curiously. "What story?"

"You know, high achievers looking to go to college."

"Is that true?" Sabrina interrupts. "Do you want to go to college?"

Remy blushes. "More than anything. I just took the NPE."

"I'll leave you two to talk," Ben says. "I'll be right over there."

It's a success, of course. Most of his ideas are. He watches from an armchair as Sabrina and Remy speak for ten, twenty, thirty minutes, their heads close together like sisters, their smiles disarmingly similar. After Remy, Sabrina speaks to the other students, one by one, and finally to Caleb, who is less self-assured than Ben has ever seen him, talking too loudly, stumbling through sentences, making one bad joke after another. Sabrina must be used to this, too, for she reacts as though nothing is wrong, smiles flirtatiously, even laughs at his terrible jokes.

When she's finished conducting interviews, Sabrina returns to Ben, glowing. "Thank you," she enthuses. "That was perfect."

"No problem," he says as he escorts her out of the library. "You know, you really have a knack for that. Interviewing people. Making them feel at ease."

"Do I?"

He is caught off-guard by the sincerity of the question. She's not fishing for a compliment. She really doesn't know.

"Yes," he answers. "More than anyone I've ever seen."

"Huh," she says. "I guess I'm still surprised any time someone thinks there's more to me than my looks."

"What about your boyfriend?" He is fishing.

"Ha! He's with me for my looks. They all are."

"Parents?"

"Dead," she whispers. "Both of them."

"I'm sorry," he tells her. "I don't have parents either. My dad died four years ago, and my mom left us."

"What happened to your dad?" Sabrina asks.

"Drank himself to death."

She's silent for a moment, absorbing what he's shared.

"How did you feel?" she asks. "When he died?"

Ben pauses. His dad has always loomed large in his imagination, a malevolent god controlling his fate. Vance had condemned his family to homelessness. He'd kept them on the streets long after it had become apparent that there were no jobs, years after the Compounds had opened and welcomed the needy. How does any child view a parent who unnecessarily deprives them? Misguided at best, but more likely tyrannical, unjust, cruel.

"Shocked at first," he tells Sabrina. "But then relieved. I hadn't realized what a burden he'd become. How much harder he made life."

"That's funny," Sabrina says. "That's how I feel, too. I shouldn't. My dad was a good man, and he adored me."

"But his adoration became a burden?"

She smiles at him, pleased he's understood. "Exactly. Because the thing is, he never really adored me. He adored my beauty. My mom was the same. She never told me I was smart or funny or nice. Everything she said to me was about looks, mine or other people's. She wasn't very kind about it. When my parents were alive, all my goals centered around not letting them down. I couldn't get enough validation. I still can't. I can't bring myself to give up Immortality or modeling. But without my parents looming over me, I think I might be able to someday. After a lot of therapy."

Ben laughs.

She blushes as she hands him her card. "You've done so much for me today, Ben. If I can ever help you, call me, okay?"

Ben's phone rings two weeks later as he is finishing a sandwich in the cafeteria. He doesn't recognize the number.

"Ben? This is Sabrina Davenport with the *Los Angeles Times.*"

"Shabrinhuh. Hi," Ben says through a mouthful of turkey and mayonnaise. Why had he taken a bite before answering? He must sound like an idiot.

"So? I assume you saw the story about your sister?"

"Yeah, I did," he says. Like most articles about Compound 78, it had gone unnoticed by the average Cruor, but the Hudsons had been proud. They'd printed the article, which was almost entirely about Remy and attached it to the wall of their living space with Scotch tape.

"It was great," Ben adds as an afterthought. He's not used to reporters calling him for feedback.

"My readers thought so, too," she says. "I've never gotten such a positive response. Tons of emails poured in. Everyone wants to know what happened to Remy. Did she pass the NPE? Where's she going to college? A few even offered to help with tuition."

Ben sets his sandwich down. "Are you serious?"

"Of course I am. Why would I make this up? Anyway, my readers are dying for a follow-up, so I was hoping I could visit again. Specifically, on March sixteenth, the day NPE results come out? I'd like to be there to record Remy's reaction when she learns her score and interview her family and friends. It would be a real feel-good piece. And then, a couple of months later, I'd write a third article about her going to college."

Ben can barely contain himself. "Yeah," he stammers. "Of course. We'd be glad to have you."

But later, when he tells Remy, she is not glad. "No," she snaps, incredulous. "I don't want a reporter here when I get my NPE Results. Are you out of your mind? This is stressful enough already."

He knows she is haunted by Malachi's failure. She cannot mention her NPE performance without mentioning him. Ben doesn't understand it. Malachi is a different person who took the test in a different year. His performance has no bearing on hers.

Ben persists, and in the end, Remy relents. It's the promise of help with her tuition that sways her. "I don't think I have a choice," she says. "A little extra money could go a long way."

Eight of them gather in the Hudsons' living space to await the NPE results. Ben and Caleb sip beers and fight for Sabrina's attention while Henry talks to Miguel's parents, who have dreamed of having their only son attend college since immigrating to the U.S. a dozen years ago. Remy and Miguel sit beside each other on the sofa, doing their best to make polite conversation, but their mind is on the NPE. Neither one of them can stop fidgeting.

Although Remy and Miguel are the most visibly nervous, almost everyone in the room has a lot at stake. Ben alone is mostly indifferent to the results. He knows Remy wants to go to college, and so for her sake, he hopes she passes. But to him, the outcome doesn't matter much. Worst case scenario, she remains in their comfortable apartment and Donates blood once a week. It could be a lot worse. Fifteen years ago, it would have been.

"Hey, Ben, have you seen Zeke?" Henry asks. "I thought he'd be here for this."

"No," Ben says. "But you know Zeke. He probably forgot."

Ben turns away from his brother, eager to get back to Sabrina, but before they can resume their conversation, Remy lets out a shriek. "They're here!"

The room falls silent as everyone crosses their fingers and holds their breath. They move toward Remy and Miguel, hovering above them, trying to catch a glimpse of their screens. Remy and Miguel struggle to open the secure text message they've each received. Their hands are trembling, and Remy's eyes are blinking and unfocused. Ben wonders if she's going to faint.

Miguel manages to access his results first. The shift in his expression betrays the outcome. "I failed," he says. He flips his phone over so it is face-down on his lap and stares at the floor, avoiding everyone's gaze.

"Oh, honey," his mom says. She kneels down on the floor in front of him and pulls him into her arms.

The others step in and step up, patting Miguel on the shoulder, expressing their regret and disbelief. They are so focused on Miguel that, for a moment, they forget about Remy until she whispers, "Me, too."

The room falls silent again. Henry is shaking his head back and forth as though he can't quite believe it. Caleb looks ill. Sabrina is gnawing on her pen, with a pensive look on her face, as though she is trying to figure out how she can spin this story now. They were disappointed that Miguel failed; they are stunned that Remy has. The mood shifts from concerned to doomed. Everyone wants to believe they've misheard, that Remy has misread the results or is playing a joke on them. Remy keeps rubbing her eyes as if willing herself to wake up from this nightmare, but it doesn't do any good. It's all over. She tucks her head in between her knees and takes deep, audible breaths.

Ben rests his hand on his sister's back. "It's okay, Remy," he says. "It's not like it was before when it was either college or starving on the streets. We have a home here, a good home, and you can have a good life. This stupid test, it just doesn't matter."

Remy sits up abruptly. "You don't get it," she says, her eyes boring into Ben. "You never have. I've spent my entire life working toward college. It's all I have ever wanted. I want to learn. I want to find a career I love and be successful at it. I want to know that when I die, I've left the world better than when I found it. I want options and opportunities. And now I won't have any of that. My entire life will be contained within these four stupid walls."

Her speech ends with a sob, deep and guttural, as tears overtake her. Henry tries to comfort her, attempting to wrap his arms around her trembling body from behind, but she pushes him away.

Ben stands helplessly in front of his sister, feeling like an idiot. He remembers the time he had run away to a Compound at fifteen, how it had felt to be so close to attaining something he wanted so much only to have it yanked away at the last minute. He had wanted to scream at the injustice of it all. But his dream had only been delayed. Hers has become impossible. He doesn't know how Remy will pick herself up from this or where she will go from here. Nowhere, he realizes. There is nowhere to go from here.

"No," Caleb says suddenly, his voice rising above Remy's sobs. He looks at Remy and then at Miguel. "No way. When Malachi failed last year, I couldn't believe it, but I thought, you know what? Shit happens. He could have had an off day. There could have been an error. Who knows? But I accepted the results because, with one student, anything is possible. But now you two? Both of you? No. There's no way."

Henry nods the slow nod of a detective piecing together evidence in a crime. "He's right. One of you failing? Okay. Both of you? Unlikely, but sure. Both of you and Malachi? It's not possible."

Sabrina, who has tucked herself away in a corner, watching this scene unfold, speaks up. "But Cruors have traditionally underperformed on the NPE, haven't they?"

Caleb and Henry glare at her. "Not these Cruors," Caleb snaps.

"You guys, let it go," Remy begs, embarrassed. "It's over. We failed."

"No." It's Ben who's speaking this time before he fully realizes what he is saying.

"No," he repeats. "We're not letting this go. They're right. Something's off here." His indifference lends him credibility. Henry and Caleb are too invested. When they protest, the others hear desperation. But Ben has never cared whether Remy passed, and yet, he realizes he had always assumed she would. His sister is smart. Even in Santa Monica, in a school full of rich kids with the best tutors, she had been at the top of the class. Caleb and Henry are right. There's something wrong here.

"But what can we do?" Miguel's mom asks.

"Your mom works in testing," Henry says to Caleb. "Can she help?"

"I'll call her," Caleb says.

But Jennifer Wentworth is no help at all. "I'm so sorry to hear this," she says. "I read about Remy in the *Times*. I was pulling for her. But an unexpected outcome doesn't mean something is amiss. In fact, it's more common than people realize. The stress of the exam often pulls scores down, especially compared to practice tests."

"I don't think you understand," Caleb says. He is frustrated with her, impatient. "They didn't even make it past triage."

"I'm sorry, sweetheart," she says, drawing her words out in a way that strikes Ben as condescending. "I know how much you'd invested in this. But for Cruors, college is always a long shot."

When he hangs up, Caleb looks even worse than before. His pale skin has become ashen, and he begins to totter from foot to foot as though he is unbalanced or weak. He sinks onto the nearest chair, thoroughly defeated.

"A regrade," Henry says suddenly. "That's what we do. It's an option, isn't it?"

"It is." Caleb hesitates. "But not a good one. A regrade costs $5,000, the same as a retake, and regrades almost always fail. If we're going to spend that kind of money, we might be better off using it toward a retake and working harder than ever for next year to make sure this doesn't happen again."

"No," Remy says, rising from the couch. Everyone turns to look at her, surprised by the vehemence in her voice. "I'm sorry, but I'm not retaking the exam. I was prepared. You know I was. Whatever happened here, it wasn't that I was unprepared."

"How does the regrade process work?" Henry asks.

"You submit a regrade request form, along with $5,000, and two different graders, neither of whom can be your original grader, review your exam," Caleb explains. "If they both agree that your exam grade should have been different, it can change the outcome, but again that's extremely rare."

"If your regrade is successful, you get your money back, right?" Miguel asks.

"Right, but again—" Caleb begins.

Remy interrupts. "Caleb, will you sponsor my regrade? I'll find a way to pay you back, I promise."

Caleb hesitates.

"I'll pay for your regrade, Remy," Henry says. "I have enough money. I've been saving since we got here."

"Well, that's all well and good, but what if she really has failed? She won't be able to afford a retake," Caleb points out.

"She didn't fail," Henry says. His eyes lock with Caleb's in an uncomfortable standoff until Caleb looks away, ashamed.

"I'll pay for your regrade, Miguel," Sabrina offers.

Everyone turns to her, surprised. Sabrina had only met Miguel an hour ago. She'd asked him a total of three questions and hadn't seemed particularly interested in him. Remy had been her focus, her story.

"Thank you, Ms. Davenport," Miguel's father says, squeezing his son's shoulder. "But may I ask why you're doing this?"

Sabrina shrugs. "The results of this exam mean everything to you. But to me, it's a couple of designer dresses, a day at the mall. I couldn't not pay."

"Thank you," Miguel's mom echoes. She hadn't cried when her son had failed, but she is crying now, big, soft, silent tears.

"Oh, now, stop that," Sabrina says awkwardly. "I'm only trying to give him the chance he deserves."

Caleb looks uncomfortable. Despite his expertise, he has become the odd man out. "I really think we'd be better off investing in retakes."

"No," Remy and Miguel say simultaneously.

"We were prepared, Caleb," Remy says. "If we didn't pass this time, we can't pass at all."

CHAPTER 5

Then

Darcy is relaxing on the couch with a glass of zinfandel, her bare feet on the coffee table. The news is on, but she isn't watching it. She is reflecting on her weekend with her nephew. A feeling she is unaccustomed to and cannot name warms her belly.

"What do you want to do this weekend, Dom?" She'd asked the exuberant five-year-old as soon as they'd waved goodbye to his parents Friday afternoon.

"Disneyland!" he'd yelled, as though the louder he said it, the more likely it was to happen.

She'd had to look away so he wouldn't see her cringe. When she'd turned to face him again, she'd been all smiles. "Disneyland it will be."

For Dom? Anything. It had been worth it, too. She'd never seen anyone that ecstatic. He'd never stopped smiling; he'd barely blinked. He'd talked of nothing else since, and he'd asked to see the pictures over and over again. She envied him. She wished she could find something, anything that made her feel that way.

The door opens. Prince and Tina are home.

Darcy feels an unexpected pang of disappointment at their return.

Now she has to leave the warmth of their beautiful Victorian—the walls covered with Dom's art, the den covered with his toys, the fridge covered with pictures of him—and return to her cold apartment, with its neutral greys and beiges and no pictures of anyone or anything. Usually, she welcomes its solitude, but spending the weekend with Dom has given her a glimpse of what she's missing. It will pass, she tells herself. Feelings like this always do.

Her brother and sister-in-law are exhausted but happy, each carrying a dozen bottles of wine in a crate. Tina is a full shade darker, and she has freshly painted turquoise nails.

"Welcome back," Darcy says, standing to greet them. "How was Santa Barbara?"

She only half listens as Tina raves about the historic inn, the restaurants, the wine tasting.

Darcy never takes vacations. She doesn't understand the appeal. To her, there is no place more relaxing than home, where she knows her bed will be comfortable, her shower steaming hot, the cheese and wine to her liking.

"How was Dom?" Prince asks. He is stacking the bottles of wine in the wooden wine rack they bought last year, dividing them by color, arranging them by grape.

"Good. Great. We had a really fun weekend," Darcy says. It's true. She is more comfortable with her five-year-old nephew than she is with any adult. He is always excited to see her, and he never flinches in embarrassment when she reaches for another French fry or asks for a second scoop of ice cream.

"I have something for you," she remembers. She goes to retrieve it, ignoring Tina's protests that she shouldn't have.

She returns, holding a mahogany picture frame and thrusts it toward them. Proud, like a child with a good report card. The frame contains three pictures. In the middle, a close-up of Dom's face, eyes shining, mouth agape, happier than his parents have ever seen him. To the left,

Dom and Mickey Mouse, arms wrapped around each other with the familiarity of old friends. Dom's smile almost reaches his small, pointy ears. To the right, Dom and Minnie. She's leaning over. He's kissing her cheek, a five-year-old Don Juan.

Darcy is beaming at her brother and sister-in-law, proud of the photographs she's taken, printed and framed, delighted to be sharing these newly formed memories with them. But when Prince and Tina look up, they aren't smiling.

"You took Dom to Disneyland?" Tina asks. She says it as if Darcy has done something wrong as if she's allowed Dom to scribble on the walls and is calling it art.

Darcy's smile falters. "Well, yeah. I asked what he wanted to do. He said, 'Disneyland.' I thought he was old enough. Should I have asked first?"

"Should you have asked first?" Tina inhales but doesn't release, trapping her frustration in her chest.

"Darcy," Prince says. "Come on. It really didn't occur to you that Tina and I might have wanted to be the ones to take Dom to Disneyland for the first time?"

No, it hadn't. If anything, she had thought she'd been doing them a favor. She had paid the absurdly steep entrance fee, stood in two-hour lines for two-minute rides, endured hordes of anxious parents and screaming children crowded together in a surprisingly small space underneath the merciless California sun. Their reaction stings. She's getting slapped when she'd expected a hug.

"Honestly, Darcy, we leave Dom with you for one weekend, and this is what happens? Really? I thought we could trust you." Tina is inclined toward hyperbole, and Darcy, unable to comprehend her dismay, assumes she must be exaggerating.

"It's not like we burned the house down, Tina."

Tina's fists clench, her turquoise nails digging into her palms. "You've stolen a memory from us," she screams.

Darcy takes a step back and looks to her brother for help, but he is trying to comfort his wife.

"It's just Disneyland," Darcy mutters, still bewildered.

"Spoken like someone who isn't a mom," Tina hisses. She buries her head in Prince's chest.

Darcy recoils. Normally, Tina's comment would be a paper cut, painless and unimportant, but now, coming off the incredible weekend with Dom, it is a knife wound.

Darcy backs away and goes upstairs to collect her belongings. She stops by Dom's room to say goodbye, but she can't bring herself to open his door. Before tonight, she'd known where she stood in his life. She was the beloved favorite aunt, a third parent, and a frequent babysitter. Now she feels like the badly-behaved pet, at risk of being locked out of the house.

Downstairs, Prince and Tina have moved to the sofa, where a heated discussion is taking place.

"—didn't mean anything by it—"

"—our memories, not hers—"

"—stupid, not malicious—"

Darcy doesn't want to hear any more, and she doesn't have anything more to say to them. She slips out the back door and around the house to her car. As it drives away, she glances back at Prince and Tina's Victorian, feeling wistful, trepidatious. This will blow over, she knows, but she is equally confident that someday there will be an incident that doesn't.

Now

In the hallway outside her office door, Darcy can hear her colleagues laughing as they make their way to lunch. As usual, she has not been invited. She tries not to care.

In many ways, her job is ideal. She has a private office. She reports to Elwood directly and rarely interacts with anyone else. She controls her own hours, which usually means working more, not less, than her co-workers, but when she does need to slip away midday, no one notices or cares. She likes being left alone to manage her time and responsibilities, trusted to deliver a high-quality product by a deadline. Most of all, though, she relishes the work, particularly her latest assignment.

In the U.S., Hemodyne runs the blood collection process. At their Compounds, everything is safe and regulated, and there is no advantage to trying to give more than once a week. In Western Europe and a handful of East Asian nations, Donation is similar, carefully managed by either Hemodyne or the government, ensuring both Donor safety and the quality of the blood. But in other countries, abuse is rife. Regulations aren't enforced. Bribes are rampant. As a result, people Donate more than they should. The blood supply is not properly screened for contamination. The poor are exploited. Under-aged Donors, too young to be giving at all, often end up dead.

Darcy's reports, which document both Donor abuse around the world and instances in which bad blood has led to illness or death, are intended to encourage Hemodyne, foreign governments, and international organizations like the United Nations, to become proactive in fighting corruption in developing nations and shutting down the black market for blood.

Darcy is so passionate about the cause that she often loses track of time. She'll look out the window and realize it is already dark outside, that her colleagues left hours ago, that she has missed dinner. Lately, she works more and eats less. She has lost fourteen pounds.

The phone rings shortly after her colleagues have left for lunch, as Darcy is finishing up her report on the Central African Republic, where a rebel group, which may or may not have the unofficial backing of the government, is setting up roadblocks around the country and demanding blood in exchange for safe passage.

Annoyed, Darcy checks to see who's calling. Being taken away from her work is jarring, like being woken by a fire alarm.

"Hi, Prince," she says. She tries not to sound impatient, fails.

Prince doesn't notice. "Darcy. It's Dom."

Darcy considers hanging up. Since their father died, Prince has been calling with medical updates on Dom any time he so much as breaks a nail. Dom has fallen out of his wheelchair and injured himself. Dom has pneumonia. Dom is feeling down that he can't go out for the soccer team. Dom has been reading a lot of books about death. Dom was crying last night when he didn't think anyone could hear. She is being forced to consume the diary of a dying child. It is painful, tragic. Manipulative.

She tries to be polite. "Prince, I know Dom is having a hard time, but I'm—"

"I'm sorry," Prince interrupts. "I know you're busy, but Dom is in the hospital, and I can't reach Tina. He wasn't breathing. I don't know if he's—if I got him here in time. Please, can you come?"

Darcy considers saying no. This could be another one of her brother's attempts to solicit pity, taken to the extreme. She wouldn't put it past him.

On the other hand, Dom does get sick a lot. His life is fragile. He is a tightrope walker without a net. She wants to be there for him, if not to catch him, then to comfort him, to make sure he knows she loves him.

"I'm on my way."

She saves the file she is working on and grabs her handbag. She stops by Elwood's office to tell him there's been a family emergency.

"Darcy," he says as she opens the door. "Have you seen the latest Brian Sa article?"

Darcy resists the urge to roll her eyes. She had told Elwood about the Eternity Column, for crying out loud, had begged him to read it for weeks before he finally found the time.

"Um, actually, I'm stopping by to let you know that there's been a family emergency," she says. "It's my nephew, Dom."

He leaps to his feet and pulls her into a hug. "What's going on?" he asks. "Is he going to be okay?"

"Later," Darcy promises. "I need to get to the hospital." Although she is neither crying nor frantic, Elwood seems pleased that she is putting something before her job. When her father died, she had missed only half a day of work, even though he'd begged her to take more time.

Another hug before she can leave. She endures but does not return it. She finds her coworkers' sentimentalism cloying. They go through tissues the way chain smokers go through cigarettes.

She often thinks Elwood would prefer a less reliable, more relatable employee to someone like Darcy, who is diligent and thorough but stoic and detached. He'd teased at the holiday party last year that she was the office sociopath, "cold and completely devoid of emotion." Everyone else had laughed, and she had forced a smile, but the comment had hurt a little. Controlling emotions is different from not having them. Remembering the incident, she makes an effort to look upset as she waves goodbye to Elwood, then she hurries to her car.

She gets to the hospital fast and makes her way through the bright blues and greens of the children's ward until she finds the waiting room, where her brother is staring vacantly at the television, taking sips from a flask when he thinks no one is watching. When he sees his sister, he is visibly relieved.

"Darcy." He inhales her name like a breath of fresh air. Clings to her for so long she begins to perspire. Reeks of bourbon. Sometimes she wonders if giving Dom Immortality would be saving two lives.

The waiting room is pea green, with jungle animals painted on the walls. The television is turned up loud enough to be heard over the thunderous air conditioning, and it smells of stale grease, the deep-fried meals of frightened parents half-heartedly consumed as they await news of their children.

Prince and Darcy are alone but for a large man with red-rimmed eyes, holding a ragged stuffed elephant and watching them enviously. Darcy wonders if he has anyone. She's glad she has shown up for Prince.

When Prince, at last, unwraps himself from her, she asks what has happened. He explains in slurred words and broken sentences. Found Dom. Slumped in a wheelchair. Not breathing. CPR. 911.

Darcy pulls her brother to her again. As his body moves towards hers, she notices his expression. Surprised. Grateful. She is disinclined toward physical contact, but she can see he needs it.

They sit beside each other on a bright blue sofa, its back too rigid to be comfortable. The television is tuned to *The Price is Right*, where a perky co-ed is trying to win a formal dining room set that looks like it belongs in the home of a stuffy suburban mom. Prince clings to Darcy's hand as if letting go would cause him to fall to his death. Darcy forces herself not to pull away. She'd held hands with a boy like this once in college. She'd hated it then, too. There's nothing romantic about crushed fingers and sweaty palms.

Minutes tick by. Darcy glances at her brother. His leg is tapping now, and a stream of sweat trickles down the left side of his face. When, a few minutes later, he stands abruptly and tells her he needs to use the bathroom, he leaves his cell phone but takes his flask, hidden underneath his sweater in the band of his pants.

The room is over air-conditioned, and without Prince's body against hers, Darcy shivers. The overweight man notices. "You're cold?" he says. "Here, take my sweatshirt."

Before she can object, he is pulling his red-and-gold USC sweatshirt over his head. "Us regulars know to bring an extra layer. It's always freezing in here."

Although he is large, too, she worries that the sweatshirt will be too small, but in fact, it's enormous on her. He's wearing a wedding ring. Darcy wonders what his wife would say if she walked in now and saw some other woman wrapped in her husband's sweatshirt. Would she be the anxious, jealous type like Tina? Or the kind who never seems bothered by anything like Sabrina?

"What's your kid in for?" he asks, as though they are parents picking their kids up from detention. Johnny pulled the fire alarm. Suzie cut gym.

She smiles ruefully. "My nephew, Dom. He has Tay Sachs."

"That terminal?"

She is amazed by how direct he is. Do parents of sick children share their diagnoses like soldiers show battle wounds? Is there a perverse kind of bragging right in having the kid with the bleakest outlook? Or maybe they hope to find someone whose child is even worse off than theirs, so they can say to themselves, At least my son doesn't have that.

Darcy nods. "Yes," she says. "It is terminal. He'll die within the next few years."

The man sucks his breath in through his teeth. "Jesus. I'm sorry."

"Thanks. My brother's taking it hard."

"It's nice that you're here for him. He have a wife?"

Darcy nods. "He does, but he hasn't been able to reach her."

"Oh. I thought maybe she left him like my wife left me."

"I'm sorry," Darcy mumbles, wondering why he is sharing this with her. "What does your child have?"

"Brain tumor," he says, choking up. "She's only six years old. Can you believe that? Six years old and the sweetest little thing you've ever met."

He takes out his phone and shows her a picture. His daughter is pig-tailed, dimpled, buck-toothed. She looks small for her age—if asked, Darcy would have guessed she was three or four. Maybe it's an old picture, or maybe it's infirmity, taking its toll.

"She's precious," Darcy says.

"Isn't she?" He strokes his daughter's photo with his thumb. "The other day, I was watching a talk show about kids who think they're entitled to Immortality. They come from families that can afford it, but their parents don't plan to give it to them for whatever reason. Sometimes it's religious; sometimes they don't think the kids deserve it. Anyway, you should have heard these brats. Spoiled rotten, every one of them. Saying they hate their parents and want them to die. Screaming at the top of their lungs that they deserve eternal life. And I kept thinking, they're whining about forever, while all I want is for my little Zoey to make it to her seventh birthday."

The speech is so well-said, so poignant, so relevant that Darcy suspects a con. Her brother has hired an actor and placed him in the waiting room, told him to strike up a conversation, to slip in this heart-wrenching little soliloquy. She keeps her eyes on the man, waiting to see if he'll slip out of character, but he is either authentic or very, very good.

"Do you have any other pictures of your daughter?" Darcy asks.

He smiles. "You bet I do." He fidgets with the phone and passes it back to her. She scrolls through photo after photo—Zoey at the beach, Zoey as a princess for Halloween, Zoey in a leotard and ballet shoes. He has dozens of pictures, but still, something seems off. They're too recent—Zoey is roughly the same age in all of them—and too expected. If there were a checklist of stock photos parents keep of their daughters, beach, Halloween, ballet would all be on there, along with in soccer uniform and opening presents at Christmas.

Darcy shivers. Is she overthinking this? It wouldn't be the first time. This man's presence here could be a coincidence, his daughter in a room somewhere, having a tumor as large as her fist blasted with radiation. He could be sitting three seats over, thinking she's interested in his dying kid, when in fact, she's merely playing detective, trying to determine if he's telling the truth.

Prince returns looking guilty. About his drinking or the plant? She can't tell. He glances at the man once, briefly, but his expression doesn't change. "No sign of the doctor yet?" he asks.

"None," Darcy replies.

And then the doctor walks in. She is slender with short curly hair and laugh lines around her eyes. With a job like hers, Darcy thinks, you'd have to laugh to keep from crying.

Prince springs to his feet. "Dr. Kuhn, how is he?"

"Fine. He'll be fine. He's resting now. I'll show you to his room, and we can chat on the way."

Darcy waves goodbye to the large man as she follows her brother and the doctor out the door. He waves back, his face crumpled and pathetic like he has lost his only friend.

The doctor leads them down the hall, her bright pink sneakers tapping rhythmically against the linoleum floor. The children's wing is designed like a bicycle wheel: an epicenter surrounded by spokes that extend in every direction. The closer they get to the center, the more chaotic it becomes. Darcy cannot imagine working here.

They stop outside room 327, where Dominick's name flashes in neon orange above the door on a scrolling marquee. As if he's scored a goal or hit a home run. Prince reaches for the doorknob, but Dr. Kuhn stops him. "Let's talk here a minute."

Prince glances anxiously at the door.

"Don't worry. Dominick is fine, but he's resting. Talk to me for a few minutes and then you can see him."

Prince nods, distracted.

"Dominick's dysphagia is getting worse," Dr. Kuhn begins, her voice matter-of-fact, clinical.

"I'm sorry, doctor," Darcy interrupts. "His what?"

"His dysphagia. It means he's having more and more trouble swallowing his food. It's caused three bouts of pneumonia in the past year, and today it resulted in him nearly choking to death." She turns from Darcy back to Prince and puts an unmanicured hand on his shoulder. "Prince, I know you've been reluctant in the past, but at this point, if you want to extend your son's life, a feeding tube is the only option."

A look of rage crosses Prince's face as if he wants to strangle the doctor, to punish the bearer of such bad news. But it passes quickly, and the old Prince returns: wretched, defeated.

"He wouldn't be able to eat anymore?" Darcy asks.

"He would get the nutrients he needs through a tube instead. We'd insert it through his abdomen and into his stomach." She places a hand on her own stomach to demonstrate where the tube would go. "Once the tube is inserted, it should result in less frequent pneumonia and reduce the likelihood that he'll choke or have trouble breathing. But I want to be upfront. Complications can arise. There can be leakage, which can cause any number of problems from skin irritation to peritonitis. Septic shock may result, and in children, we sometimes see malnourishment. The decision is yours and Tina's, Prince, but you should know that a number of parents decide not to proceed with the feeding tube at all."

"They give up?" Prince asks, horrified. He is looking Dr. Kuhn in the eye for the first time. Darcy pities the poor doctor. There is something wild in her brother's face, some unchecked desperation mingled with years of pent-up rage.

Dr. Kuhn must be used to this. She doesn't even flinch. She meets his gaze head on, her bedside manner exceptional. "I wouldn't say that," she says. "I'd say they accept the fact that, sooner or later, their children will die. To them, a feeding tube is prolonging the inevitable."

Darcy nods. She remembers how much Dom had struggled to eat a popsicle, his fury when it had shattered to the ground in a sweet, icy mess. She can't imagine not being able to eat at all would make him any happier.

"Unbelievable," Prince fumes. "These are children we're talking about. This is my son. He's not some dog to be put out of his misery. A cure for Tay Sachs could come along tomorrow. I want him to fight. Giving up, dying, it's not an option."

"Okay," Dr. Kuhn says with a quick nod. "Do you want to talk to Tina about this?"

"Tina will agree with me," Prince insists. "Get the tube."

Dr. Kuhn doesn't say anything more, but her face—slight frown, hesitant eyes—betrays her disapproval. "You can go in and see your son now," she says as she turns and walks away.

Inside, the light is off, and the drapes are drawn. The only light in the room slips beneath the door from the brightly lit hallway. The bed closest to the door is empty now, but the bedside table is covered with stuffed animals and handmade cards encouraging a child named Farouk to Get Well Soon!

Dom is in the second bed, curled up on his side, arms around a stuffed gorilla. When he's asleep, he looks like any other teenaged boy. There's no evidence of his disease or the stress it has caused. Darcy gazes at him fondly, amazed to see that he still resembles the little boy who used to reach for her hand every time they crossed the street, who would beg her to kick the soccer ball back and forth with him for hours on end, who had, until he was ten, given her a gift for Mother's Day every year, along with a note that read For My Second Mom. She misses him. She reaches down to brush the hair from his face, but Prince seizes her wrist.

"Don't touch him," he snaps, his voice low but angry.

She looks over at him, taken aback by his tone. He has the flask in his hand. He's no longer bothering to hide his habit.

"Prince, is this really the time? When Dom wakes up—"

"Don't say his name. Don't you fucking say his name!" He is managing to control his volume, if not his temper. Dom remains asleep. Darcy takes a step back.

"I'll never forgive you for this," he whispers. "How can you look at him there, my little boy, and think some fucking cause is more important than his life? What kind of monster are you? For years, I defended you against Mom, who couldn't stand to look at you. Against Dad, who regularly called you a bitch. Against Sabrina, who found you repulsive. Against my own wife, who thought you were cold and unfeeling. I insisted you had a soul. I defended you and defended you and defended you. I was there for you when no one else was. I'm the only person besides that little boy right there who's ever loved you. And what do I get in return? A freak who'd rather see our dad's fortune go to saving the whales than to saving my son."

Darcy feels her heart constrict. Prince isn't wrong. She has alienated one of the two people who loves her, and she's about to kill the other. As she watches Dom's chest rise and fall, as she looks at his lips, curled into a soft smile, as she remembers not his temper tantrums of late but his love from earlier years, she begins, for the first time, to doubt her resolve. Can she really let him die when it's within her power to save him?

Around her neck, she's wearing a necklace he gave her, concocted out of twisted wire at summer camp the year before all of this began. She fingers it gently, looks down at it with fondness. And then, beneath it, she sees the red and gold USC sweatshirt the man in the waiting room has lent her. She thinks of his daughter, of Zoey with the pigtails and buck teeth, and the reasons she opposes Dom's Immortality come flooding back to her.

She knows nothing she says will ever make Prince understand, but she tries again anyway. "Prince, Dom is in a wheelchair. He struggles to communicate, and he's losing his motor skills. He doesn't have much energy. He's miserable most of the time. In my opinion, and I know you disagree, but in my opinion, that's no way for anyone to live. It's a half-life. It's bad enough that he has to endure that temporarily, but you want to do it to him permanently, and I won't have any part of that."

Prince turns to her, eyes blazing. "Who the fuck are you that you think you should get to decide whether my son lives or dies? Who the fuck are you to decide what's best for him? You think you're God? Some fucking God!"

Darcy's heart is pounding. She hates this, hates everything about it: her brother's rage, her nephew's illness, her role in this drama as the worst villain imaginable. She longs to let out a violent scream, just one.

She takes a deep breath instead. It is woefully inadequate.

She is trembling as she turns to her brother. "Disagreeing with you doesn't make me a monster," she whispers. "When you called, I came. I love you, and I love Dom, but that doesn't mean I'm always going to agree with you or do what you want. I'm following my conscience just as you're following yours."

"You don't have a conscience."

Darcy sighs. No good can come of prolonging her presence here. "I'm going now," she says, turning to leave.

He grabs her by the sweatshirt, the bright red USC sweatshirt that belongs to the man in the waiting room. "You're not going anywhere until you agree to give my son Immortality," he hisses.

She pulls away, but he grabs her again.

"Dad, stop it," Dom slurs from his bed. They turn and see that he is awake, watching them as he struggles to sit up.

Prince releases Darcy. "Dom, you're okay." He forgets about his sister and rushes to his son, pulling the boy's shoulders toward him in a relieved embrace.

Darcy watches, envious, desperate to hug Dom, afraid of reproach if she tries.

Dom seems to sense this and slowly extends his arms toward her. She smiles and bends to hug him. Prince, resigned to his son's wishes, steps aside.

"I heard what you were saying," Dom says. He turns to Prince. "Why didn't you ask me? It's my life. Doesn't what I want matter?" He is speaking loudly and slowly, which makes his voice clearer than usual, but still Darcy has to focus to understand him.

"Of course, it matters, Dom," Prince says, resting his hand on the boy's head. "I didn't mention the possibility of Immortality to you because I didn't want to get your hopes up. It was only going to become an option if my dad died, and for a long time, that didn't seem likely. Then, when he did die, well, his will was written in such a way that it complicates things."

"Uh-huh. I see," Dom says. "The thing is, Dad, it's not complicated, not to me. Aunt Darcy's right. I don't want Immortality. I hate my life."

"Don't say that, Dom," Prince says. "You're so bright, and funny, and—"

"Shut up, Dad," Dom interrupts. His face is not angry but weary, as though he has been through all of this before. "You keep shoving inspirational books and movies down my throat, stories about children who manage to live meaningful, fulfilling lives despite their illnesses and handicaps."

"Yes, exactly," Prince says.

"No," Dom says. "It's not like that. My life isn't like that." He continues, but as he gets more agitated, he becomes harder and harder to understand until Darcy can't make out his words at all, only the frustration in his tone. His face is scrunched and purple like a prune, and a stream of spittle dribbles down his chin.

He takes a deep, shuddering breath as Prince looks on, transfixed, tears flowing silently down his horrified face. "Dom—"

"Shut up, Dad," Dom begs. He is crying, too, but he has regained control of his speech, and Darcy can understand him again. "Don't you get it? I can't even get off the fucking toilet by myself. Living like this forever sounds like the worst thing in the world. I'd rather die."

"You don't know what you're saying," Prince says. "What do you think happens after you die?"

"I don't know and neither do you," Dom slurs. "But you know what? I don't care. I don't want this life, even if it's the only one I get. I don't want to live forever. Don't try and make me."

"What about your mom and me?" Prince asks.

"What about you? Look at you. You're already falling apart. You drink all the time. Mom has become a raging bitch. You're a mess. Both of you!"

Dom turns to Darcy. "Aunt Darcy? Whatever he says, don't give in. I don't want Immortality."

She places her hand on her nephew's. "You have my word, Dom. I hope you know that I love you. That not supporting your Immortality doesn't mean, has never meant, that I love you any less."

"No," Dom says. "It means you get it."

"Darcy, can you give us a minute?" Prince asks. He is still crying, but his anger seems to have dissipated.

"Of course," she says. She squeezes Dom's hand and leaves the room.

She walks out into the hallway, closing the door behind her, then leans against the wall, trying to process all that has happened. She should be relieved. Instead, she feels guilty.

The hospital is unbearably hot all of a sudden, despite the overactive air conditioning. Darcy fans her face with her hand, wipes her brow. She reaches for the sweatshirt she's been wearing and tugs it over her head, then flings it to the floor before realizing that it's not hers.

She picks it up and makes her way back to the waiting room to return it to the friendly man with the sick daughter, but when she gets there, he's gone. The space is populated by three new parents, all tense with tired eyes, disappointed when they see the person entering the room is not a doctor bringing them news but another aggrieved visitor with another sick kid.

CHAPTER 6

Then

After school, Zeke kneels on the floor, playing with multi-colored wooden blocks. His teacher, Ms. Ingram, is sitting at her desk in a dress that he recognizes from the secondhand store. It's a distinct orange-soda orange, covered in tiny yellow flowers. It's sunshine captured in fabric, and it suits cheery Ms. Ingram perfectly. Zeke's mom had tried that dress on, too, but it hadn't suited her at all.

His mom is here now, sitting beside his dad, in two student-sized chairs that have been arranged to face Ms. Ingram's desk. They have dressed up for the occasion, his mom in her newest dress, a dour maroon number that suits her beautifully, his father in clean jeans and a t-shirt, which is about as dressed up as he gets.

There have been a lot of parent-teacher conferences about Zeke, not because he misbehaves but because his teachers don't know how to reach him. These meetings make his father drink and his mother pray.

Zeke has discovered that his parents worry most when he has no tastes or preferences. So, over time he has learned to make them up, to feign interest in matters he cares nothing about. What is your favorite subject? Color? Animal? Art. Blue. Dog. They always seem relieved, as if the discussion has proved his teachers wrong. There's nothing wrong with Zeke, they say to each other. He does have preferences; he's just shy about expressing them.

This is the first parent-teacher conference Zeke has been allowed to attend. Ms. Ingram has given him the Tupperware container full of the blocks he loves so much and told him to play quietly while she talks to his parents. Zeke is thrilled. He forgets all about the conference, retreats to the corner, and gets lost in the world he is constructing one block at a time.

Ms. Ingram cuts to the chase. "Mr. and Mrs. Hudson, I've looked at Zeke's file. It's full of concerned reports from his previous teachers, saying that they have trouble engaging Zeke, that he, well, that he seems a little lost."

Zeke is hearing without listening. He has finished the skyscraper, moved on to the police station.

Ms. Ingram continues. "I think they're wrong."

The police station is too tall, Zeke decides. He dissembles the top couple of layers, makes the building go out instead of up. The police station in El Desierto is only one story, a small, squat little hole-in-the-wall not much larger than a three-car garage.

"Look at Zeke over there now, playing with the blocks," Ms. Ingram instructs. "A couple weeks ago, Zeke got ahold of those blocks, sat in a corner of the room all by himself, and played with them for the entire twenty-minute recess. At lunch and afternoon recess, he did the same thing. He's played with those blocks every chance he's had since."

"So, what you're saying is our son doesn't care for schoolwork, but he likes blocks?" Zeke's dad asks, bewildered.

The house he's building for him and his family is almost as grand as the skyscraper. That's silly, he knows, but he likes the idea of living in a place that nearly touches the sky.

"Not quite. I'm saying Zeke isn't unreachable. He just has very specific interests, and they're not the interests we're used to seeing in kids. Most of my boys like soccer, a few basketball. One is enamored with books. But I've never had a student as obsessed with blocks as Zeke. They command all his attention, almost to the exclusion of anything else. Think back to Zeke's early childhood. Were there ever unusual toys or objects that he seemed particularly attached to?"

They answer simultaneously: "Toilet paper."

He makes the school large because it is large, but, like the police station, not tall. If it's too tall, it will be too big for the little children who go to school there. It should be child-sized. Approachable.

"Toilet paper?"

"Toilet paper," Ilene repeats. "For about two years, he had a roll with him all the time. Found a million uses for it. He'd pretend it was crepe paper and decorate the house, wrap himself in it like a mummy, ball it up like a snowball and throw it at his brothers. He loved toilet paper."

"That's a perfect example," Ms. Ingram says. "An unusual interest, to be sure, but one that he was passionate about to the point of obsession."

"So, what does this mean?" Vance asks.

He makes the grocery store the biggest building of all, bigger even than the skyscraper. It has to feed everybody. He doesn't want anybody to go hungry anymore. He makes it as wide as the school, then builds it higher and higher and higher.

"It means most people aren't going to understand Zeke. That his teachers will continue to dismiss him as passionless because he doesn't display any of the usual enthusiasms boys his age do. What I want you to get from this meeting is that he's not. Passionless, that is. Watch him closely. Pay attention to the little things he becomes obsessed with. The key to finding a path for Zeke isn't to try to make him fit the mold but to let his interests guide him to something he truly loves."

"What do you mean?" Ilene asks.

"Well, he sure loves those blocks. Maybe that means a career as an engineer or an architect."

Vance snorts. "Can you really imagine Zeke in college?"

"Well, a contractor or construction worker, maybe," Ms. Ingram suggests. "What specifically he does isn't the point. He's only in the second grade. For now, watch him, take note of his interests, and use them to steer him in the right direction. Zeke doesn't think like most people. Being aware of that will help you understand him when he seems indifferent to the things that matter to the rest of us or becomes fixated by things the rest of us consider mundane."

In the corner, Zeke is frowning. He's run out of blocks and his grocery store isn't finished. He should have built it first, before the skyscraper and the police station.

A hand touches his shoulder, and he jumps.

"Ready to go, Zeke?" his dad asks.

"Okay," Zeke says, though he isn't really. He would stay here all day if he could.

"Let's get these put away." His mom knocks over the skyscraper and the grocery store in one quick swoop. Zeke blinks back tears. He's beginning to sense that progress is impossible, his task hopeless. Everything he creates is destined to be destroyed.

Now

Zeke is irritated when Remy's phone rings during one of his detective shows. He spends less time at home these days, has fewer hours to devote to this beloved hobby. As a result, his television time has become sacrosanct. He turns to Remy and glares, but she isn't looking at him. Frustrated, Zeke pauses the TV.

"Yes, this is Remy Hudson."

Zeke waves his hands to get her attention. She doesn't notice.

"I did?" she asks in a small voice.

Zeke lets out an exaggerated sigh.

Remy ignores him. "Thank you," she is saying. "You have no idea what this means to me."

You have no idea what it would mean to me if you hung up the phone, Zeke thinks. When had Remy become so exasperating? He turns back to the television screen where Detective Han is suspended mid-sentence, his mouth agape, his dark hair covering his left eye. He'd just noticed something on the victim's body—some clue or unexpected injury.

Remy hangs up, and Zeke resumes watching his program, but he still can't hear it. Remy's making noise in the background. He pauses the show again. He turns, intending to ask her to be quiet, please, but he discovers she is sobbing.

Zeke stares at her, wondering how he should proceed. Is she sick or hurt? Upset about something he did? Should he check on her or give her some privacy? Henry or Ben would know what to do, but neither of them is home. She appears to be okay, physically at least, but emotions Zeke can't make sense of play across her face.

He feels like a voyeur watching a very personal, embarrassing display. He turns away and stares at the paused television program, praying silently that this will end soon, that one of his brothers will come home, that Remy will disappear.

And then his sister is standing in front of him, taking his hands in hers. "Zeke," she says. "I passed."

"Passed what?" Zeke asks, confused.

She gives him a look he recognizes, a look he's been receiving his entire life. Haven't you been paying attention, Zeke?

He offers the same response he always does: an embarrassed half smile, a shrug. I know I'm a dolt. Forgive me.

"The exam, Zeke," Remy says, and when he still doesn't appear to follow, "The NPE?"

"Oh, right. Of course," Zeke says. He wishes Remy would take a step back. She is in his personal space now, too close for comfort.

Remy gives him another look. Disappointed this time, maybe a little hurt. "I'm going to call Henry."

"Could you do it in your bedroom?" Zeke asks. "I want to finish my show."

"Sure," Remy says. But she sounds annoyed.

The killer is holding Detective Han at gunpoint when Henry comes home carrying a bottle of champagne and a cluster of balloons.

"Remy!" he calls out as he comes through the door.

Zeke scowls and pauses his show again.

Remy emerges from her bedroom and runs to Henry, throwing her arms around his neck. He lets go of the balloons as he returns her hug, and they drift up to the ceiling, a kaleidoscope of color.

"Would you believe the drug store doesn't sell balloons that say congratulations?" Henry tells her. "Only happy birthday. So I got the plain ones without any writing."

"They're wonderful," Remy replies. "I've never gotten balloons before."

"You deserve it. I'm so proud of you."

Zeke stares up at the bright, helium-filled spheres. They remind him of circuses and birthday parties, trips to the zoo or the park. A childhood he knows about only from television and movies, not one that he or anyone he knows has lived. He studies the balloons curiously. No, he doesn't understand the appeal. They're not edible. They'll float away if you let go of them and shrink in a couple of days if you don't. What's the point? What a silly gift.

"What did they say?" Henry is asking Remy. "Tell me every word. Who was it that called?"

"Her name was Linda something. She manages regrades for the NPE, and she—Henry, she actually apologized to me. She said my grader must have made a mistake. My case wasn't even close. My score is high enough to qualify me for an Ivy."

Zeke gets up to go to the bathroom. Maybe by the time he returns, the living space will have fallen silent again, and he'll be able to resume his show.

"An Ivy?" Henry is saying as Zeke leaves. "Remy, that's incredible."

When Zeke returns, the apartment has become even more crowded. Ben is home now, and Miguel and his parents are there. Everyone is talking over each other, laughing and hugging and kissing. Zeke turns to leave, but Henry stops him.

"Zeke, come on in," he yells.

"That's okay," Zeke mutters. There is another television in the lounge downstairs. Maybe he'll be able to watch his detective shows there.

"Come on, Zeke," Henry says. He reaches for Zeke's arm, tugs him into the room. Zeke's eyes dart around anxiously. He feels trapped, like an atheist surrounded by missionaries.

"Can you believe it?" Henry asks.

"Sure," Zeke replies. "Remy passed the NPE."

"So did Miguel," Henry explains. "We're celebrating. Sabrina is driving in from Los Angeles. We've got reservations at the Desert Rose."

Zeke frowns. Then there's no chance of reclaiming his living space until dinner.

"Zeke," Henry says. "This is good news. It's like—imagine how you'd feel if you got Immortality. That's how Remy feels now."

Zeke tenses. Has Henry found out? But no, now Henry's back to talking about the NPE and Remy's promising future. Zeke glances wistfully at the door.

"Don't even think about it," Henry says. "Tonight is Remy's night. Tonight, we celebrate."

The day drags on. Caleb brings more champagne and several six-packs of beer. Sabrina arrives with a fancy cake, a message written in cursive across the top: Congratulations Remy and Miguel!

Zeke sits on the sofa staring at the television that Henry turned off hours ago, recalling his favorite episodes of *Law & Order* and *The Immortal Murders*. When somebody speaks to him, he responds, but mostly he sips his now-flat champagne and stares at the blackened screen.

Around him, everyone else is talking. He tries to tune them out, but they are too loud, the space too small.

"What are the odds?"

"Weird that they were both failed—"

"Does it matter? They passed in the end."

Henry's analogy is bothering Zeke. Is passing the NPE the same as getting Immortality? No, he decides. Not at all. Passing the NPE is a step on the way to Immortality, the first stone when rock hopping across a river. But Immortality is landing safely on the other side, knowing you'll never stumble into the currents, you'll never die.

"—some problem with the grader—"

What does Remy hope to get out of this? Zeke wonders. Does she think she'll ultimately become Immortal? If so, there are easier ways. He wonders if he should talk to her, help her.

"—Malachi's exam regraded. If he passes, too, we'll know—"

But maybe she's in it for the money, not eternal life.

"—talk to my sister, Darcy. She's an Immortality lawyer—"

If she's not interested in Immortality, he doesn't want her to know his secret. She might tell Ben or Henry. They might force him to stop.

"—something's off—"

Can they do that? Can they make him stop? He's a grown man now, isn't he? Isn't it his decision? But Zeke has never quite understood the rules of adulthood. Maybe they can make him stop somehow. Maybe they can ruin everything.

The next morning his alarm goes off at 5:30 a.m. Zeke groans. The party to celebrate Remy's success hadn't died down until well after midnight.

"Shut that thing up," Ben grumbles from his bed.

"Sorry," Zeke whispers, reaching over to silence his phone.

Ben doesn't have to put up with his brother's alarm often—he usually doesn't sleep in his own bed—but when he does, he complains. The alarm is a tinny cowbell, reminiscent of their traumatic childhood.

Ben asked Zeke once to change the alarm to a favorite song, a shrill ring, anything but the cowbell, that haunting call to prayer that echoes through his mind for hours afterward. Zeke, always eager to oblige, had complied, making his alarm instead the sound of a police officer calling through a bullhorn "Come out with your hands up!" over and over again.

When Ben had made a second appeal to his brother to find something better, Zeke had apologetically explained that he could not. Years of living on the streets had trained him to sleep through almost anything—sirens, car alarms, a teacher's droning voice. The two exceptions are the sound of a police officer's voice and his mother's dreaded cowbell.

Ben had reluctantly deemed the latter preferable to the former, and now, three times a week, they are transported back to El Desierto, to knees chafing against threadbare carpet, to tired eyes and empty stomachs. Sometimes, Ben swears he cannot only hear their mother every time the cowbell sounds but see and smell her, too.

"What does she smell like?" Zeke had asked once.

"Bleach, of course," Ben replied. "Same as she always smelled." But in Zeke's mind, she smells not of bleach but of wax, the remnants of the prayer candles she'd lit every day.

This morning, as Ben rolls over, turning his back on both his brother and the pre-dawn light streaming in through the window, he mutters, "This girl better be worth it."

That is what Zeke has told Ben, that he wakes up every morning to go to the gym because he is trying to impress some new girl he's dating. That's where he claims to spend all his time, too, with her, at her place, anywhere she is. "But don't tell the others," he'd begged. "Not yet."

Ben, who never could keep anyone else's secret, told everyone.

"A girl, huh?" Henry had teased. "I thought you were going into the city to look for a job."

Zeke had blushed but hadn't said anything. Aside from the occasional jesting comment, his family let it drop. He could tell they were pleased that he had a girlfriend even if he wouldn't discuss or introduce her. To them, it was a sign of burgeoning normality; it could only be good for Zeke.

"Be back by nine," Ben reminds him now as Zeke eases out of the room.

"Sure," Zeke replies, even though he knows he will not be. The others are going into the city today to meet with some lawyer about the NPE. Even if Zeke didn't have to work, he'd try to get out of that. What's the point? What could he possibly contribute?

Into and out of the shower in five minutes. He pulls on khakis, a polo shirt, dress shoes. Departs before Ben wakes again and wonders why he's dressed for an engineering convention when he's supposed to be going to the gym.

Down the elevator and out the door, across the Compound and onto the first shuttle of the day, the 6 a.m. There are four others on board today. Often, he has it to himself. Nobody takes the first shuttle unless they have to, for a medical procedure or a court date. Otherwise, Cruors sleep in. There is no rush. In their lives, with so few obligations, time practically stands still.

On the bus ride into Los Angeles, he watches detective shows on his phone. This early in the morning they're aimed at the elderly—less blood and guts, a spry septuagenarian as the protagonist. On the Compound, Zeke steers clear of old people. They are so close to death they frighten him. They're shriveling up like rotting fruit. Their movements are slow. Their skin no longer clings to their bodies but droops and sags, giving the impression that, like tender, slow-cooked beef, it might fall off the bone any minute. They are so visibly knocking on death's door that the sight of them alone is enough to make Zeke shiver, to bring back memories of his father's horrifically decomposed body, to reinforce the notion that nothing is more important than staying alive forever.

But the elderly people on the morning detective shows don't have the same effect on Zeke. They are better put together, with carefully powdered skin that conceals their wrinkles and blemishes. Moreover, Zeke assumes that if they are television stars, they must be rich, and if they are rich, they must have Immortality. Their age is just a number, not an indicator of how close they are to death.

He is not ten minutes into the first show when a man seated behind him whistles. "You're looking mighty fancy. It's too early for a date. What, you got a job?"

Zeke turns to look at the man. He is middle-aged with thinning hair and a thickening mid-section. Ruddy skin and a workman's clothes. A glimmer of resentment leering permanently in his eyes. He reminds Zeke of his father.

Zeke knows how to talk to men like him. "A job?' he says, incredulous. "If only. Made the mistake of voting in the last election. Now I've got jury duty."

The man chuckles. "I don't know of no other Cruors that vote," he says. "What's the point? What they do don't affect our lives."

"Yeah, believe me. I regret it."

The man leaves him alone. Zeke breathes a sigh of relief. He's never voted in his life. Had the man asked who he'd voted for, he's not sure he could name a single politician.

When the bus pulls up beside the library, Zeke is the last person off. "Good luck with jury duty," the middle-aged man yells to him.

"Thanks," Zeke mumbles. He turns in the direction of the courthouse in case the man is watching.

Zeke, who never used to worry about much of anything, has become paranoid about everything. He doesn't like it—feeling like a fugitive, looking over his shoulder, taking a nonsensical route up and down the streets of Los Angeles to avoid detection. These high-stakes games of cat and mouse wear him down.

Several minutes later, he arrives at Min Lee's Dry Cleaning. It is small, inconspicuous, under-utilized. A shabby little store no wider than a shopping mall kiosk, tucked in between a discount jewelry store and a vegan restaurant in a neighborhood that's perpetually on the verge of gentrification.

Min is always at the dry cleaners no matter which shift Zeke works, dressed in faded, oversized clothes, feigning broken English to whoever stops by. She scurries back and forth like an industrious ant, head lowered, subservient smile on her face, the poster child of the dutiful immigrant, fresh off the boat and determined to make something of herself in a country she doesn't fully understand.

When Zeke walks through the front door, setting off a bell, claim ticket in hand, she shuffles toward him as if he is a customer.

"Mr. Zeke. Is good to see you again," she says, bowing her head.

"Hi, Min," he replies. "Is my dry cleaning ready? I'm about out of clean shirts."

It's a code. If anything were amiss—if, for example, he suspected he was being followed—he has a different line. He's never had to use that line before and isn't sure what would happen if he did. He hopes he never has to find out.

Min nods. "Your belongings are in the back. Get changed, get moving. You're already ten minutes late." Now her English is perfect, crisp, like biting into an apple on a summer's day. She has shifted from one Asian stereotype to another. She's no longer the dutiful immigrant trying to make it in America but the over-zealous tiger mom, a bossy micro-manager who runs a tight ship.

Zeke, ever the dutiful son, hurries through the shop and out the back door to see who he'll be today. He has been a masseur, a tutor, an interior designer, and once a Jehovah's Witness, any profession that will excuse his presence in a series of random homes for up to thirty minutes. Zeke likes this aspect of his job. It makes him feel like an undercover detective in one of his shows. He takes the roles more seriously than he should.

Today he finds navy cargo pants and a matching t-shirt, work boots and a baseball cap that reads "Three Js Plumbing." His ID indicates that he is one of the three Js—Jeff Holt from Tarzana. His vehicle—a white van with the Three Js logo on each door—is already stocked with a double-decker toolkit. Zeke opens it, checks his inventory. On the top layer, haphazardly tossed tools—wrenches, pliers, screwdrivers, several that Zeke, who isn't confident he knows how to use a plunger, doesn't recognize. Underneath is his inventory. He counts the number of clients on his list, totals the vials. The numbers match. He is good to go.

He directs the van to the first address. Nicholas and Michelle Parker. Maple St. Beverly Hills.

The van makes its way through downtown LA to the I-10, heading west. Of all the suburbs of Los Angeles, Beverly Hills is the most zealously oblivious to the world's problems. Its overstaffed police force pulls over suspicious looking vehicles, fines litterers as steeply as drunk drivers, discreetly deports the homeless. The city remains pristine, with tree-lined streets and beautiful buildings and stores carrying items that only Immortals can afford.

As the van exits the freeway, Zeke's phone buzzes. Henry: *Where are you?*

Zeke is staring at the message, debating how to respond, when the phone buzzes again. Ben: *Zeke, we're waiting for you.*

Zeke is at a loss. He usually moves through life unseen, the world equally indifferent to his presence and his absence. He has been gone for entire days without anyone noticing. Why are they looking for him now?

He cannot think of how to respond, so he decides not to. He puts his phone in his back pocket and gets out of the van. He has work to do.

The Parker home is stucco, not large, but comfortable, with a pool out back and a carefully maintained rose garden in front. In another city, it would belong to a middle-class family, a teacher's home or a civil servant's. But in Beverly Hills, it belongs to two successful attorneys; it's probably worth six million dollars.

Zeke removes his toolkit and walks to the front door. He takes in the aroma of roses, lets their scent calm his nerves. He's been doing this job for nearly six months, but still, it makes him anxious. Every time he approaches a house, he feels like a bank robber, entering a different branch of the local savings and loan, hoping to pull off a high-risk heist. Henry would say if a job makes you feel this way, you probably shouldn't be doing it, but for Zeke, quitting has never been an option. It's a game of Russian Roulette with a bullet in one chamber and Immortality in the other five. He'll take his chances.

The front door opens before he can ring the bell. Nicholas is waiting for him with his darting, suspicious green eyes.

"Jeff, good to see you," Nicholas says, patting Zeke on the back.

Zeke cringes. Most people don't know their plumber by name. Moreover, there is a protocol, a series of comments and responses that Zeke and his clients are to exchange every week. But Nicholas has never had the wherewithal to follow protocol.

"You have a plumbing problem, Mr. Parker?" Zeke asks because he is supposed to, in case the room is bugged. In case Nicholas is.

But Nicholas doesn't respond. He is already making his way through the house, leaving Zeke to follow. The Parkers' home is all white marble and crystal chandeliers—an attempt to compensate for size with opulence. The house intimidates Zeke, but it also improves his posture. To him, it's regal, like a palace or a fancy hotel.

At the back of the house is a small den with a television as wide as the wall and nearly as tall. Zeke always hopes it will be on during one of his visits. He longs to see his favorite television characters projected to nearly his size in high definition. But the television is never on.

Michelle Parker sits on the sofa, legs crossed, toes painted, gossip magazine in her hands. She doesn't look up when Zeke enters.

Zeke sets his toolkit on the floor and extracts two vials and two sterile needles. He places them on the TV stand with care. If any of them break or spill, it's his neck.

Behind him, Nicholas sits in a wooden rocking chair, urging it back and forth with vigor as though it is a playground swing. His eyes dart from the door to the window and back again. Zeke knows he's looking for spies, cameras, audio recorders. It's a silly habit. If anyone wanted to bug the Parker home, Nicholas would have no way of knowing it. Zeke tries to ignore him. Nicholas's anxiety can be contagious.

As Zeke approaches, Nicholas stops rocking, plants his feet firmly on the floor, rolls up his sleeve and stares at the television screen with such intensity that Zeke glances back to see if he's turned it on. He has not.

One quick injection a week, that's all. Simple. Except, if caught, the penalties are stiff. Armed robbery stiff. Like Zeke, Nicholas Parker and his wife will be robbing a bank every week for the rest of their lives.

"I never have liked shots," Nicholas says as Zeke injects him. He says this every week.

"But it's worth it, right?" Zeke asks, smiling at him as he removes the needle and moves onto Michelle.

Nicholas looks at him and nods. "For Immortality? Absolutely."

Zeke doesn't know where the blood comes from; he only knows it's cheaper. How much cheaper? About two-thirds, apparently, or at least that's what they charge their clients. Zeke doesn't ask questions. It's one of the reasons Min hired him.

He found the job through one of the Compound's resident thugs, who was well-connected in the underworld and knew desperation when he saw it.

"So, I go into LA three times a week, give a bunch of people the Infinity Serum, and in exchange, get Immortality myself?" Zeke had asked, repeating the offer almost verbatim to be sure he understood.

"That's right," his contact confirmed. "It's black-market shit. Imported from China, probably. A billion people over there who'll do anything for a buck."

"Why are you giving this job to me?" Zeke had asked. "Why aren't you doing it?"

His contact had shrugged. "I got enough on my plate right now. And to me, Immortality ain't the be all end all, you know?"

"You'd rather have money than live forever?" Zeke asked.

"What's the point of living forever if you don't have money?"

Zeke does the job for Immortality, but he likes the work, too. He goes from house to house through his client list. The Barbers are filthy rich but always on the lookout for a bargain. Brandon Figueroa has leukemia, and

Mary Ann Justice's ovarian cancer has spread throughout her body. Eve Bryant is the mistress of some Hollywood bigshot who agreed to gift her Immortality, but only the cut-rate, black-market version.

These are his most vocal clients, the ones whose stories come bursting out of them like soda from a shaken can. There are plenty of others who are more like the Parkers—edgy, nervous, barely able to get a word out—and still others who are calm but discreet, afraid that anything they say may be used against them. Zeke prefers the clients who speak, but he doesn't mind the silent ones either. He dreads only the difficult ones, like John Mosley, the scrawny little accountant who always wants to examine the vial of Infinity Serum before he's injected. Who asks questions Zeke can't answer, like 'Why is it lighter this week?' and 'Where does it come from?' Sometimes he asks for a different vial of blood; sometimes he refuses the Serum altogether. "It smells funny," he'll say. Or "It looks off."

"You might as well take it, Mr. Mosley," Zeke will reply. "You've already paid for it."

"I want a refund," he'll insist, crossing one leg over the other. Twisting his head until his chin is over his shoulder.

"You know it doesn't work like that, Mr. Mosley," Zeke says.

Then John Mosley, depending on his mood, sulks or yells. Once, he threw a vial of serum at Zeke's chest, shattering it against his pale blue shirt, making him look like the victim of a violent attack. "You're trying to poison me," he'd screamed, and Zeke, frightened that his neighbors might hear, had fled. There had been no point in staying anyway. John Mosley had already destroyed his weekly allotment of Infinity Serum.

Every Monday, when Zeke is given his client list, he hopes John Mosley's name won't be on it, that he's someone else's problem for once, but his name is always there, a persistent weed lingering in the garden, even as the flowers around it come and go.

As Zeke's van approaches John Mosley's apartment, his phone buzzes again. He's been getting messages all day. First urgent, then annoyed, now concerned. Before he gets out of the van, he types a quick response. *I'm fine. With girlfriend.*

Before he makes it to Mr. Mosley's door, he receives four more messages.

Henry: *What???*

Ben: *You dumbass. You were supposed to come into the city with us today. How about a little solidarity?*

Remy: *Okay. Glad you're okay.*

Henry: *Seriously, Zeke?*

Zeke turns his phone off. He doesn't want to think about his family right now.

Mr. Mosley, who has no family, lets Zeke into his spotless, mid-century modern living room, then retreats to his couch without a word. Zeke's nose perks up at the scent of baking bread. It always smells like food in Mr. Mosley's apartment.

"Hi, Mr. Mosley," Zeke says.

Mr. Mosley nods in acknowledgment, but he neither speaks nor looks up.

"Here's your Infinity Serum," Zeke says, removing a vial from his tool-kit. "Do you want to inspect it?"

Mr. Mosley shakes his head. "No," he says. "Go ahead, Jeff. Stick it to me."

"You seem down today, Mr. Mosley," Zeke says as he injects the liquid into his client's vein.

"Do I?" Mr. Mosley asks. "It's kind of you to notice. My rabbi has asked me not to return to synagogue. Can you believe it? A rabbi asking that of one of his congregants. I thought a house of worship was supposed to be a refuge for anyone, but apparently, if you're odd or unpleasant enough, you can be kicked to the curb, like a drunk trying to board an airplane."

Zeke does his best to act surprised. "Did he tell you why?" he asks as he repacks his bag.

"He says I'm 'ruining services for everyone else,'" Mr. Mosley huffs, his fingers bent in air quotes. "Look, I'm a little vocal. I know I am. I can be nosy, suspicious. I have no volume control. But I'm not malicious. I'm not some pervert who gropes women or leers at little boys. I don't spit or swear. I never fall asleep during services. I try. I'm just a little vocal."

"Well, can you go to another church?" Zeke asks. He doubts it. If John Mosley is anything like Zeke's mom, there is only one place of worship for him, one rabbi he trusts, one place he feels he belongs.

Sure enough, John Mosley shakes his head. "It's not the same. I've been going to Beth Shalom since I was a little boy. My grandfather went there. My parents met there. It's like the IRS repossessing the family farm. Something that's always been there, that I thought would always be there, swept out from under me like that." He snaps his fingers, lowers his eyes.

"I'm sorry," Zeke says.

"Thank you." He looks over at Zeke curiously, eying his scrawny provider from head to toe. "Tell me something, Jeff," he says. "Why do you still come around here? I've treated you abominably."

Zeke frowns. "Well, it's my job, Mr. Mosley."

"It's your job, sure, but every provider I had before you stormed out in a huff, vowing never to work with me again. Hell, somebody from Hemo-Imposter even called and said if another provider refused to work with me, they'd cut off my service."

Zeke shrugs. "I'll never refuse to work with you, Mr. Mosley." It had never occurred to him that he could. To him, difficult clients and quirky personalities are part of the job.

"Thank you," Mr. Mosley says. "But to be honest, I'm starting to wonder what I'm doing here. My whole life I've pinched and saved, so I have plenty of money, but I have no family, no friends, and now I don't even have my synagogue anymore. What's the point of living forever if you don't have anything to live for?"

Zeke answers intuitively because, for him, it has never been about loved ones or a greater purpose. "The point of living forever," he says, "is that the alternative is death."

The van pulls into Min Lee's and Zeke gets out, leaving his toolkit to be refilled for the next plumber. Min is waiting for him, sitting at her small desk with nothing but a computer, a notepad, and a pen amongst the array of large dry-cleaning machines that whiz and whirr continuously. She told him once that the sound of the machines drove her crazy. The next time he'd come, he'd given her noise cancelling headphones. The gesture had brought tears to her eyes.

"Hi, Min," he greets her.

She nods. "Come on, Zeke. Let's pay you and send you on your way."

He follows Min through the laundry to the small apartment at the back, a room with twin beds and tulip wallpaper, a King James Bible on the nightstand. Zeke sits on the bed and rolls up his sleeve while Min goes to the bookshelf, removes a book, and extracts a vial of Infinity Serum hidden inside.

Zeke extends his arm and watches as she injects the thick red liquid into his veins. He imagines he can feel it coursing through his body, making him stronger and better, making him invincible. Hard to believe that just fifteen years ago, Immortality had been nothing more than a super-power, reserved for the spandex-clad heroes of comic books.

"Rest for thirty minutes," Min advises as she finishes up.

Zeke nods and stretches out on the bed, not bothering to peel back the covers. He is asleep within minutes. But Zeke no longer dreams of homelessness, or of torturous deaths and rotting corpses. Now his dreams are of daredevils and superheroes and the promises of eternal tomorrows.

CHAPTER 7

Then

"Maybe I should get a real career," Sabrina speculates as they lie in bed together watching the sun set over the Pacific through the window.

"What are you talking about?" Patton asks, running his fingers through her hair. "You have a real career."

"I mean, I do, I guess. But I thought it might be nice to try something different. I've been modeling since I was twelve." She leans back, resting her head against him. He has a firm, broad chest that is better than any pillow.

"Like what?" he asks. "An actress?"

No. She cannot act. She never could. She'd been in three school plays growing up, and every time she'd been given a part with no lines: a tree, a lamb, a life-sized doll.

"I don't know. A journalist, maybe?"

Patton groans. "Why? Nobody even likes journalists."

She sits up, indignant, and pulls the sheet up over her breasts. "That's not true," she insists. "Journalists can do a lot of good."

"And they can annoy the hell out of people," he tugs gently on her elbow, coaxing her back into his arms. "I didn't mean to upset you. I only meant that we should all play to our strengths. I excel at making money, so I'm a banker. You are one of the most beautiful women in the world. You should be a model."

"But what if I'm a great writer, too?"

"And what if I'm great at archery? Any of us could have hidden talents. Sure. But you have to spend years, decades even, honing your skill. You can't just pick something up and expect to be good at it."

Sabrina frowns. "So, I'll work at it and get good."

He kisses her on the forehead. "Don't," he tells her. "Stay beautiful and delightful and fun."

The next morning, after he leaves for work, she slips into his terrycloth bathrobe and tiptoes around the house, exploring. She looks in drawers and closets, opens doors to rooms she's never seen before. You can learn a lot about a man from his house. Her last boyfriend, Ricardo, had been a closet nerd with stacks of *Dungeons & Dragons* books in his mancave, posters of wizards on the walls. Nikhil, ostensibly vegan, had hidden packets of beef jerky in his underwear drawer. Zibrek had a collection of troll dolls and a box of blond toupees. Some of her friends had found worse digging through their lovers' belongings: evidence of wives that had never been mentioned, whips and handcuffs, cameras planted throughout the house, including in the bathrooms, and once, a stash of child pornography.

But so far, Patton doesn't appear to have any secrets. Is he above board or boring? She can't decide. When she'd asked, on their first date, what he liked to do for fun, he'd snorted. "I work eighteen hours a day, six days a week. When I'm not working, I spend time with my daughters. Hobbies are for children."

But all work and no play makes Patton a dull boy. There must be more to him than that.

As she makes her way down the hall, she opens an unmarked door to her left. Inside, there is a blast of color so at odds with the careful off-whites of the rest of the house that Sabrina has to wait for her eyes to adjust before entering. At first, she thinks she has discovered the chink in Patton's armor. His creative or playful or strange side. But no, this room isn't his. It belongs to his daughters.

Sabrina doesn't know much about them. They are nine and eleven, prefer the beach to the park and the mall to both. The older girl has just started wearing bras; the younger one sometimes steals them, puts them on and stuffs them with tissue paper. Patton doesn't know how to handle any of this, so he doesn't. He waits until the weekend is over and then reports back to his ex-wife who keeps the girls most of the time.

Sabrina steps tentatively into the room. She has never felt guilty snooping around the homes of boyfriends, but breaching the trust of two little girls she hardly knows feels wrong. She considers turning back, but curiosity gets the better of her.

The room is such an aggressive shade of yellow that it feels like it's trying to force cheeriness on its inhabitants. The bedspreads are tributes to bands Sabrina has never heard of. The wall is covered with digital posters of teen idols. In the closet are dresses and sweaters from the teen lines of high-end designers, knee-high boots, two- and three-inch heels. A shared vanity is covered in make-up and hair products. A full-length mirror occupies a prime position against one wall. Underneath it, a scale. On the small wooden bedside table, a stack of magazines threatens to topple over: *Teen Vogue, Seventeen, Modern Teen.* Under the pillows, diaries.

Sabrina picks one up and flips through its pages. *Mom won't let me dye my hair blonde. A HOT LIST got passed around school today. I was 9th. That bitch Natalie was 7th. I don't care if she has c-cups, I'm prettier than her!*

I've gained 3 pounds since the last time I visited Dad. When he first saw me today, he pinched my side and said I was getting fat. Must try Celery Slimdown. DISCIPLINE!

Sabrina sets it down and reaches for the other one. *I've decided I will be a movie star when I grow up because I want to be beautiful. Like Lola Kidd. She's so pretty. Dad is always talking about how gorgeous she is. When I tell him I want to look like her, he says I shouldn't count on it because I have my mom's nose. But that's an easy fix. I just have to get a nose job.* Seventeen *says purple lipstick is in, but all of my lipstick is pink. Is it better to wear pink lipstick or none at all? Must get purple lipstick!!! I wish Jake would look at me the way he looks at Dara. Is it wrong to pray to be pretty?*

Sabrina, who has always been the most beautiful woman in the room, cannot relate to these girls. Sabrina, who has been imprisoned by beauty her entire life, relates to these girls perfectly.

She replaces the journals and slips out of the room, closing the door behind her. When she returns to the master bedroom, she finds her phone and calls her editor.

"Jonas? This is Sabrina. You know your idea for an Eternity Column? I'll do it."

Now

It wasn't easy asking Darcy for a favor. Her sister is so arrogant, so condescending, so confident that Sabrina is nothing but a porcelain doll, pretty and fragile with an empty head. Darcy hadn't made it easy for her either. She'd asked so many questions. "What do you mean, suspicious regrade results? Who are these people? How do you know them? What makes you think this is legitimate?"

Sabrina dodged and demurred until, at last, Darcy agreed to meet them, all of them, the next day for lunch at some cheese-heavy Italian restaurant Sabrina wouldn't normally set foot in. When Sabrina hung up, she wondered if she'd made a mistake. Two misgraded examinations isn't evidence of much, but her gut tells her there's more here, and she sees no harm in digging a little deeper on the off chance she's right.

The Cruors, in the midst of celebrating Remy and Miguel's regrade results, slightly drunk off cheap beer and champagne, had been happy to travel into LA

"I can't believe there's a lawyer who'll talk to us," Remy had said, amazed. The others were equally incredulous. Only Ben had ever spoken to a lawyer before, a public defender, once, when he was caught shoplifting. To the others, an attorney was as inaccessible as a celebrity.

Now, as they all settle into a large, round table crammed into the back of the restaurant, Sabrina expects her sister to be skeptical. When she was a child, Darcy could eat an entire chicken, picking the meat off the bones with her teeth, faster than Sabrina could finish a drumstick. Sabrina suspects she and the Cruors will receive the same treatment as the chicken. Darcy will strip them down to their bare bones in a matter of seconds, ripping through any bullshit or bias they might be clinging to.

But as it happens, Darcy has long been skeptical of the NPE. "I saw an article a year or two ago suggesting steps the NPE should take to ensure fairness in the exam. One involved randomly distributing exams across the country so that any grader might get exams from anywhere instead of from his local district. Another was to remove any identifying information from the exams, including school attended. The NPE declined to do either." Her food remains untouched on the table. She sips water from a transparent plastic glass as she thinks.

"I think you're right that there's something suspicious here. If fewer than ten people nationwide pass the NPE on regrade in any given year and now two students from the same school have, well, it may be a single incompetent grader, but it may be something more."

She turns to Malachi, who has accompanied the Hudsons and Miguel into Los Angeles. "Let's send your exam in for a regrade, too," she suggests. "I'll pay."

"Thank you," Malachi says. He has been transformed by the news that Miguel and Remy have passed on regrade. The fire has returned to his eyes, the confidence to his voice.

"Is there anything we can be doing in the meantime?" Remy asks. "The regrade process takes at least two weeks."

"There is," Darcy replies. "The NPE publishes the passage rates for every high school nationwide. What we need to do is investigate the data, going back to when the Compounds opened, and look for irregularities in a school's performance. Have certain Compounds gone multiple years in a row without a single student passing? Have other high schools seen a sudden, sustained boost in their performance, not just for one year—that could be the result of a particularly strong cohort—but for several years in a row?"

"Why do we need to look at the data nationwide?" Miguel asks. "We know the person who misgraded our exams is in Southern California District 8."

Remy answers him. "If this is happening here, there's a chance it's happening elsewhere, too."

Darcy nods. "Exactly. It's a lot of data. It's not going to be easy. But we'll divide it up and make our way through it. Don't sacrifice thoroughness for the sake of speed. We don't want to miss anything. Once we have the results, we'll reconvene to discuss how to proceed."

Sabrina watches the scene before her unfold, fascinated. She has never seen her sister in a professional capacity before. The Darcy here bears little resemblance to the sarcastic blob who used to grumble through family dinners.

Darcy turns to Remy. "So, you're the Remy Hudson I read about in the *Los Angeles Times*," she says.

Remy blushes and nods. Sabrina clutches the bottom of her seat.

"I was devastated when I read that you'd failed. I wrote a letter to the editor ranting that if a bright, motivated student like you couldn't get into college, the Compounds are clearly failing to educate Cruor children effectively."

"You did?" Remy asks. Sabrina is constantly surprised by the Cruors' humility, their inability to believe that anyone on the Outside would take an interest in them.

"Sure. It wasn't published, but it should have been. Is Brian Sa going to write a follow-up telling the world you passed?"

Remy looks at her curiously. Ben turns to Sabrina. Miguel and Malachi exchange glances.

Sabrina isn't sure why she hasn't told anyone about her new job. Initially, she was afraid that taking a position with the *Times* might be seen as a sign that she wasn't serious about modeling anymore, that Xiomara Khan might let her go, that designers and photographers would feel uncomfortable working with her knowing that anything they said or did might end up in the paper.

Then there was the matter of Immortality. The men who gifted her eternal life wanted a certain kind of girl. She was their arm candy, their trophy, the pretty bimbo who didn't understand much but giggled a lot. Journalism was none of that. Journalism suggested intelligence, resourcefulness, a level of self-reliance that would have made even the best of her ex-boyfriends uncomfortable.

She'd worried, too, that she wouldn't be able to cut it. She had no journalism degree and no experience. She hadn't written much of anything since high school. She'd gotten the job not because the writing sample she'd submitted had blown anyone away but the way she'd always gotten everything: by sleeping with the editor. If she told people she was a reporter, she'd have to tell them if she got fired, too, and early on, she was certain that she would be. She was pretty, not talented. She felt like an impostor.

In the end, it had simply been easiest not to tell. Her secret had made her feel like a spy with an alter ego, and that had given her a certain freedom that made her a better reporter. She didn't have to worry about what anyone would expect from someone like her; she didn't have to consider what they would think. Her articles could be open, honest, intelligent.

But now the jig is up. She'd known by introducing the Cruors to Darcy she risked exposure, but she'd done it anyway. It was worth it, she'd decided, in case there was something bigger here. As she prepares to confess, she feels threatened and vulnerable, but she also feels relieved.

"Darcy," she says, looking at her older sister, her arch nemesis since childhood, the one person who has been consistently immune to her charms. "I'm Brian Sa."

She expects her sister to laugh or snort. To Darcy's credit, she does not. She contemplates Sabrina's words, puts the pieces together. "Brian Sa is an anagram," she realizes. "And that's how you know these guys," she says, indicating the Cruors.

Sabrina nods.

"How long?"

"Since the Eternity Column started." She pauses, uncharacteristically self-conscious. "I started it, basically."

"It's fantastic, isn't it?" says Henry.

"Yes." Darcy looks at him then back at Sabrina. "It is."

After the others have returned to the Compound, Sabrina and Darcy walk around the city, having a real conversation for the first time in their lives. Sabrina has little faith that they will get through it without an argument. Their shared history has left them uncharitable toward one another. One insensitive remark threatens to derail any progress, but at least they're talking.

"I love the Eternity Column," Darcy says. "I read it every week. I email it around the office. I never would have guessed you were capable of something like that."

"No, why would you have?" Sabrina says. You never took me seriously, she thinks. "That's not how Mom and Dad presented me when I was small. That's not how I presented myself when I got older."

They pause at a stoplight. "I'm sorry," Darcy mutters. "I guess that was rude."

"Don't worry about it," Sabrina replies. "In fact, why don't we not worry about anything we've said or done to each other in the past. Why don't we start fresh?"

Darcy hesitates. "I'd like that," she says, "but there's something I need to tell you first."

"What is it?" Sabrina asks, suddenly nervous.

Darcy takes a deep breath. "Dom doesn't want Immortality. Prince is out."

The next morning Sabrina decamps to a local coffee shop before her boyfriend Milo wakes up. She has work to do, and he would hinder it. He can't sit still, can't stand it if other people are sitting still. Even when he's learning his lines—he's the star of a hit television show—he paces the room looking aggravated. Half the time, he can't be bothered to learn his lines at all. If Sabrina were to try to work at home, he would talk to her, encourage her to go hiking, go surfing, go swimming, have sex in the pool. She's convinced every new guy she dates is stranger than the last.

Sabrina heads to a coffee shop on the other side of the freeway, an untrendy chain that Milo would never set foot in. She plans to be wonderfully productive today, to discover the extent of the NPE scandal, to find any smoking gun that might be out there. Darcy has assigned her to analyze test scores in California, which means she should find suspicious results in Southern California District 8 if nowhere else.

She begins her work with the best of intentions, but her mind wanders. She hadn't been able to sleep last night or to focus during the evening. She's consumed by dread. It's her father's will. If Dom is out, it's between Darcy and her. No, it's between some as yet unnamed cause of Darcy's and her. One step away from Immortality and her position has never been weaker. A model needs Immortality. She has to stay young and attractive or she's out of a job. But a journalist can age without consequence; grey hair lends dignity, the occasional wrinkle gravitas. The truth—that beauty is so firmly intertwined with Sabrina's identity that she can't bear to give it up regardless of professional necessity—will not be convincing to Darcy. She'll tell Sabrina to get over it, to tell Xiomara Khan to shove it, to spit in the faces of Milo and Leroy and Hayes and every guy like them. But Darcy still doesn't get it. To Sabrina, losing her beauty is like Samson losing his hair; it would render her weak and powerless, a shell of her former self.

She is so distracted by her father's will that she can't focus on the NPE scandal. She jots down arguments for her own Immortality in bullet points. She is pleased when Xiomara's assistant calls to tell her she's been booked by Brikon H, the gender-neutral designer who's made tulle in casual wear trendy. But when she hangs up, she realizes she's dreading the shoot. It's become more difficult for her to pose for hours at a time. She doesn't have the patience for it anymore.

That evening, she has a phone conference with Darcy and the Cruors to discuss progress. Sabrina tells them, truthfully, that she hasn't found anything yet but fails to mention that she hasn't really looked. Remy, Ben, Henry, and Miguel have all come up empty, too, and Sabrina's heart sags. She has sent them all on a wild goose chase in search of a story that isn't there.

"So, we're the only Compound this has happened to?" Remy says. "None of us have come across any other suspicious data?"

"I have," Darcy says. "In New England. Three Compounds there used to have passage rates of between twenty and thirty percent. The last six years, those rates have been cut in half."

"But there are still Cruors passing?" Remy asks.

"There are," Darcy acknowledges. "My guess is that the grader there is savvier than the one here. He doesn't triage students like Remy who are so strong that their failure would raise suspicion. He only nixes students who are borderline."

"Smart," Miguel says. "If Remy and Malachi had passed, but I hadn't, no one would have raised an eyebrow."

It's exactly what Sabrina was thinking, but she would never have said it.

"What I haven't been able to find," Darcy continues, "is any school or schools with a corresponding jump in scores."

"Maybe the students who are benefiting don't all go to the same school. Maybe they have the same tutor or attend the same church or live in the same neighborhood," Remy suggests.

"That's a good point," Darcy says. "A network of cheaters could come about in a hundred different ways."

"Well, let's keep going," Sabrina suggests, gazing guiltily at her computer screen. "We've barely scratched the surface."

Over the next couple of weeks, the evidence trickles in: nearly three dozen Compounds with passage rates that have plummeted with no obvious cause, and twenty-five schools that have seen an inexplicable and sustained jump in scores that began the same year the passage rate at the local Compounds declined.

"I never imagined it would be this widespread," Sabrina exclaims. She had expected to find evidence of cheating at two or three schools in one or two locations, but nothing like this.

"It's not quite the Wagner-McQuaid Robotics Scandal, but it's pretty bad." Darcy, who always assumes the rich screw the poor where they can, is surprised they haven't found worse.

For the first time since she became a journalist, Sabrina fully comprehends the significance of what she's doing. She's uncovering injustices, changing lives. When Darcy had talked about her various human rights projects, they'd always seemed distant and abstract. But Remy isn't abstract. Miguel and Malachi aren't abstract. Sabrina wraps her arms around her body, anxious, suddenly, about the gravity of what she's undertaken. She has to get this right. It's the most important thing she's ever done.

Two weeks in, Malachi announces that his regrade results have come back. He has passed, too, his score even higher than Remy's. They are relieved but not surprised.

As Sabrina combs through her data, she discovers that both Compound 78 and Compound 4, about twenty miles to the north of it, have had one hundred percent failure rates for the past decade until Remy, Malachi and Miguel's regrades. They are in the same district with the same grader. Still, it takes another week before Sabrina discovers the school that's benefiting from their failure.

"It's called Fasching Prep," she tells the others, her voice breathy with excitement. "It's a private school in the Inland Empire. Their passage rate went from fifty-eight percent to eighty-one percent exactly a decade ago, and it's remained high ever since."

The others cheer. Every time they have discovered another school that cheated, it has felt like a victory, but this time—this school, this victory—feels different. It is so much more personal. Finding Fasching Prep changes everything. They're eager for action now, impatient to bring the cheaters down.

"What's next?" Henry asks. "Do we turn everything we've found into the NPE or the police or the FBI?"

"First, we finish going through the data," Darcy insists.

"Okay, but then what?" Henry presses.

"We'll look at what we have when we're done and decide," Darcy says.

But Darcy has a shortcoming, Sabrina realizes. She is used to writing reports that document abuses but don't change anything. She doesn't expect anything to come of this. She is not an advocate but a witness and a jaded one at that. She has gotten them this far but can lead them no further.

"I have another idea," Sabrina says. "I'm going to speak to my editor and tell him what we've found. Maybe the *Times* can scrounge up some money to pay for more regrades, for other Cruors at other schools. If we find that Cruors have been systematically failed when they should have passed, it'll be the final nail in the coffin."

"And those Cruors will get to go to college," Remy adds.

Sabrina blushes. She had been so focused on the crime, she had forgotten the victims.

"It does seem especially cruel to target Cruors, doesn't it?" Miguel says. "We can't afford to get a regrade or retake the exam. We're out of luck when something like this happens."

"That's why we were targeted in the first place," Remy says. "We don't have any recourse. They're much less likely to be caught."

"But it is pretty damn heartless," Sabrina says. "I wonder what these graders got in exchange for screwing poor Cruor kids."

As her car pulls into the garage at Milo's, Sabrina is lost in thought.

She has secured $25,000 for regrades from the *Los Angeles Times*, $5,000 from Remy's brother Henry, and Darcy is tossing in another $10,000. Sabrina wants to put $50,000 total into the regrades, enabling them to submit ten at a time, so she chips in the last $10,000 herself, even though she can't really afford it. She's never accumulated much in the way of savings. Still, they expect to get most of the money back, to be able to submit more names for regrades. She is not naïve enough to think they can identify every Cruor who has been cheated out of a future, but they have to try.

Sabrina is so lost in thought that she doesn't notice Milo sitting in an armchair in the dark until he says, "Where have you been?"

She jumps and drops her keys which clatter against the concrete floor like discordant wind chimes "Milo, Jesus," she says. "I didn't see you there."

He doesn't get up. He doesn't even move, and Milo is always moving.

"Can I mix you a drink?" Sabrina asks. She can tell that he's angry, that something is seriously wrong, but she can't imagine what it could be.

"I asked where you've been," he repeats. Even his lips are still. He has become a ventriloquist's dummy, perched atop a leather chair.

"Various places. Why?" Sabrina doesn't like any of this. It reminds her of the haunted houses she used to go to as a teenager, where something frightening could jump out any minute, where dread, more than fear, was a constant companion.

"What were you doing at the *LA Times*?" he asks. He stands, moves toward her in three long steps, and seizes her arm with unexpected force. "Huh?"

"Let go of me," Sabrina says, tugging her arm away. "I was helping a friend, that's all."

He looks hesitant, as though whatever he was expecting it wasn't that. "Which friend?"

"Nial Mandel. He's the gossip columnist," she says. "He missed the after party at London's last night and asked me to help him reconstruct it."

Milo believes her, she can tell, but he also doubles down when wrong. He seizes her arm again. "Were you doing a tell-all about me, you little bitch? Sharing my habits and secrets and what I'm like in the bedroom for a measly ten grand?"

Sabrina rolls her eyes at Milo as if he's being ridiculous. "The *LA Times* isn't a tabloid. They don't pay for celebrity gossip."

Milo seems off-balance, torn between pursuing this and backing off.

"How did you know where I was anyway?" Sabrina asks.

"I tracked your phone," Milo answers. He is honest because he doesn't think he's done anything wrong. To him, as to all of the others, she is property; he can do with her as he pleases.

"I didn't give you permission to track me," Sabrina whispers. Quite the opposite, in fact. When they'd first started dating, she had listed unauthorized tracking as a deal breaker. She'd had too many possessive boyfriends over the years, too little privacy. She has suspected for some time that Milo has disregarded her wishes. Now, she knows he has. She feels a headache coming on. She can't do this anymore. She yanks her arm free again and turns toward the door.

"Where do you think you're going?" he asks as she turns the handle.

"Anywhere but here," she replies. "I'll send someone for my things."

"You walk out that door, you can say goodbye to Immortality."

Sabrina freezes in the doorway. She turns to face him and sees that he's grinning, his eyes dancing with victory. *I've got you now, haven't I?*

Sabrina is sickened by the sight of him. She is sickened by herself. "I'm not your whore," she says, pushing the words out of her mouth before she loses courage. And then she walks away, closing the door in Milo's face.

She slips into her car, hopped up on adrenaline. She wants to laugh, to dance, to spar, to scream. She has never stood up to a boyfriend before. Not like that. Usually, she sneaks out in the middle of the day when no one is around to see or stop her. Her exes return home to discover her half of the closet empty, her cosmetics no longer crowding the medicine cabinet. She never leaves a note; it would be overkill. Then the phone calls begin, angry, apologetic, desperate. But by then, it's too late. Sabrina never likes any of these guys enough to go back to them.

There is something freeing, Sabrina decides, in calling it quits to a guy's face, in leaving him behind, standing there, staring after you. She only wishes she had recorded the encounter, so she could show Milo's adoring fans what he's really like.

Sabrina's liberation is short-lived. As she settles into her Tesla, she realizes she has nowhere to go. She could check into a hotel, she supposes, spend the night soaking in a bubble bath and ordering room service. But for once, Sabrina doesn't want luxury. She wants a friend. A friend and a bottle of wine. A shoulder to cry on. A wedge of chocolate cake. She hasn't had chocolate cake in over a decade. The trouble is Sabrina doesn't have friends. That is, she has tons of friends, but she doesn't trust any of them. They're all too much like her, or like she was: shallow, untrustworthy, cut-throat. She directs her car to the little boutique in West Hollywood that only A-listers know about.

Her phone dings. Darcy: *I've listed the names and contact information of the relevant Compound principals in the attached spreadsheet. Let me know if you need more. D*

She stares at the message for a full minute and then redirects the car to her sister's place.

She doesn't intend to stay. She plans to eat her sister's chocolate cake and triple cream brie and then flee to that West Hollywood boutique. She doesn't expect Darcy to offer either. Her sister likes her privacy; her sister doesn't like her.

Sabrina doesn't think to call first—if she's honest, she's still not very good at being considerate. She shows up at the entrance to her sister's building, buzzes to be let in. She's never been to Darcy's place before, she realizes.

Darcy, in faded navy pajamas with soft yellow ducks on them (she looks absurd, Sabrina thinks), shows no surprise at finding her little sister on her doorstep.

"Come on in," she says. Just like that. No questions asked. Sabrina, who had been preparing a monologue to explain her presence here, follows her inside gratefully.

The apartment looks like a hotel lobby, safe and inoffensive. Beige furniture, generic landscapes on the wall. You couldn't learn anything about the person who lives here by looking around this room, Sabrina thinks, except that she doesn't care about décor.

"It's bland, I know," Darcy says apologetically, handing her sister a glass of wine.

"No," Sabrina corrects. "It's neutral. You're choosing not to make a statement here, that's all."

"No, not here," Darcy agrees. "When I make a statement at all, I do it through my work."

Sabrina cannot help but think there is something admirable about this. It reflects an impressive depth, especially for an Angeleno.

"Can I get you anything else?" Darcy asks as Sabrina sinks into the couch.

"Cheese," Sabrina answers. "And chocolate cake if you have any."

Darcy looks at her suspiciously.

"Another break-up," she explains, hoping that will suffice for now.

Darcy nods and heads to the kitchen.

"So, why's this one different?" she asks as she returns to the sitting room juggling two plates, a box of crackers, three cheeses and a chocolate cake.

Sabrina shakes her head. "He's not. I am."

Darcy looks at her thoughtfully. "Yes, you are."

Sabrina cuts a generous wedge of chocolate cake, then brings it up to her face and takes a bite out of it, smearing chocolate frosting across the bottom of her nose.

"Oh my god," she mutters, her mouth gooey with sugar and butter. "That is divine."

Darcy watches, amused, as her sister takes a second bite and then a third.

"So, I dumped him," she says when she has paused to cut another slice.

"Don't worry," Darcy says, picking at crumbles of stilton. "I'm sure the next one will be along soon."

"God, I hope not. I could use a break."

Darcy raises her eyebrows. Sabrina hasn't been single since she was a child. "Really?"

"You don't think I can manage without a man?"

"Oh, I know you can," Darcy says. "I've always known that. But you've never wanted to before."

Sabrina thinks about this, pushing her lower lip out slightly. "No," she says. "I suppose I haven't."

"Have you considered taking a break from modeling while you're at it? Focusing on this budding journalism career instead?"

Sabrina answers without thinking. "If I go long enough without a boyfriend, I'll have no choice but to give up modeling."

And Darcy, sharp, clever Darcy, puts two and two together. "Oh, I see," she mutters. "Well, it wouldn't be the worst thing in the world, would it? To age? To give up modeling and have a successful career as a journalist instead?"

"I can't imagine it," Sabrina admits.

She expects Darcy to chastise her, to accuse her of being vain and superficial. But instead, Darcy says, "Well, lately, it seems like you've been doing all sorts of things you never imagined you would."

The bottle of wine is empty now, and Darcy stands to recycle it and get another one. "I have a spare bedroom," she says when her back is to Sabrina. "You can stay as long as you want."

It is such an unexpected offer that Sabrina feels tears spring to her eyes. She can't remember the last time someone went out of their way to help her.

Sabrina is grateful to Darcy, both for taking her in and for helping with the NPE investigation, but Darcy's caution and adherence to procedure are starting to impede their progress.

"Determining which Cruors deserve regrades is the problem," Darcy laments one morning as she passes Sabrina a cup of coffee. "There's probably a correlation between their grades and their NPE performance, but we can't access their grades without permission. We could file a subpoena, I suppose, but on what grounds?"

Sabrina is always nervous about contradicting Darcy. Her sister's confidence and experience are daunting. But now, Darcy is complicating something that should be simple; she's thinking like a lawyer, not a journalist.

"Why don't we just phone the principals?" Sabrina suggests, hoping she sounds more assertive than she feels. "We can ask them for a list of students who deserve a regrade."

Darcy is startled by the suggestion. "You think they would talk to us?"

Sabrina shrugs. "It's worth a try."

Sabrina's first call is to Dolores Cantwell at Compound 92 in Alabama.

"Hello, Dr. Cantwell, my name is Sabrina Davenport, and I'm a reporter with the *Los Angeles Times*. I have reason to believe that over the past decade a number of Cruors across the nation have been erroneously failed on the NPE."

"Oh, praise the Lord," Dr. Cantwell says. "I knew something was wrong. First Jason, then Philip, and then the Hopkins twins. Something had to be wrong. It had to be."

"I think so, too, Dr. Cantwell," Sabrina affirms. "And we'd like to offer to pay for regrades for your most deserving students."

"Are you serious? Oh, Lord. Thank you, Jesus."

Sabrina blushes, touched by the principal's gratitude. "Who would you like to retest?"

"Those four, please. Jason Brown, Philip Kistler, Braza and Biso Hopkins. Them and poor little Anya Garcia. Her parents scrimped and saved for her to retake the exam, and then she failed it again. Poor thing was so upset she tried to kill herself."

"You're kidding," Sabrina says. She is horrified, though she supposes she shouldn't be. Wealthy kids kill themselves all the time when they underperform on the NPE.

"Mmm hmm, slit her wrists with a pair of scissors. Hasn't been the same since."

Sabrina can picture it. A bright girl with all the potential in the world, letting her parents down not once but twice. Can't bear to tell them the second time. Can't disappoint them again, not when they've spent their life savings on her retake. Doesn't see much point in living anyway. What kind of future does she have? A pair of scissors in the wrong place at the wrong time, the sharp tip digging into her fragile skin.

She will submit not only Anya's first exam, but her second, too.

Some principals don't trust her. "Why are you getting their hopes up?" Mr. Hoelster out of Oklahoma asks. "It's cruel."

Others are uncooperative. "We have many bright students here at Compound 185 High School. I'm sure I couldn't single any out," says Ms. Silva in Tennessee as she hangs up the phone without giving Sabrina a chance to respond.

One or two are clueless. "You'd have to ask the counselor about that. I'm not sure which of our students, if any, deserved to pass the NPE," Mr. Finley in upstate New York admits.

But most seem relieved by her call. They have names on the tips of their tongues, students they'd always wondered about, failures they'd never understood. Eleanor Hoag in Virginia had won fourteen national essay contests. Meadow Rivera in Washington had been taking college level math since she was twelve. In Texas, Denny Ogburn had designed an algorithm, since implemented by all the Compounds, to maximize the efficiency of blood donation.

"I thought I was crazy," Ms. Eakes in Pennsylvania says, her voice choked with tears. "They've been screwing our kids, haven't they?"

The answer is a resounding yes. Of the first ten tests submitted for re-grades, all ten pass overwhelmingly. Six of them qualify for the Ivy League. In the second and third batches, nine out of ten students pass. Anya, the girl who'd attempted suicide in Alabama, passes twice.

"We've submitted thirty-three regrade requests if you count Remy, Malachi and Miguel. Thirty-one have passed. That's ninety-four percent. Of non-Cruors submitting regrade requests, less than one percent are successful," Darcy summarizes.

"I'm ready to run with my article as soon as we call the NPE for comment," Sabrina says.

But the NPE has no comment. Despite her best efforts to reach someone higher up in the company, she's only able to access a low-level PR rep who answers the questions Sabrina puts to her like a mindless automaton. "The NPE has been perfected over the past two decades. It is an accurate indicator of skills acquired in high school and of future performance in college, and I don't make that claim lightly. We have dozens of studies confirming as much."

"Okay," Sabrina says patiently. "But I'm not claiming the test is invalid, I'm saying you have a cheating problem."

"The NPE monitors the test closely for evidence of cheating," the PR person parrots.

"Not by students," Sabrina says. "By graders."

"All graders are carefully screened." Sabrina pictures this idiot sitting in a windowless cubicle reading her responses off a screen. They may as well replace her with a machine.

"May I speak to your supervisor?" Sabrina asks at last.

"She's unavailable right now," the automaton chirps.

"Of course she is."

Sabrina runs the story with the NPE quote, 'All graders are carefully screened.' It sounds so dismissive a simple 'no comment' would have been better.

As her editor rereads her article one last time before it's published, he is close to tears. "If this isn't Pulitzer Prize winning stuff, I don't know what is."

CHAPTER 8

Then

Lunch is served on the east side of the church, the needy asked to enter by a separate side door instead of through the elegant archways that lead to the main meeting room. There is a queue today, probably fifty deep, occupied by people like Henry, unemployed and unclean.

Henry gets in line, prepared to wait his turn. He glances over to the main entrance, where a stream of well-dressed older women are flooding out after a choir practice or committee meeting. As they make their way down the steps, they are accosted by a young boy in tattered clothes, his hands cupped and extended. The women reach into their purses, smiling at their own beneficence.

Ingenious, Henry thinks, watching the boy stuff his pockets. How can they not give with both God and their church friends watching?

The boy turns in pursuit of another handout, allowing Henry to see his face for the first time.

"Shit," he curses.

It is Zeke, his hair ruffled, his face smeared with dirt. Twelve years old but small for his age, with oversized brown eyes and an impish smile, Zeke is perfect for this task. But he's supposed to be in school.

Henry leaves the lunch line and moves toward his brother, who has finished collecting money and is sitting on the bottom step counting his earnings.

"What are you doing, Zeke?" Henry asks, grabbing his brother by the arm. Startled, Zeke drops the stack of bills, which begin to blow away in the breeze.

Zeke frees himself and scurries after the money. Before he can get ahold of his brother again, Henry is seized from behind and thrown to the ground. He lands hard, his elbow crashing into the church steps, his head striking the iron railing. "You keep your hands off my boy," a familiar voice bellows.

Henry—elbow sore, head aching—looks up and into his father's eyes. "Dad?"

"Henry?" Vance Hudson says, taking a step back. "What are you doing here?"

"I was getting lunch. What's he doing here?" Henry asks, indicating Zeke, who has collected the scattered money and is folding it neatly into thirds.

"He's begging. What does it look like he's doing?"

"He should be in school," Henry protests.

Vance shakes his fist at Henry as if Henry is a snake oil salesman trying to con him for the second or third time. "Oh no you don't. Your education for Remy's, that was the deal. What happens to Zeke ain't your concern."

He's right, Henry knows, but he's wrong, too. "Come on, Dad," he says. "Don't you want Zeke to go to school? To have a shot at a future?"

"I want my boy to stay alive, that's what I want," Vance tells him. "I never should have made that deal for Remy, but I did, and I'm gonna honor that. But Zeke is mine. Zeke does what I tell him. Zeke does what he has to do to help this family survive. Is that clear to both of you?" He aims his finger first at Zeke who nods dutifully and then at Henry, who can't bring himself to agree. He knows he can't win this argument, but he had fought for Remy. Shouldn't he fight for Zeke, too?

He has to pick his battles, he tells himself, and Zeke isn't Remy. Zeke hates school. Henry looks away. "Yeah, it's clear," he mumbles.

He turns and makes his way back to the lunch line. His headache amplifies, but he makes no attempt to quell it. He deserves the pain. It is his punishment for failing to save Zeke.

Now

In all the hubbub about Remy, they had forgotten Zeke. No, Henry thinks as he sits in the office of some Compound administrator, head in his hands, throat dry, they had always overlooked Zeke. The story of the Hudson family was that of four children walking atop a balance beam, surviving as long as they did not fall. Henry had watched out for Remy. Ben could take care of himself. And Zeke had brought up the rear, wandering haplessly after them, ignored but for the occasional warning to keep his head out of the clouds.

They had gotten it wrong, Henry sees now. Remy is bright and focused. She is destined for great things with or without her brothers' watchful eyes. But Zeke had needed more from something or somebody, and nobody had been there for him.

"He needed a father," Henry says.

Ben doesn't disagree. "I'm sorry," he whispers. His voice is an octave lower than usual, the way it sounds when he first wakes up.

"Why are you sorry?" Henry asks. He is the oldest. Zeke was his responsibility.

"You had Remy. Zeke should have been mine," Ben replies. "You even asked me to look after him."

The door opens, and a woman walks in. Red hair, hardened face. "I have some good news," she says, and Henry lights up, thinking it's all been some terrible mistake, that Zeke is on his way home.

"The police are prepared to release Zeke's body, and some friends of yours, the Davenports, have offered to pay for cremation."

Henry lets out a pained cry. Zeke is on his way home, alright, in an urn.

When Henry sleeps—after three sleepless nights, with the help of a pill—he dreams he has become Zeke. He injects himself with the illegal Infinity Serum and relaxes, savoring the prospect of eternal life. And then he starts to cough. Just a little bit at first. He thinks it must be the air or that he swallowed wrong. But the coughing develops into hacking, which in turn becomes dry heaves, desperate chunks of bile fighting their way out of his system. His stomach is wrenching, and he doubles over in pain. His attempts to call for help are strangled in their infancy. The room becomes pitch black; he can't see anymore, and he can't breathe. He wonders why the Infinity Serum hasn't kicked in, why it isn't saving him. He never realizes that it is the culprit, that it is what's killing him.

Henry wakes up sweaty and short of breath. He knows it didn't happen like that. The police said that Zeke died in his sleep, that he didn't suffer. But dreams are more compelling than a few hastily uttered words. Whenever Henry imagines Zeke's death, it is the death of his nightmares.

With Henry incapacitated by grief, Ben steps up. He plans a memorial service in a generic multi-purpose room on the Compound. He enlarges a photograph of Zeke and hangs it on one of the walls. Remy lights candles to mask the scent of feet that lingers from the hot yoga class that had met in this space immediately before them and makes homemade fans to combat the stuffiness. They set up twenty-five folding chairs, arranged in five neat rows, but the only people who show up are Caleb, Darcy, and Sabrina.

"Nobody's here," Henry whispers. He finds the turnout distressing, a symbol of how little Zeke mattered.

"So what?" Ben says. "Zeke is dead. It's not like he cares."

Henry attempts to eulogize his brother, standing unsteadily before the meager crowd to read the words he had written the night before. He doesn't get far. The reality of what he is saying and doing hits him—Zeke is really gone, forever—and he can't bring himself to go on. He hands his eulogy to Ben and walks off the stage in a daze. Ben shares the remainder of Henry's words before adding a few of his own. Remy reads a Dylan Thomas poem. The service lasts less than ten minutes.

"He couldn't get past death," Henry mumbles to Ben afterward.

"What do you mean?" Ben asks.

"As long as he thought he was going to die, he couldn't live."

"Well, that's stupid," Ben says. "What did people do before Immortality? They all died. They all knew they were going to."

"It doesn't matter. That wasn't Zeke's reality. Zeke knew he didn't have to die. Our hopes and expectations are products of when and where we live."

But, Henry realizes, thinking back to the ill-attended memorial service, even when Zeke had Immortality, he didn't live. He drifted. His one ambition satisfied, he was content to float through life for eternity. The world is neither better nor worse without him.

A therapist with a unibrow tries to convince Henry that this is not his fault.

"You're what? Six or seven years older than him?" he says. "You were his brother, not his father, and under no circumstances his keeper."

"The label doesn't matter," Henry mutters. "I should have been there for Zeke."

The psychiatrist prescribes anti-depressants. Henry throws them away.

He keeps Remy at arm's length.

"Why is that?" asks his new therapist, Prince Davenport.

Darcy and Sabrina have arranged for him to see their brother as an act of kindness. ("Everybody knows Compound therapists are no good," they'd said when he'd told them the psychiatrist had given him pills and sent him on his way.) He doesn't have the heart to tell them that their brother doesn't exactly seem to have a thriving practice these days. When Henry arrived, the waiting room was empty. The receptionist had been let go. Prince's breath reeked of alcohol, and Henry had discovered upon stepping inside, so did his office, which looked like it hadn't been cleaned in weeks.

Henry shrugs. He hates therapy. If he knew the answers to his problems, he wouldn't be here. Prince waits.

"I don't want to see Remy right now," Henry says.

"Why not?"

He pictures Remy walking along beside him, smiling up at him, her hand in his. And then he pictures Zeke tagging along behind them. His stomach wrenches.

"I chose her over Zeke," he whispers. It's a relief to admit it out loud. "I watched out for her. I made sure she went to school. I took care of her. But Zeke? I never did anything for Zeke."

After three or four sessions with Prince, Henry can no longer pretend he doesn't notice the persistent stench of alcohol, the burdened countenance and defeated mannerisms.

"Are you okay?" he asks, placing his hand on his therapist's shoulder.

Prince smiles and starts to lie. "Yes, thank you. I'm," he pauses midsentence, his tortured eyes gazing into Henry's. "No," he admits. "My son is dying."

Henry already knew. He'd heard from Darcy or Remy. Still, he is glad his therapist has confided in him. He prefers mutuality to a one-sided relationship in which he does all the talking.

"I'm sorry," he says. "Whatever you do, don't resort to black market Infinity Serum to keep him alive."

It's the first joke he has attempted about his brother's death.

Prince forces a sardonic smile. "Your brother was healthy. His death from contaminated Infinity Serum was a tragedy. For my son, any extra time, every day that he's stable and not declining, is a blessing."

Henry freezes and stares at his therapist.

"What?" Prince asks. "What is it?"

"Thirty-four people died besides my brother. Thirty-four. All this time, it's felt like he was a suicide bomber. I've lost him, but I've also had to live with the fact that he killed thirty-four people."

"Not intentionally," Prince interjects. "And those people weren't innocents. Every one of them signed up to receive illegal Infinity Serum despite all the warnings."

"Maybe," Henry acknowledges. "But my brother was their supplier. He gave them the injection that ultimately ended their lives. Regardless, I guess I'd always pictured the victims as people like Zeke: young and healthy, dying in their prime for no good reason. But maybe some of them were terminally ill. Maybe they would have died sooner without the Serum. Maybe before he killed them, my brother kept them alive."

"Almost certainly," Prince says. "Your brother gave them a chance when no one else would."

Henry is crying now, and Prince takes him by the shoulder and guides him to a chair.

"This is the first time you've mourned Zeke?" Prince asks.

Henry nods.

"Good. Believe it or not, that's progress."

"Thank you," Henry mutters through his tears.

"No, thank you," Prince replies. "This is the most meaning I've gotten from my job in years."

Caleb moves in with the Hudsons two days later. It's not what they had hoped for. They had thought Caleb would take Remy's bed when she left for college, that the move would be an occasion for celebration. Instead, the Hudsons are reluctantly accepting Caleb into their apartment because he is better than a stranger and because they know Hemodyne would not have let Zeke's bed stay empty for long.

At first, Henry can't figure out why Caleb would want to live with them. A house of mourning is never a fun place to be, and when the dead is young and the death unexpected, it is worse still.

But Caleb moves in anyway, not because he is as eager to live with his friends as he once was and not because of the solitude and silence their apartment will provide. He comes out of loyalty because he can see that the Hudsons are going to need help to survive this.

He is good for them. He invites Ben out for drinks and sends him home with a woman who has a reputation for being up for anything in the bedroom. He gives Henry a dog-eared copy of *One Hundred Years of Solitude*, enabling him to forget about Zeke for the first time in days. He pours over college guides with Remy, trying to get her to refocus on the future.

Henry is amazed by how quickly the others revert to their normal selves. It's as if Zeke's death is no different from watching *Schindler's List* or *Hotel Rwanda*. It's upsetting. They cried. For some time afterward, their moods were noticeably subdued. But then they grabbed a slice of pizza or a can of beer and let themselves be tugged back into the present, gratefully embracing reality and moving on. They haven't forgotten Zeke, of course, in the same way that they haven't forgotten the slaughtered Jews or Tutsis. But they don't dwell on his death either.

Henry understands now how Zeke must have felt when the rest of them had gotten over their father's death and he had not. The haunting feeling that lingers in the stomach, the dread that never seems to go away. Zeke had been imprisoned in that parking garage with their dad's corpse. Immortality had been his attempt at escape.

One afternoon, the others come in jubilant, talking over each other in their excitement, laughing at everything. Caleb is clutching a bottle of champagne.

"What are we celebrating?" Henry asks, standing, eager to retreat. Celebrating in the midst of tragedy seems inappropriate. Being happy feels wrong.

"The downfall of Urban Jacinski," Caleb says, triumphant.

"Who?" He has heard the name before, but he can't place it.

"Urban Jacinski. We told you about him, remember?" Remy says. She is surprised that he has forgotten, maybe a little hurt.

"He's the corrupt NPE grader. The one who failed Remy," Ben explains.

Remy is holding up a hard copy of the *Los Angeles Times*. The cover story features pictures of twenty-four people in three rows under the headline "These Are the NPE Graders Who Cheated." It is the sixth or seventh article Sabrina has written on the scandal, each more damning than the last. Henry had stopped paying attention when Zeke died, but by then, the resignations at the NPE had already begun rolling in: the CEO, the head of the Cruor division, the entire examination auditing board. The exam itself is expected to survive, but only once some serious changes have been made.

Henry hadn't realized the others were pursuing the topic again. In the days following Zeke's death, the NPE investigation had been pushed aside. Henry had never intended to resume it, the same way that he never intended to resume *Homage to Catalonia*, the book he'd been reading when he first learned the news, or watch a detective show again.

"Right," Henry mutters when it becomes clear the others are all waiting for him to speak.

They talk over each other in their eagerness to tell him what has happened.

"Sabrina called to interview him—"

"He didn't even try—"

"—confessed and started crying—"

Amongst their jumbled sentences, one stands out: "He didn't do it for money like the others; he did it for Immortality."

Henry stops listening. He pictures a frightened little man in a small apartment, trembling, with a tear-streaked face, and he feels a pang of sympathy for him. Urban Jacinski could be Zeke, desperate to live forever with no realistic way to afford eternal life. He'd seized the one opportunity he'd been given just like Zeke had. Different victims, different consequences.

Wrong, but understandable.

Around him, the others are popping the cork on the champagne. Someone passes Henry a glass, which he accepts but doesn't drink. He wants to help Urban Jacinski, to save him from himself. But he's too late. Once again too late. He drops the glass of champagne, which splatters to the floor, spilling its contents across his feet. The glass, made of plastic, doesn't shatter but rolls beneath the couch.

The others are staring at him, recognizing at last that something is wrong. Someone helps him to the couch. Relieved, he closes his eyes, but he can still hear them talking above him. He wishes they would go somewhere else. Half-asleep, he sees Zeke in Urban Jacinski's apartment injecting him with Infinity Serum. Then Zeke injects himself. A murder-suicide. Revenge for what has happened to Remy. Urban and Zeke. Zeke and Urban. Sometimes rivals. Sometimes friends. Sometimes becoming one.

For another week, they leave him alone. He mopes around the apartment, unbathed and unshaven, declining to speak to anyone. He refuses to go into LA to meet with Prince, so in an act of extraordinary generosity, Prince travels to him.

"You seem to be backsliding," Prince says. "Any idea what's triggered that?"

They are meeting in the Compound coffee shop, a ploy, Henry is convinced, to get him out of the apartment.

Henry shrugs. "I don't know." Or, at any rate, he doesn't want to talk about it.

"Well, when did it start?"

He doesn't say anything. He's tired of talking about Zeke. He's tired of talking.

"You were fine at last week's appointment, right? So, it's something that's happened in the past seven days?"

Another shrug.

"Does this have anything to do with Remy? Or Urban Jacinski?"

Henry's body contracts at the name. He can't help it. Prince notices.

"Urban Jacinski tried to cheat your sister out of a place in college. How does that make you feel?"

Prince's phrasing enrages him. "He wasn't trying to cheat Remy. He wasn't trying to cheat anybody. He's a good man who was afraid to die. That's all. But everyone keeps trying to villainize him. He's not a monster, okay? He's just a man who made a mistake."

His defense is too vehement. Everyone in the coffee shop is staring at him. He rests his forehead against the table and wraps his arms around his head—a child's attempt to hide.

He hears Prince's voice above him. "So, what you're saying is that everybody is condemning Zeke, and they shouldn't be. Is that right?"

"Yes!" Henry exclaims, sitting up. Relieved that Prince, at least, understands.

"Zeke or Urban Jacinski?"

Henry pauses, confused. "Both," he says at last. "Either. Ultimately, they're the same, aren't they?"

"Are they?"

Henry hesitates. "I think they are. Desperate men, desperate measures."

Prince nods. "I can see why you think that. Of course, there is a difference, isn't there? Zeke only gave the black-market Infinity Serum to people who consented to receiving it. The students Urban Jacinski cheated had no choice in the matter. They were deprived of a future against their will."

Henry thinks about the distinction, concedes it's not invalid. "But Zeke's actions caused more harm."

"Only against people who had assumed the risk."

Henry nods. "Urban isn't Zeke."

He is speaking to himself, but Prince responds anyway. "No," he says. "He isn't, and there's nothing wrong with mourning Zeke while condemning Urban."

The phone rings during one of Henry's therapy sessions, and he shudders. Prince's ringtone is the same as his, the default, and although it is hardly rare, every time Henry hears it, he is transported back to the day the police called to break the news about Zeke.

"Sorry about that," Prince says, reaching down to silence his phone. He pauses. "Actually, do you mind if I get this? It's Dom's nurse."

"Go ahead," Henry says, trying to pull himself together. He can't keep hiding from the things that remind him of Zeke—cowbells, detective shows, Immortality.

Across from him, Prince has turned pale. "I'm on my way," he says as he hangs up. He turns to Henry. "I'm sorry. I have to go. It's Dom. They think he might not—they think this might be it."

Prince turns his phone's speaker on and dials as he haphazardly tosses his belongings into a leather bag: glasses, a sweater, a book. He extracts a bottle of bourbon from the bottom drawer of his desk. He stares at it for a moment, then packs it. Unpacks it. Packs it again.

Henry sits frozen in place, reliving his own unbearable phone call. He watches Prince, who is manic with fear, his eyes darting anxiously from the bourbon to Henry to the phone, always circling back to the bourbon.

Is this better or worse than what I went through? Henry wonders. He can't imagine watching someone die, the life evaporating from them like boiling water on a stove. On the other hand, he wishes he could have said goodbye to Zeke.

Tina answers the phone, but the connection is spotty. "What is— birthday—" They hear through the static.

Prince closes his eyes. "Tina's on her way to Vegas. It's her best friend's fortieth birthday this weekend. Shit."

"Prince?" Tina says. "—thing okay?"

"Tina?" Prince yells into the phone. "It's Dom. He's—You've got to get back here now. They say he's not going to make it."

It takes four efforts for Prince to convey his message. When he does, Tina panics, ill-prepared for a death she's known was coming for years. She's 150 miles away, and she'll hit rush hour on her way back. She can make it in three hours if she's lucky. Four or five is more likely.

"Keep him alive for me, Prince," she begs. "Don't you dare let him die."

Prince doesn't promise anything. When he hangs up, instead of rushing from the room, he collapses back into his chair and sobs. Henry watches him, wondering whether he should stay or go. Help Prince to his car? Phone somebody else?

At last, Henry gets up and goes over to his therapist, cautiously placing a hand on Prince's back. "I'm sorry," he mutters. "What can I do to help? Should I call Darcy or Sabrina?"

Something shifts. Henry doesn't know what it is exactly, but Prince's expression hardens. The grief is still there, but there is some other emotion now, too. Prince, who has mostly struck Henry as kind but ineffectual, suddenly looks like he could strangle someone with his bare hands. The shift catches Henry off guard, and he takes a step back.

But even angry, Prince is pathetic. He knocks the items on his desk— two framed photographs of his son, a mug full of pens, an inexpensive lamp—to the floor in one great sweep of fury and then bursts into tears again. Henry pities him, but he wants to slap him, too. If Dom really is dying, they don't have time for this.

Henry takes control. "Prince, we have to go. You need to be there for your son."

Prince nods, then lets Henry pull him to his feet and steer him toward the door, stopping only to grab his bag and to look wistfully at the bourbon.

"Take a swig," Henry tells him before they proceed. "It will help."

Prince greedily obeys. Then he looks back at Henry, awaiting his friend's instruction.

"Okay," Henry says, realizing what's going to be required of him here. "Let's move."

In the car on the way to the hospital, Henry again offers to call Darcy or Sabrina.

"Don't," Prince hisses, and Henry, who understands now that something is seriously wrong there, backs down.

"I'll stay with you," he offers instead. "If you want me to."

Prince's expression softens. "Thank you," he whispers. He drinks some more bourbon. By the time they arrive at the hospital, the bottle is half gone.

In the ICU, everything is a chaotic blur. Dom's nurse, a small, round woman with soft, sad eyes, breaks down when she sees them. "Mr. Prince, it's my fault. I helped him to the bathroom. He told me he'd call when he was done. When he doesn't call for a long time, I go to check on him, and then I find him passed out on the floor. I'm so sorry, Mr. Prince. I should not have left him. I should have checked on him sooner. I'm so sorry, Mr. Prince."

But Prince doesn't seem to hear her. He only wants Dom now. He only wants his son.

Dom is lying comatose in a hospital bed. His breath shakes and rattles like a car trying to start. His right hand is resting across his heart. Prince shakes him gently. "Dom," he pleads. "Dom." But Dom doesn't stir.

Prince looks at Henry. What do I do now?

"Talk to him," Henry suggests. "Just because he's not responding doesn't mean he can't hear you."

Prince nods and turns back to his son. "Dom," Prince says. His voice is loud and slow as if he is talking to a small child or someone who doesn't speak English well. "Dom, you're all I've ever wanted. You're my whole life. I know that you're okay with going, that you've made peace with death, but I—Dom, I haven't. I'm not ready. I don't know how to live without you. I don't know what to do. God, Dom, please don't go. Please. You're all I have, Dom, please. I love you so much. God, I love you so much."

Henry watches and listens. He imagines it is Zeke lying in the hospital bed instead of Dom. He mentally crafts his own apology, his own goodbye.

Dom never regains consciousness, and he dies four hours later, twenty minutes before his mom arrives.

Dom's death hits Henry hard. That it was expected doesn't make it any easier. That he never really met the boy doesn't dull his pain. He knows all too well how Prince must be feeling. He worries his therapist will drink himself to death.

Henry, Remy and Ben travel into Los Angeles for the funeral. The bus ride is torture. Henry stares out the window, wondering what he'll say to Prince, trying to remember what he wanted to hear after Zeke died. Remy's words had helped the most, but they don't apply here: "Zeke died believing he was going to live forever. Really, that's a pretty good way to go, thinking you've gotten everything you ever wanted." Zeke had been lucky compared to Dom. He'd never seen it coming.

Henry has never seen so many teenagers at a funeral. They are Dom's former classmates, he realizes, paying their respects. They are the picture of grief, with their grim faces and dark suits and dresses. Prince's wife Tina thanks them for coming, but Prince, looming in the background, only glares. "Where were they when he was alive?" he hisses. One of the schoolgirls overhears him and drops her eyes in shame.

Prince, Tina, and Tina's parents all deliver eulogies. The high school choir sings an old Venn Diagram song about dying young. Dom's doctor reads a poem. Neither Darcy nor Sabrina participates. Henry glances around the church and finds them, huddled together toward the back. They are hollow-eyed and hunched over. Sabrina's smudged makeup stains her face. Darcy keeps her eyes closed and a fist in front of her mouth as though she is afraid she'll be sick. Henry wonders what they did to anger Prince so much that he has denied them the opportunity to pay tribute to their nephew.

Somehow, the Hudsons end up back at Prince's home for the reception, even though Henry longs to go home. He sits in an armchair in the corner of the living room, holding a plate of uneaten baked goods, watching Prince and Tina greet the well-wishers streaming into their house. Tina seems grateful for their presence. She opens her arms to them, accepts their condolences with a sad smile, dabs at her eyes with tissue. But Prince might as well be enduring a root canal for all the comfort this is giving him. His eyes shift toward the kitchen with startling regularity. He is trying to stay sober today, but it is costing him.

When there is a lull between visitors, Prince makes his way to Henry and hisses, "I needed their support when Dom was dying. Now, all I want is to be alone."

But that isn't how people operate, Henry thinks, watching the mourners. People have experience with death. They know what to say and do and bring. A terminally ill child is so much harder. Do you attempt optimism? Ignore reality? Express regret for the inevitable outcome? Dealing with dying is infinitely harder than dealing with death.

An hour in, Prince begins to tremble. Tina doesn't notice, but Henry does.

"Think you could use a break, Prince?" he asks.

Prince looks at him gratefully and follows him from the room.

When they are upstairs, sitting beside each other in a dust-covered guest bedroom, sipping Irish coffees, Prince tells Henry about the ten-million-dollar inheritance, his sisters' refusal to help Dom, Dom's eventual rejection of Immortality.

"I can't let it go," he admits. "I'm trying. I know I need to. I know it's what Dom would want. But how do you forgive someone who could have saved your only child and didn't?"

You don't, Henry thinks. If Ben and Remy could have knocked the vial of Infinity Serum out of Zeke's hand, if they could have stopped him from getting involved in the black market or squelched his obsession with Immortality, and they had chosen instead to let him proceed down the path that would ultimately end his life, Henry isn't sure he'd ever get over it. But he knows that's not what Prince needs to hear.

"You keep trying," he says at last. "You talk to them. You think about what Dom would want. You think about how much worse your life would be without them, and you keep trying."

They work to get over their grief.

"I've joined Alcoholics Anonymous," Prince announces.

Henry is surprised. For a therapist, Prince had always seemed skeptical of twelve-step programs. A week or so after Dom died, he had told Henry he was giving up alcohol cold turkey on his own, no support group necessary. Last time they'd talked, he'd been nine days sober.

"Oh? What's prompting this?" Henry asks.

"The other night, I thought to myself, 'Maybe I'm not an alcoholic. Maybe I was drinking a lot because my son was dying. There's no reason I can't enjoy a glass or two.'"

"What happened?"

Prince hesitates. "I drank an entire bottle."

Henry laughs. "Well, at least now you know," he offers.

But Prince doesn't find it funny. "Now I know," he says gloomily.

At six days sober, Prince suffers another blow.

"Tina filed for divorce," he says, and Henry can tell he's been drinking. He's trying so hard to keep his voice from slurring he's comically over-enunciating his words.

"Why don't I come into the city?" Henry offers.

"No, that's not necessary," Prince insists. "I'll be okay."

"You'd rather have your bottle, huh?"

Prince pauses, embarrassed to be caught. "Maybe you'd better come," he concedes.

"How's life as a Cruor?" Prince asks a few weeks later.

Henry tenses. "Why do you ask?"

"I'm thinking of giving up my practice."

Henry hadn't realized he had much of a practice left. He shakes his head at how casually Prince talks about walking away from a job. He still has memories of his father, trudging from business to business in El Desierto, willing to do anything that was asked of him.

When Henry responds, he can't keep the resentment from his voice. "Do you have a cleaning bot, Prince?" he asks.

"What?"

"Do you have a cleaning bot?"

"Of course."

"Great, then you know how he works. You turn him on. He cleans your house or office as directed. He powers down. End of story, right?"

"Right," Prince agrees.

"Being a Cruor is like being a cleaning bot. We wake up once a week to give our blood and then we power down again. In between there's nothing. We're not working toward anything. We give blood. We eat and drink and watch TV and have sex. But we don't grow or develop or contribute. We don't have any meaning." Henry takes a deep breath. "I fight it. I read a lot, and I try to educate myself, but I still feel empty and pointless an awful lot of the time. I don't understand why you or anyone else would ever choose this when you have other, better options. This isn't rehab or a spa. This isn't a place you come to recover or take a vacation. This is a place of last resort."

"Okay," Prince says reluctantly. "I get it. I'll, well, I'll keep trying, I guess."

"You have to," Henry says. "You'll get through this, and when you do, you want options. You don't want to find yourself trapped on a 150-acre Compound wondering why you're alive."

When they hang up, Henry looks up and sees Caleb looming in the doorway. "What am I doing here?" he asks.

"I've been wondering that for a long time," Henry replies.

At Darcy's behest, Henry convinces Prince to meet with his sisters. They convene in a neighborhood park with empty tennis courts and a deserted playground on a scorching mid-summer day. They sit beneath an oak tree at a wooden picnic table—Henry and Prince across from Darcy and Sabrina.

The sisters offer hesitant smiles. Prince glares at them. "I'm only here because Henry made me come," he mutters, but Henry knows that's not exactly true. When he had suggested this reunion, Prince had refused at first, but it had been a reluctant refusal, as though he wanted to reconcile but didn't think he should. He must be lonely. Between his divorce and Dom's death, he has lost everyone but Henry, and he is no good at a life without loved ones. He is a family man; he's said so himself on numerous occasions. He reminds Henry of the girls who come to the apartment looking for Ben—their desire for his brother at war with their recognition that he has wronged them.

"We're glad you're here," Sabrina says, looking at her brother with large, sympathetic eyes. "And we're so sorry about Dom."

"We miss him," Darcy adds. "We think about him all the time."

They mean it; Henry can feel their grief and sincerity. He pictures Dom's well-attended funeral, all the people who had loved him or at least cared enough to show up. He can't help but contrast it with Zeke's, where Henry's voice had echoed through that empty auditorium and the only tears shed had been his own. Does anyone miss Zeke? Henry doubts it. Not even his siblings. Not even him. He feels terrible that his brother is dead, but he never finds himself thinking that he wishes he could talk to Zeke or that there is something missing without his brother in his life. How could anyone be so inconsequential?

Prince's grief-stricken voice pulls Henry back to the present. "You let him die," Prince says, but he chokes on the word 'die,' and then he is crying, his strange, silent tears that Henry finds haunting in their restraint.

"I'm sorry," Sabrina whispers through tears of her own. She is staring at her hands, a look of unbearable sorrow on her face.

"We know nothing we say or do can ever make this right," Darcy says. "But we wanted to propose something that may help."

"Have you found a way to resurrect my son?" Prince sneers.

Darcy takes a deep breath and shakes her head. "No. But," she hesitates, "we have agreed on what we'd like to do with Dad's fortune."

She extracts a manila envelope from her bag and slides a stack of papers out. On top, there is a photograph of a homely woman with limp brown bangs. "This is Dr. Laura Gold. She—"

"—is the top Tay Sachs researcher in the world," Prince interrupts, wiping the tears from his eyes with the back of his hand. He is sitting up a little straighter now, leaning over the photograph of Dr. Gold.

"That's right," Darcy says. "She's a geneticist who hopes to rid the world of Tay Sachs."

"If you agree, Darcy and I would like to use Dad's money to sponsor her Immortality," Sabrina explains. "We know that nothing will bring Dom back and that you may never forgive us for not saving him when we had the chance, but we love you, Prince, and we loved Dom, and we want to do something to honor him."

It had been Sabrina's idea, Henry knows. Darcy had been reluctant at first. Tay Sachs isn't cancer. Couples can genetically screen for Tay Sachs before they become pregnant. Fetuses can be screened for it in utero. It is preventable in a way that so many other conditions are not. But Sabrina had convinced her, pointing out that Dr. Gold meets her sole criterion— she engages in work that could change the world. She is focused on Tay Sachs for now, but with Immortality, a brilliant geneticist like her could go on to conquer any number of diseases.

Prince is crying harder now, his tears no longer a stream but a river. Henry suspects he could not speak even if he wanted to. Sabrina and Darcy watch him, their expressions anxious but hopeful.

Prince stands abruptly. He looks at his sisters and then at Henry. He pauses for a moment as if unsure what to do next. Then, he steps over the picnic table bench and trots through the park toward his car.

"It could have been worse," Sabrina says as they watch him go.

None of them hear from Prince for nearly a week. Then he sends them all a four-word text: *Yes to Dr. Gold.*

CHAPTER 9

Then

The sixth-grade field trip will be to Hemodyne Enterprises.

"We'll tour their labs and have lunch in their cafeteria," Mr. Nguyen tells his class. "And, as a special treat, Dr. Odili himself will do a question-and-answer session with our class."

He turns to Sutton North, Remy's academic rival. "A special thanks to Sutton's parents for making this incredible opportunity possible."

"My dad was college roommates with Uncle Nate," Sutton explains, lifting her chin a quarter inch as she speaks.

Remy is stunned. To her, Nathan Odili has never been an actual person. He is a historical figure like Stephen Hawking, or a fictional genius, like Sherlock Holmes, not someone who could ever walk the same streets as she does, breathe the same air.

She has so many questions for Dr. Odili. Will the Infinity Serum become more affordable? If so, does he worry about overpopulation? Can he restrict who becomes Immortal? In particular, what about nations that have dictators who will not step aside? Once upon a time, they would die eventually. Now, what if they never do? She is fascinated by Immortality and its unintended consequences.

She is grateful now that her parents have moved them to Santa Monica, that she can attend a fancy public school that has the money and connections to make something like this possible. It never would have happened in El Desierto. She doesn't remember the schools there having field trips at all.

She asks Henry to sign the permission slip because her parents' disdain for Immortality is so fervid she is almost certain they'd refuse. Henry does so happily; he is practiced at forging their father's name.

"You're really going to meet Dr. Odili?" he asks again and again, unable to wrap his head around such an incredible opportunity.

"If I could ask him one question," he mulls, his voice drawn out and pensive, "Immortality has had a lot of unexpected consequences. Which of them do you regret the most, and is Hemodyne doing anything to mitigate the damage?"

Remy is always in awe of her brother. For someone who dropped out of school, he is so bright, so thoughtful. His question encapsulates all of hers. "It's perfect," she says.

The morning of the field trip, Remy wakes before dawn, quivering in anticipation. She does not bother trying to fall back to sleep. Her family has stayed in a shelter, and she tumbles out of her cot and patters barefoot to the bathroom, dodging thrashing sleepers and stepping around belongings stuffed in plastic bags. The shower still has hot water at this hour, and she scrubs her body clean with the unscented bar soap provided. She rinses her mouth with Listerine. She fiddles with her unwieldy hair before pulling it up into a tidy bun and slips into the new used dress she has saved up to buy and new flats, half a size too small. In the mirror, she sees a nice, put-together eleven-year-old. No one would know she was homeless just by looking at her.

She gets to school as the sun is rising and paces until her feet start to hurt in her too-small shoes. Then she settles onto the front stairs to wait, crossing and uncrossing her legs, drumming her fingers against the concrete steps, imagining Dr. Odili being so impressed with her question that he takes an interest in her, adopts her, and whisks her away from poverty, as though he is Daddy Warbucks and she is Annie, except she has actually earned her place in his household; Annie just got lucky.

"Remy, I don't have your permission slip," Mr. Nguyen tells her as she prepares to board the bus at last.

Remy frowns. "I turned it in weeks ago."

"I have the school's permission slip," he agrees. "But yesterday afternoon, we were made aware that Hemodyne has a permission slip of their own. We Zapped every student and their parents about this."

Mr. Nguyen is looking at her expectantly, waiting for her to pull out her phone and check her Zap account or send a quick message to her dad, instructing him to Zap the permission slip over right away. How does she explain that she doesn't have a cell phone or regular access to the internet and neither do her parents?

"I guess we didn't see it," she mumbles.

She realizes this means she will not be able to go on the field trip she has been looking forward to for weeks, but she will mourn later. For now, she needs to protect her family. Mr. Nguyen cannot discover how destitute they are. Child Protective Services removes homeless children from their parents, separates them, and houses them with families of dubious quality. Remy prefers the devil she knows.

"Why don't you call your mom or dad now?" Mr. Nguyen suggests, trying to be helpful.

"I can't," Remy says. Her mind is racing as she struggles to come up with an excuse. She's lost her phone. Her parents have lost theirs. They have an important business meeting. They're at a funeral. They're in Bogota.

"They don't like it when I bother them at work," she mutters at last. "Unless it's an emergency."

"I think this constitutes an emergency, don't you?"

Remy shakes her head. "Not to them."

Mr. Nguyen looks concerned. He must think her parents are monsters. "What do they do again?"

"Their jobs?" Remy blushes. What has she gotten herself into? "You know what, I'm being ridiculous. Let me give them a call."

He looks relieved as she steps to the side and digs through her backpack, ostensibly for her cell phone. She glances back, making sure his attention is elsewhere and fakes a call.

Things like this happen all the time. She'd missed a party invitation posted on Besties by one of her few friends. That friend hasn't spoken to her since. A boy she'd liked had Flirted with her on Crush. By the time she found out, he had Flirted his way into another relationship. She'd studied for a postponed math test and missed virtual tutoring sessions for science and failed to enter an essay contest with a one-thousand-dollar prize. She wants to scream at the misery of it all. She wants to smash her head into the wall with frustration. Like Immortality, poverty has so many unexpected consequences.

Now

Remy almost doesn't recognize Dallas when he turns up at her door. It is because his head is not tilted back, she realizes. He is no longer trying to look down on her.

She is not sure what he's doing here, but she assumes it has to do with Zeke. Dallas had managed the Hudsons' intake all those years ago. Now, he is here to manage Zeke's exit.

Dallas smiles and extends his arms toward her as though he is expecting a hug. "Remy!" he exclaims. "Just the person I was looking for."

Remy sidesteps the hug and gestures for him to come inside because that seems like the polite thing to do, but she doesn't trust exuberant Dallas any more than she trusts elitist Dallas.

"So, good news," he says, propping himself on the edge of the sofa and crossing one leg over the other. "Nathan Odili himself is going to visit

Compound 78 next month."

"Nathan Odili?" Remy repeats. Her mind is traveling back to her sixth-grade field trip. Watching the school bus pull away from the curb had been the nadir of her childhood, worse than the day they had been evicted or the day her mom had disappeared. It had felt, in that moment, as though nothing was possible, as though everything could be taken away. Incredible the way her life has come full circle, for lately, she has come to believe that anything is possible, and the news that Nathan Odili is visiting the Compound seems to confirm as much.

"I know, right?" Dallas enthuses. "And you haven't even heard the best part. He's coming because of you!"

"Me?" she says. But she already knew. What else would draw him to Compound 78? She has been in the news constantly for the past few months, not only in Sabrina's articles but also in those of countless other reporters. She has been applauded on daytime talk shows and interviewed by late night hosts. This is the fifteen minutes of fame she had never asked for and isn't sure she likes, but so many people have become invested in her story that she feels she owes it to them, as a kind of thank you for caring.

Dallas is explaining that Nathan Odili will meet with Malachi, Miguel, and her for half an hour after delivering a televised address in which he will praise their accomplishments. Remy nods along. She will process all of this later after Dallas is gone.

When Dallas finishes sharing the details of Dr. Odili's visit and delivering instructions ("You should wear a modest dress. Do you have a modest dress?"), he stands and, appallingly, pats her on the cheek. "Congratulations, kid," he says. "You should be proud."

And then, as though as an afterthought, he adds, "Oh, and maybe don't mention Zeke to Dr. Odili. There's no way that would go over well."

As he walks out, Remy glares at the back of his head. She hadn't planned to mention her brother, but now she's considering it, just to annoy Dallas.

As it turns out, Nathan Odili already knows about Zeke. When he meets Remy briefly before his address, he takes both her hands in his and says, "I was sorry to hear about your brother."

Remy is so charmed she can barely speak. "Thank you," she manages, with effort.

The speech takes place indoors, in a sterile conference room, tucked in the bowels of one of the Compound's administrative buildings. Cruors, dressed in their Sunday best, have filled every available folding chair. Remy is impressed by the turnout – she didn't think this many Cruors cared about education or current events – until she learns from Ben that Dallas has discreetly paid them to show up, doubling their weekly income for attending a twenty-minute press conference.

The Cruors cheer dutifully as Dr. Odili walks to the podium. Remy wonders how many of them even know who he is. Zeke would not have, despite his obsession with Immortality.

Dr. Odili's address is well-delivered and inspiring. He has the charisma of a politician as he speaks with pride about the role of the Compounds in facilitating opportunity, praising their schools and their libraries. He ignores the absence of honors classes and the low literacy rates, and, when he asks Remy, Malachi, and Miguel to join him at the podium, he does not invite Caleb or acknowledge his contribution. Remy understands that this is because Caleb is too much of an anomaly to fit Nathan Odili's narrative. Caleb does not inspire hope the way Remy, Malachi, and Miguel do because he is rare and irreplicable; other Compounds do not have access to a Princeton-educated tutor.

Still, Remy thinks it is important to be honest about the ingredients in their recipe for success. Other Compounds may not have Caleb, but they should at least know that they need to find a substitute. She considers mentioning this to Dr. Odili when she talks with him later, but she already knows she won't. It feels inappropriate, out of place. He is here to honor her, not solicit her advice.

There is a private reception afterward, to which Remy, Malachi, and Miguel are each allowed to invite four guests. Malachi and Miguel are there with their families, but Ben has no interest, so Remy brings Henry, Caleb, and Sabrina, and Darcy, who is practically foaming at the mouth at the prospect of meeting Dr. Odili.

The reception is down the hall from the press conference, in an intimate room that cannot fit more than thirty. It has been furnished with a series of standing tables, each topped with a vase of calla lilies. Serverbots circulate, offering hors d'oeuvres. As Remy samples her first crab cake, her first lamb chop, her first goat cheese crostini, she finds herself wishing that Ben had come after all. He would have loved all this fancy finger food.

Nathan Odili arrives ten minutes after everyone else, and instinctually, they applaud at his entrance, all except Darcy, who has such a sour expression on her face that Remy begins to suspect that inviting her was a mistake.

Dr. Odili works the room, shaking hands and congratulating proud relatives. He never stops smiling and cocks his head as he listens to others speak. There are rumors that he may run for office, which makes Remy wonder if his gestures are natural or practiced, sincere or calculated. She watches him move from Miguel's family to Malachi's and waits, with a thumping heart, for him to get to her.

He seems especially taken with Malachi, and as the two men speak, Malachi's family recedes, and the conversation becomes between him and Dr. Odili alone. Ten minutes pass, then twenty. She envies Malachi, who is brilliant and science-minded, and tries to come up with topics of conversation that will captivate Dr. Odili, too, but nothing comes to mind. In fact, she can't think of anything to say to him at all.

When, at last, Dr. Odili gets to Remy and her unconventional family, Remy is desperate to impress him, but she never gets the chance. The conversation quickly spirals out of control. When Dr. Odili tries to thank Darcy for her work on the NPE scandal, she is not star-struck and receptive as the others have been. She is a balloon, filled to bursting; she tries to release all that she has been holding in slowly, in a well-thought out, oft-rehearsed speech, but within seconds she bursts, and her speech becomes a tirade.

"Everything you said was a lie," she rages. "Cruors almost never attend college. You're not creating social mobility; you're taking advantage of a few exceptional students to bolster the reputation of your Compounds while ignoring the vast majority of the people who live on them. Less than one percent of Cruor children attend college. That's hardly providing opportunity."

Remy blushes. She hadn't expected Darcy to be so combative.

Nathan Odili's pleasant smile is replaced by a flash of annoyance, but only a flash. Then, he is smiling again, even more effusive than before. "I have always wanted the Compounds to be a nice place to live," he says. "Perhaps the fact that nobody leaves suggests that they are."

"Oh please," Darcy huffs. "You and I both know they don't have any other option."

"That's not exactly fair," Caleb intervenes. "Most people really do seem happy here. I have been."

Remy's shoulders tighten and hunch. She doesn't mind debate, but the setting is all wrong. This should be a place of peace, a moment of joy. She attempts a compromise. "Most people are happy here, but for those who aren't, it can be hard to leave."

"I agree," Nathan Odili says, beaming at her through his tortoise-shell glasses as though he is a professor and she is a promising young student.

Remy is surprised that he has agreed with her. The notion that Cruors can find themselves trapped on the Compounds runs counter to everything he had said in his speech not half an hour before.

"May I tell you a secret?" Dr. Odili continues. He accepts a glass of champagne from a Serverbot, then waits until it has left to continue. As though it's human, Remy thinks. As though he is afraid it will overhear him.

Dr. Odili leans in, and the others do the same, the proximity of their heads forging an unexpected intimacy. "When I opened the Compounds,"

Dr. Odili begins. "I thought I was clever. The masses were struggling. The wealthy were indifferent to their plight and would not back the sort of tax hike necessary to get them back on their feet. We needed subsidized housing, well-funded schools, plentiful food banks."

Darcy nods along vigorously, her head bouncing up and down as though it is on springs.

"The rich did not want to pay taxes, but they did want Immortality. Demand for Infinity Serum was through the roof right from the beginning—the exorbitant price was no impediment—and so were my profits. My CFO and I were looking at our balance sheet one day, patting each other on the back at how successful we had become, and he remarked that with numbers like ours, we could house every homeless person in America and still turn a healthy profit. It was just an offhand remark, but it triggered something in me. Why not? I said to myself. Why not house every homeless person in America?"

"In exchange for their blood," Darcy interjects, wagging her finger at him as if she has caught him trying to pass pyrite off as gold.

"We are a corporation, not a charity," he says unapologetically. "But we did not have to construct the Compounds. Even in America, people were willing to donate blood for as little as five dollars a pint. We pay them fourteen times that, in addition to room and board."

Darcy crosses her arms, unconvinced, but Remy thinks she might like to marry Nathan Odili.

"I am proud of what we've done," he continues. "My company has solved one of the nation's most intractable problems. But I've found that, in life, as soon as you solve one problem, a new one arises. What Darcy says is true. Very few people leave the Compounds. Their children do not leave the Compounds, and I suspect their grandchildren won't either. This keeps me up at night. What if, instead of ending poverty, we have unintentionally entrenched it, creating a permanent underclass?"

His words silence them, sadden them. He is Frankenstein, and the Compounds are his monster—brilliant but uncontrollable. Remy had thought Dr. Odili had come to Compound 78 so that Hemodyne could capitalize on the positive press coverage she has received. Now, she sees that he is here not for Hemodyne but for himself. He needs flesh and blood proof that there is a way out of the Compounds, that they are not just a refuge but a place of hope.

"I think you made them too nice," Caleb interjects. "The Compounds, I mean. Life here is really good, too good. Maybe if it weren't, maybe if it were barracks and bunk beds and beans and rice for every meal, people wouldn't be so content to stay."

"You're suggesting he make the Compounds worse?" Darcy says, incredulous.

"No." Caleb scratches the back of his neck. "Well, kind of, I guess. Yeah."

"Making living conditions worse doesn't seem like the solution to anything," Dr. Odili says. "This problem tortures me. How do I break this stalemate? How do I create social mobility?" He looks around at each of them as though he genuinely hopes one of them might suggest a solution.

Henry catches Remy's eyes and gestures toward Dr. Odili with his chin. Remy blushes. She knows he wants her to share her idea for a boarding school for academically motivated Cruors, but she can't. She won't. She is afraid it is too far-fetched, too fantastical.

"It isn't your fault," Sabrina is saying. "If people don't want to leave the Compounds, you can't force them."

"I know," Dr. Odili acknowledges. "But when I look at the children here, it discourages me. What chance do they have?"

Again, Henry silently urges Remy to share her idea, but again she demurs. Instead, it is Caleb who speaks. "What I've learned from my time on the Compounds is that the people who want to leave find a way. It isn't easy, but they manage."

Caleb's comment irritates Remy. It's so simplistic. It ignores the Compound's problematic culture, the absence of role models, how few of her classmates have family members like Henry encouraging them to make something of themselves. "That isn't true," she says before she can stop herself.

"What do you mean?" Nathan Odili asks, turning to her.

"As I see it, there are two problems: vision and opportunity. On the Compounds, people lack both. A lot of children have barely left the Compound. They've never seen what the world has to offer. The schools don't bring in speakers or go on field trips. Their parents can't encourage them to think about the future because they don't think about the future themselves. After years of poverty, they're grateful just to have a bed."

Remy can hear the frustration in her voice. She doesn't sound like herself. She sounds like Darcy. But she isn't finished yet. "Then, for the handful who do hope to leave, they find no support from teachers or counselors, and the Compound curriculum is two years behind the public schools. The test prep books are insufficient, and if they take practice exams, there's nobody to grade them or provide feedback. We got lucky here on Compound 78; we had Caleb, but not everyone does."

Darcy and Henry nod along as she speaks, while Caleb looks surprised, but she can't gauge Dr. Odili's reaction. When he doesn't speak right away, she begins to think she's over-stepped.

"Interesting," he says at last. "So, what do you suggest?" He is looking at her differently now, and she gets the sense that he is taking her more seriously.

She gulps. "I don't know," she says. "I think they need a different environment or subculture, one that encourages and supports achievement." It is the closest she can bring herself to sharing her dream.

Nathan Odili smiles. "Yes, I'm sure that is true," he says. "But it is easier said than done."

He moves on then to some other, less consequential topic, and before she knows it, he is congratulating her once more and departing. Remy watches him go, hoping she has said enough, knowing she should have said more.

That night, Remy wakes to the sound of Henry crying. She sighs. Henry's grief is quicksand; every time she thinks he has begun to emerge, he sinks a little deeper.

"Are you okay?" she asks, rising from her bed to sit on the side of his. She rests her hand on his shoulder remembering her early childhood when he would comfort her this way after a bad day or a nightmare.

"I was just thinking about what Dr. Odili said today," Henry tells her. "About education and motivation. I motivated you, Remy. I pushed you to get an education. Maybe if I'd pushed Zeke, too, he'd be in college now."

"He wouldn't," Remy says.

"How can you be sure?" In the dark his voice sounds younger and farther away.

Remy gives his shoulder a sympathetic squeeze. "Zeke was never interested in school, and he had no aptitude for it."

"But maybe if I'd encouraged him—"

"You tried," Remy interrupts. "Don't you remember? When we were small and still living in El Desierto you used to encourage all of us to do well in school. Ben and Zeke and me. You had some teacher who'd motivated you, who told you she'd gotten out of poverty by working hard and getting a good education. And you wanted that for all of us. The reason you focused on me wasn't because I was the youngest or because I was a girl. It was because I was the one who listened. Ben and Zeke weren't interested, not then, not ever."

Henry opens his mouth, then closes it again. He scratches at his beard. "You're right," he admits. "Zeke was never going to go to college."

"But you still could," Remy says. "Your guilt over Zeke isn't doing anybody any good. It can't bring Zeke back. All it can do is destroy your life, too."

She finds his hands in the darkness, takes them in hers. "It's time to move on, Henry."

EPILOGUE

The East Coast has finally warmed up, but still, Remy shivers. She is so excited she has made herself anxious. She bounces up and down, gnaws on her fingernails, gets distracted by every new sight or sound.

Years ago, when they were destitute, underweight children, she and Henry would take walks along the Santa Monica Pier and dream aloud of everyday things, like warm beds and full bellies, and of grander things, like college degrees and stable jobs. Often, the everyday things had been so hard to come by that the grander things had seemed not just impossible but absurd. Amazing, Remy thinks, to have come so far, to be on this gorgeous gothic campus, knowing her childhood dreams are dreams no longer.

The Hudsons, the Davenports, and Caleb arrive on campus three hours before the graduation ceremony to block off the best seats. Ben brought, and had confiscated, a megaphone. Sabrina has made a congratulatory sign. She confided in Remy last night that she wished she had gone to college.

"It's not too late, you know," Remy had told her.

But she had shaken her head. "I think it might be."

Remy hadn't pressed, but she'd made a mental note to mention college to Sabrina again.

More and more people arrive. Graduates in navy caps and gowns, attempting to spend time with their families while also saying goodbye to their friends. Lost relatives wondering where they are supposed to be. Administrators ushering people around, doing what they can to ensure the ceremony proceeds smoothly. Remy loves the mild chaos of it all, the celebratory spirit in the air.

She catches Henry's eye, and they both grin. He is bursting with pride. She is near tears. This is their moment.

The ceremony starts, but Remy only half listens. She is so consumed by memories of the past and the promise of the future that it is almost impossible to focus on the present.

And then she hears his name. Henry Vance Hudson. Yale University. Bachelor of Arts. Magna Cum Laude.

They have dinner at an upscale Peruvian restaurant with dim lighting and pop music blaring in the background. It is overflowing with Yale graduates and their families, and by some oversight, they do not have a reservation. Sabrina, still gorgeous even though she has aged six years, flirts with the manager, who shifts and rearranges until he finds a way to squeeze them in. Caleb has procured several bottles of non-alcoholic sparkling cider in support of Prince, who is eighteen months sober. Darcy brings a cake, then passes it to Remy as her phone rings.

"Hi, Nate," she says, walking outside to take the call. The others roll their eyes, used to this.

"I miss her old job," Sabrina complains as she clears a space on the table for the cake. "She controlled her own schedule, and nobody liked her enough to contact her when she wasn't in the office."

"Yeah, but how many people get to call Nathan Odili 'Nate'?" Caleb says.

Remy sets the cake down and takes a seat beside Sabrina. "Does he call her often?" she asks, a hint of envy in her voice.

"All the time," Sabrina moans. "She's not just Hemodyne's Chief Ethics Officer; she's Odili's right hand man. He consults her about everything."

"That doesn't sound like Darcy," Caleb remarks. "The reason she took this job was to keep Hemodyne in line."

"Oh, don't worry. She does. You should hear her." Sabrina's voice becomes deep and bossy. "'No, Nate. No. I don't care if it's not illegal; it's still immoral. You've got to take this seriously, Nate. This is really important. It's really, really important.'"

Darcy returns. "Sorry I took that call, but it was really, really important."

The others burst out laughing.

"What's so funny?" she asks, but they only laugh harder.

Prince and Ben arrive together as the others are ordering appetizers. They are sharing a hotel room because neither can afford one of his own. Ben still makes seventy dollars a week donating blood and spends every cent of it, while Prince works as a therapist on Compound 78, a position Ben had procured for him after he lost his previous three jobs for showing up to work drunk.

"How's he doing?" Sabrina asks Ben when Prince isn't paying attention.

"Good," Ben says as he pours himself a glass of apple cider. "Really good. He's actually great at his job."

"He is," Sabrina agrees. "If he can stay sober."

"The new girlfriend helps. She's kind of boring, but she's more loyal than a robo-pup, and she doesn't drink, which—"

"Is exactly what he needs," Sabrina says, nodding. Her brother is a serial monogamist—he can't stay single for more than a month—but his past girlfriends have been problematic. They've walked all over him or kept alcohol in the house or been impatient with his grief. A dull teetotaler who adores him sounds perfect.

"Does he still donate his salary?" Sabrina asks Ben.

"Half of it, every month."

They all tithe to Tay Sachs. In addition to sponsoring the Immortality of geneticist Dr. Laura Gold, Darcy and Sabrina donate ten percent of their salaries, as do Caleb and Remy. Ben and Henry, who have no money, volunteer ten hours a month instead. For Darcy and Sabrina, this has been a form of continued atonement, for the others a show of support.

Such gestures had been important in the early days of their makeshift family. Since they were not bonded by blood, they'd had to prove their devotion in other ways. They'd sent presents for birthdays and been careful not to fight. They'd been fond of big gestures. Darcy had convinced Nathan Odili to fund Remy's fledgling non-profit. Sabrina had gotten Caleb a book deal for his memoir. When Ben had married, they'd all chipped in to pay for his wife's dream wedding at Disneyland, and when he'd divorced four months later, Prince had helped him through the emotional aftermath. Now, six years later, they are more like a regular family. They send cards instead of presents for birthdays; they squabble.

Over dinner that evening, they talk the way families do, the familiar mix of fond memories and future plans. Henry retells a story from Ben's bachelor party. Remy complains about the dating scene in D.C.

Darcy's phone rings and the others say, "Hi, Nate," in unison. Darcy sticks her tongue out as she steps away to take the call.

While the others dig into their starters, Sabrina, who has ordered only a main, shares photos from a recent trip to Japan, where she had been researching a story for her Eternity Column. "This eccentric eco-warrior billionaire has been injecting a rare maple with Infinity Serum. He believes preserving this tree is his calling."

"Does the Infinity Serum even work on plants?" Henry asks, helping himself to a bite of Remy's ceviche.

"Probably not," Sabrina admits. "But it makes for an interesting story."

Darcy returns. "How's Nate?" Sabrina asks, as though Nate is a crush or a boyfriend.

"That was Warner, actually," Darcy says. "Dominique hit her head on the side of the crib, and he panicked."

"You left Dominique with Warner?" Prince asks, incredulous. "Does he have any experience with kids?"

"As a matter of fact, he does," Darcy says. "He paid his way through law school by working at the university daycare, and anyway, he's been watching

Dom since she was born."

"Don't call her 'Dom,'" Prince snaps. His grip on his spoon visibly tightens, and his knuckles turn red. Today was always going to be difficult for him. Had his son lived, he would be graduating from college this year, too.

Darcy blushes. "Right, sorry." But they all call her Dom behind Prince's back. Dominique is too much name for such a little girl.

Darcy had discussed the adoption with Prince before proceeding. She had explained that she missed having a child in her life. She missed Dom. "Whose fault is that?" Prince had asked, still bitter, still not entirely over it. He had been conflicted about the adoption, about naming the baby after his son, but he had reluctantly agreed to all of it.

"Let's see Dominique. She must be getting big," Henry says. He is the closest to Prince, but he is also the least likely to tiptoe around his friend's feelings.

Darcy extracts her phone and shows the others a photograph of a chubby baby, her face and clothes smeared with bright orange puree, her lower lip extended in displeasure. "She's your daughter alright," Sabrina jokes.

The others ooh and aah at the frizzy-haired girl as they pass Darcy's phone around, all except Prince, who hands the phone to Remy without looking at it. He is staring at Remy's pisco sour with a longing that makes her nervous. She moves the glass away from him, wishing she had stuck with cider.

She returns the phone to Darcy and changes the subject. "Henry, are you sure you won't work with Caleb and me for a year or two before grad school? We could really use a bright Yale English major on our team."

Henry looks bemused. "From what I've read, you're oversubscribed. You have more tutors than you know what to do with."

Remy nods. "Ever since the *Times* called us the new Teach For America, we've had four times as many applicants as we have positions." The Cruor tutoring company she and Caleb have started is not the boarding school she still dreams of opening, but it was cheaper and easier to get off the ground, and she is proud of it.

Caleb snorts and takes an aggressive swig of cider.

"What?" Remy says.

"I don't know. Before the stupid *Times* article, our candidates applied because they really cared. Now, most of them are just looking to add a line to their resumes."

"I don't care why they're tutoring as long as they do it well," Remy says. "But Henry, the data has shown that our best tutors are the ones who are ex-Cruors themselves."

She gazes at her brother with pleading eyes, silently imploring him to reconsider.

"Sorry, but no," he says. "I like campus life better. I fit in here."

Ben shakes his head. "I love you, Henry, but I don't think I'll ever understand you."

Remy smiles. No, she thinks, of course he doesn't understand. While the rest of them work eighty hours a week and still fail as often as they succeed, Ben is never stressed or tired or disappointed. He still lives on the Compound, and he is the happiest person she knows.

Prince seems to be thinking along the same lines. "Maybe you should become some kind of guru, Ben," he jokes. "Teach us all how to live simpler lives." Prince has forgotten Dom for the moment. He is focusing on the family he does have.

Remy looks around, smiling. Remarkable, she thinks, the ties they have forged, the meaning they have found in each other.

Henry and Remy have plans to meet later that night after the others have retired to their rooms. Remy is running a few minutes late, and she finds her brother waiting for her on a bench in front of the library, a small paper bag in his hands. He stands to greet her.

"Congratulations again, Yale grad," she says.

"Thanks," he replies. He hasn't stopped smiling all day. "I have something for you."

"Henry, this is your day, not mine. You shouldn't be getting me any-thing."

"It's our day," he corrects. "You set the example. I followed in your footsteps."

He extends the paper bag he's been holding toward her.

She takes the bag and extracts a book. "*Les Misérables*," she reads.

"Don't you remember? It's the first book you ever gave me, back on the Compound when I was bored and miserable."

A bookmark is sticking out, leather, engraved with the Yale crest. She opens the book to the page it's holding, where two sentences have been highlighted in yellow. "It is nothing to die. It is frightful not to live."

And scrawled in the margin, in Henry's crisp hand: "To Remy, who has found her purpose in helping Cruors live."

Acknowledgments

To my husband, Danny, the love of my life, who encouraged me to quit law and become a writer, who supports me financially and emotionally, who always drops anything he is doing to read and provide feedback on my work, and who, as a result, has read everything I've written almost as many times as I have. To my amazing daughter, Eyer, who inspires me to be the best that I can be at everything I do.

To my in-laws, Teri and Phil Oppenheimer, who are and always have been incredibly loving and supportive.

To my literary agent, Victoria Skurnick at Levine Greenberg Rostan, who believed in this book and in me right from the beginning. To my TV and Film Agent, Shivani Doraiswami at Grandview and to my publicist, Jocelyn Kelley at Kelley and Hall.

To the team at Stillhouse, who have made this novel into an actual, physical book. A special shout out to Linda Hall, who has supported and encouraged me throughout this process, and to my editors Tara Fritz and Kate Steagall, whose enthusiasm for this novel buoyed me, and who pushed me to make this book the best that it could be.

To my writers' group: Katie Aspell, Stacey Closser, Jessie Ren Marshall, Kristin Walrod, Kate Weinberg, and Sarah Zoric, who excel at balancing encouragement with critical feedback, who are ceaselessly generous, who have not only made me a better writer but have also become dear friends.

To my beta readers: Sara Etchison, Becky Ferrer, Alice Foy, David Jacobs, Julia Lauper, Nicole Shelton, Jillian Thomadsen, Shea Van Boskirk, and Michael Wynn, who read this novel in various stages, provided thorough, invaluable feedback, and pushed me to keep working on it.

To my mentors Liam Callanan at Bread Loaf and Tyler Dilts at The Community of Writers at Olympic Valley, who were everything good mentors should be—thoughtful and honest and supportive. And, especially, to Brad Felver, both a cherished mentor and a good friend, who is always willing to do whatever he can to support me as a writer.

Finally, to my parents: my dad, John Eyer, who has thought I should be a writer since I was very young but had the patience and wisdom to let me figure that out for myself, and to my mom, Mary Eyer, my best friend and tireless supporter, who was all the things a mom should be and then some, without whom I would not be the person I am.

Thank you, all of you.

About the Author

T.N. Eyer is a graduate of Yale Law School and worked as a corporate lawyer in London and Los Angeles before transitioning to writing fiction full time. She now lives in Pittsburgh with her husband and daughter. This is her first novel.